continued . . .

"Ms. Byrd does a fantastic job of balancing the stories of these two couples. Both women are captivating heroines, both men irresistible heroes . . . I look forward to the next book in this intriguing, well-written series."
—*The Best Reviews*

PRAISE FOR
Beauty in Black

"Delightful . . . witty . . . hooks the audience."
—*Midwest Book Review*

"The social whirl of Britain's Regency era springs to vivid life . . . Charming."
—*Publishers Weekly*

"Another delightful tale by the multitalented Nicole Byrd . . . Heartwarming, humorous at times . . . a well-written page-turner."
—*Romance Reviews Today*

PRAISE FOR
Widow in Scarlet

"Nicole Byrd scores again with her latest Regency historical . . . an exciting and engaging almost Cinderella-type story with touches of suspense, sensuality, and the exotic."
—*The Romance Reader's Connection* (4 Plugs and a Star)

"A romantic tale filled with suspense and enough characters and plot to have you quickly turning the pages . . . A superb Regency tale you won't want to miss."
—*Romance Reviews Today*

Titles by Nicole Byrd

ROBERT'S LADY
DEAR IMPOSTOR
LADY IN WAITING
WIDOW IN SCARLET
BEAUTY IN BLACK
VISION IN BLUE
GILDING THE LADY
SEDUCING SIR OLIVER
LADY OF SCANDAL

A Lady
of Scandal

Nicole Byrd

BERKLEY SENSATION, NEW YORK

THE BERKLEY PUBLISHING GROUP
Published by the Penguin Group
Penguin Group (USA) Inc.
375 Hudson Street, New York, New York 10014, USA
Penguin Group (Canada), 90 Eglinton Avenue East, Suite 700, Toronto, Ontario M4P 2Y3, Canada
(a division of Pearson Penguin Canada Inc.)
Penguin Books Ltd., 80 Strand, London WC2R 0RL, England
Penguin Group Ireland, 25 St. Stephen's Green, Dublin 2, Ireland (a division of Penguin Books Ltd.)
Penguin Group (Australia), 250 Camberwell Road, Camberwell, Victoria 3124, Australia
(a division of Pearson Australia Group Pty. Ltd.)
Penguin Books India Pvt. Ltd., 11 Community Centre, Panchsheel Park, New Delhi—110 017, India
Penguin Group (NZ), 67 Apollo Drive, Mairangi Bay, Auckland 1310, New Zealand
(a division of Pearson New Zealand Ltd.)
Penguin Books (South Africa) (Pty.) Ltd., 24 Sturdee Avenue, Rosebank, Johannesburg 2196,
South Africa

Penguin Books Ltd., Registered Offices: 80 Strand, London WC2R 0RL, England

This is a work of fiction. Names, characters, places, and incidents either are the product of the author's imagination or are used fictitiously, and any resemblance to actual persons, living or dead, business establishments, events, or locales is entirely coincidental. The publisher does not have any control over and does not assume any responsibility for author or third-party websites or their content.

A LADY OF SCANDAL

A Berkley Sensation Book / published by arrangement with the author

PRINTING HISTORY
Berkley Sensation mass-market edition / February 2007

Copyright © 2007 by Cheryl Zach.
Excerpt from *A Lady Betrayed* copyright © 2007 by Cheryl Zach.
Cover art by Leslie Peck.
Cover design by George Long.

ISBN: 978-0-425-21425-1

BERKLEY SENSATION®
Berkley Sensation Books are published by The Berkley Publishing Group,
a division of Penguin Group (USA) Inc.,
375 Hudson Street, New York, New York 10014.
BERKLEY SENSATION is a registered trademark of Penguin Group (USA) Inc.
The "B" design is a trademark belonging to Penguin Group (USA) Inc.

PRINTED IN THE UNITED STATES OF AMERICA

10 9 8 7 6 5 4 3 2 1

For my editor,
Cindy Hwang,
with great appreciation for her years of
support, friendship and definitive editing skills

One

The North Country coach rumbled into the London innyard almost two hours late. Just in time, too, the passenger in the far right corner thought, as the mole on her nose seemed about to drop off.

The gray-haired dame dressed all in rusty black pushed the offending article back up with one long finger. Her legs were cramped from sitting so long in the confined space, and her maid had to help her rise. From beneath her battered bonnet she peered with suspiciously keen eyes as the serving girl guided her down from the crowded public coach. Back bowed with age, she used her cane to support herself as she at last set foot on the dusty ground. She looked about her as she waited for her servant to follow.

The nondescript posting house where the coach had ended its long journey was neither the best nor the worst of its kind. Aromas of baking bread and mutton stew, mixing with heavier scents of ale and less savory stable odors, beckoned the weary travelers who emerged from the vehicle. Her back ached—she ached all over!—but the lady in the worn widow's weeds also felt the emptiness in her stomach after the long, jolting ride, so she hoped the food would taste as good as it smelled. Eager to go inside and see about refreshment, she looked around for her companion.

Her maid had barely stepped down from the coach when the girl jumped and her eyes widened. The pudgy man in the puce waistcoat was behind her, the same one who had bedeviled her through most of their long ride south. It took only a glance at Cordelia's set lips to know that he had pinched her bottom again, the louse!

The gray-haired dame narrowed her eyes. Despite the fact that she had spent her whole life in the barren reaches of northern Yorkshire, she knew his type—one look at a pretty face and shapely figure and he couldn't keep his hands to himself! He assumed that a maidservant had no recourse when advances were made by a so-called gentleman—and, judging by his disheveled and half-drunken appearance, he barely deserved the title. He'd been gulping rum from a silver pocket flask through most of the journey.

She would show him differently.

She raised her walking stick and took two quick steps forward, striking the lout about his shoulders with a vigor unexpected in one so advanced in years.

He yelped with pain. "Here, now, have do! 'Tis only a serving girl!"

"I'll teach you to respect a lady . . . I mean, a female, serving girl or not, you reprobate!" she answered, in a surprisingly youthful voice. Belatedly, she realized she had straightened to her full height, forgetting her posture of old age and infirmity.

The stable lad who had come out to hold the heads of the coach's forward pair, the coachman, and two servants from the inn, as well as the last of the passengers who had not yet gone inside, all stared at her with varying expressions of shock and surprise.

She allowed her shoulders to drop forward again and her back to bend, and the end of her stick to drop to the ground. "It's my doctor's syrup for the rh-rheumatism," she said, putting the faint quaver back into her voice. "Works w-wonders, it does."

"More like the devil's work, it is," the stable boy muttered. "I 'eard of witches comin' from the north, I 'ave!"

One of the other servants crossed herself nervously. The remaining spectators continued to gape. With surprising boldness for a mere servant, her maid took her arm and pulled her away from the group.

"You've done it now, Ophelia," she muttered. "We'll have to find another inn for the night."

Swallowing her chagrin, Ophelia Applegate felt the mole on the end of her nose wobble once more. Twitching her nose and wishing she could give it a good scratch, she turned her head and hastily pushed the artificial blob back before it fell off. That would really send her now too-attentive audience into hysterics!

Then she followed her twin sister as Cordelia picked up their carpetbag and set off down the narrow London cross street. Remembering to use her walking stick for its intended purpose—but, my, it had felt good to dust that leach's fat toad-like frame and see the look of shock on his face—she hobbled down the lane beside her sister. Perhaps putting pebbles into her shoes to insure that she minced along like an elderly lady had been too much verisimilitude. Perhaps, after all, one could get too deeply inside a role! Although forgetting that she was supposed to be bent with age had been a serious slip.

And now, where would they spend their first night in London?

Her twin was saying just the same.

"It's not as if we know the city," Cordelia worried aloud as they walked. "And this neighborhood does not look the best."

"It's not so bad," Ophelia argued, glancing about them. Although the ramshackle buildings that lined the cramped byway—it looked like more of an alley than a street—were not reassuring, she had a habit of contradicting her sister that was familiar to both. Cordelia didn't even seem to notice her statement. She had focused her attention on avoiding a pile of horse manure.

"Hold on a moment," Ophelia added. "Let me empty these rocks out of my shoes. They're killing my feet."

"I told you that was a foolish idea, Miss Future Toast of London," Cordelia muttered, but she paused to allow Ophelia to lean against her and take off first one shoe, shaking the small pebbles out of her leather boot before sliding it back on her foot and relacing it, then repeating the action with the other. She added a few more words under her breath, and Ophelia didn't have to make them out to know what her twin had said.

"Yes, I know what you think of my plan to come to London. You could have stayed safely at home!" she snapped.

"And let you go off to town alone?" Cordelia raised her lovely brows with their delicate arch. As Ophelia watched, it was almost like staring into a looking glass. They both had hair of a sadly indifferent shade of brown, but at least with a pleasing natural wave that made it curl about their faces, and eyes that were colored an uninteresting if changeable hazel. Their features were regular and pleasing enough; certainly there had been besotted young men who had called them beautiful, even if the same eager suitors did sometimes confuse them one for the other, though family members who knew them well did not. But of these men she had found no one in their isolated shire who had stirred her heart or caught her fancy.

Or who had distracted her from her most cherished dream—the dream she had not dared to share with her father or her older sisters because she knew what they would say: how impossible, how unattainable, even shocking it was.

She wanted to tread the boards, to go onstage, to act out the wonderful stories that played inside her head!

But she knew what her older sisters would have told her, with a great deal of unnecessary lectures: the sad fact was that ladies did not become actresses. To do so would be to put oneself beyond the pale of Society—and she knew that well enough. She would be cast off from her family, unable to be received in Polite Company, despite the fact that her sisters would no doubt still love her. Despite their familial bonds, they would not be able to see her or acknowledge her, and thinking of that fact made Ophelia's eyes dampen. Perhaps there would be some way they could smuggle letters to her, once her father, sadly, with reluctance, had disowned her, cast her off, as he would be forced to do. She had braced herself for it, prepared herself, though she knew she would shiver and cry—she would not be able to help herself—when it happened. She was sensitive that way, and besides, she adored her father.

But when she became a great actress (the Toast of London), as Ophelia knew would occur, and soon, she was sure, she would set up in nice rooms, no, a house of her own in Mayfair— she had read about the fashionable part of the city in the occasional newspapers that sometimes came their way—and she would keep a guest chamber (a score of them!) and just perhaps, she could send money so that her sisters might slip away and visit her. . . .

And how would they explain that to their father? The more practical side of her mind inquired, in a voice that sounded annoyingly like her sister Cordelia's.

They would make up a ruse, she told it, pushing the commonsensical voice away. They could say they were visiting a relative.

And what relative did their own father not know about? came the answer.

Ophelia frowned, trying to come up with a response, and not looking what she was about, stubbed her toe on a loose stone.

"Ouch," she exclaimed. She stopped and looked about them. The buildings were only growing more shabby, and there was still no sign of a decent inn. Shaking her head, Ophelia lifted her foot and rubbed her abused toe as well as she could through the leather of her worn boot.

Still, if they were destined to wander about the town, and one of the most shabby neighborhoods, too, they could at least make good use of their rambling. Ophelia knew where she wished to go, and it was also one place where she was sure that no one would be in bed at an early hour.

The next time the narrow lane crossed a bigger street, she led her sister into the larger avenue where they could feel less alone. And she waved down a passing hackney as if she were an experienced traveler.

"Ophelia," her sister said, her tone urgent. "What are you doing? We do not have enough funds to spare the coin to hire a vehicle!"

"Yes, we do," she retorted. The cab fare would take a big chunk out of their carefully hoarded purse, true, but if her plan worked, they would then not need to pay for their night's lodgings. And besides, her feet hurt.

"We wish to go to the Malory Road Theater," she told the driver, who nodded as they clambered into the hackney.

The theater she wished to visit was not as grand as Covent Garden or Drury Lane, but it was still a creditable venue for a new actress's debut, and dreaming of her first performance on that wonderful stage, she kept only half her mind on the shops and houses that slipped by them, or the other carriages and wagons that crowded the streets. There would be time enough for shopping later, when she was the toast of the town and had riches enough to buy all the beautiful clothes, fetching hats and flashing jewels that she wanted!

Beside her, Cordelia clutched their bag and peered at the passing buildings as they bounced over the pavement until they reached the theater. Then Ophelia paid the driver, and they climbed down again.

Here the street was crowded with vehicles and people coming and going. She saw ladies in fine gowns and heavy evening cloaks, gentlemen in tall hats and dark jackets and sleek pantaloons, as well as urchins running here and there to brush away the horse pies and collect a penny or two as their reward for leaving the pavement clearer for patrician feet to make their way unsoiled into the theater.

On the street, vendors called out, "Hot pies, gents, ladies!" and "Get'cher roasted chestnuts right 'ere!"

The rich and savory aromas reminded Ophelia, whose stomach rumbled painfully, that she and her sister had had no dinner.

But what was an empty stomach compared to the chance to at last realize the dream of a lifetime? To convince the manager of this grand theater—well, it was mostly a plain wooden building, but in front was a long row of arches which added a facade of grandeur—that she was a gifted actress who deserved the opportunity to set foot on the stage of a real London theater? No, it wasn't actually licensed, but still, it was a place to start!

Ophelia's heart beat fast at the very thought. "We must buy tickets," she told her sister. "Then I will see the manager and—"

"No, we will not!" Cordelia said, her tone firm.

Ophelia felt as if her most cherished dream had collapsed about her ears. "But, Cordelia, I must—"

"You spent enough money to pay for a night's lodging on that cab ride, Ophelia!" Cordelia frowned. "Or, at least, I think you did. I'm not sure about London prices. But we don't dare spend another farthing. We don't want to end up penniless and on the streets! It's dangerous enough to be here without family or friends to go to."

"But I must talk to the manager," Ophelia tried to get her twin to see reason.

"Surely you can do that without buying a ticket?"

Ophelia bit her lip. Normally, she could persuade anyone to listen to her, anyone except her sister. For example, convincing the squire back home, their middle sister's father-in law, to allow them to go into the next market town had been child's play, though once he found that they had run away from home, he might not be so persuadable next time, she thought. But Cordelia knew her twin too well to bend to her wiles.

And a perfect stranger—it might take a little time; she had wit enough to know that many girls might want to become actresses, and the manager of the theater might receive many petitions from young ladies (young women) wanting to go on the stage. So she must have enough time to speak to him at length, to display her charms and be sure she had the chance for a proper audition, and she didn't know how these things were done. Plus, she was slightly disadvantaged at the moment, still decked out as an old hag. She had meant to change her clothes, wash her face and present herself at her charming best.

But perhaps she could make the disguise work for her: if he

could see her act as an elderly widow, poignant and alone, if she could make that role convincing, surely he would see her potential as an actress.

She had been in a church pageant once when she was small, and she had acted in private theatricals, of course, wonderfully moving dramas which she had written herself, acting out the best parts with the help of her older sisters in the smaller roles—Cordelia always refused to participate in such folly, as she called it—but that was not the same as a public play.

But since ladies didn't do such things, there was no way she could have garnered experience in provincial companies. And there was no point in running away to join a company of thespians in York! No, it had to be London or nothing. And as for ladies not going onstage . . .

She was so tired of hearing that sad refrain. She shook her head so vigorously that a shower of powder drifted into the air. She sneezed.

Her twin waved her hand to diffuse the cloud of fine particles. "Mind what you do, or you'll have no gray left in your hair at all. Your precious disguise will be for naught."

Ophelia refrained from moving her head, but she frowned. "You don't understand," she told her sister, with more anger in her voice than she'd intended.

A gentleman nearby, who had been eying her sister with appreciation, raised his brows. Ignoring him, Ophelia made her way to the entrance and spoke to the man who guarded the door.

"Ticket, ma'am? Last night of the play's run! Two shillings for—"

"No, I wish to speak to the manager."

"I'm afraid the manager is occupied, ma'am." The man coughed. "If you won't wish no ticket, please do not block the entrance."

"But—"

"Step aside," he said again, and someone behind her pushed so she found herself jostled willy-nilly away from the doorway.

Frowning, she turned back to her sister. "There must be an-

other entrance," she said. She led her twin toward the corner
of the building, although they had to take a circuitous path as
they avoided a crowd of well-dressed ladies and gentlemen
who were headed toward the front doors. One of the women
glanced at their modest traveling dress and sniffed in apparent
disdain, which made Ophelia stiffen. She had found her
widow's disguise in the squire's attic, relics of his late mother-
in-law, good woman that she undoubtably had been.

After they turned the corner, Ophelia spotted a side door
and hurried to it, knocking on the wooden panel. When a man
opened the door, she said quickly, "I wish to speak to the manager of the theater."

The man inside looked over her shoulder to leer openly at
Cordelia. "Got a prime 'un, 'ave you? How much?"

"No, indeed." Annoyed at the constant attention to her sister, Ophelia was wishing intently for her own clothes, clean
hair and a face unadorned with fake warts and wrinkles. "*I*
wish to speak to the manager. I wish to audition for a role on
the stage."

He guffawed. "Don't need any old 'ags, today, Grandma.
Best be about your business."

And before she could protest, he shut the door in her face.

"Oh!" Ophelia gasped in indignation.

"I think your disguise has worked too well, Ophelia," her
twin pointed out. "You'll have to come back tomorrow in your
own clothes and, well, your own face."

Ophelia was forced to nod, though she bubbled with frustration. "I suppose so," she said. But now they still needed a
place to spend the night, and their store of coins was very
light. As she turned back, she glanced about her. At first Ophelia saw only a mangy dog sniffing at a puddle and a pile of
crumpled newsprint, but then she looked farther and what she
saw made her stiffen.

"Good God," she breathed. "Cordelia, look!"

Her sister turned to stare, and her eyes widened. "Oh,
heavens, Ophelia. Someone is breaking into the theater!"

Ophelia gasped. It seemed impossible, but it was true—if
not the theater auditorium itself, the smaller building attached

to it at the rear. The sunlight, never strong as the buildings blocked the sinking sun, was dimming, but even in the growing twilight, she could just make out the form of a man as he worked at an upper window, his shape barely discernable against the darkening shadows.

"Thief!" she shrieked. "Housebreaker!"

At first, no one seemed to take notice of her shrieks. The alley was empty, so she ran to the corner and shouted again.

Then someone did take note and repeated her warning.

"Oy! 'Ousebreaker!"

Someone else in the crowd shouted, too, and there were more noises of alarm. Faces appeared as men ran around from the street, peering down the alley.

Other people gazed out of buildings nearby.

The man at the window dropped down, like a spider on a web, to the window beneath—how did he do that?—and then he somehow disappeared.

"Come along," Cordelia muttered into her sister's ear. "People are staring at us."

"We didn't do anything except save the theater from being burglared. They should thank us!" Ophelia said, her tone indignant.

But any thought of thanks, of being invited in for a private meeting with the manager, of receiving an introduction and finding the perfect opening for her audition, vanished abruptly and painfully as a portly man in a dark suit, his expression harsh and frowning, came out of the side door of the theater and turned to stare at them.

Ophelia instinctively stepped back.

"Perhaps he thinks we're part of the gang of criminals," Cordelia said, keeping her voice low.

"That makes no sense. If we were, why would we alert him to our own company of thieves?" Ophelia argued. But she had no desire to put the argument to the man with the dour glare. If he was the manager . . . oh, dear. This all might be much more difficult that she had imagined.

She was feeling very tired, and they still did not know where they were going to spend the night. The darkness grew more dense with every passing moment, and now she had to admit that her grand scheme might, just possibly, have a few holes in it. Perhaps coming to London with no friends to meet them, very little money, and no idea where to stay might not have been the best plan in the world.

They walked down the side street and turned a corner, but the cityscape did not improve. The buildings on either side were narrow and unappealing. The walkways were becoming more crowded, but not with the types of people the girls were accustomed to seeing.

The men wore dusty threadbare clothes, and some of the women she glimpsed wore low-cut gowns, and their glances were brazen.

"Don't look back, Ophelia," her sister whispered, her voice uneasy. "I think that man in the tattered coat is following us."

Ophelia felt a coldness in her middle that had nothing to do with the coolness in the damp night air.

And now the man in the shabby brown hat and ragged coat stepped up into their path.

"Need lodgings for the night, mum?" he said. "If ye be new to town, I can show ye to some rooms."

"That's very neighborly of you, but—" Ophelia began. Her mouth felt dry, and she glanced wildly toward her sister for help.

"Thank you kindly, sir, but my mistress is meeting relatives," her *maid* said.

"That is, yes, thank you, but I am meeting someone, and we . . . I am already late," Ophelia amended, in a firmer tone. But as she was about to turn away, she found that the man reached out to clutch her arm. She tried to break free, but he tightened his grip.

For a moment they struggled, then he gave her a shove that sent her sprawling to the dirty street. Before she could do more than gasp in outrage, he had laid hands on Cordelia.

"Ye be too long in the tooth, ye old crone, but yon maid should fetch me a good few coppers."

Now Cordelia struggled in his grasp. While she fought to release her arms and kicked at his shins, Ophelia, cold with fear, grabbed her walking stick and jumped back to her feet. She struck the man on his back and hit him again on his side as he shouted in surprise. But although he hesitated, another man, thin and dressed even more shabbily, pushed Ophelia aside and joined his mate in the attack.

Despite her resistence, they were pulling Cordelia toward a twisting alley. If they took her away to some dark and terrible fate, Ophelia might never locate her twin!

Ophelia cried, "Oh, help us!"

Two

No one seemed to even notice their plight, much less Ophelia's calls.

Cordelia, who had taken the measure of this London neighborhood long ago, did not waste her breath on cries for help. Poorly dressed passersby averted their eyes, and no one seemed to take note of a mere case of kidnapping. No, no one would help them here. She and her twin would have to look out for themselves.

Oh, why had they come to this miserable city! Kicking and punching, Cordelia fought for her life, sure that if these two villains succeeded in parting her from her sister, she might never see light of day again. After an evil assault, her throat would be cut and her body thrown into the Thames, or else she'd be taken away and given over to some living hell of a brothel, and even if she had the chance to escape, she might be too wounded in body and spirit to seek out anyone who knew her—

She fought harder.

She kicked the first man in the groin with her heavy boot and was gratified to hear him grunt in pain. But although she clawed next at his face, the man—wiry though he might be—was stronger in the arms and shoulders than she. Despite her efforts, soon he was pinning her arms back against her body.

"No!" Ophelia shrieked from just beyond. "Help, we must save my sister!"

She threw herself upon the first man, trying to pull him away from Cordelia. But the assailant tossed her off as if she were as light as the merest autumn leaf, then the second man punched her in her stomach, causing her to fold in two and collapse on the street.

With no help at all, Cordelia bit back a moan of despair. The men were scrawny as ill-fed roosters, but there were two of them, and they knew every trick. Although she bit and kicked and scratched and pummeled, they pushed her arms down, evaded her feet and pulled her steadily toward a twisting alley. Stunned and helpless, Ophelia lay still in the dirt, and no one else was here to care—

"Got spirit, this un 'as," the first man muttered. "I should get extra blunt for such a wildcat."

"Yeah, be sure to tell Madam Nell that, won't ya?" the other man answered, curling his lips. "I bet she'll be right struck."

They chortled, their breath rank upon her face.

These words were so ominous that, terrified, Cordelia was spurred to a last burst of furious energy. For a few moments her struggles kept them all rooted to the pavement as she fought with every ounce of strength in her. But again, the men, through sheer brute force, pushed her hands down and forced her toward the next alley with its denser shadows. Cordelia thought she could glimpse inside the blackness a future too appalling to imagine.

Perhaps she should try another tack. Cordelia shut her eyes and let her body go limp.

"Eh, she's swooned. 'Bout time, too, the little hellcat. You pick up 'er feet and we can make better time," the first man ordered his henchman.

To her disappointment, the other man still held her firmly by the upper body. But as the first villain bent to take hold of her legs, she lifted her feet and kicked him hard in the stomach.

"For Ophelia—" Cordelia muttered, then turned her attention to wresting loose of the other assailant's hold.

Almost, she did it.

But the first thug recovered too quickly, and the second man would not let go, although he puffed at the exertion as she pulled against his grip, swearing as she kicked his shins.

"Od's bod, that smarts, that does. Have do, girl!"

"I got 'er!"

The first man had recovered. Now he held a compact but nasty-looking bludgeon in one hand, and his expression was ugly. "Don't like to mar the goods, as it were, but sometimes, we got no choice, eh, Dinty?"

"Don't kill 'er, mate, or we won't get nutting for our pains. I got bruises from this 'ellion, and I want me coppers for 'er," the smaller man argued, although he eyed the weapon with resignation.

Cordelia's eyes widened, and she held her breath as the ruffian raised the club. Waiting for the blow to fall, she was so focused on the weapon in the man's fist that she hardly noticed the newcomer glide up from behind until he hooked the man's feet out from under him and sent the villain crashing to the ground.

The club fell on the man's own shoulder instead of upon Cordelia's head.

The ruffian shouted in surprise and pain, but the newcomer gave him two quick jabs that seemed to put him rapidly out of the fight. Then before the second villain had as yet moved, Cordelia found the newcomer's strong hand gripping her upper arm and his steely gray eyes accessing the situation.

"I would suggest that you unhand the lady," the stranger said. He had handsome if somewhat rugged features with a firm jaw and arching dark brows.

The smaller thug stuttered. "I-I got a knife, gov," he said. Fumbling in his ragged clothing, he pulled out a blade about six inches long.

Cordelia, who had enjoyed the briefest taste of relief, now held her breath again.

"Oh, come," the stranger said. "How uncivil." Dressed in fashionable evening clothes, he lifted an ebony walking stick.

The second thug chortled, and Cordelia swallowed hard.

"You gonna bow to me, next?" the man sneered. "Should I run away screamin' in fear or drop 'ee a curtsy, like?"

The newcomer twisted the top of the cane and pulled out a thin, silvery blade. The ruffian's laughter stopped abruptly. He swore again, then suddenly released his grip on Cordelia's arm and pushed her toward the new arrival.

Afraid she would be skewered like a roasted piglet, she exclaimed involuntarily. But the stranger lowered the thin sword in time. Cordelia found herself propelled into his arms as the second thug took to his heels and disappeared down the twisting alleyway.

For a moment Cordelia thought she might swoon for real. She swayed as the stranger slipped the long blade back into the walking stick and reached to steady her.

But it would be a shame to waste the touch of his hand on her arm, or the feel of the other arm that now wrapped itself around her shoulders. He felt firm with muscle, like a weapon himself, ready to protect a lady alone in an alien and dangerous city.

You don't even know this man, she scolded herself. Have a care, Cordelia; remember your common sense!

I know he has come to my aid, she answered herself, at a time when I was never more in need. The fear had been so deep, and her peril so real. It still lingered in the back of her mind, leaving her knees rubbery and her limbs strangely weak.

Finding it a little hard to take a breath, she clutched at the coat fabric that covered his well-muscled chest.

"It's all right," he murmured into her ear. "Take long breaths, slowly. I know you've had a shock. But you are safe now."

Unable as yet to command her voice, she nodded. She clung to him, feeling more secure inside his arms than she had ever felt in her life. She might have felt this protected as a child perched on her father's knee, but this man was not in the least fatherly, and what she felt, standing so close, inhaling the masculine scent of him—clean linen and the faintest hint of male skin, perspiration and soap in a somehow pleasing mixture—was nothing like what a child would feel . . .

Surprised at the feelings inside her, Cordelia found she was blushing, and she looked away from the cool eyes that seemed to see too deeply inside her. And yet—

"It was you!" She stood up straighter inside the circle of his arms, and even the realization that shocked her did not— she only realized later—make her break out of his hold. "You're the man we saw trying to break into the theater! Are you a thief, sir, an ordinary housebreaker?"

He lifted those dark arching brows. "So it appears. And you cried out for the crowd, alerted them to my presence. They would have shouted for the Watch, tried to have me charged, leaving me both poorer and with my neck in certain jeopardy."

She felt a ridiculous urge to protest. "But—"

He ignored her interruption. "Under the circumstances, do you not think it noble of me to save your honor, perhaps your neck, too, regardless that you so recently put mine at risk?"

He lifted one hand and touched her neck lightly, just beneath her chin. His fingers felt so warm against her skin that she shivered, and while she should have been appalled, perhaps even afraid, she found she still felt strangely conflicted.

His odd-colored eyes were mocking, and his tone . . . seemed to be mocking, too, she wasn't sure. But he sounded like an educated man, a gentleman. How could he be a thief? Yet they had seen him at the window. He didn't argue with her label. And if he were, how could she in good conscience associate with such a man?

Yet how could she not be grateful to a man who had just saved her from such villains? And he held her firmly but so gently, and his nearness caused a strange weakness inside her and his touch on her skin sent ripples of awareness through her whole body, causing a curious thrill all the way down to her belly . . .

She blushed even more deeply. "Yes, I must thank you for your fortuitous rescue, sir. We would not have been here at all, it was just that my sister was determined to have her chance to go onstage—oh, heavens, my sister!"

They found Ophelia moaning and holding her stomach. Cordelia helped her up, disturbed to see that the Future Toast of London still looked green and had to cling to her sister in order to stand.

"Are you all right?" Cordelia asked, remembering how weak she herself had felt.

Ophelia tried to nod. "And you?" she asked, her voice barely above a whisper. "Those awful men . . . what . . ."

"This man . . . I-I'm afraid I don't know your name, sir?" She almost hoped that Ophelia would not realize just who their Good Samaritan was, and, in fact, at the moment, her twin did not seem inclined to stare closely at his face. Besides, it was now so dark in this back lane that it was hard to see anyone's features closely. Cordelia had heard that more prosperous parts of the city had modern gas streetlights, but this lane showed few lights of any kind, and the ones she had glimpsed were old-fashioned lamps with oil wicks, and even they were few and far between.

The stranger gazed about them. "We had better be on the move, ladies. This is not a prosperous neighborhood, and there are worse than those two thugs about."

At his warning, Ophelia shuddered.

"Do you have someone to stay with, an address I can escort you to?" he asked.

The girls looked at each other.

"Surely you didn't come to London without a friend or relative to take refuge with?" He sounded incredulous, and well he might, Cordelia thought, her spirits sinking even lower.

"You expected to present yourself to the manager of the Malory Road Theater and obtain a position at once?"

"I am, sir, a fine actress!" Ophelia straightened her shoulders, regardless of her gray powdered hair and black weeds, which he could not see well anyhow.

"Really? And just where have you played, my dear?"

He appeared to have penetrated her sister's disguise, Cordelia thought.

Bristling at the intimate tone—but then, he thought he was

talking to an actress, not a lady, so what could she say—Cordelia bit her lip as she waited for her twin to reply.

Ophelia hesitated.

"I thought so. It's not that simple, my innocent country miss, and Mr. Nettles, the manager of the Malory Road Theater, will eat your liver for dinner and have the rest of you, body and soul, for dessert, if you don't look out. We suspect it's not just plays that he makes his blunt off, and a pretty young thing with no one there to protect you—you'd be gist for the flesh mills, I'm afraid. If not his, someone else's."

Cordelia had been following behind the man, eyes down as she tried to see the rough stones of the pavement, clutching her sister's hand so that Ophelia would not disappear again, and for a moment the meaning of their rescuer's cryptic words eluded her. Then Ophelia stopped abruptly and she, too, paused as their meaning became clear.

Join the ranks of the demimonde? Good heavens!

"Never!" Ophelia declared, her voice carrying her usual theatrical flourish.

"Certainly not!" Cordelia agreed, with less drama but a firm tone.

"Indeed?" She could hear his skepticism. "Your sense of virtue is commendable, but an empty belly has vanquished many a conscience ere now, I fear. Come along. You don't want to be lost in this neighborhood."

They ran to catch up. The night air was damp, and they had to almost hug the buildings to avoid the occasional carriage that went by. In the carriage lights, she noted that fog was forming in wispy patches.

It seemed that they walked a long way, and Cordelia's imagination, never as wild as her sister's, was nonetheless working just fine. Where was he taking them? To his own rooms? They could not stay with a man, a perfect stranger, much less a man of ill repute, a thief, even if he had saved them from kidnappers and, likely, white slavers.

Yet, even if she demanded that they be taken to a reputable hotel, she was not sure that any hotel in this rundown part of town would be safe. Even if such a thing existed, she was not sure they had enough money left to pay for two people's lodgings.

Oh, they should not have spent their coin on that hackney, drat Ophelia's ambitious schemes, anyhow! Their coach fares south had cost more than they'd expected, and then there had been meals along the way; they should have just gone hungry and saved their money. Remembering meals of overdone mutton and stringy chicken, she swallowed. Posting houses dreadfully overcharged travelers who had little choice in venue, but going without meals had been surprisingly hard to do when one's stomach was empty. She thought of his warning and sighed again.

Frowning, Cordelia considered their current situation. At least she had a last desperate card up her sleeve. Lord Gabriel Sinclair, their half brother, might still be in London. Even though they barely knew him, he would surely lend them enough money to get them back home to Yorkshire, at least if she could convince her sister to go! Even Ophelia must see that she had tried to get an audition and what more could she do? She could not condemn herself and her twin to starvation and death on the London streets—enough was enough!

After all, they had almost been abducted over this foolish scheme. Cordelia was no longer in humor for indulging lifelong dreams, even for a beloved sister, not when it led them into such perilous straits.

But where was this man taking them? How long would they trek through the dark?

"Need a good time, gov?" a female voice inquired out of the darkness.

Cordelia jumped. They were approaching a rare streetlight, and she saw the woman standing at the edge of the small circle of yellow light, her face rouged and her dress low-cut. She was a streetwalker.

She felt Ophelia shiver. Was this someone whom hunger had forced into the direst of fates? Cordelia felt a stirring of pity. If the kidnappers had had their way, this could have been her—

"No, thank you," the man who led them said, his tone polite.

"Guess not, you already got a damn 'arem," the prostitute said as she made out their shapes in the growing mist. "Lawd, 'ow many women you need, gov?"

"I am a man of surprising talents," he answered, his tone smooth.

Her laughter faded behind them as they walked on.

Cordelia found she was clenching her fist. Wonderful, perhaps he was a white slaver, too, she thought darkly. Beside her, she sensed her sister's growing tension. Where was he taking them?

She should not have told him that they had no family here.

"We have a half brother who is a lord," she said, her voice a little too loud.

"And I am a gentleman of means," he agreed, in his usual sardonic tone. "But taking two young ladies home with me could cause gossip. For tonight, you should be safe where we are going."

But they had only his word for that, the word of a stranger.

He saved you from the men who attacked you, she told herself. Perhaps only for his own ends, she answered herself. He was a thief, he had not denied it. No one even knew they were here. If they disappeared, who would know—

"What shall we do?" Ophelia leaned closer to whisper.

Cordelia wanted very much to box her twin's ear. "I don't know!" she answered, keeping her voice low. "We can't sleep on the street. We don't have the money to try to locate our half brother tonight, if he's even in London. This plan was madness, Ophelia, didn't I say so?"

They walked a few more feet in the darkness, the clouds above them scudding across the sky and the moon flicking in and out.

Ophelia suddenly tightened her grip on Cordelia's hand. "Run!"

Three

*A*cting on instinct, Cordelia clung to her sister's hand, her other holding the carpetbag, and ran for her life. They pounded down the pavement, away from the man whose guidance they had been following, and plunged farther into the darkness.

Only when they had—she assumed—left him behind and not until her side ached from running did her sister slow, and they both stopped, leaning against each other to take ragged breaths. She could make out no clatter of footfalls behind them, although she listened anxiously to detect any signs of pursuit.

"Ophelia, didn't we just say we cannot spend the night on the street? What are you thinking?"

"You also said we don't know if we can trust our Good Samaritan or not; he may be a knight in shining armor or a wolf in sheep's clothing," her sister said dramatically, although with a sad mixing of metaphors. "We are not going to sleep on the street!"

"But—"

"No, listen. When the moon came out a moment ago, I saw a church steeple!" Ophelia was still short of breath. She paused to take a breath again, and then she spoke more slowly. "We can find the church, it's not far away. There should be a rectory nearby, and surely they will give us aid, Cordelia. If not, perhaps we can find a way into the church itself."

Feeling a great wave of relief, Cordelia nodded. At last, something they could do for themselves, without having to rely on the doubtful help of a man they did not know and were not sure they could trust. It wasn't a foolproof plan, but it was a plan.

"Very well," she whispered. "But be very quiet. We don't want to alert him to our position." Was he looking for them at all, or had he given up in disgust? Perhaps he would think them too much trouble, whether he was being helpful or had more nefarious motives.

So they stood clutching each other for support and listened hard. The street was strangely quiet, for a city at night. Cordelia could hear faint noises of distant carriages, faraway clangs and clatters of unknown origins, but the houses on this street seemed to slumber along with their residents. The fog was rising, smelling of sewage and stable odors and making her wrinkle her nose, and it blurred the buildings around them and did not help their search. The darkness was growing more murky with every moment, and the moon was a capricious ally, hidden once more behind the clouds.

It had to emerge again, in time, Cordelia told herself, scanning the gray clouds just visible against the darker sky. Surely. So they waited, and she tried to convince herself that their rescuer—they did not even know his name; surely an honest man would have told them his name!—was not about to reach out and grab them from every shadow.

The clammy cold seemed to seep inside her cloak. It had been ripped during her struggle with the two would-be kidnappers, and she tried to draw it closer around her shoulders, but she shivered anyhow, partly from the damp chill as the fog thickened, partly from the fear that threatened to slow her thoughts.

Only the feel of her twin's answering tremors kept her from total panic. Ophelia was frightened, too. Cordelia had to be brave for her sister's sake.

"In what direction did you see the church spire?" she whispered. They had been standing here for some time, and still the obdurate moon had not reappeared.

"That way, I think," Ophelia pointed.

Cordelia ignored the slight tremor of the finger that her sister held out. "Then we must make our way in that direction," she decided.

Ophelia did not object.

Better to proceed the wrong way than to stand here until they were too terrified to take action at all, Cordelia thought. So, hand in hand, they walked along the pavement. Between the darkness and the fog, which now swirled about them like a kind of dry bog—at least it could not catch their feet and hold them prisoner like the marshes at home—they had to almost feel their way along the edge of the street.

With painful slowness, they inched along the pavement. The darkness was unabated, and Cordelia began to fear they were going the wrong way. She almost said as much, then hesitated to increase her sister's fear as well as her own.

But presently, Ophelia voiced her concern, too. "It was not this far, Cordelia. I think we have overshot it."

Cordelia swallowed hard and they both stopped. Now what?

And at last, the moon showed its coy face. The faint light was as welcome as any delinquent lover. Cordelia whirled and tried to look in every direction at once. Thank God for church steeples that reached high toward the heavens, she thought, when the tall distinctive shape caught her eye.

"There!" she cried, then clapped one hand to her mouth as she remembered the need for quiet. The stranger who had been escorting them had likely long ago gone about his own affairs, but there might be other miscreants about the streets, and they did not wish to meet them. She did not expect honest men to be out at this hour.

"We were going the wrong direction. Come on, before we lose it again," she urged her twin, and they set off again as quickly as they could. Within a couple of minutes, the moon disappeared, taking its scant light with it, but this time, at least

Cordelia believed they were traveling in the proper direction, so she was more sanguine about finding their destination.

The darkness was its own obstacle, however. Cordelia, who was slightly in the lead, stumbled over a loose paving stone and almost fell to her knees.

"Are you all right?" Ophelia cried.

The pain was too great for Cordelia to reply at once. She blinked back tears, wondering if her toe was broken. Drawing deep breaths, she leaned against her sister, at last able to say, "It is . . . just a trifle." She leaned forward to put her hands on her knees, and in a minute more could straighten and move on, this time more slowly.

At least she detected the pile of wood in their path, and they edged around it.

Next, a dog growled and barked like a demented soul. Cordelia felt her heart hammer in her chest at the sudden fierce sound. Was it penned or free—and if so, would it attack?

She could almost feel its teeth rending her flesh. And Ophelia was particularly afraid of big dogs.

Her sister clutched her arm. "Oh, Cordelia!"

"Stand still," Cordelia whispered. "We don't know where it is."

The dog continued to bark, but the sounds did not seem to advance. Perhaps it was behind a fence or on a rope or chain.

Then moonlight glinted through patchy clouds. Cordelia looked around. She could not detect any sign of the dog, but . . . "There, we can cut behind that house, and I see the church itself. If there is a rectory, it should be close."

She grabbed her sister's arm—Ophelia still clung to her—and sprang over a low stone wall while she could still see it. They half ran, half stumbled over a littered piece of ground and made it almost to the back of the church's grounds before the moon disappeared behind a cloud, taking its faint light with it.

Cordelia paused, and her sister with her. Once more they edged forward through inky blackness. Moving one foot at a time, feeling her way, she mouthed words most inappropriate so close to a church. Surely they could not get lost again. Yet it seemed to take a very long time to cover what had seemed such a short distance.

Had they gone the wrong direction again? In the darkness, it was so easy to become disoriented. Cordelia inched ahead, Ophelia holding on to her skirt, both too miserable to talk. Then something white loomed up out of the blackness, and she almost fell over it.

Catching herself against it, she drew a deep breath. It felt cool beneath her palms, seemed to be some kind of stone and she detected indentations in the gritty surface.

"It is a gravestone," she said.

Behind her, Ophelia gasped. "Oh!" she said. "I hope not another poor lost lady who followed a strange man who promised to help her—"

"Ophelia! This is not the time to be spinning tales," Cordelia snapped. "This means we are still on the church grounds." She backed away from the grave marker. "Now, if we can just find the church and not keep going in circles . . ."

She shut her eyes for a moment, thinking of their parish back home. Didn't the graves usually face the church? If so . . . she turned and led the way again, with her sister still holding on to her. If they became separated . . . no, she didn't want to think of that!

Presently, she felt smoother ground beneath her feet, then—

"Ouch!"

"What is it?" Ophelia demanded.

"A rose bush," Cordelia said. "Mind the thorns." She rubbed her arm where the bush had caught her and edged around it. They made it a few feet without more obstacles, then the roughness beneath her feet tripped her before she could catch herself. Ophelia was too close to stop, so she tumbled after her, landing on top of Cordelia.

"Oh, rats!" Cordelia said. "Ouch, have a care—that's my stomach you're leaning on."

Something gritty moved beneath her hands as she tried to scramble up.

"What is this?" Ophelia complained, coughing. "I'm all dusty."

"I think," Cordelia said, trying to shake off her skirts, "we have fallen into the cinder pile."

"Oh, lovely," Ophelia grumbled. "As if we were not dirty enough."

"No one would recognize you now, that's for sure." Cordelia suddenly had an insane desire to laugh.

Her sister giggled. "Nor you."

"And we must be near a kitchen, so the rectory must be nearby."

"Oh, that's true." Ophelia sounded more cheerful.

A circle of light appeared a few feet away. It came from a lantern, held up by a man who stood in a doorway.

"Who is there?"

They had forgotten to be quiet, Cordelia realized with chagrin. They had been talking and laughing like lackwits. Was it the man who had led them through the darkness? No, this man was tall and broad-shouldered, too, but he was fair and his voice more mellow.

"Oh, we are looking for the church, seeking assistance, if you please. We are two ladies left adrift by no fault of our own," Ophelia said quickly.

"You'd better come in," the man said. "Not to the church, which is cold and empty at this hour. Come across to the rectory."

Oh, they had found it, at last!

With his lantern to guide them, it was a ridiculously simple matter to follow the path from the church across to the simple stone rectory and into the side door, while they gave him a shortened and simplified version of their misadventure.

The tall and surprisingly youthful vicar, who introduced himself as Giles Sheffield, put down his lantern and took their cloaks. Mrs. Madigan, his motherly housekeeper, clucked over them, mercifully did not comment on their grimy clothes and blackened cheeks and even dirtier hands, only offered them warm water and soap and a towel to wash off the grime of their passage through the dark, and promised hot tea and sandwiches very shortly. When they were more presentable, the vicar guided them down the hall toward the parlor.

"My cousin is visiting, too, but you needn't mind him," he said cheerfully. "How upsetting that you should have arrived in London and found your relations not here to greet you. The city has many dangers for young women alone, without family or friends to protect them. By all means, you must spend tonight here. We will make up a guest chamber for you."

"You're very kind," Cordelia said, her relief so palatable that it seemed as bright as the candlelight that at last vanquished the darkness they had struggled through for so long. "We have been through some difficult hours."

"Yes, you are an angel," Ophelia added, with her usual hyperbole. "I was so terrified!" She also seemed very taken with his fair good looks, smiling at him often.

The vicar opened the door and showed them in to the parlor. It was a long room with well-worn wing chairs and a plain deal table and a fire in the hearth, which warmed the air. And seated before the fire was another gentleman with dark hair, his back to them. He turned and rose when they entered.

It was their rescuer.

Four

"*You!*"

"You have met my cousin?" the vicar asked, his tone surprised.

Unable to stop herself, Cordelia glared at the thief, who grinned at her, apparently quite unrepentant. "You were bringing us to a church?" she demanded, remembering her unsettling fears as they had walked through the foggy darkness.

"You don't like churches? This is the rectory, actually. And I told you you'd be safe here."

Hearing herself, Cordelia blushed at her tone of outrage. "Of course I like churches, I mean . . . but you could have said where you were taking us!"

"I didn't think you'd believe me."

He was surely right, and she almost admitted as much. But to think of him sitting at his ease in front of the fire while they had been stumbling about through the dark, falling over rocks and tumbling into the cinder pit . . . well, really!

"And were you not even going to look for us?" she demanded, seething.

"If you did not care for my escort . . ." he murmured, then

gave her a devilish grin. "Yes, if you had not turned up very soon, I would have come looking once again, such a Good Samaritan that I am."

Oh! But he was still speaking. She tried to swallow her fury and pay heed.

"I am Ransom Sheffield; the vicar, as he has likely already told you, is my paternal cousin, the Reverend Giles Sheffield," he said.

He leaned back against the far wall, where shadows covered half his face, giving him the look of a saturnine gargoyle, stretching his handsome features into something that appeared evil and deformed. No, she was allowing her imagination to run away with her; it was Ophelia who made up silly melodrama! She was the sensible one, even if she was livid with repressed anger just now.

And he had left many questions unanswered. She still was not sure what sort of man he was. He had made no attempt to explain the robbery attempt; did his clergyman cousin know about that? Was Mr. Ransom Sheffield a thief or not?

"Giles likes taking in strays from the street," he was saying. "So I thought you two would make an excellent fit. I'm afraid I didn't ask your names . . ."

"Now, really, Ransom, that is no way to speak to these ladies." The cleric gave a reassuring nod toward Cordelia. "They will think you are quite deficient in manners."

"I am M-Miss Cordelia Applegate," Cordelia stuttered, trying not to take out her annoyance on the poor vicar. "And this is my sister, Miss Ophelia Applegate. As you may infer; my father is fond of Shakespeare."

Giles Sheffield glanced at Ophelia in her black weeds and gray-powdered hair, but was too polite to ask about the odd disparity of appearance. At least she had washed her face in the kitchen. "Yes, Shakespeare. Your father seems a man of excellent taste. But he did not travel with you?"

She exchanged a quick glance with Ophelia. "Sadly, no. Our father is an invalid; he is back on our small estate in Yorkshire."

"And you said the relative or friend you were to stay with

suffered some mishap and that you were not met, as planned, when you came into town?"

He assumed that no lady in her right mind would come to London without a safe place to stay. She shot an "I told you so" look at her sister, who turned toward the fire and held out her hands, pretending not to see.

"Ah, yes, that is, we have a half brother who has a house in London, but he . . . he does not appear to be in town, and we foolishly neglected to be sure he was home before we set out. And then we had a dreadful fright on the street, and your, ah, cousin did come to our rescue, so even though he is not being very gentlemanly right now, I admit we do owe him a debt of gratitude." She described the abduction attempt, which made the rector look grim. He looked toward Ransom Sheffield.

"Madam Nell's boys, do you think?"

"I should not be surprised," he agreed. "Especially as the sisters had just come from Malory Road, and someone might have followed them."

Cordelia gasped. The kidnapping was not a matter of happenstance? How many evil people there were in this city!

Ophelia pulled off her ancient black bonnet and shook her hair free of its knot, sending a cloud of gray powder into the air. When she faced them again, she looked almost her normal youthful—and pretty—self.

The vicar's eyes widened at this sudden change in Ophelia's appearance.

"Do not blame my sister. It's all my fault," she announced, with an air of contrite confession. Her eyes, just now a melting hazelnut color when seen in the soft candlelight, were opened wide and seemed to glint with tears.

Acting again, her twin thought cynically.

"You see, I had such a desire to go onstage—and I know, I know, ladies are not supposed to tread the boards—but I wanted it so badly. So I dressed as an older lady, to avoid notice on the coach. My sister only came along because I longed so for my chance that she thought I would waste away, fall into a decline and lose my health. She came with me so that I should not be alone and to protect my reputation. I was so selfish that I allowed her to come. I am truly filled with remorse."

This time a tear did slip down her cheek, and Cordelia was not at all surprised to see the vicar hurry forward to press Ophelia's hand.

"Now, now, my child, you're very young, and I'm sure we've all made mistakes in our time."

Since he appeared to be no more than perhaps five and thirty himself, Cordelia had to bite back a smile at this fatherly—or at least big brotherly—pronouncement, but perhaps it was an attitude that came with his chosen profession.

He was still responding to the murmured expressions of contrition uttered by her wretchedly wicked twin.

"We shall contact your half brother and see about getting you back to your family. In the meantime, you will be safe here. My housekeeper, a very good woman, is making up a room for you and your sister. It was most providential that my cousin was able to save you tonight. There are very real dangers in town for young ladies without escort, as you have seen, and I think you have certainly learned a valuable lesson . . ."

He went on talking as he led Ophelia to a chair in front of the fire, seated her and then pulled up a chair for himself. He sat down close to her and continued to talk in a soothing tone, apparently not noticing that he still held her hand.

The other Sheffield cousin observed the pair with a cynical gleam in his eye. "Does she always cast this spell over men?" he asked, his voice low.

"Oh, yes," Cordelia replied, watching the two as she tried not to reveal her resignation. And this time it was a vicar, no less. Perhaps it was just as well that the resident churchman in their parish back home was in his nineties, she told herself. And even he pattted Ophelia's hand quite a lot, she remembered. "It helps, of course, getting rid of the disguise. The warts were a bit off-putting."

He chuckled. "I suppose so." But this time he looked at her, instead of toward Ophelia, and Cordelia was chagrined to find herself blushing. He had caught her staring intently at his face.

"Do you find my countenance disgusts you? I haven't found any warts of late, but—"

"Of course not," she replied, trying to keep her tone dignified. As if he didn't know how good-looking he was! "Why were you trying to break into the theater building?"

"Ah, that." He took his time about answering, but he seemed quite unembarrassed; his cool gray eyes did not slide away from her accusing stare but met her gaze and held it easily.

"Surely," she continued, daring him to contradict her, "you are not a mere housebreaker; I mean, you cannot make a habit of breaking into other people's rooms?"

"You think not?" he answered, keeping his voice low. "What would you judge me to be, then?"

"A gentleman, of course!" she retorted. "You dress and talk like a gentleman, and your bearing is so upright. And then there is the way you came to our aid, with the sword cane and so handy with your fists! You might even be a military man."

Although, she thought, perhaps it would take a thief to understand street brawling . . . How could the man be such a contradiction?

"You do me too much credit," he told her, his long dark lashes half-veiling those strange-colored eyes. "I mean, a handsome coat, a good change of linen, hardly enough on which to judge my character. How do you know I didn't simply lift these clothes from within an honest man's bureau while he slept? Easy enough to do, I wager."

"You seem remarkably eager to claim the title of thief!" She bit her lip, glancing at the other couple, who still appeared engrossed in their own conversation. "Does your cousin the vicar know of your disgraceful occupation?"

He paused for a moment, and she felt that she had scored a hit. "Shall I tell him?" she pressed her advantage.

"A pity to worry the overworked vicar." Ransom Sheffield demurred. "He has enough wretched sinners to worry himself about in this parish. Let's not fret his mind with another."

"Since you are so intractable?" Cordelia suggested.

"I fear so." Ransom smiled down at her, and something in

that predator's grin made all her instincts tingle with a warning: this was not a man to trifle with. She should collect her twin and take them both straight up to bed, she told herself, before that strange and unfamiliar spark inside her surged into a raging flame.

"I imagine I am every bit as docile and biddable, as willing to follow the rules of polite society, as your sister," Ransom Sheffield told her, smiling once more.

"There is no need to insult my sister!" Cordelia snapped.

He raised his brows.

Aghast at what she had implied, Cordelia flushed and looked away. Fortunately, the other two did not seem to have heeded any of their words. Then the door opened, and the housekeeper appeared holding a tray laden with plates of food and a teapot and cups.

"I have tea and sandwiches, Vicar, as you said, and the young ladies' room is ready."

"Thank you, Mrs. Madigan," the young vicar said. He turned to look toward Cordelia and his cousin, and it seemed natural for the two of them to approach the fire as the housekeeper drew up a table and set down the food.

Cordelia found she had a great hollow place where her stomach should be. No doubt that was why she felt so odd inside, when she stood next to the irritating, perhaps totally immoral Sheffield cousin. She tried not to look at him, tried not to be aware of how his arm brushed her shoulder as he bent closer to the table, or of the masculine smell of him as he leaned across to pick up a sandwich from the platter. But it was no use. Her pulse jumped almost as erratically as it had when he had pulled her away from those horrid thugs in the alley . . .

With enormous effort, she pulled her thoughts back to the hot cup of tea the housekeeper had poured out for her and the very welcome plates of sandwiches and small cakes. Oh, she was ravenous. She sat down in one of the smaller chairs and pulled it close to the fireplace, enjoying the waves of warmth, not even caring that—judging by the conversation—Ophelia now seemed to have talked the vicar into allowing her to return to the theater for one more try at an audition. So much for scrupulous moral standards and learning her lesson about rash conduct. . . .

Ophelia would never give up. That came as no surprise to Ophelia's twin. The sandwiches were thickly cut slices of bread layered with chicken and ham and quite delicious. Cordelia took a large bite and consigned her sister to her fate.

After they had finished the light repast, the Applegate sisters said good night. Ransom Sheffield was still staring into the fire when they departed. He turned long enough to make them a polite bow, his expression just a trifle too bland. Somehow, even his courtesies always seemed to hold a sardonic edge.

The vicar showed them upstairs to the Spartan but clean bedroom, set down their carpetbag at the doorway and said good night. Suddenly aware of how weary she was, Cordelia sighed. The endless coach ride south, the long walk through London's streets, the dreadful attack and the fight for her life, and then the bickering with her unsettling savior and their mad dash for safety—her limbs felt heavy and her eyelids leaden.

Tempted to crawl into bed in her traveling costume, she yawned. Pulling off her cloak and bonnet, she shed her outer clothes and tugged her nightgown on over her shift. The room was chilly, even though a minute fire had been lit on the hearth. No doubt the vicar's housekeeping budget was too small to allow for many luxuries, and it was kind of the Reverend Sheffield to indulge his unexpected guests.

She held out her hands to the warmth before turning to the basin on the dresser and splashing water from the jug onto her face and hands, then drying them on the linen towel and hastily crawling between the covers of the bed.

While Ophelia took her turn at the basin, Cordelia shut her eyes. But although she had expected to slip immediately into blissful sleep, instead a mosaic of disjointed images from their chaotic day swam before her closed lids. The horrible men who had attacked her with their loose leering mouths and evil eyes, the shocked stares of the other passengers on the coach when Ophelia had lost her temper and thrown off the trappings of her disguise, and more, so much more.

Ophelia crawled into the other side of the bed. They huddled together, back to back, waiting for warmth to spread, and Cordelia thought again of the infuriating Ransom Sheffield. Was he really a thief? He seemed so obviously a gentleman. He could not be a criminal, could he? And the vicar, who seemed so good-hearted, or was that a sham, too? If not, did he know that his cousin was a housebreaker? The question kept returning . . . felon, or not? And how could the two men, close relatives, be such opposites?

She was too tired to worry over it now. But the shifting images that played inside her closed lids still would not fade, and she blinked in frustration. The chilly air touched her face. Outside, a cat yowled somewhere in the alley, and faintly, a dog barked.

Inside, in a softer rustle of sound, a coal broke on the hearth. Pinpricks of ruby light from the dying fire danced against the blackness, throwing patterns of light against the dark wall. Shivering, intensely thankful that she and her sister were not sharing the alley with the cat, she slipped even lower beneath the blankets and stared at the galaxy of tiny sparks, which slowly faded together as sleep overcame her.

And then she was blinking against full golden sunlight. Good heavens, how late was it? She realized she did not sense another person in the bed. She looked over her shoulder, but the other side of the mattress was empty. Alarmed, Cordelia looked at the rest of the bedroom, just as bare as it had been last night. A small chest of drawers, a clothespress, a straight wooden chair and small table, but no sign of her sister. Oh, no, what was Ophelia up to, now?

Pushing back the bedclothes, Cordelia jumped out of bed and dressed hastily. At least this time she did not have to pretend to be a lady's maid. Not that her own gowns were much better in quality, she admitted, sighing as she pulled on a faded muslin day dress. And it would have been easier to dress if her sister had been here to help her with stays and buttons. Cordelia frowned, but she managed, although with some difficulty. In a few minutes she was hastening down the plain wooden staircase.

To her relief, she found Ophelia in the dining room, eating toast and tea and chatting amicably with the vicar.

"But you must agree that God expects us to use our talents," she noted.

"I can appreciate your argument," the churchman said, smiling a little. "Even if I must point out that the talents mentioned in the parable were actually coins. The translation—"

"Even so!" Ophelia refused to give in to a mere matter of superior scholarship. She took a small bite of toast and continued, not the least abashed. "One still should not bury one's talent, whether metaphoric or genuine."

"I will grant you the point. But you know that ladies do not generally engage themselves as actresses—"

"But I feel a calling. I know I dare not compare it to your noble profession, sir, but indeed, I have thought of this for years, and I do feel that I simply must make the attempt. And I have come so far. It would be a crime, really, almost a sin, to stop now—"

If his acquaintance with Ophelia continued, he would learn that it was quite hard to finish a sentence in her company without being a good deal more ruthless than he was at present, Cordelia thought cynically. She couldn't help wishing that someone would—just once—push a piece of toast down her lovely twin's throat until she choked, just a little.

"Do not tell me that you are going back to the theater?" she interrupted.

Ophelia frowned at her. "Did I not just say—"

"I know, I know, you've been called to use your talent. Were you called to be attacked in a back alley of London? Or to get your sister kidnapped by white slavers?" Cordelia shivered to remember the assault, so narrowly averted and met her sister's outraged stare with a hard look of her own.

Ophelia flushed. "You know I would never choose to see you threatened in any way, Cordelia. But I have come so far—"

"*We* have come so far," Cordelia corrected, picking up a plate and helping herself to toast, meat and a coddled egg. The reverend's cook was really not bad at all, she thought as she sat down again and took a bite of eggs and ham.

The vicar himself poured her a cup of tea.

Ophelia at once changed her tactic. Instead of looking outraged, she threw herself into the chair next to her twin and gazed adoringly into her sister's face. "Oh, yes, it was so incredibly good of you to come along, only for me, darling Cordelia! She risked her own life and reputation to safeguard mine, you see," she told the vicar. "She is really the most devoted sister in the entire world. I truly do not know what I should do without her."

So that if she refused to go along with Ophelia's plans today, she must forfeit this noble crown? Frowning, Cordelia sipped her tea. She was quite ready to do so! But then she looked up and saw Ransom Sheffield in the doorway, his posture erect as always, wearing his usual half-twisted smile, his eyes aloof and cool.

Somehow, it was harder, then, to be as calm and determined—even heartless—as she needed to be to stop her sister's wild plans.

The vicar took advantage of the moment of silence. "Yes, an admirable quality, sisterly devotion, but you know that ladies of quality do not join thespian troupes—"

Ophelia said at once, "We met a gentleman back home whose mother was an actress! No, it is true. When her husband died, she supported herself and her children by her performances."

"But a widow, an older woman, especially one in need, and a young lady just beginning her life, that is quite different," Reverend Sheffield tried to explain.

Cordelia could see her sister was not listening.

"I must go back to the theater this morning. Just one more try, then I promise I will take the manager's response as final." She fluttered her long lashes at the vicar and gave him a sunny smile, and reverend or not, he had no more chance than the next man Ophelia choose to brandish her smiles and her wiles upon. Cordelia stabbed her ham with unwonted vigor.

She found that Ransom Sheffield had put down his teacup

and seated himself at the chair next to her—they did not seem to stand on ceremony in the rectory—and he offered her a small but sharp-looking table knife.

"Just in case your frustration needs more outlet," he muttered.

Shocked, she looked up at him. "I would not carve up—"

"Your ham?" His expression was innocent, now.

She grinned unwillingly, and some of her irritation eased.

"I will admit that sometimes I get very annoyed with my . . . ham," she admitted, glancing down a little at her plate.

"Yes, hams will do that," he answered, taking a bite of his own.

"Do you have any at home?" she couldn't help asking.

"What, hams?"

The tiny maid who came in to bring a wire rack of fresh toast looked at them as if they were mad. Cordelia bit her lip to keep from laughing and waited to hear his answer.

"No, only several brothers, and we express our differences freely, usually by means of a hammerlock around the neck or a right cross to the jaw," he assured her.

"Too bad I cannot do the same," Cordelia muttered.

But when Ophelia was ready to depart for the theater, Cordelia was, of course, at her side. She really could not allow her brilliant, addlepated sister to depart alone. And when she found that Ransom Sheffield was coming with them, she felt a strong rush of gratitude.

"I have a long list of sick to visit today," the vicar told them. He had already donned his hat, too. "So I fear I cannot join you."

"Of course your errands are far more important," Ophelia assured him.

Cordelia suspected that her twin was simply glad not to have him watch as she buttered up the manager with her usual flirtatious manner. As for herself, she smiled in gratitude at the other cousin, remembering his strong arms and prompt actions yesterday. Then she recalled his attempt to slip inside the rear theater building's upper floor, and her smile faded. Or was he simply using their visit to get inside the theater for his own ends?

She couldn't be sure.

His escort did have its uses. He hailed a hackney and told the driver the address of the theater, and they crowded into the vehicle. This time Cordelia watched the London streets with more interest. Knowing that they were not homeless and destitute allowed her to look at the city without a sense of panic drowning out her natural curiosity.

And when they came to Malory Road, quiet at this time of the morning, he led them to the side entrance, and they were admitted easily into the theater. Ransom Sheffield passed over a few coins to the man who opened the door and said something in a low voice that she couldn't hear. The old man opened the door wider, and the sisters followed Sheffield quickly inside.

Ophelia's expression was triumphant. Cordelia sighed. She knew her sister was already decorating her dressing room and planning her stage wardrobe. Surely this insane venture would not be a success? She followed her twin on toward the stage area until Ophelia came to an abrupt halt. A group of at least a dozen girls of different sizes and ages, but none older than five and twenty, waited at the side of the stage.

"What's this?" she demanded.

"Said you wanted to try out, didn't you?" the old man croaked. "Well, 'ere be the morning tryouts, lovie. You be the last in line. We already had closed the doors, but your gentleman friend, 'e persuaded me, like, to open 'im again." Chuckling as he palmed his bribe, the old man went back to his post at the door.

The other girls were staring hard at a wrinkled page of script and muttered to themselves as they memorized the words on the page. Ophelia found another copy for herself lying on the dirty wooden floor. She picked it up and scanned it, her lips moving as she mouthed the words, shaking her head as if she didn't think highly of the scriptwriter's talent.

Cordelia hoped her sister would at least get through the audition before she tried to rewrite the play.

She walked a little apart from the group of would-be actresses and leaned against a stack of stage flats, out of the view of anyone in the audience. In a minute or two, Ransom Sheffield joined her.

"Unlike your sister, you have no dreams of thespian glory, Miss Applegate?" he asked, his tone polite.

She glanced at him suspiciously. "No, indeed," she said. "One of us has to be sensible."

"That must get boring," he noted.

Stung, she raised her brows. "Should I run after impossible dreams, like Ophelia?"

"No, but I should hope—for your own sake—you do have dreams to pursue?" He turned his luminous gray eyes on her for a moment, and she forgot to be annoyed. If he ever looked at her like that in earnest . . .

But someone was speaking, onstage, and she had to shift her position so that she could listen. Just as well, as her pulse was jumping in a very strange manner. . . .

A skinny girl with sallow skin and dark hair was holding her page in front of her and reciting, as if it were a lesson she'd learned by rote.

"Nomylord,myhandhemayhavebutIcannotgivemyheartto-himforIloveanother—"

"Stop," a harsh male voice called from below the stage. "Again, slower."

"NomylordmyhandhemayhavebutIcannotgivemyheartto-himforIloveanother—" she said, again without appearing to take a breath.

"That's all," a short man at the side of the stage said. "Off you go, then."

The girl, still apparently pale with terror, was persuaded with some difficulty to give up her near death grip on the page of script and pointed toward the door.

"The next girl has to be better than that," Cordelia muttered.

"One must hope," Ransom Sheffield answered from beside her.

The next girl on stage had a wide smile and wider hips, but at least she seemed more at ease with the situation. She recited the line more slowly, her accent broad and harsh, accompanied by a cheery smile.

"No, my lord! My 'and 'e may 'ave, but I can-not give my

'eart to 'im, for *I* lo-ve a-no-ther!" she announced with cheery determination.

"She makes it sound as if her heart is a new wheel of cheese," Ransom Sheffield whispered from beside Cordelia.

Cordelia choked back a gurgle of laughter.

"Yes, not bad. We'll let you know," the voice in the pit said.

Looking disappointed, the girl walked off the stage.

Two more girls spoke the lines, then another with a voice so faint they could hardly hear her, then one who croaked like the ravens on Tower Hill, Ransom Sheffield said, sending Cordelia into more stifled giggles. Wicked man!

But really, Ophelia had to be better than any of these, unless she threw it all away by—

When her twin finally had her turn, Cordelia found she was holding her breath.

Ophelia walked slowly and with apparent calm to the center of the stage, smiled out at the unseen person in the pit, and began.

"I cannot give him my hand, my lord." Sounding distressed, her voice as patrician as any princess's, she batted her lovely eyelashes at an unseen guardian and put one hand to her brow.

Silence while Cordelia bit back a groan. Of course, hadn't she known it would happen! Oh, well, perhaps they could borrow coach fare home from the vicar.

The man in the audience said, his voice annoyed. "Can't you read? I said only girls who can read. That's not what the lines say!"

"I know; I've been revising them. They make no sense!" Ophelia pointed out, her tone matter-of-fact. "She can't give him her hand but not her heart; he won't care if he has her heart, which is to say her love or not, he only wants her body and her property. He's obviously the villain, for heaven's sake!"

The man who'd risen to approach the stage paused. It was the disagreeable man with the square jaw from yesterday. "Er, right, but—"

"So, she has to protest right away, and then he can start browbeating her, and the audience will feel for her at once—not all the way down the page, and the scene can build tension—there's no point in wasting all this time. Now, look."

She came closer and pointed out more changes she had penciled in, and Cordelia could no longer hear all the exchanges between the two. The manager seemed to be listening.

She sighed.

Beside her, Ransom Sheffield raised his slashing dark brows. "I'll be damned. Don't tell me your sister is actually going to get herself a part in this ridiculous farce?"

She didn't answer, but her expression must have said enough.

"I take back everything I said. Perhaps just surviving as the sister to such a chameleon is ambition enough?" To her surprise, he suddenly reached for her hand and lifted it to his lips. She had slipped off her gloves while she waited—obviously a mistake.

His mouth felt warm against her hand, and hidden in the shadows at the side of the stage, she felt a peculiar kind of intimacy. They stood so close, and as she looked up at him, she saw him gaze into her face, and he showed no sign of his usual easy flippancy.

He held her hand to his mouth, to his supple warm lips, and something inside her ached beneath his touch. She was suddenly aware of his masculine energy in a more intense way than she had ever known before.

She was holding her breath.

He lowered her hand, still gripping it, and leaned closer.

He was going to kiss her.

This was insane—she hardly knew this man!

Did it matter?

But instead of pressing his lips to hers, he brushed her lips with one long sun-bronzed finger. Her lips had somehow fallen open as if in anticipation. She blushed at the thought of being so obvious about what she had hoped for. Then he whispered a word she could not even make out. Blood was thundering in her ears as her pulse pounded. He turned away rather quickly, leaving her blinking as if she had wakened from a trance.

Was he a hypnotist?

She felt as at sea as a sailor washed overboard in the far

reaches of the Magellan Straits. Her head was whirling and her knees weak. Taking deep breaths, Cordelia leaned against the wall again. Good God, she must have lost her mind. And he would think she was an abandoned flirt, instead of a concerned sister, whose only purpose in coming to London had been to watch out for her twin's well-being.

And . . . and good gracious, where was her sister? Cordelia glanced about her and drew a long breath when she saw her twin still speaking to the theater manager in the middle of the stage. The strange interlude that had seemed to go on for half an hour had, in fact, only been a matter of moments. It had merely been her consciousness that had been so warped by Mr. Sheffield's nearness. She must stay away from that man!

Cordelia was promising herself just that when Ophelia, smiling broadly, bustled off the stage.

"I suppose you have a part," Cordelia muttered to her sister.

"Just as I said," her twin agreed.

"I am pleased for you." Cordelia hugged her sister, knowing how long Ophelia had waited for this moment. "We will have to look for rooms; we cannot depend on the vicar's charity forever. How much are you getting for your role?"

"Um, perhaps we can stay a little longer? He seems quite happy to have us in the rectory," her sister argued as she walked ahead toward the outer door.

"Ophelia?" Cordelia had to almost run to catch up. "You are getting paid?"

"Of course. And I'm sure in time—"

"How much?" Cordelia ran around to stand in front of her twin, forcing her to stop. "How much, Ophelia?"

"Twenty shillings. But I'm sure in no time I can persuade—"

"Twenty shillings a week? We'll never be able to exist on such a salary!" Cordelia stared at her sister in dismay.

"Actually, it's for a fortnight," Ophelia corrected, not meeting her sister's horrified gaze. "So, I think that yes, it would be most kind of the vicar if he would put us up for just a wee bit longer."

"Unless he wants to see us melt away to skeletons," Cordelia grumbled. "The Toast of London, indeed!"

They had reached the street before she remembered to wonder where Ransom Sheffield had taken himself to, but he caught up to them at the corner. She raised her brows, but Ophelia was too busy telling him about her new role for Cordelia to quiz him, and it was only later, after he had hailed another hackney and they had ridden back to the rectory and shared a nuncheon of bread and cheese and apple tarts, that Ransom admitted that he, too, had secured a small part for himself.

Cordelia dropped the last crumb of her tart onto the plain deal table. "What? You, an actor?"

He regarded her with a wounded look. "Really, Miss Applegate. Do you think I am such a clumsy dunderhead that you find it impossible to imagine me onstage?"

"No." She lifted her chin and met his stare with a cool one of her own. "I think you play a role very well!"

But whether he was a thief pretending to be a gentleman or a gentleman pretending to be a thief, she had not yet discerned.

"I think you will make a wonderful captain of the guard," Ophelia added, her tone merry. "It's not a large role, so it will not tax your acting powers too greatly, though I will be sure to add more lines to the part. I have several ideas already to improve the play, I assure you!"

"But, as a lady of quality, are you not concerned—" The vicar shook his head at the rashness of this development. He had obviously not expected her to obtain a role.

"Oh, I have thought of an answer to that, too," Ophelia explained, her tone unconcerned. "I am rewriting the play; it will be a play within a play and I will wear a mask to conceal my identity. That will be part of the fun, you see, as the audience tries to guess who I am!"

"And has the manager agreed to this?" Ransom Sheffield asked, his tone dubious.

"Not yet, but he will," Ophelia predicted, taking a bite of her tart, her tongue pink as she licked a bit of apple off her finger. She continued, explaining her own role to the vicar.

Ransom Sheffield turned back to Cordelia and lowered his voice. "I felt I should stay close to your sister, you see. She may think she can control the situation, but she will still be under the thumb of a man who is much less than a gentleman, and I am not at all sure her mask strategy will suffice to protect her reputation."

Cordelia felt a surge of renewed alarm. "Then I must be there, too!"

"Oh, I think she plans for you to be," he muttered, and something in his tone made her wary.

She glanced back at her twin. "Ophelia, you did not tell that horrid man . . . that is, you did not tell the manager of the theater that I also plan to act, did you?"

"Without asking you, of course not. Besides, you didn't even try out. But I said you would look out for the wardrobe; he said he'll give a few shillings for the job," her sister said merrily. "I knew you would want to contribute."

"Oh, did you?" Cordelia said, swallowing a more caustic retort before she disgraced herself utterly in front of a man of the cloth.

Ophelia smiled sweetly. Cordelia returned the smile with one just as bland, promising herself she would tug her sister bald later, when they were alone.

It was her need to control her own temper that made her turn away abruptly, and it was for that reason that she caught the look on Ransom Sheffield's face. That dark look in his eyes—why did he look so dire? It was more than a moment of sibling annoyance that turned his gray eyes dark with dangerous rage.

She did not wish to be the one who stirred his ire!

Five

The four of them enjoyed another simple but hearty dinner in the rectory dining room, and after the two ladies excused themselves and went into the sitting room, the gentlemen rejoined them promptly.

Cordelia had just told her sister that they should go up to bed early.

"Why on earth?" Ophelia had replied. "Just so you can scold me all evening? I thought you would be pleased about the wardrobe position. You said you wanted to be close by."

"I do, but—"

"So, you can be there every day. And besides, I want to play cards, or at least charades, do something fun, for goodness' sake! They are both handsome men, even if he is a vicar. Such a waste!"

Which left even Cordelia, accustomed to her sister's artless statements, speechless for a moment. And then the men joined them. But before Ophelia could put forth her ideas for the evening, the vicar himself took charge.

"The fire is low in my study, but the room is still warm. It might be a good time if you ladies would like to write letters in some privacy," he suggested. "There is paper, ink, sealing wax, everything that you would need."

Cordelia exchanged a quick glance with her sister.

"I'm sure your father will be waiting to hear that you are safe," the vicar reminded them gently. "And I know you are eager to reassure him that all is well. And you must wish to know if your brother is returning to town soon. He will like to learn of your whereabouts, too."

His tone was pleasant. Still, Cordelia hoped her cheeks had not reddened, and her sister looked abashed.

"Of course, you're too kind," Cordelia agreed, trying not to look as guilty as she felt. They followed him to the smaller room where she pulled a chair up to the desk as the vicar took out paper and showed them the quills and ink and penknife and other items they would need. Ophelia took another chair and sank into it without speaking.

Giles Sheffield went out and shut the door softly behind him. The twins looked at each other.

"They may not even realize—" Ophelia began.

"You cannot be sure. They could easily know we are missing by now!" Cordelia interrupted. "Don't fool yourself."

"But you told Madeline we were going back to stay with Lauryn at the squire's manse, and I told the squire we were going home, so—"

"Even so, Lauryn writes to Madeline often, so by now, our family may have put two and two together and discovered a missing pair of Applegate sisters, Ophelia!" Cordelia hissed at her twin, then lowered her voice and glanced at the door, glad that it looked so solid and thick. The last thing she wanted just now was for the good-hearted vicar to learn that they were not only in London alone and unprotected but here without the knowledge of their kinfolk. Ophelia might enjoy the man's masculine good looks, and while a civil flirtation was acceptable in polite society, they could not abuse his help and good intentions too far.

She fixed her sister with a firm stare. "We cannot know

how long it will be before they realize we are gone, Ophelia, or if they already have. They will be most distressed whenever they do find out. We must write to reassure them we are safe; the vicar is quite right."

"It's your fault for telling him we have a father," Ophelia muttered.

"What did you expect me to do?" Cordelia retorted.

"We should have said we were orphans, alone in the world . . ."

"That would be a lie. Besides, we're close enough to that now," Cordelia argued, and she looked in distrust at her sister's dreamy-eyed expression. She was getting that look . . . "No, you don't!"

"Don't what?" Her twin asked absently, twirling a piece of hair around one finger as she stared at a small crack on the wall.

"Don't start making up stories again. We have to write letters. You must write to our father and confess what we have done. Tell him we're very, very sorry for running away; we're safe, we're staying here at the rectory and we'll be home very soon."

"No, we won't! Not till the play is over, at least, and I expect it to run a good long time!" Ophelia fired back. "Anyhow, why can't you write to Father? You can do a better job of asking forgiveness and expressing contrition than I, since I'm not really sorry. I had to come, you know that!"

"You're the writer," Cordelia answered. "Anyhow, I have to write to our half brother, Lord Gabriel Sinclair, a man I have met only once, briefly, and who has probably forgotten I even exist."

"Oh," her sister said, her expression changing abruptly. "No, no, I can't write to him. After I made such a bad impression at Juliana's wedding—"

"It was an accident, Ophelia, anyone could have done it," Cordelia tried to reassure her, but despite her brave words, she played restlessly with her quill until she found she had spoiled the point, and she had to reach for the penknife to sharpen it again. She had no idea what she would say. There was no doubt that their new relation was intimidating. Lord Gabriel was such an elegant, handsome man, and his wife . . .

"Yes, but I was the one who did!" Her sister was saying.

"You spilt wine on him, that was all. I'm sure he's already forgotten it."

"I haven't! The look he gave me—I felt like a schoolgirl. I haven't been so mortified since I twisted my ankle at the Butterford's Michaelmas ball and showed everyone the rip in my petticoat!" Ophelia shuddered at the memory.

"Then write to Father. Unless you would like to switch with me?" Cordelia looked down at her still blank sheet of paper.

"No, no indeed, you are right. I should write to our father!" Ophelia agreed quickly.

They each dipped a quill into the ink pot, took a sheet of paper and bent over their difficult writing assignments.

What could she say to the no doubt top-lofty Lord Gabriel Sinclair? No, that was surely not fair. She knew he had been very kind to her sister Juliana, even if Jules had been frightened half to death of him when she'd first come to London to visit with their newly discovered half brother. But that had worked out all right, and Juliana's wedding had been very pretty . . .

She and Ophelia would quite likely have gotten an invitation to come and visit, too, in time, and so she had argued to her sister. If Ophelia had a scrap of patience in her, she would have listened and waited.

Cordelia threw a resentful glance across the table, then shook her head and bent over her sheet of paper again. She couldn't blame everything on Ophelia. Perhaps Cordelia had wanted to come, too, had not wanted to wait, had not wanted to be sensible. Perhaps the annoying Mr. Sheffield had been right. Perhaps she was weary of always being the sensible sister. She looked down at the paper and sighed.

So far all she had written was: *Dear Lord Gabriel.*

How—precisely—did one inform a barely legitimate relation that one had invited oneself to London without so much as a whisper of invitation? Not that they'd really planned on staying with him, but to admit they'd come without any plans at all was almost worse. He'd think them scarlet women before they'd even touched the polished boards of the stage.

And if Ophelia did act in the play, as planned, perhaps Lord Gabriel would choose not to acknowledge them! Oh dear, she'd better prepare him for the worst, right away. Cordelia gave up trying to choose her words carefully and tried to put it all down, amid a jumble of past and present and perhaps future plans, and finally sealed it all up without even reading the letter over, sure she would throw it into the dying fire if she had to reread it. And she knew the vicar expected to see two letters, sealed, of course—he was too much a gentleman to read their correspondence.

"I wish he hadn't been so helpful," Ophelia complained about their host as she finished her own letter, after, she complained, crying real tears over it.

"If you've shed real tears, it must be because you've pricked your finger with the penknife," Cordelia shot back. "And you didn't mind him being helpful when he offered us a room!"

Her sister frowned. "Harpy! No indeed."

The clock on the wall had struck the hour before they had put down their quills, sealed their letters with wax and left the study together.

They gave the letters into the vicar's hand, and Ophelia especially was profuse in her thanks for his help in sending them on.

"No, indeed, it is my pleasure," the young churchman told her, his blue eyes gleaming with the smile that lit up his whole face.

Ophelia smiled back at him. "And now that our letters are written—"

"I'm sure the ladies would like to retire," Cousin Ransom said from behind them, his voice solicitous, though his gray eyes were mocking.

"Of course," the vicar agreed. "How inconsiderate of me, to keep you standing in the drafty hall. We should not wish to overtire you."

Ophelia pursed her lips, and even Cordelia considered a tart comeback, but decided that the other man had them boxed into a corner. And really, she was tired. And heaven only knew what tomorrow would bring during the first rehearsal.

She murmured good nights to the two men, who bowed politely, and turned toward the stairs. Like a seasoned actress, Ophelia did not waste a good exit, offering her hand to the vicar, who bowed over it, and also to Ransom Sheffield, who not only bowed but went so far as to lift it to his lips.

Looking back at her sister, Cordelia caught this rakish gesture and felt a stab of jealousy streak through her. A ridiculous conceit, she thought, and fought to keep her expression neutral. She would not give the man the satisfaction of allowing him to see that his action had rankled.

At last Ophelia followed her up the staircase, and they could enter the bedroom together.

Cordelia made a hasty toilette and climbed into bed, too annoyed to want to chat. She pulled the covers to her chin, shut her eyes and pretended to be asleep. But her sister said nothing. Perhaps she was not inclined toward conversation, either, and had other things on her mind.

Tonight she was tired but not totally exhausted, and Cordelia was more aware of the noises outside the rectory, city noises that seemed to go on into the early hours of the morning.

Horses clip-clopped over the paving stones. Wagon wheels clattered. Unaffected by the nearness of the church, men shouted and laughed and swore, their voices heavy with rum or cheap gin, and she could swear she heard prostitutes plying their ancient trade, calling out to the men, trading jests and sometimes insults when they were passed over.

Every time she dropped into a restless sleep, a new sound would rouse her. Her sister seemed to be having the same problem; she turned and twisted on the other side of the bed, once poking Cordelia painfully in the ribs.

"Ouch," Cordelia said. "Mind your elbow."

Ophelia pulled her pillow over her ear and didn't answer.

Cordelia tried to go back to sleep. The faintest streaks of pink streaked the gray sky, and she still felt leaden with fatigue.

Now heavy wagons creaked along the street outside, and street vendors shouted their wares. Perhaps Ophelia had the right idea.

She pulled her pillow up over her head, too, and shut her eyes, dozing off again.

When she woke, the morning seemed far advanced. Someone rapped on the door.

"Come in," Cordelia muttered, trying to push her eyelids open.

She saw a skinny maid carrying a tray with a teapot and two cups. "The master says as 'ow you'd best be stirring, miss, if you wish to be back at the theater by 'leven o'clock. And Master Ransom says as 'ow 'e's leaving in ten minutes and 'e's not waiting for you if you be late, and pardon me for repeating such, but that was what 'e says."

"Yes, thank you," Cordelia managed to answer. She pushed herself up a little farther and glanced out the window. Gracious, it was late. But after the restless night, she had been so tired—and what about her sister?

Turning, she saw the lump under the covers. "Up." Cordelia prodded the lump with one finger. "We have to hurry, or you'll be late to rehearsal."

That brought a tousled head up from beneath the covers. "Oh, my," her twin said, blinking drowsy eyes. "What a dreadful night! No one ever told me London was so horridly noisy!"

They drank the tea and swallowed almost whole the buns the maid had brought up, then hurriedly washed, did up their hair and dressed, lacing up each other's stays, then donning gowns and doing up each other's back buttons as they always did at home. Snatching up bonnets and shawls, they almost ran down the steps. Ophelia was a few steps ahead, but only just.

They found Ransom Sheffield at the front door of the rectory with one hand on the latch. He looked them up and down. "I see you can move rapidly when you are forced to," he observed, his tone dispassionate. "My regards, ladies, and good morning to you."

"Good morning, Mr. Sheffield," Ophelia told him, giving

him a sunny smile. "It is so good of you to offer us your escort and protection."

Cordelia was polite if somewhat less cordial. But then, she was still not sure if he was being chivalrous or simply underhanded. Did he want access to the theater to more easily rob the manager? Ophelia had a dreadful habit of seeing only what suited her. Should Cordelia, in good conscience, warn Mr. Nettles? Yet she felt better having Mr. Sheffield's protection, too. Although, if he were really a thief, how much was such protection worth?

The man who was causing her so much indecision hailed another hackney and they set off for Malory Road. When they reached the theater, they entered through the side door. The old man who guarded it nodded at them and passed them on. In the space of one day, they had become accepted as members of the troupe, it seemed.

Cordelia remarked as much to her sister, and Ophelia smiled broadly at the notion.

"Isn't it delightful?" she agreed, her tone blithe, and she wandered off to find the dressing rooms.

Backstage, other actors and actresses rambled about, too, looking for missing pieces of costume, complaining about warped looking glasses and the need for better candles in the dressing rooms.

A fair-haired young woman with blue eyes outlined in black and a low-cut gown shook her head. "I smell like a bloody tallow factory, I do!"

"Not to worry, love," a skinny lad carrying a long thin canvas-covered flat told her as he maneuvered behind her and the young actress ducked to avoid being smacked by the spare bit of scenery. "You smell so high any 'ow, no one would notice."

She made a hand gesture that even Cordelia knew was rude, having heard old Thomas scold the hired harvest hands for using it in her presence.

Just then a handsome dark-haired woman with a deep bosom came forward, then paused in front of Cordelia. She looked down her long nose, leaving Cordelia with the faint notion that she was expected to curtsy, as to royalty. "What's this, then? Are you playing the ingenue role and sewing up costumes, too? That's too penny-pinching even for Nettles!"

"No, no, that's my sister Lily," Cordelia explained quickly, giving her sister's stage name. "I'm Clara; I'm only sewing."

The matron sniffed and handed her a long cloak. "I need this back at once."

"Pardon me?" Cordelia blinked in surprise.

"You're the new wardrobe mistress, are you not? So, Nobby said." The woman nodded toward the old man who guarded the door. "I am Madam Tatina, lead actress, and I must have my cloak repaired at once, so don't allow anyone to put a costume ahead of mine."

"I assure you I will make tending to your cloak my first priority," Cordelia promised, hiding her impulse to grin at the woman's theatrics, onstage and apparently offstage.

The grand dame lifted her chin and showed her fine profile. "I expect no less!" she declaimed, with the kind of force she must use to reach the back rows of the theater, then she swept away to her dressing room.

"I suppose I have my orders! But where on earth is the sewing mistress's room where I'm to commence my work?" Cordelia muttered aloud.

Sighing, Cordelia went to ask one of the other crew members about its location. She was directed to a tiny, dark room hardly the size of a broom cupboard. Several pieces of costume had been tossed willy-nilly into a basket. An assortment of pins, dingy spools of thread and some needles—a few still usable—were stuck into a pincushion. Pulling a three-legged stool into the doorway where the light was better, Cordelia sat down to sort out the sewing basket so she could see what she had to work with. Then she would sew up the slit in the back of the prima donna's damaged cloak—she suspected the woman had outgrown her costume—and try to put it to rights.

She was putting the last stitches in the velvet cloak half an hour later when Ophelia came by, now wearing a low-cut and scandalously short scarlet dress that exhibited most of her calves and revealed a clear view of the stockings and silk slippers that she wore.

"You can't wear that onstage!" Shocked, Cordelia stared at her.

"Of course I can," her reprobate sister argued cheerfully. "I'm an actress, this is not the real me, silly."

"But why did you put it on already? You don't need a costume for rehearsals; even I know that."

"I'm trying it out. I have to get in the mood. And they say Mr. Nettles likes to get an idea of how his actresses will look."

Seeing how much flesh was exposed, defying all decorum, this gave Cordelia a very dim view of the manager's morals. She bit her lip against more sisterly warnings. She knew this mood too well. Right now, her twin was too exultant over her first taste of the theater to heed even the most heartfelt cautions.

Ophelia was speaking again. "This is important. I need you to take this bit of silk and fashion a mask for me."

"Oh, yes, your wonderful plan to remain incognito." Cordelia frowned as she tied off the cloak's seam and then bit the thread. "Have you informed Mr. Nettles about this scheme, yet?"

"Not yet, but I'm sure he will agree," Ophelia said, her tone confident.

"You do, do you?" Cordelia muttered under her breath. "I'm not sure he's as concerned about your reputation as we are, Ophelia."

But her sister had already turned away. Praying that this mad venture did not destroy her sister's good name and reputation, or do even more vital harm, Cordelia took the bit of silk fabric and attacked it with scissors and such savage intent that a scene shifter walking by eyed her with alarm.

She soon decided she needed heavier fabric to back the silk, so she dug into her basket of scraps in the back of the tiny sewing nook. She was still there when her twin found her again.

Ophelia seemed still in good spirits. "Oh, nice work, Cordelia," she said, looking down at the finished half mask. "I should have a spare or two, I think."

Her twin was scanning the dark nook and glancing over the twisted pile of grimy costumes and odds and ends of thread and trim with which Cordelia was to make miracles. "What fun you'll have here. You always were clever with a needle."

"Liar. I'm not half as good as you." Cordelia pointed out, but kept her tone polite. "And if you want more masks, you'd better sit down and help."

Ophelia sighed, but she seemed to know better than to argue with her sister. "Very well." She drew up another stool and threaded a needle. Soon she had cut out another mask, and they both worked while Ophelia chatted about the cast members she had met.

"They're quite nice, Cordelia. Mostly from London, of course. Venetia, that's her stage name, is from Whitechapel. She had thirteen brother and sisters and they all lived in one room, with no heat, just fancy! And we thought we were poor. Her stepfather beat her, so she ran away when she was twelve, brought one sister with her, and managed to survive."

Cordelia stared at her sister.

"Your mouth is open," her twin noted.

"That's a very sad story," Cordelia said slowly. "I just . . . Ophelia, I don't know if you should be . . . well, associating with people like . . . like . . ."

"For pity's sake, Cordelia, you're not going to go all prim on me, are you? I'd expect that of Madeline, who tries so hard to mother us, as if to atone for our poor mother dying soon after our birth, but not you! Because we're ladies of quality, you think we're too good to speak to poor girls like Venetia, who have struggled to survive? She's not a bad person, Cordelia!" Ophelia's eyes flashed.

Cordelia felt ashamed of herself. "I didn't mean that she is . . . only, well . . . what Father would say . . . and really . . . in the eyes of Society . . ."

"Society be damned!"

For once, Cordelia was not sure that her often rebellious twin might not have the right of it. Still, she couldn't help being shocked to hear her swear so openly. What on earth would

Madeline say when they returned home? She concentrated on her sewing, and they worked side by side in silence. When the half masks were completed, Ophelia thanked her a bit stiffly and took them away.

Cordelia continued to work on other costumes in her basket, and presently, she looked up to see that Ophelia had returned. She had changed back to her muslin day dress. This time, her expression seemed less tense.

"Here." She took out a wrapped bundle she had concealed beneath her dress and offered her sister a juicy half of a still-warm meat pie.

"Thank you," Cordelia said quickly, feeling that the food was also a peace offering. Besides, her stomach did feel remarkably empty. "Does Mr. Nettle provide a luncheon for his staff?" Cordelia took a bite, attempting to eat the pastry without dropping crumbs and drops of gravy all over her apron.

It was Ophelia's turn to look skeptical. "Mr. Nettle, I'm told, does nothing that forces him to spend a farthing he doesn't have to. No, Mr. Farmer, the second male lead, bought this for me from a street vendor when I told him I was famished."

Cordelia almost dropped what was left of the pastry. She swallowed her mouthful as quickly as she could. "Ophelia! You should never have accepted. You know what he must expect in return—"

"A kiss, or more, I know. But it doesn't mean that he will get it!" Ophelia lowered her lashes and affected a coy smile. "Men are the same in London as in Yorkshire, Cordelia; don't think I'm that innocent, for pity's sake."

Looking down at what was left of the pie, Cordelia shook her head, then ate the last few bites and wiped her hands on her handkerchief. "Mind you don't let him maneuver you in a dark corner, then," she warned, keeping her voice low as she glanced around.

Ophelia only giggled. "Look," she said, and to Cordelia's astonishment, she pulled a small dagger out of her sash. "Venetia gave me this. We have to get one for you now. Venetia says you should never be without a weapon, and don't let the men-folk know you have it, either. She says she's been attacked in the streets, too. I told her about our narrow escape in the alley. She says . . . well, she says lots, I'll have to tell you later."

Ophelia dropped her voice, even though she was speaking in a quiet tone. She glanced behind her, and Cordelia felt a shiver run up her spine.

"Venetia's got a younger sister here. Mr. Nettles wants her to act, too, but Venetia says she's too young as yet. Venetia says she's going to keep her sister out of the stews if she dies for it!"

"Good heavens," Cordelia said faintly. "What are the stews?"

"I'm not really sure," Ophelia admitted, her eyes wide. "But it sounds quite bad. Maybe it's one of the debtor's prisons? I did gather that poor Venetia has worked very hard ever since she was a girl, and I think perhaps she works after hours, too."

Cordelia frowned. If the theater paid as badly as that, Ophelia's dreams of making a fortune to share with her family might be doomed to failure from the beginning. And fame kept no one's stomach full. Even the play's leading lady was wearing a ratty cloak which was several sizes too small. Of course, this small playhouse was not one of the legitimate theaters like Drury Lane or Covent Gardens, but still—

Another thought interrupted. "Where is Mr. Ransom Sheffield?" she asked, trying to keep her voice casual. "Not that I expect him to provide for our every need, but he'd said he was here to keep us safe, after all."

Ophelia shook her head. "I think the guardsmen were practicing their drill, but that was some time ago. I don't know if he's still with them or not."

So much for their protector, Cordelia thought. She frowned. Was he practicing his paltry few lines, or was he in the back, trying to break into Mr. Nettles's private rooms? What was the man really after?

Mr. Nettles's assistant, the skinny young man with the spotty face, came to the doorway of her small nook. "Mr. Nettles wants you . . . you . . ." He looked back and forth between them uncertainly as if not sure which was which.

"Yes?" Ophelia straightened her chin with an imperial pose worthy of a princess and the assistant fastened his gaze, with obvious relief, on the actress.

" 'E wants you on stage, so 'op to it."

"I am coming at once," Ophelia said, but she rose with great dignity, laying aside the mask on her lap and following him toward the stage.

Cordelia took it and made a quick job of the final stitches. She had to see her sister's first rehearsal. She followed, lagging behind several steps, just in case someone should see her and give her another job to do.

On the way, she came across their missing guardian. Taking off the large helmet with the face piece which hid much of his face while onstage, Ransom Sheffield looked disgruntled.

"Where have you been?" she said, before she thought. Then, aware that her tone had been sharp, she wished she could retract the impulsive query. He would think she expected much too much of him.

"Drilling in the alley," he retorted. "With the saddest excuse for a pocket infantry I've ever had the misfortune to serve with, on or off the stage!"

She remembered that she had suspected he had fought in a real army, before Bonaparte's defeat, and felt a pang of sympathy that eased her irritation. "They are rough in their steps, are they?"

"Rough does not begin to describe them, Miss Applegate. In fact, the words I would use to evoke them could not be spoken aloud in front of a lady." A passing scene shifter glanced at him curiously, and Sheffield added quickly, "Or any other female. Not only are they incapable of telling their left foot from their right, they have no idea how to handle their wooden swords. None have served in the real army—otherwise, we would all likely be speaking French by now!"

She laughed.

"What were their occupations previously, or are they real actors?"

He grimaced. "I believe one was an assistant in a taproom and broke one too many mugs, and the other two . . . I'm not sure they have ever had gainful employment. I have been jabbed in the back, in the ribs, by their swords and nearly lost an eye. I'm just thankful to Providence the weapons are made of wood instead of steel. I'll be black and blue as it is. And one of my fellow guardsman, with whom I'm supposed to duel onstage, cannot stay erect long enough to make my victory appear even halfway convincing. He keeps stumbling over his own feet."

She laughed again at his expression.

Then someone closer to the stage yelled, "Shut yer traps!"

"Shhh," she told him, taking his arm and drawing him to the side, stepping back behind a leaning stack of canvas flats where she could peek at the stage but not be too obviously glimpsed herself. "I want to see Ophelia rehearse," she whispered.

Ransom Sheffield nodded and stepped back to stand beside her. He was silent, although she was very aware of his presence. A hint of perspiration from his exercise in the alley overlay his usual odor of soap and clean linen and the general male scent that was uniquely his own. Why did something move inside her when he came so close?

She bit her lip and tried to think only of her sister, ready at last to claim her childhood's ambition. Cordelia narrowed her eyes and watched Ophelia draw herself up like a queen in the center of the stage.

If Ophelia was nervous, she covered it well. Her shoulders were back and her chin up, and she didn't even need that ridiculous costume.

"Know yer lines?" came the harsh voice of Mr. Nettles himself from the seats in front of the stage.

Ophelia nodded. "Of course."

"We'll see," the man muttered. "Okay, from the top of page ten."

"Lord Toplofty, I can never forsake my aged father." Ophelia put one hand to her forehead. Her tone was modulated and her voice sounded delicate and sincere. "How can you ask it of me? I must protect—"

"What?" The manager interrupted. "Them's not the lines in the script!"

"I rewrote it," Ophelia explained. "She needs motivation—"

"Don't you never just say the lines I give you?" the manager grumbled. "Anyhow, we'll get back to that, later. First, Jutes, tell her about the back rows."

"What?" Ophelia wrinkled her nose. "What about the back rows?"

"They got to 'ear you," the spotty assistant told her, looking smug. "Can't make out yer words if ye whisper."

"I wasn't whispering," Ophelia argued, sounding indignant.

"Might as well 'ave been," the man insisted. "Ye got to project yer voice, throw it out from yer gut, like . . ." He moved closer, holding a wooden club that might have been left over from the guardsman drill. "I'll show ye. Try it again."

Looking puzzled but determined, Ophelia turned to faced the audience of one and drew herself up to an imperial pose. "Lord Toplofty, I can never forsake—"

Jutes swung the club and punched her lightly in the stomach.

Ophelia gasped and doubled up.

Cordelia cried out. She took an impulsive step forward, but Ransom Sheffield grabbed her arm.

"Let go of me!" she protested. "They are attacking my sister!"

"It was only a slight blow," he muttered. "Quiet, or we will all be out on the street, and your sister will have lost the role she coveted so badly."

"But—"

"Shush. Let her make the choice."

Unwilling, Cordelia pressed her lips together and turned to watch the scene unfolding on stage. Her face tinged a faint shade of green, Ophelia straightened.

"There," Jutes said, looking as if he had enjoyed the blow. "That's where ye 'ave to talk from."

Ophelia nodded and swallowed hard.

Cordelia hoped her twin wouldn't lose her breakfast in front of everyone. What a way to start her first day on the stage!

But Ophelia was made of sterner stuff than that. Although her face was still pale, she drew a deep breath. She tried again, and although her tone was not quite as sweetly pathetic, it did seem louder and more vibrant.

"Lord Toplofty, I can never forsake my aged father," she said.

"You're getting the notion," Nettles said from his seat out front. "Ye don't want to shout; that'll just strain yer throat and ye'll end up with no voice at all, on opening night, no doubt, and leave me in a fine pickle. Breathe from yer toes and pull yer voice from there, too. Try again."

Ophelia drew another long breath and then spoke once more, in a voice that did seem pitched toward the back of the auditorium. "Lord Toplofty, I can never forsake my aged father—"

"Oh, well done!" Cordelia muttered, burning with pride for her twin's resilience, for not giving up, for not crumbling before such harsh tutelage.

Beside her, Ransom Sheffield nodded, too. And now that her concern for her sister had lessened, she remembered how distracting his nearness was, and how alarmingly his closeness moved her.

She turned abruptly away.

"I should get back to my mending," she explained when he glanced at her, his dark brows raised in surprise.

Without looking back again, she hurried on to her cubbyhole of a room and picked up her sewing, sitting down on her three-legged stool. But it was hard to concentrate on her stitches when the memory of his closeness still lingered in her mind. Thinking about the strange effect he had on her, she stabbed the needle into her finger instead of the fabric. She cursed, putting the afflicted finger into her mouth.

Damn!

Where was the cursed man now?

He had never explained why he had been trying to break into the upper rooms over the building behind the theater. And now they had helped him gain entrance to the theater buildings. Perhaps that had been his motivation, not a desire to offer chivalrous protection to two young ladies alone in London. Motivation, as Ophelia often said about her fictional characters, was everything! Perhaps she and Ophelia had been ridiculously naive. Should Cordelia go to Mr. Nettles and explain about Ransom Sheffield? Yet, Mr. Nettles hardly seemed a saint, either.

Finger still in her mouth, looking no doubt like an infant, Cordelia hesitated, not sure what to do. Whom could she trust? Perhaps no one . . .

She would go and find Mr. Ransom Sheffield and demand an explanation, a full and complete explanation this very moment. And if that eased her longing to be close to him again, to experience again that quiver than ran down her back, the weakness in her belly that came upon her when he stood so close. . . . Well, no, that was not her motivation at all, she told herself firmly. Nor did that delightful feeling mean that he was honest or trustworthy—

She stuffed her sewing into her sewing basket just as a shadow in the doorway made her look up. To Cordelia's relief, it was her sister. "Rehearsal over already?"

Ophelia nodded. "He only wanted to see how I spoke and moved, he said," she explained, plopping down on the stool her sister had abandoned. "Oh, I felt such exhilaration, Cordelia! I can hardly imagine what it will be like when there are real audience members in the seats!"

Cordelia nodded somewhat absently. "I have an errand to run," she said. "What are you doing now?"

"I want to hide out and work on some new lines for the script. You don't mind if I stay here? The women's dressing room is very noisy and crowded with the other actresses and dancers moving about."

"Certainly. I'm going to look for Mr. Sheffield. I want more detailed answers about his attempts to housebreak." She explained her plan, and her twin nodded.

"I will sit here with mending close by, and if anyone comes, I'll grab it and cover my paper," Ophelia said, her eyes twinkling. She picked up a gray shawl and draped it over the papers in her lap. They had often, when they were younger, taken on each other's identity for short periods and fooled people who did not know them well. "They will think I'm you, and no one will order me away to practice that stupid May dance we have to do after the last act. That's the worst part about not being a licensed theater like Drury Lane or Covent Garden; we have to show musical and other variety acts as well as plays."

Cordelia bit back a grin at how easily the *we* came to Ophelia's lips. She regarded herself as one of the cast already.

"Won't you get in trouble if they can't find you?" she pointed out.

"I doubt it," Ophelia predicted. "Mr. Nettles is strict on some things and very lax on others." However, she diluted her confident statement by adding, "Just don't stay away too long."

"I'll try to get back within the hour."

Her twin nodded, then Cordelia slipped away.

It took only a quick surveillance to see that Ransom Sheffield was not onstage, which was just now occupied by two fair-haired young ladies singing an off-key song.

He was not back in the men's dressing room. She asked a young man dressed in a guard's costume to check. He was not in the alley outside. She went into the rear building and found the rickety stairs and hurried down to the cellar. Except for the smell of damp and grime, and a slight rustle along the edge of the far wall that suggested rats—she shuddered—it was empty of inhabitants.

She climbed up again and kept going past the ground floor. Here the landing was bare and quiet. She stepped off the stairwell and hesitated. She had no excuse to be here, where she had been told the manager had his rooms, so she listened hard before she went any farther, but detected no footsteps and no murmur of voices.

So she stepped into the hallway, hugging the wall, ready to dart back toward the stairwell if she heard anyone coming.

Then a shadow made her pause, and what she saw caused her eyes to widen. There was someone ahead.

Ransom Sheffield bent over an inner door, his hand on the knob. He seemed to be doing something to the door—no, to the lock. Surely he was not jimmying the lock?

He *was* a thief!

Six

*W*hatever should she do? Mr. Nettles was rude and coarse and unpleasant and a bully, but he was still the manager and part owner of the theater, and she could not stand by and watch him be robbed.

She would have to run and fetch help. Of course, that was what she should do, Cordelia told herself. Yet she did not move, and her feet seemed frozen to the floor.

Very well, she would scream to alert others in the household, as she and her sister had done the first time they had caught this—this *criminal* trying to break into Mr. Nettles's private rooms! She opened her mouth to scream.

"Help!"

But somehow it came out as a faint and plaintive bleat. What was wrong with her? The man bent over the lock turned at once and took two long steps to reach her, grabbing her by the shoulders. She gasped in fear.

"Hush, do not raise an alarm. It is not what you think!" he told her, his voice sharp with urgency.

"What else could it be?" she whispered back. Still, she could not seem to get her voice to work properly, and she found that she was shivering with shock or—or some other emotion just as primitive. He was grasping her so tightly between his two hands that she could not move even if she had desired. No, no, of course she did not wish to be so constrained. She could see the fine hairs of his thick brows and how densely they grew, and how his quicksilver eyes glittered as he stared down at her, his manner cool and contained even though surely he must be alarmed to be caught in such a compromising position.

Yet he never seemed to lose his head, the amazing Mr. Ransom Sheffield. What had his rank been in the army, she wondered in some distant corner of her mind. Captain, major . . . His soldiers would have followed him through hell and back, the vicar had said. And no wonder, if he had faced danger with this kind of cool insolence. She would follow him anywhere, too, if he met his fate with such dancing, daring eyes . . .

And now she felt him stiffen, then she heard it, too, another—heavier—tread on the staircase.

Oh, dear Lord. Someone was coming.

"Damn!" He breathed the word as Cordelia looked around wildly.

She saw another door farther down the hallway, and she opened her mouth to suggest taking refuge inside a different room, but he shook his head before she could voice the thought. "It's locked as well," he muttered. "I checked earlier."

"Oh, dear!" She felt as helpless as a rabbit caught on the open moor with no hole near enough to dart into when a hawk is diving. "We're trapped!"

Sheffield's expression was grim, and the heavy footsteps seemed nigh on to reaching the top of the stairs. Was it Mr. Nettles himself? What on earth would he say? What could they say? There was no reason for them to be found lingering outside his private rooms—

With one smooth motion, Sheffield pulled her into his arms and pressed his lips against hers. Cordelia forgot everything else.

His lips were firm and warm against her own. For a moment she simply stood still and allowed him to kiss her.

Despite all the tales told around the shire about the scandalous Applegate twins, she had never kissed a man. Ophelia had kissed a right few—and come home to share the stories, laughing and protesting that most boys were too sloppy about it, too awkward, too boastful of their prowess when few could stir her blood.

But Cordelia had been too reserved, too shy to try such debaucheries herself. And now it was her turn, though she had never thought it would happen so suddenly, that she would be taken unaware by a man who did not have the decency to ask her leave first!

But despite his lack of gentlemanly scruples, she found that his touch sent a thrill through her, not just her lips or her mouth but through her whole body. She felt the shivers run up and down her torso and her legs, touching even the tips of her toes. She leaned into the kiss and discovered that she was kissing him back, seeking more from his firm solid lips than he was giving, and she knew at the very moment when he perceived the difference and pulled her even closer, demanding more from her, and she strove eagerly to deliver.

And now she was also aware of his arms about her, the strong corded arms that held her so firmly, thrilling her yet again, allowing her to feel wrapped in his embrace as never before. Her elder sister would say this was not proper, the small voice of her conscience warned her dimly, very dimly. Cordelia consigned her conscience to the devil and concentrated on giving her best effort to the kiss.

How long was a kiss supposed to last? She wasn't sure, but he seemed in no hurry to break away, and she found herself loath to break the connection. In fact, if anything, she found that she seemed to want to press herself more closely against him. . . .

Now his tongue slipped between her lips, and she jumped a little in surprise. But no, after a moment, Cordelia found it a rather heady sensation. He tasted faintly like salt and red wine, and his tongue was strong and probing, curious, seeking—just like the rest of him, no doubt—and the thought that followed next was so shocking and unmaidenly that her cheeks red-dened. She was glad that he could surely not see them since they were pressed so closely together, and just to ensure that he could not, she kissed him even more heartily, allowing her tongue to follow his example, a little shocked at her own daring. But he seemed to like her conduct just fine. . . .

"What the bloody 'ell do ye think yer doing?" A voice roared into her ear.

Cordelia jumped, and they parted abruptly. She had forgotten where they were and who was standing before them. She blinked now in honest bewilderment to see the theater manager scowling at them both.

As Ransom Sheffield released her, she looked up to see Mr. Nettles's red face contorted into an expression of angry disgruntlement.

"No, I see well enough what yer doing, but go do yer messing about on the lower levels, dammit all! These are my private rooms!"

"Sorry, sir, we was just looking for a quiet corner for a-a little chat," Ransom Sheffield muttered, playing a part more effectively than he had done during his mock drills in the alleys, she thought wildly.

Cordelia blushed and looked away, but Ransom gripped her hand. With him in the lead, they slipped down the stairs and quickly out of the manager's sight. She was silent. She wasn't sure whether to break into nervous tears or hysterical laughter. So it was only to evade suspicion from Nettles that Ransom had kissed her?

Of course, she should have thought of that.

By the time they reached the stage level and crossed over to the theater side again, pausing to allow a group of chattering dancers to walk past them, Cordelia was trying hard to pull herself together. No matter how this man affected her, she could not allow Ransom to observe it. She had some pride left!

Afer all, he must certainly be accustomed to kissing women. It had all been a ruse, she told herself. He had not kissed her because he wanted to, it had been a maneuver, a feint, a quick-thinking move by a clever tactician to explain their presence on the upper floor.

So when he turned to her, she had put on an expression of—she hoped—smooth serenity. "That was a clever stratagem, Mr. Sheffield," she said, keeping her voice low. They stopped at the edge of a pile of lumber, a distance from the other cast and crew members.

His eyes glinted as he looked down at her. "You think that was all it was?"

"Wasn't it?" She threw the words back at him.

"Perhaps that was how it began," he admitted. "But you were kissing me back, Miss Applegate."

"Perhaps. And perhaps my sister is not the only actress in the family," she suggested, managing with immense effort to keep her gaze level with his.

He leaned closer, putting out one arm to pin her against the rough inner wall of the theater. "Not even your sister is *that* good an actress, Miss Applegate," he told her, so near now that she could feel his breath warm against her temple. The curious hunger inside her stirred again. "And you came close to making me forget the whole purpose of my mission."

And that—his mission, the purpose of it—was what she had meant to find out! But as she opened her mouth to ask, he started to turn away.

With a daring she didn't know she was capable of, she grabbed the sleeve of his coat and held him back.

He looked at her in surprise.

"If you can use me as a decoy, Mr. Sheffield," she said, keeping her voice pitched low. "Then I have the right to ask you what your mission is. Why were you breaking into Mr. Nettles's rooms?"

He lifted one of those arching dark brows. "You don't believe I'm simply trying to lighten the manager's purse? It would be the most obvious explanation."

His gray eyes glinted, whether with wickedness or only gentle teasing, she couldn't be sure.

"It is hard to apply the word obvious or simple to anything

that you do," she said, hearing a certain grimness in her own voice. "But I want . . . I believe I deserve . . . an explanation. This is the second time I've caught you in the act of house-breaking. If I am to have any faith that you are an honest man, I need to know what this is about!"

"You were good enough not to cry wolf on me this time," he said, nodding. "I suppose you deserve something for that."

And for the kiss, she thought, what about the kiss?

"Mr. Nettles has something of mine," he told her, his tone abrupt, and his silver-colored eyes suddenly turning cold and hard. "Something of great value to my family. I mean to get it back."

This was so unexpected that Cordelia had no response ready. She stared at him, unprepared for his change of demeanor. It was if the great theater curtain itself had dropped down, cutting off the dawning connection between them. Suddenly, he was cool and detached again, just as he had been when they first met.

Not knowing what to say, she hesitated. With two long strides, he was gone before she could gather her scattered wits to ask.

Talking loudly, two scene shifters came up to move the pile of wood.

Cordelia stepped aside. The illusion of privacy had vanished, just like their chance for a tête-à-tête, even if he had still desired it. She could not run after Ransom Sheffield, nor be-rate him with angry questions as she would have like to have done. She pressed her lips together and walked on to her tiny sewing nook.

Her twin looked up. "Good, you're back. I need to go see if I have to rehearse that dance." Ophelia tucked the script changes into her pocket and corked the bottle of ink. "Bessy wants her jumper mended."

Cordelia took the garment and nodded absently. She sat down with the sewing basket and threaded her needle, trying to concentrate on her mending, but she kept sticking her finger instead of the fabric.

Frowning, she shook her abused finger, wishing for a thim-ble, which she had not been able to locate. Why not wish for tougher skin, she thought, or a man with fewer mysteries? What was he after, the enigmatic Ransom Sheffield? Why did he wish to break into Mr. Nettles's private rooms? How could a common thief make her heart beat faster? And why was a man obviously born a gentleman reduced to the status of a housebreaker anyhow? Had he no character, no conscience at all?

And she was a great one to talk, kissing a thief in plain view of a common huckster like Mr. Nettles, who was nonetheless her employer, so she supposed she shouldn't be calling him names. Strange as it was to think on, she and her sister were employed in a theater company. Cordelia paused to rub her hand over the wrinkled garment in her lap, shaking her head as she considered.

If that were common knowledge back in their home shire, they'd be the talk of the county! Actresses were generally considered barely one step above prostitutes, and sometimes not even that.

Holding the needle still, Cordelia bit her lip. She did hope the mask idea would work, and no one found out that Ophelia, a lady by birth and of respectable if impoverished family, was acting onstage, and not even in a licensed theater. . . .

A burst of noise—if one were charitable, one supposed one might call it music—came from the direction of the stage. The sounds came from a small pianoforte, which served as a substitute for the orchestra that usually would play when an audience filled the theater; Mr. Nettles was too cheap to pay musicians for the rehearsals. The girls commenced the dance that filled the space between Act One and Act Two.

Did they have to sing, as well? It sounded for all the world like a quartet of quarreling cats.

Cordelia sighed and, in order to save her fingers more abuse, directed her thoughts to her mending.

They did not have another chance to get access to the manager's rooms, but Cordelia thought all day about what the man could have that belonged to Ransom Sheffield and how he could have acquired it. An item of great value . . .

Mr. Nettles kept the actors late, and when he finally released Ophelia and Ransom and the other cast members, and

Cordelia could put away her sewing, a fine rain was falling. There did not seem to be a hackney to be had. So in the end they made their way home on foot through the London twilight, tramping along the crowded pavements shoulder to shoulder with other tired, damp Londoners.

It was a strange sensation, being one of the working populace, and Cordelia said as much.

"I'm sure it's good for our character," Ophelia pointed out, her tone blithe as she circled a woman herding half a dozen children and calling to the laggards to keep up with the rest. "Women don't usually get the opportunity to earn a living, you know."

"Ladies don't, you mean," Cordelia corrected. "Women of the lower classes might well have to work for their bread, Ophelia, if they wish to eat."

"Oh!" Ophelia looked startled. "What do they do, then?"

Cordelia rubbed her sore fingers; she was developing calluses on her fingertips. "They sew, they bake, they work in shops. The new factories employ many women and children, too, the vicar was telling us at dinner last night. And, well—" She thought of the two ruffians who had tried to kidnap her on their first day in London and shivered.

"There are other hazardous occupations," Ransom Sheffield finished for her, "as dangerous as the factories, I fear, where the machines may snatch off your fingers or indeed, your arms, if the women, or the girls and boys who operate them, do not pay strict attention."

Cordelia glanced at their escort curiously. She had not been surprised that the good-hearted vicar should know about the poorer classes of London. In his position he would be called upon to help the unfortunate. But how did his more cynical cousin come to know about the woes of the working classes?

"Oh, dear." Ophelia's eyes widened. "I certainly prefer the theater. I might forget a line, but at least no one will cut off my fingers!"

"True." Ransom Sheffield guided them around a steaming pile of horse droppings as they crossed a street and stepped back up to the sidewalk. They had almost reached the rectory, and Cordelia thought with longing of a hot dinner. It had been a long day.

"Nor will working in a factory make you the Toast of London," Cordelia added beneath her breath, throwing a rueful smile at her sister.

Since Ophelia had achieved her goal of obtaining a part, they had heard less about her dreams of glory. The reality of sharing a dressing room with girls who dropped their *h* and who smelled of liver and onions seemed to have brought her ambitions down a notch or two, although Ophelia still appeared to be thoroughly enjoying her time in the theater company.

If all went well, perhaps her sister could act for a few weeks, protected by the anonymity of her mask and fake stage name, then they would go home to Yorkshire and no one would be the wiser, Cordelia told herself. As she thought it, she glanced at Ransom Sheffield and felt a pang at the thought of leaving him behind. But she had no business thinking of the man with his mysteries and his illicit conduct: she had only his word for it that he was not an absolute criminal! And he certainly did not seem eager to confide in her. So . . .

She looked away, determined not to allow her feelings to betray her just because the man made her shiver, made her tremble when he kissed her; she hadn't yet confessed to Ophelia that she had kissed Ransom Sheffield. Her biggest romantic adventure to date, and she hadn't told her sister!

That was unheard of. They told each other everything.

What was wrong with her?

There hadn't been time, Cordelia told herself. Backstage, with its bustle and listening ears, was no place for telling secrets . . . and . . . and . . .

The church was just ahead. She pushed her thoughts away. Ransom Sheffield stepped a little faster to reach the iron gate first and push it open.

"Thanks goodness," Ophelia said. "I'm famished, and I'm sure I couldn't walk another step. Too bad we couldn't flag down a hackney tonight."

Cordelia nodded. She turned and followed her sister through

the side door and into the rectory, which already seemed to feel like home.

A savory smell of cooking food made her empty stomach twist. Cordelia sniffed with appreciation and took off her damp cloak, hanging it and her bonnet on the pegs in the hall as her sister and Mr. Sheffield followed suit. Then she and her sister went upstairs to wash their face and hands before dinner.

The evening meal was plain but savory and filling. The vicar greeted them as pleasantly as always, and did not remark on the fact that his guests seemed to have settled in for a prolonged visit, although Cordelia was feeling a trifle guilty about their stay. When she tried to say as much, he waved away her worries.

"I would hardly turn you out on the pavement, my dear," he assured her. "Until your brother returns to town, you will be safe here—"

Feeling another surge of guilt, Cordelia looked down at the table. She had no reason to think that Lord Gabriel's return to town was imminent, so she still felt they were taking advantage of the good vicar. The housekeeper, now that she'd had more time, had prepared another room, so the twins now could have separate chambers.

If the good-looking vicar's blue eyes lit up at the sight of her sister, and if Ophelia seemed particularly pleased when in his company, well, her sister was a confirmed flirt, so Cordelia did not put much stock in such signs. In fact, she really needed to remove her sister before the good churchman had his heart broken, as many a young man in Yorkshire had done before him!

After dinner, Ophelia announced that she had to work on rewriting script pages. The vicar looked disappointed but accepted her early withdrawal with his usual good nature. Cordelia couldn't stay downstairs with the vicar alone— Ransom had already gone out—so she also said good night and went upstairs, taking a book from the vicar's bookshelves that she could read before bedtime.

She and her sister helped each other with buttons and stays

and when they had donned nightgowns, Ophelia curled up with her paper and quill to work on the changes she planned for the script.

Cordelia said good night, then, in the new bedroom, took her book in hand and climbed into her own bed. She glanced at the curtains drawn over the window and wondered briefly in which gambling hell—or worse establishment—the other Mr. Sheffield amused himself.

In fact, Ransom Sheffield was not at all amused. It was not until the ladies had withdrawn after dinner that his cousin had broken the news.

"What do mean, Avery has gone out? Bloody hell, he's supposed to be staying out of sight!" Ransom said, putting his wineglass down so hastily that some of the ruby liquid sloshed over onto the bare wood and swearing aloud. "Is this how he thinks to repay all our efforts?"

Giles, who was more forbearing, simply eyed the puddle of red wine on the wood surface. "A good thing the cover has already been removed. If you could hear my housekeeper on the subject of wine stains—"

"Don't change the subject! We're talking about my feckless younger brother's bloody neck! No, you're quite right. Perhaps your household linen is of more significance!"

"I know it's frustrating, Ransom. I wish he would listen to reason. He promised me that he would be back before sunset. And he has been in hiding for some time; you know it's hard for him to say indoors and—"

"I should have stayed here, not gone off to the theater; then he wouldn't have gone at all!" Ransom snapped. "If I had to tie him to his bedpost!"

Giles looked grave. "Yes, but I'm sure I should have—"

"It's not your fault," Ransom added, knowing that his cousin would assume all the blame. "After all I've done, am still doing, you'd think that my idiot brother—"

He stopped and took a deep breath. "Very well. I'd better go out and hit some of the obvious places. I might be lucky enough to stumble across him."

"I can come, too," Giles offered.

Ransom shook his head. "No, stay here. You might receive a more urgent call for help, from, Lord knows, a more deserving complainant!"

And, still swearing beneath his breath, he left the dining room quickly before he could be forced into offering some mendacious explanation to the ladies in the sitting room.

He'd lied more in the last fortnight than in his entire life, it often seemed . . .

It was another damp, cool night. Late summer might be turning into early fall, but already cool evenings had claimed the last brave sunny afternoons. Yet Ransom was so angry that he carried his own heat inside him and barely needed the cloak he had shrugged on over his evening coat. He walked until he found a hackney in reasonable condition and hired the man to take him and wait when he went inside the first club to look over the men inside, then came back out and went on to his next destination. He would likely have a lot of territory to cover.

Damn Avery, anyhow. When was the young cub going to learn some sense? If this misadventure hadn't taught him . . .

He tried White's, and two other clubs—not that Avery belonged to them, but he could have gotten in with friends. No luck. And anyhow, they were too sedate for his madcap brother's tastes, Ransom realized belatedly. He was wasting his time.

He headed for some of Avery's favorite gaming hells. These were crowded and noisy, not at all sedate, but they were more in line with his brother's tastes. And if he found the younger man in any of them, flaunting his face in front of the very people he was supposed to be evading, Ransom might kill him himself, here and now!

A woman in a brassy-hued, low-cut gown whose shade almost matched the color of her hair tried to catch his eye as he glanced over the tables of card players and hard-drinking spectators.

"What's yer 'urry, love?" She leaned closer, putting one hand possessively on his arm. "I can show you a good time. Why not stay around for a while? 'Ave a drink, try the cards. Or we can 'op upstairs first thing, if you want."

He looked at her without smiling. Her face was not ugly,

though her chin was weak and her eyes tired. And her breasts sagged a little under the low-cut dress, as if they, too, were tired and had had too much handling. She leaned even closer to him, as if inviting him to be the next man to touch her bosom, to trace the vee that ran down between the swelling mounds, which smelled of sweat and a strong musky perfume, or the nipples that peeked just beneath the neckline and which he would no doubt find rouged. At Avery's age, perhaps he would have found her arousing—good Lord, had he ever been that naive?

He hoped Avery had not been here tonight; if so, he had probably left with a good case of clap, or worse. Ransom described his younger brother to the prostitute and asked if she had seen him.

"No," she said, her eyes suddenly wary. "Not me. Why you askin'?"

From necessity, she was such a habitual liar, it was impossible to tell if she lied now or not.

Ransom kept his expression impassive, though perhaps his eyes gave him away because she stiffened.

"You don't have to look at a girl like that!" she snapped. "I'm just earning an honest living, gov."

"No doubt," he said, and this time his voice was softer.

She still glared at him.

He took one more glance around the room, then returned to his waiting hackney. He tried three more spots, gaming hells and taverns, but without success.

Somehow too restless to sleep, Cordelia read until at last her eyelids felt heavy. The long day at the theater had been tiring, and the rectory seemed a quiet refuge. It was a relief to at last have time to herself. Being with her twin was one thing; having so many strangers about her was quite another. She was just about to shut the book and reach to snuff out her candles when a sudden creak made her pause, arm already extended.

The noise seemed to come from inside the wall.

For a moment, her skin crawled, and she wondered if the rectory housed any restless spirits, departed souls who did not rest easily?

That was silly. It was an old building, and buildings made noises as day darkened into night and the air cooled, that was all, she told herself stoutly. Except suddenly she felt less sleepy and much less inclined to blow out her candles' flames. But now the words on the page could not hold her attention. She put the strip of linen which served as a marker into her volume and closed the book, placing it on the table beside the bed. Glancing about the bedchamber, wishing that the shadows at the edge of the room did not dance so much in the candles' flickering light, Cordelia found herself holding her breath.

She was being foolish, she scolded herself again. It was nothing—

Another creak sounded even more loudly, and she jumped, clutching the bedcovers and pulling them up to her chin. She stared at the far corner of the room where the shadows pooled deepest, wondering if she should call for help or even run to fetch someone.

And tell them what? They would think her a child seeing ogres in the dark.

Nonetheless, perhaps she would go and sit a while with Ophelia in her bedroom, Cordelia told herself, just until her nerves steadied. She was not usually one to fancy strange phantasms. Perhaps it was only—she was about to slip out of bed when she heard a bump and then a long nerve-wracking screak like the sound of a rusty bolt being pulled back.

A panel opened in the wall, and a looming figure stepped out of the darkness.

Seven

Cordelia tried to scream. But her throat felt scratchy and dry as if she had been changed, like Lot's wife, into a pillar of salt. A strange sort of hiss was all that emerged. Perhaps she needed acting lessons, too, or a punch in the stomach like Ophelia, she thought in a corner of her mind removed from the panic that threatened to overwhelm her.

"Hallo," the stranger said.

The innocuous greeting, and the fact that the set of his shoulders looked oddly familiar, plus the circumstance that, as he stepped into the candles' faint circle of light and out of the shadows trailing him from the inner chamber, he no longer seemed to be seven feet tall—Cordelia found that her chest no longer felt constricted by invisible bonds.

A bit light-headed, she concentrated on breathing while the man, the young man, ogled her.

"Didn't know anyone was in this bedchamber. Used to be my room, you see, my bed. Sorry if I startled you," he said, his tone diffident. "I say, are you that actress?"

She stared at him. Tall and slim, he had medium brown hair and a pleasing set of features marked by a brave attempt at a mustache. He seemed . . . her thoughts suddenly skewed in a totally different direction, and her alarm returned in full force.

With a calm matter-of-factness, he had turned back the sheet and was climbing into bed beside her!

"Awfully cold in that damned passage. My hands and feet are turning into bloody icicles. And I haven't seen a girl as pretty as you in simply ages. Would you mind if I took a turn in your bed tonight?"

She grabbed the covers—all that she could snatch of them—and pulled them up to her neck, dreadfully aware that all she wore was a thin cotton nightgown. "Of course I mind, you . . . you reprobate! What do you think you're doing? Get out of my bed this instant! I shall scream for help!"

She followed her threat with a shriek that was satisfyingly loud. At least her throat was working again.

The young man's eyes widened, and he slid away so quickly that he fell out of bed, his backside hitting the floor with a thud. "Ouch!" Holding his hands in front of him and waving them like flags of truce, he scrambled up from the floor.

"I say, don't sound off again, if you please! You'll have the servants in hysterics, and Giles will give us all a lecture. I did wonder how it was he was turning a blind eye to Ransom's little, eh, well, I mean . . . not like him at all. Giles, I mean, quite like Ransom—"

"I have a dagger hidden about my person, sir! If you approach me again, you shall have it in your heart!" Cordelia warned him, just wishing that her threat were true. "I am a virtuous lady of good family and good character, and I do NOT welcome strange men, or any men for that matter, into my bed."

"Oh, maybe I've got the wrong end of the stick, here, I mean—" The stranger colored, and for a moment he looked absurdly young. Cordelia almost relented, then reminded herself he had not been too young to climb into an unknown lady's bed! Plus, she remembered her own moments of genuine fear, even if that emotion was now fading into a milder blend of anger and annoyance and even, she had to admit, a reluctant desire to laugh, since the young man looked so confused and perhaps even embarrassed.

"But if you're not the actress, who—"

"Stop repeating that!" she interrupted him, her voice sharp. "My sister is the actress you have apparently been told is staying here, and if you must know, not all actresses are fallen women."

"If you say so," he muttered, but his tone sounded unconvinced.

"And I am her chaperone!" Cordelia added.

Looking totally befuddled this time, he blinked at her.

She hear a sharp rap on the door. "Miss Applegate, are you all right?" It was the vicar, and he sounded concerned.

"Oh, God, it's Giles; I've had it, now," the young man muttered beneath his breath. "I don't suppose you'd let me just vanish back down the passage?"

"Don't you dare move, or I shall scream my lungs out!" she told the intruder, reaching for a shawl to drape about her shoulders before she called, "Come in, please."

The door opened. The vicar, a frown on his face, stood there in slippers and a robe. And beside him loomed Ransom, still fully dressed. The darker Sheffield cousin seemed to carry the cooler air of outdoors about him, and his scowl was truly alarming. He looked at the young man in her bedchamber with an expression that boded no good for the newcomer.

"I've been turning London upside down, and I find you here, distressing our guest in her own bedchamber!" He took two long strides, grabbed the younger man by his collar and jerked him back.

The vicar directed a grave glance toward the young man, who stared piteously at Giles as if asking for reassurance.

"I say, I didn't know—" the younger man began.

"Do you suppose you can find any more trouble to fall into, Avery, you damn fool?" Ransom Sheffield asked, his voice cold. "If I had to be cursed with a young nitwit for a brother, I would have preferred one with a minimum of common sense!"

"Do all your guest rooms have secret passages?" Cordelia demanded at almost the same time, plagued with too many warring emotions to cloak them with polite dissembling.

Giles Sheffield turned to her. "I do beg your pardon, Miss Applegate. I hope you were not too alarmed. I had no idea that my young cousin would make such a dramatic entrance." He looked over at his relation. "I am relieved that you are back, but the side door would have sufficed, you young fool."

The newest Sheffield to make an appearance lifted his chin. She should have known! He had the same set of good shoulders and the same handsome look as the others, even though his features were somewhat different, and his hair not as dark as Ransom's but not as fair as Giles.

And for the first time, Cordelia realized she could smell a faint aroma of strong spirits that lingered about his person. The young man was foxed.

"I was staying out of sight; you told me to stay out of sight," Avery Sheffield complained, his voice plaintive. "I didn't mean to frighten anyone."

"Out of sight means just that, staying quietly at home with a good book in front of the fire, not running off to drink and gamble with undependable lowlifes. That's how you got into this tangle in the first place," Ransom Sheffield snapped, reaching out again to lift the younger man by the back of his coat, for all the world like a mother dog picking up a long-legged puppy and giving it a shake.

"Here now, this coat's from my best tailor. I owe him a fortune," Avery muttered. "And if you don't find that damn snuff-box soon—"

"If I don't, you won't have to worry about your tailor bills," Ransom pointed out, his voice cool. "Now come away and allow our guest to get some sleep. Miss Applegate, I will see that passage—it dates back to the days of the Civil War when sudden escapes were often necessary—closed off. Like my cousin, and my wretched younger brother, I do apologize."

Bowing, the three men left without more ceremony. Avery's steps were somewhat unsteady and his brother still gripped the back of his coat and pulled him along.

Cordelia shut the door to the hall and locked it, then, with some huffing and puffing, slid the clothespress in front of the panel. Hoping it was the only secret access to her room, she at last crawled back under the covers. And then she sat in bed and hugged her knees and thought.

Avery was Ransom Sheffield's younger brother? And despite the cold tone and the attempt at an indifferent expression, he was concerned. Something was wrong, if Avery Sheffield was supposed to be hiding out, there was a danger that was real. She had glimpsed it in Ransom's steel-colored eyes, even in the softer blue eyes of the vicar as the two older men had regarded Avery Sheffield—despite their cool expressions—with compassion and concern in their eyes.

And the snuffbox—what about the snuffbox and why was it so important? And did it just now reside in Mr. Nettles's apartments? Was that why Ransom had been trying to pick the lock, and was it the object he meant to search the manager's rooms to find?

Weary as she was, it was still a while before she could fall asleep.

The next morning Cordelia was wakened by a terrific lowing and stamping of hooves outside her window. It did not sound like the usual London street noises.

She yawned and rubbed her eyes, then, sure she had been dreaming of the barnyard back in Yorkshire, turned over and tried to go back to sleep. But no, the noises came again, and she smelled—surely she smelled *cows!*

Cordelia pushed the sheet aside and stumbled over to the window, which had been left open to catch the nighttime breeze. Oh, my, yes. The air was redolent of animals—in fact, it smelled strongly of barnyard scents. And when she looked down, the street below her rectory window was packed from one side to another with cows, who strained for space and mooed and lowed and tossed their horned heads. A few men with staffs and stout sticks yelled and waved the pack of animals onward.

She rubbed her eyes, wondering if she were dreaming still. But the noise continued, and the dust that drifted up made her cough, so she drew her head back and shut the window, despite the closeness of the room. Otherwise, the chamber would soon be filled with the smell of cow manure and the thick gray dust that billowed up from the street.

She washed and dressed quickly, and when the young housemaid appeared to finish the buttons at the back of her gown, Cordelia said, "Bess, there are cows on the street!"

"Yes, miss. They be taking 'em to market, It 'appens every week on Haymarket," the maidservant said, as if it were the most ordinary thing in the world. "Noisy, though. But the butchers 'ave to get 'em from somewhere, don't they, miss?"

"I see," Cordelia muttered, though she certainly didn't. She also wondered how on earth she would get to the theater, though surely most of the other streets would be clear. "Is my sister up yet?"

"Oh, she left early, miss. Said she 'ad a special appointment to see Mr. Nettles afore the re'earsals started."

"What?" Cordelia felt a frisson of alarm run up her back. "Did Mr. Sheffield go with her?"

The maid shook her head. "No, miss."

Cordelia had to press her lips together to keep her words of worry and censure from tumbling out.

Why hadn't Ophelia consulted her? She would have told her sister in no uncertain terms not to go off alone. Had her sister not learned anything from their near disastrous encounter with the white slavery gang? The streets of London held so many dangers—

Oh, Ophelia would never change!

"Where is Mr. Ransom?" she asked the maid before hurrying downstairs. "Is he up?"

"Oh, yes, long ago. He went out after Miss Ophelia," the maid told her.

That was something. Perhaps he would have caught up to her sister by now, Cordelia told herself, in which case her worries were not necessary. She went down the stairs and helped herself to a cup of tea and a slice of ham and some bread and butter, then set out by a side street for the theater, hoping she would find her sister, safe and unruffled.

And she would hug her, and then give her a thorough scolding, Cordelia told herself.

Ophelia had wakened before the sun had topped the darkened city. Often an early riser, she loved the freshness and promise of the early morning. Slipping out of bed, she pulled a shawl around her shoulders and went to the window to look out over London's sprawling rooftops. A few faint streaks of rosy light showed to the east.

Remembering Mr. Nettles's cryptic commission, she turned away from the window, eager to find out what her appointment with the theater manager might portend. Did he intend to increase her role in the play? Perhaps he had seen such promise in her acting ability that he was going to increase the prominence of her part and the number of her lines, as she had been hinting for him to do?

She grabbed a few bites of bread and butter and soon hurried up the lane toward the theater, too impatient to wait for an escort. She had become accustomed to the city streets and now felt less frightened by every bystander.

In fact, the street seemed unusually empty this morning, with fewer carts and coaches about than normal. Once she heard an unusual sound in the distance, and it seemed almost that she could feel a vibration in the ground. But likely she was letting her imagination get away from her, Ophelia told herself. It was all very well to make up stories, but this was real life, and no fairy tale.

Sure enough, she reached the side door of the theater without incident. She had to bang on the door before Nobby, the old man who sat beside the door and guarded the entrance, finally opened it.

"You out early," he muttered. "'Aven't even 'ad me porridge yet!"

"Mr. Nettles wanted to see me," she explained, her tone cheerful. She stopped at the dressing rooms to check the looking glass and make sure her hair was tucked into place and her gown presentable. The other actresses had told her how the gentlemen would come backstage, once the theater was presenting nightly performances again, walking unannounced into the actresses' dressing rooms, ready to flirt and make assignations for dinner and perhaps even more intimate tête-è-têtes. Ophelia's mind conjured up a handsome young lord who would have eyes only for her . . .

Then, she pinched her cheeks to make them pinker, applied a touch of paint to her already red lips and, ready for her interview, she hurried to the manager's office and rapped on the scarred oak door.

"Come in, then," the manager growled.

She opened the door and walked in. Mr. Nettles sat, or to be more accurate, sprawled in front of a desk heavily laden with papers, empty bottles and several pieces of dirty crockery. His eyes were bloodshot and his neckcloth crooked. His coat hung over the back of his chair, and he smelled.

She wrinkled her nose. He smelled.

She rather thought Mr. Nettles had had a long night.

"You asked me to come in early?" she reminded him. "Did you have something you wished to discuss with me, perhaps?"

He appeared to be trying to focus his eyes.

"It's Miss Applegate, Mr. Nettles," she reminded him a little desperately, beginning to feel annoyed, "You said you wished to speak to me. About the play!"

"Oh, yeah." He waved his hand toward the biggest pile of paper on the desk. "Got some handbills for you to give out."

Ophelia blinked. "Handbills—me?"

The manager looked pleased that he had remembered. He pawed the pile and then found a silver pocket flask in an inner pocket and, lifting it, took a long gulp. "That's right."

"Surely you can hire a street urchin for such a job!" Ophelia bit back her disappointment. "Are you sure you didn't intend to speak to me about something else? About my part in the play, for example? If you remember, I suggested adding some lines in the second act—"

He shook his head. "Later, maybe. Right now, we have to scare up an audience, first, don't we?"

"But, a boy can—"

"Always better to use a pretty girl," he insisted.

To Ophelia's dismay, he stood, a bit unsteady on his feet, lifted the hefty stack of paper and shoved it into her arms. "On your way, girl. I want you back smart in time for rehearsal. Don't dawdle."

Frowning, Ophelia found herself shoved back outside the office door, still holding the unwieldy stack of handbills.

"Get them to as many streets and as many men as you can," the manager added before he burped—he smelled of cheap spirits—and shut the door abruptly behind her.

For the love of heaven! Ophelia shifted the pile in her arms and almost dropped the whole stack. She would love to dump the pile into the privy out back, but if Mr. Nettles found out, he might fire her, and they did need an audience for their play, she conceded reluctantly.

Could *she* hire a street boy to hand them out? Would the manager discover it if she did?

Oh, dash it.

Apparently she would have to do this, as undignified a task as it was. She stomped off to find the small, lace-trimmed half mask that her sister had sewn for her. She would certainly not hand out bills without her disguise. Did Mr. Nettles not remember that she intended to remain anonymous?

For the first time, a flicker of doubt crossed her mind. Did the theater owner support her resolve to keep her true identity a secret?

She would do it with or without his help, Ophelia told herself. Putting her mask into her reticule and hanging the latter over her wrist, she picked up the stack of handbills, which announced in bold black letters:

A new and delightful comedy of manners and wit,
starting at the Malory Road Theater a week from today!

Smaller print listed the actors and lauded the play itself, "... *which has been exhibited with UNBOUNDED AP-PLAUSE to audiences around the provinces.*"

Seeing her stage name listed in tiny letters made her heart beat faster, and Ophelia felt less resentful about her errand. She tucked one of the handbills safely into her reticule to save for herself.

She didn't want to take all day about this; they still had rehearsals as usual, and she still had to convince Mr. Nettles that she needed more lines in Act Two.

Sighing, Ophelia put the handbills into a basket and put it over her other arm, then headed back out of the theater and turned toward the main street. She had gone only a few steps when again, strangely, the ground beneath her seemed to vibrate. Pausing, she turned, and what she saw made her freeze in her tracks.

Eight

S norting and tossing their horned heads, a solid line of cows trotted toward her. The street was wide, but the animals were packed so solidly that she saw no way to avoid the heaving mass of heavy bodies. And if she fell beneath their hooves, she would be trampled, surely maimed or killed.

In the middle of London, who would have expected such a thing? Where had they come from? She rubbed her eyes for a moment, wondering if she were dreaming.

No, she could feel the pavement vibrate from the stamp of their hooves, and the air stank of the heavy smells of manure and animal hides. The lowing of the cattle and the shouts of unseen men who urged them on would drown out any cry of hers, and there was no one in sight to help her. She was on her own, and, although she turned her head, looking in vain for a way to flee, she saw no way to escape.

She could step inside a doorway of one of the buildings alongside the street, but that would gain her only a few extra inches, not enough to protect her from the press of the cattle as they passed. She dare not risk it.

Ophelia picked up her skirts and ran, but the cows were

moving at a steady pace, advancing even faster than they had first appeared. She could hear them coming closer and closer. The back of her neck crawled as she felt the warmth of the animals, crowded together as they were, approaching nearer with every passing minute. She sensed the heavy smell of their bovine breaths on the air.

Trying to run faster, she stumbled over a loose rock in the street, almost falling. No, she dare not fall. She would surely be killed if she lay helpless in the street; there would be nothing to stop them from trampling her supine body. She caught herself and regained her balance, huffing a little as she fled once more.

The irony of it was, Ophelia thought, she had grown up in the country. Even though, not caring for country chores, she was less likely than her other sisters to be found in the barn or stable, she nevertheless knew her way around the farm. She could milk a cow if necessary, gather eggs, put a broody hen back on the nest. She was much less likely to panic in this situation than a pampered London miss, but no one could be really calm before scores of bawling cattle packed into a solid mass of tossing horned heads and trampling feet!

So far, Ophelia had managed to keep ahead of the moving wall of animals, but her breath was coming fast, her heart pounded and her side ached. There, just ahead, a side street; surely there at the intersection she could get away to safety—

But three or four cows had the same instinctive urge to escape the drive to their slaughter. One young bridled animal galloped ahead of the rest, pushing past the leaders of the herd and brushing against Ophelia. Its right horn ripped her sleeve and she felt the tip of it tear at her skin, and the force of the impact came near to knocking her off her feet.

Gasping, Ophelia grabbed at the animal. Somehow with one hand she grasped one of its ears and with the other she reached for the top of its head, holding onto the short bristles of hair that covered its hard crown.

The cow bawled in protest and shook its wide head. It tossed Ophelia about like a last autumn leaf clinging by the merest whisper to the tree and now buffeted by a north wind.

Knowing that she would fall beneath its hooves if she lost her grip, Ophelia held on for dear life. Grimly, she fought with the cow, and the animal shook her again, then pushed her back against the nearest building.

Ophelia grunted in pain as the brick wall scraped her back. The rest of the cows were catching up with them; she would be crushed in the press of the beasts. But she dare not let go and be flung to the pavement!

"Damn you!" she swore briskly. She redoubled her grip and when the cow pushed her again back against the brick she fought for a toehold against the uneven wall. Somehow, she found a step up, then another. Afterward, she would never remember exactly how she did it, but knowing that she dare not go down, somehow, she scrambled up—and in another breathless moment, Ophelia flung one leg over the broad back of the cow.

Her skirt had already been ripped in a dozen places as she'd fought with the cow and the brick wall, so she could straddle the beast without any hindrance from her lightweight muslin skirts.

Clinging to the animal's ears and horns, she found that she still had the basket, though its shape was sadly crushed, and the bills were falling, one or two at a time, beneath the hooves of the cows to be crushed into the muck of the street. Oh, what would Mr. Nettles say? For a moment, she actually worried more about that than how she would get out of this ridiculous, and dangerous, predicament.

Then she saw a boy gaping at her from an upper window.

"Ma, come look! A woman is riding a cow!" he yelled.

She held up her hand to him, thinking he might be able to pull her up, but he only waved merrily back to her.

"Can you stand on your 'ead, too?" He called. "Ma, there's an eh-equilibrist on the cows, come and see! Maybe she'll do some tricks."

Now more windows were being pushed open along the street as the cow trotted along, falling back in line with its herd, and more heads poked out to see her pass. Oh, heavens, Ophelia thought, what a spectacle she was making of herself.

She felt her face go red with embarrassment, and she coughed as the dust rose from the cattle's passing.

"Can you help me?" she called to the next window, where a woman looked out who appeared reasonably sensible. "I want to get down!"

But the woman only smiled and waved back.

Probably, with the sounds of the cattle rising about her, the people in the buildings couldn't make out her words, Ophelia thought. She was doomed to ride a cow, at least until they reached wherever these animals were being taken to be sold and handed over to the butchers. And half of London was going to stare at her in the meantime!

A man at the next window leered, and she realized how much of her legs were exposed, due to her shredded skirts and the unladylike posture she had had to assume to stay on the cow's back. She tugged at her skirts, trying to cover up more of her limbs. She suddenly remembered her reticule and the half mask it contained. Was it still in the basket?

With one hand, she released her death grip on the cow she rode long enough to poke into the basket and—to her immense relief—found the mask and tied it about her head. She had no desire to be remembered the rest of her life as the demented woman who'd ridden a cow down the streets of London!

But as more and more people leaned out of windows and called and waved to her, it occurred to Ophelia she might as well take advantage of this insane predicament. She recaptured the handbills which were leaking from the misshapen basket and tossed them toward the windows.

At once, eager hands leaned out to catch them from her.

They should certainly have plenty of people talking about their new play, Ophelia thought with the first hint of satisfaction she had felt all day. And plenty of people buying tickets!

"If we come to see you next week, will you ride a cow onstage?" a fat woman called down to her after taking a handbill and scanning it.

Startled, Ophelia managed a mysterious smile and didn't answer.

Even on the back streets, Cordelia found it slow going.
All the vendor's carts that usually crowded the main avenues
had been pushed into the side streets this morning, and most
of the morning traffic had flowed this way as well. Any experienced Londoner apparently knew to avoid Haymarket and
its cattle herds. So she had to fight the packed pavements on
her way to the theater, and she resigned herself to being late.

At an intersection of two back streets, she found a group of
children crowded around a tall thin man whose arms and legs
were long and spindly, like a wooden doll which bends at odd
places. His faded blue coat had large pockets and his hands
were large, too, with long agile fingers, and they were engaged
now in juggling, with reasonable expertise, three colored balls.

Cordelia paused a moment to watch the circling orbs. The
tall man kept up a running patter of silly jokes that made the
children laugh.

"And this one, this one is wanting to run away and eat cakes
all day, just like the pretty miss with the lace on her kerchief—"

A little girl at the edge of the crowd giggled in appreciation. She had chubby cheeks and no doubt did like cakes,
Cordelia thought, grinning.

"And the blue ball, methinks the boy in the blue coat would
mayhap dream now and then of a life on the open sea? The
blue ball wants to fly away over the sea so blue—"

The blue ball suddenly darted away into the crowd of children, who squealed and ducked. The boys scrambled to find it
and after a short but lively scuffle to see who could wrestle it
away from the other reaching hands, one of the urchins had
the prize and tossed it back to the funny-looking man. He
caught it deftly, and the children applauded. Cordelia joined
in, and some of the adults standing around tossed a few pennies
into his soft cap, put on the pavement beside him for just this
purpose.

With his head uncovered, you could see that the man had
longish hair whose locks tended to stick out in odd directions,
everywhere except just above his forehead, where a balding

spot made Cordelia think that, along with his round eyes and his habit of nodding toward his audience, he looked a good deal like a crane with crumpled feathers.

"Another trick, if you please," the little girl with the kerchief called. "I want to see the white mouse again, please, sir!"

Her father, who was standing just behind her, brought out a tuppence from his purse and tossed it into the cap.

Ah, the man was a conjuror, too, as well as a juggler, Cordelia thought. She knew she should be on her way, but she lingered just another minute. Good conjurors had been rare occurrences in her isolated part of Yorkshire, and she enjoyed seeing a good trick.

The little man was speaking again, as he pulled colored scarves out of the air, apparently a prelude to the mouse's entrance. The little girl giggled and all the children laughed at his nonsensical patter, but Cordelia permitted her mind to wander. Was Ophelia back at the theater by now? She certainly hoped so, or at least that Ransom Sheffield was with her to protect her from any danger. Which, of course, reminded Cordelia that she herself had no escort today, but surely—

As if the thought had brought the menace to life, Cordelia narrowed her eyes and cried out, "Your cap, sir! Your coin!"

One of the same boys who had been laughing at the street magician's tricks a moment earlier had now sidled closer to the hat on the pavement while the rest of the audience watched and waited for the appearance of the white mouse. His small dirty hand darted out to scoop up the pennies inside the tattered lining, and then he took to his heels.

"Thief!" the magician roared, with a louder voice than Cordelia had heard him use yet. "Come back with me blunt, ye scurvy brat!" He took two long steps, then somehow collided with one of the taller boys and, their legs tangled, they collapsed into a heap.

"We'll catch him, sir!" Several of the other boys loped after the first one and almost at once disappeared into the crowd.

The lad who had fallen jumped up and was off, too, but the

conjurer got to his feet more slowly and limped when he tried to follow. He seemed to have turned his ankle.

"All my coin!" he lamented. "All of it! I'll 'ave no lodging for tonight, and no dinner, damn their wretched 'ides. They was all in it together, I 'ave no doubt."

He patted his pockets and groaned again. "And Milly is gone—they 'ave scared her off, damn them."

"Where is the Watch when you need 'em?" The girl's father snorted in disgust. But he turned away, too, and took his daughter's hand, apparently not interested in contributing any more pennies to the conjurer's now empty cap.

"Are you hurt, sir?" Cordelia asked in concern. "And who is Milly?"

"My mouse, of course," the man said, his tone woeful. "I spend weeks training her, and now . . ." He peered about him, and Cordelia looked, as well, but in the trash that littered the street, she saw no evidence of a mouse, white or brown.

After several minutes of poking through garbage, the man sighed and rubbed his eyes and pulled out a green silk handkerchief from one capacious pocket, paying no attention to the fact that it was connected somehow to another bright crimson kerchief which dangled just behind it.

Cordelia couldn't help staring. "I have to go," she told him. "Will you be all right, Mr.—"

"Druid," he told her proudly.

"Mr. Druid?"

"It's not me birth name, you understand," he explained, lowering his voice as if it were a great secret. "That were Smith, like me dad, who worked 'is fingers to the bone and died afore I was twelve, but who would 'ark to a 'andbill touting a prestidigitator named Mr. Smith?"

"Ah, yes, I see," she nodded, managing not to smile. "Mr. Druid, I'm afraid I have no pennies in my reticule. But I work at a small theater, and the manager does use extra acts in the interval between scenes. If you like, you could come along with me and speak to him about—"

"Oh, splendid!" The skinny man stood up straighter, like a

balloon whose hot air has been freshly infused. "Thank you, dear lady! You are an angel in disguise."

"I can't promise anything," she told him hastily. "But I can, I hope, get you in the door and then, it's up to you."

"Oh, just give me a fair chance, and I'm sure I can get me name on the program. Why, I was a smash in Birmingham, and in Leeds, they called me back for an extra performance—"

He spent the rest of the walk to the theater listing his past performances and extolling his long list of illusions and tricks. "And my experiments with second sight and 'ypnotism and anti-magnetism, why, all the crowned 'eads of Europe know me name—"

Well, he could certainly talk anyone into a trance, Cordelia told herself.

At any rate, now she had an escort for the rest of the walk to the theater. By the time they reached Malory Road, the last of the cattle were trailing down Haymarket, leaving behind even larger piles of manure than usually littered the pavements.

Cordelia wrinkled her nose at the smells and was glad to go inside. She whisked the little magician past Nobby's frowning countenance and took him down to the manager's office.

"This is Mr. Druid," she said, after knocking lightly on the door and getting a growled command to enter. "He performs tricks and juggles and, oh, lots more, and he'd like to talk to you about performing."

"Are all the handbills gone?" the manager demanded.

Cordelia blinked, not sure what the question referred to, but thought it best to simply nod.

"Good, then get yourself into costume. We'll go over that dance routine again presently," the manager looked back at his desk.

She motioned to the conjurer to go inside and made her escape. Mr. Nettles still couldn't tell the difference between Cordelia and her sister. Had Ophelia been sent to give out handbills? On the street, like any urchin?

Good heavens, surely she had taken someone with her. . . .

Cordelia headed to her sewing room to take off her hat and gloves. Where was Ophelia?

When a shadow crossed the doorway, she looked up, her heart leaping to her throat, but although Ransom Sheffield stood there, the frown on his face and the worry in his cool gray eyes told her everything.

"You didn't find her?" Her voice faltered. Oh, dear God, where was her sister?

"I've searched every street within a dozen city blocks," he said, his voice low. "I cannot think where—"

Someone else came up, and Ransom hesitated. It was the actress whom Ophelia had befriended, the fair-haired woman with the tired eyes, Venetia. "Lily?"

Cordelia shook her head. That was the name Ophelia was using to act under.

"Where's your sister, then? Ol' Nettles said if she misses another dance rehearsal she'll be out on her arse. You'd better take 'er place; 'e'll never know the difference."

Startled, Cordelia started to shake her head. "But I don't know the steps."

"Your sister don't, neither," Venetia observed, her tone matter-of-fact. "We just put 'er in the back and dance around her. Come on, we don't 'ave much time. I'll get her gown and slippers out for you in the dressing room."

She turned away and hurried back toward the dressing rooms.

Cordelia was concerned about graver matters than Ophelia losing her position in the theater company. She stepped closer to Ransom and without thinking, put one hand on his coat, feeling the rise and fall of his hard muscled chest between the smooth superfine. "Oh, tell me you don't think the worst!"

He met her worried gaze with a steady glance. Putting his own hand over hers—his sun-bronzed skin was warm against her own, and his fingers felt strong and somehow very reassuring—he pressed her hand. "Don't give up, Cordelia. Your sister has an uncanny way of surviving the most perilous circumstances. I will go out again—"

She was so thankful to have an ally; without him, where would they be, with no one in London except strangers to depend on? Surely that was why her heart beat so fast and the pit of her stomach quivered in that way it had when she stood close to him—

He lifted his other hand and brushed her cheek, and for just a moment she leaned her head against his shoulder.

"Oh, Ophelia, just be safe," she murmured.

As if she had called her up, a shadow darkened the doorway again and they pulled apart.

"Ophelia!" Cordelia gasped, then rushed to hug her sister.

She had never seen her fastidious twin look so disheveled. Her clothes were in tatters, reduced to mere rags. Her hair had come undone and trailed in uneven tendrils down her back, with so much dust covering it that it looked as if it had been dusted with powder for a masquerade. Her face, too, was covered in dust, except for a brief area around her eyes where her mask had left a pattern of clear skin, and spatters of dried spots down her cheeks showed evidence of tears.

"My dearest, were you attacked again?" Cordelia cried, throwing her arms about her sister, who swayed on her feet. She seemed ready to collapse.

"Someone must go and pay the hackney outside, or he will come in and make a commotion," Ophelia said faintly. "I had to come all the way back in from the other side of the city, and I could not walk that far, I just could not—I rode a cow, Cordelia." She put her head on her sister's shoulder and sobbed.

Not understanding this at all, Cordelia held her close. "Mr. Nettles made you ride a cow?"

"I will call the man out!" Ransom sounded outraged.

"No, no, it was an accident," Ophelia said, her voice muffled, "B-but it was so exhausting and I was so frightened—"

Cordelia patted her sister's back, holding her tightly. "Are you hurt? Do you need a physician?"

"I will see to the hackney driver and be back at once," Ransom Sheffield promised.

Thank heavens for friends with full purses, Cordelia thought.

From the stage area, a tinkle of song sounded, and Ophelia's head rose abruptly from her sister's shoulder.

"Oh, no, the dance rehearsal! I cannot miss it again, Mr. Nettles said; I was rewriting the script yesterday, and I forgot the cue. . . . But today my feet are blistered. I cannot possibly dance!"

"Venetia said that Mr. Nettles would be incensed if you did not come," Cordelia agreed. "But, Ophelia, you are in no state. If you explain—"

"You will have to do it for me," her sister said, pushing Cordelia toward the stage. "Go, quickly. He will never know the difference. Hurry!"

"But I don't know the form!"

"It doesn't matter, just show up!" Ophelia shrieked.

She sounded so agitated that Cordelia was afraid to argue. She saw Ransom coming back inside and waved him back to look after her sister. She ran toward the dressing room where one of the older ladies who was not in the dance helped her pull on the slippers and the full skirt necessary for the dance, then she ran for the stage, slipping in at the back of the other girls.

Feeling like a fool, Cordelia tried to follow along. How could she possibly fake this? She knew most of Ophelia's lines in the play, because Ophelia practiced them every night at the vicarage, but the dance steps . . . Her panic calmed a little when she saw that most of the dance set was just an ordinary country dance, slightly changed to reveal more of the girls' limbs than would have been considered decent at home—there was a great deal of lifting of skirts and kicking of legs—but if she kept a close watch on the women on either side of her from the corner of her eye, she could almost keep up.

When Mr. Nettles himself walked by and watched her, her heart beat fast again. But he nodded his head, so she breathed a little easier.

"Not too bad, not too bad," he muttered. "You're half a beat behind, mind you, so step it up." And he swung his cane and gave her a whack on her buttocks, which stung and made her jump.

She muttered a few words beneath her breath that she hadn't even known before they had, so scandalously, joined the theater troupe.

She thought of the vicar's cautions and blushed. Perhaps they *were* being corrupted. But dammit, that hurt! Being half a beat behind was the only way she could do this bloody dance!

The dance rehearsal seemed to stretch on for a year, but at last the women were released, and Cordelia could go back to the dressing rooms with the others, slipping around the diva's gentleman caller, the stout baronet whose inquisitive hands were all too apt to reach out and pinch backsides and who she now evaded without even thinking about it.

She changed her shoes quickly and hung her sister's costume back on the peg. She waited till the hallway outside was empty, then sped back to her sewing room where she could resume her own identity.

She found Ophelia, her face now somewhat cleaner and her shredded clothes hidden by Ransom Sheffield's dark cloak, sipping a cup of tea and talking in a more composed manner to their protector.

Cordelia slipped inside and gave him a grateful glance.

"So I scrambled onto the animal's back. I'm still not quite sure how I managed it, but I was desperate, as the only other choice was to be trampled underfoot. I had to ride for blocks and blocks until we came to the business district, and the cattle were sorted into smaller groups for the knackers, and someone was finally able to help me down. I am sore in every muscle of my body, I must tell you."

Ophelia explained the whole dreadful occurrence again for her sister's behalf. Cordelia hugged her sister, hardly daring to believe that she had survived such an alarming experience.

"You could have been killed! And all over a silly stack of handbills."

Ophelia drew a deep breath. "Oh, let's not talk of it. But I am more than ready to go back to the rectory. Thank you for standing in for me in the dance rehearsal, Cordelia. I did not want Mr. Nettles scolding me, too."

Cordelia nodded. "It was nothing; it hardly compared to riding a cow down the middle of London!"

Ophelia's woebegone expression melted away and her infectious laugh bubbled out.

Cordelia grinned back at her sister and gave her another hug. Not everyone could have laughed after such a day.

Ransom Sheffield raised his brows at them both. "You are an unusual pair," he said, his tone dry, but she saw that his eyes, no longer grim and concerned, had lightened. "I shall go and see about finding another hackney. I don't think our lady equestrian feels up to a long walk home."

Ophelia shuddered at the mere suggestion.

When they sat huddled together in the rented carriage, Cordelia put her arms around her sister, and Ophelia lay her head against her sister's shoulder and dozed off and on until they reached the rectory.

It took them both to help Ophelia down, as her afflicted muscles were becoming stiffer and even more sore. Cordelia felt another wave of anxiety.

"We will ask the housekeeper to make up her best mustard poultice," Ransom suggested, his tone low. "That and a hot bath will help relax her muscles. And my cousin will call his physician if you wish."

She nodded, and they went inside. But the news that greeted them was almost enough to make them forget Ophelia's afflicted physical state entirely.

"Oh, Miss Applegate, and Miss Applegate!" The little housemaid dipped a curtsy and smiled broadly at them both, as if sure she had welcome news. "Here be letters, at last—from Yorkshire."

Nine

*O*phelia felt as if she had been punched in the stomach, just as she had during her first rehearsal. For a moment she couldn't seem to get her breath.

She glanced at her sister and wondered if she had gone as
pale as Cordelia.

"Letters?" her sister muttered.

"From Yorkshire?" Ophelia repeated, thinking that they
must sound as if they had both lost their wits.

The maid stared at them. "Yes, miss."

Cordelia pulled herself together first and reached for the
post. "Thank you, Bess. We will read them upstairs."

Looking disappointed at their unenthusiastic response, the
servant curtsied and turned away while they made for the
stairs. Ophelia stumbled once going up the steps but caught
herself by grabbing the railing. Oh, what would her father
say? They had broken every commandment. Well, they hadn't
killed anyone, or committed, you know, adultery, but as for lying and honoring your father, and, well, she knew there were a
lot more—did Moses mention running away from home and

dressing up as an old lady and sticking fake warts on your nose?

Her darting thoughts, as hard to calm as a swarming hive of bees, flew away altogether when they reached the upper floor where the guest chambers were located. This time Cordelia took her hand and drew Ophelia inside her room and shut the door; then she broke the wax seal on the first letter. "This one is from Madeline," she said.

"*To Cordelia Antonia and Ophelia Quincy Applegate*," it read.

"Oh, dear, not a promising start, if she feels compelled to stick every name we have into the first line," Cordelia muttered, then she drew a deep breath and continued.

"Read it aloud," Ophelia begged. "I want to hear the worst and get it over with." Still, she put her hands to her ears as she used to as little girl when she could hardly bear what she knew was coming.

" *'I cannot address you as sisters since I feel you have forfeited the right to that title. Indeed, I am not sure I shall ever feel sisterly affection for you again!'* " Cordelia's voice quivered despite her obvious struggle to hold it steady.

Ophelia gasped.

Cordelia paused and drew a deep breath, looking over at her sister. "She is in one of her rages, you know she is. Likely she is already repenting of writing such harsh words." But her tone was not as certain as Ophelia would have liked.

"Read the rest," Ophelia urged, even though tears trembled on her lashes and she was not sure she really wanted to hear her eldest sister's condemnation.

"To do such a thing, and to impose such a fright upon our father! When the first two letters came from Lauryn after Juliana's wedding, and she talked about the pear preserves she had made and how she was drying the late summer blooms, but said nothing at all about her sisters, I wondered, but I thought perhaps you two had displeased her—it HAS been known to happen—but when

she wrote to say the young men were asking if you were coming back for the dance at the White's, which was now only a fortnight away, then I KNEW something was badly wrong. Father sent a message straightaway to the squire, and when the answer returned, he fell back in his chair and his eyes rolled back in his head and I thought he had died. I thought he was DEAD, you wicked girls!!! I could feel my heart pound in my chest, and I thought I should never be happy again, not to mention the fact that we would all be homeless, thrown out into the hedgerows, and you would be guilty of parricide and no one would ever speak your name aloud for the rest of your wretched lives and we should all wear black and if I should happen to set eyes on you, I would pull out every hair in your heads myself!"

Cordelia paused to take a breath, her eyes wide. Ophelia shuddered and this time covered her own eyes. Oh, Lord help them. To say that Madeline was angry just now was like saying the sky was blue.

Looking as if it pained her, Cordelia raised the paper and—her tone grim—read aloud once more.

"I called for the maid, and we tried to find some smelling salts, but we were both so frantic, we couldn't remember where they had been placed, and she was burning hen feathers under his nose when Papa came to himself. He told us to leave off making such a stench and called for Thomas to harness the horse and help him into the carriage. He was bound and determined to go to London himself, even though the exertion would likely have killed him, Ophelia, you selfish wretch—for I know it was you who began this insane plan—"

Cordelia paused and shot her twin a sympathetic glance. Ophelia swallowed hard, but she could hardly complain. It *had* been her idea, her plan, her deep-seated ambition that had led her to devise the scheme to run away and hope she could at last find a way to go onstage.

> *"And thus it's all your fault if our dearly beloved father is taken to death's door by the weight of this mad scheme. I sent Thomas on the donkey to fetch the doctor in the hopes of persuading him that he must not go, and we were still arguing when, by the grace of heaven, your letters arrived."*

Ophelia shut her eyes. If the vicar had not insisted that they write home when he did—oh, how selfish and irresponsible she had been. Why had she not thought more about the effect her mad flight would have on her father, on all her family? And why did she not think they would find out quickly that she and her twin were missing?

Cordelia paused and scanned the rest of the page. "There's more of the same. She does at least say that Papa is recovering. And the other letter is from him." Cordelia put down the first note and, her fingers moving slowly, broke the wax seal on the second piece of correspondence.

Inside the folded sheet were two pieces of note paper. Cordelia swallowed visibly. "One is addressed to me, one to you."

She held out one of the sheets, and Ophelia, who would rather have plucked a writhing adder from the heath, took the sheet.

She had to brace herself to look at the words, in the familiar script, at the top of the page.

Dear Daughter,
> *I am shocked and saddened that you would forget your duty to your parent and depart your home and the protection of those who love you in such an abrupt and unseemly way. Your mother, had she lived, would not be pleased to think that you depend so rarely on my instruction, nor trust my guidance so little, that you ignore all my warnings about the dangers that could befall young women without*

escort or protectors abroad in a city such as London. It hurts my heart to think of you exposed to such vice and such peril, and it wounds me even more deeply to think that I have been such a harsh and unfeeling parent—that I have failed you by not ensuring that you grew up to trust me as you should.

He had failed *them*?

Tears flowed down her cheeks, and Ophelia rubbed at them, but she could not brush them off fast enough, too quickly more came to replace the ones that she struck aside. She thought of their invalid father being carried out to the carriage and jolted painfully on the long journey toward London, and she shuddered. How could she have been so blind and so heedless, yet again, and so eternally selfish and wretched and wrong? She was indeed just as miserable, awful, dreadful, terrible and evil a person as her older sister thought she was. She dropped her father's letter and put both hands over her face, giving way to an even more hearty burst of tears.

Presently, she realized that Cordelia had put one arm around her shoulders, and when she looked up, she saw that her twin's face was also damp, although her other hand clutched a moist handkerchief.

"Papa will never forgive us." Ophelia's voice sounded anguished.

"I'm sure he will," Cordelia said, her voice faint but calm.

"Well, Madeline won't!"

That Cordelia didn't answer right away. She hugged her twin more tightly. "In time," she said. "Surely . . ."

Ophelia sighed again. She pushed herself up from the bed.

"Where are you going?" Cordelia frowned at her.

"I am going to tell the vicar the truth—that we ran away from home and are here under false pretenses. I am not lying to anyone ever again!"

"Oh," Cordelia said, her voice faint. "I do hope he doesn't turn us out into the street."

"If he does, it's only what we deserve, or what I deserve,

anyhow," Ophelia said, lifting her chin. "I shall tell him you should be spared."

Blinking, Cordelia looked somewhat doubtful of the efficacy of this plan, but she didn't argue.

Ophelia scrubbed at her cheeks again, aware that she must look horrid, but she was determined to keep her word before she lost her nerve totally. She marched down the stairs, and demanded of the startled maid the whereabouts of the vicar.

" 'E's out in the garden, miss," the maid told her.

Sure enough, she found the handsome young churchman on his knees, his hands deep in the thick foliage of a flower bed. Startled, he looked up when she strode up to him. He rose quickly and brushed the dirt off the knees of his trousers.

"Miss Applegate, are you all right?"

"Yes, I mean, no, but I have something to confess."

"I see. I mean, I don't exactly, but I am happy to help you if I can. Do you wish to confess formally? While the rite is not performed as regularly in the English church as with our Roman cousins, I do of course perform the Sacrament when it's requested. We have a booth at the side of the church. Some of my older ladies like to confess at Lenten time, although I may have to dust it out before you enter, or you might explode into a sneezing fit. I'm not sure it's been cleaned in a fortnight."

"Oh." Ophelia hesitated. For a moment, the idea of formal church confession had its appeal—with its ceremony and solemn words acknowledging her transgression, and the resulting penance to perform—but then she thought how pleasing were his blue eyes gazing down at her with such warmth and understanding shining in their depths, and she hated to shut his good-looking countenance away behind a screen where she could not regard it.

Seeing her pause, he nodded. "Perhaps you had more in mind simply talking to a friend, even though he is a vicar? Perhaps we should sit down on the stone bench which is at hand, and you could tell me what is worrying you, and I will attempt to give you counsel, if I can."

"Oh, yes, that would be very kind of you," she agreed, hoping that he would still call her a friend when he had heard the depths of her depravity.

Haltingly, she said as much, and she thought his lips threatened to curve, but he brought them under control and regarded her with not a trace of a twinkle in his eye.

"What dreadful sin have you committed, Miss Applegate?"

She gulped. "I have lied to you and to my father. I left home and came to London without telling him I was going—and do not blame my sister because it was my fault entirely."

This time he did not look tempted to smile. "That is serious, Miss Applegate. Did you not realize how dangerous such an action would be?"

"I do now," she said, biting her lip and not meeting his gaze.

"From what my cousin tells me, you came near enough to—" The young vicar stopped himself with, it seemed, some effort. "I can only thank heaven that you did not pay with your life, much less your good name, for being so heedless."

It was not she, but her sister, who would have paid, Ophelia remembered, and that made it so much worse. Hoping he would not recall that just yet, she hurried to add, "We are more thankful for your cousin's timely aid than we can express. And I assure you that since we have been here, and you have kindly offered us shelter, we have conducted ourselves with perfect decorum. It's just that for so long, I have dreamed only of going onstage! It was always my deepest and my most fervent wish."

At least the sternness in his expression had eased, and she thought she could detect a gleam of sympathy in his eyes. "I fear I must point out that some people, many people, would suggest that being on the stage is itself improper, when it is a young lady of breeding who is being discussed."

"Oh, piffle!" Ophelia reverted for a moment to her usual self. Then, reminded of her new resolve to be a better person, she tried again to look suitably meek. Meekness was apparently harder to achieve than it appeared. "I suppose the costumes are a bit . . . a bit . . . ah, a bit eye-catching." She pictured the ingenue's costume for Act One. "I will admit that the neckline is somewhat low, and the skirt somewhat high." She gathered up the skirt of the muslin day dress she now wore, trying to imitate the length of her costume, trying to estimate how much the other shorter skirt revealed—her ankles, yes, and a bit of her leg. She stared down at her skirt and tried to judge. "But not an awful lot, really."

To her surprise, the vicar stood suddenly and walked a few feet away, his hands clasped behind his back, his face turned away from her.

"Oh, I beg your pardon." She dropped the skirt hastily back into place. "I didn't mean to offend you, vicar. I was trying to estimate—"

"You didn't offend me. But, Miss Applegate—"

"Yes?" She looked up at him as he turned back to face her, his blue eyes somehow blazing.

"You must remember one thing. Whether as your vicar or as your friend, I am still a man, and you were showing a rather admirable set of ankles." He paused, his brows lifted. For a moment, he showed a striking resemblance to his rakish cousin Ransom.

She blushed and couldn't think what to answer. It was true; she had been thinking of him as if he were their own vicar, close to the century mark, frail and elderly and past any interest in matters of the flesh. How could she explain? Just because he was a man of the church . . .

He had already bowed and turned away.

Flustered, she didn't try to take a formal leave but jumped up and hurried back inside. Rushing up the steps, she didn't return to her guest room. Instead she hung out the open window at the end of the upper landing where she could look to see what Giles Sheffield was doing now.

He had not returned to the flower beds. Instead he seemed to have marched out to the wood pile, where he'd removed his coat, rolled up his sleeves and was lifting the ax and—what well-muscled arms he had!—chopping wood as if they were facing an Arctic winter. The sounds of the blade hitting the hard oaken tree limbs rang out, clearly distinguished even from where she stood. She watched him swing the ax and saw how smoothly his arms moved and his torso twisted. What strength he had, and how well his body was made—

She was still there, strangely transfixed, when Cordelia came to question her some time later.

"Well? What did he say?"

"What?"

"The vicar, what did he say?" Cordelia demanded. "Did you tell him about our running away without permission?"

"He said it was a foolish thing to do and very wrong," Ophelia answered, her gaze still directed outside.

"Did he give you a lecture?"

Ophelia hardly heard. It was getting dark now, and she'd have to meet him at dinner soon. How would she meet his gaze over the dinner table? Was it possible that the vicar—he was a man, too; funny that she hadn't really considered that before—would be picturing her ankles crossed demurely beneath the dining room table, just as she would be musing on how well defined were his arms and how broad his shoulders?

What would it be like to dance with him, to put her hands on his shoulders, run them down his back? She sighed at the thought.

"He didn't threaten to turn us out?" Cordelia went on.

"No," Ophelia told her sister. "Not at all. He only chopped wood."

Her sister eyed her strangely. But Ophelia didn't try to explain.

The dinner table was very quiet, but at least Ophelia had something to think about besides the letters from home. And for the first time, she was intensely aware of the handsome vicar who sat at the head of the table with such easy grace. All the Sheffields had it: the indefinable poise and ease of movement that made them so attractive to the eye. Of course, the vicar's attractive face, brilliant blue eyes and fair hair were already enough to draw one's eyes sufficiently without the lure of that long limbed frame, too! She did not see how any lady of his parish could keep her mind on his sermons, well-written and nicely delivered though they might be.

But she kept her thoughts to herself, of course, and if she blushed when he offered her more sauce for her brussels sprouts—with only one housemaid, the service was informal— she did not meet his eye nor try to explain her odd reaction to such a prosaic vegetable.

She slept little that night between her bruises and bumps from the cattle ride and her remorse over the correspondence from her family. She had written long letters of apology, punctuated with teardrops, and she hoped that her father, at least, would forgive her. She knew Cordelia had also written in contrite affection, though in her own note Ophelia took all the blame on her own shoulders, as she should.

But despite all her expression of regret, Ophelia did not offer to come home—not yet. She had to have her time on-stage, surely she could at least have this one play, even if she were not to be allowed a career on the London boards. And perhaps, in the back of her mind, she still harbored some hope of convincing her father . . . well, one step at a time. For now, she assured her long-suffering parent that she could not walk out on the theater manager who had given her a chance with the opening of the play only days away. Still, she told her father:

> But rest easy, we are well protected, staying in the rectory at night, and Mr. Ransom Sheffield is watching over us at the theater in the daytime and seeing us back and forth to rehearsal. Really, he has been our guardian angel, he and the vicar, his cousin.
>
> Your most repentant and sadly undeserving daughter,
> Ophelia.

The next day, she rose early, made sure her letters home were well-sealed and gave them to the housemaid to send off, then skipped down the stairs, aware of an eagerness to reach the breakfast table that had not been there before.

When she reached the dining room, her sister was nibbling on a piece of toast, and Ransom Sheffield drank tea, but the rest of the table was untenanted. Ophelia muttered, "Good morning," to them both, put some toast and meat on a plate, then sat down and allowed the maid to bring her a cup of hot tea.

"Is the vicar not up?" she asked the servant, keeping her voice low. Surely he was not avoiding her?

"Oh, yes, miss. 'E's been up for ages," the girl said cheerfully. "'E got called out to see an ol' lady who's bad with the dropsy—they don't think 'er will make it through the morning, poor ol' thing."

Ophelia nodded, feeling foolish for such self-centered thoughts. Of course, he had a job to do, more than a job. She knew he cared about the people he served. But Ophelia was conscious of a distinct feeling of disappointment as she sipped her tea and eyed his empty chair. How could she possibly have equated him to the sweet but ancient man who filled the same post in the church at home?

Sighing, she ate her breakfast, then she and Cordelia, with Ransom Sheffield's escort, took a hackney to the theater. When they entered the side door, she thought that Nobby ogled them with more than usual interest, but he only bobbed his head on its long skinny neck and croaked, "Morning, misses."

"Good morning, Nobby," Ophelia answered, and Cordelia echoed her.

"You're bright-eyed this morning," Ransom Sheffield pointed out. "Have a good evening at the dice?"

The old man tried to look offended. "W'ot makes you think I plays the bones, gov?"

"Not a thing." Ransom grinned at him and tossed the doorkeeper a coin, which Nobby plucked nimbly out of midair.

When the two girls headed toward their usual posts, Ransom Sheffield decided to snatch a few minutes while the theater manager was safely occupied below stairs—he could hear the diva inside Nettles's office complaining about her lack of adequate wardrobe allowance. Ransom had heard this diatribe before and it would last at least half an hour. That was more than enough time for him to slip up to the second floor and have another try at the lock on Nettles's private quarters. So far, despite some private practice with lock-picking in his chamber at the rectory, the damned thing still eluded him. Who said that lock-picking was so simple? They had never tried a really hard lock, then, with one ear cocked for a step on the stairs, and the necessity of not leaving any scratches on the metal to give yourself away.

Too bad that he couldn't just break in the bloody door and be done with it!

When he knew from the lengthening shadows on the wall that too much time had passed and the diva might have at last ended her monologue and released Nettles to wander about the building, Ransom rose to his feet, dusted off the knees to his trousers and hurried back down the steps, cursing beneath his breath.

He expected the stage to be filled with dancers working on the musical numbers, but it was empty, and the theater strangely quiet. As he walked past the junior actresses' dressing room, however, he heard enough chatter from inside to make up for the lack of noise outside. He glanced into the room.

To his surprise, he saw two of the dancers who appeared to be quarreling over the costume which Ophelia wore. Despite himself, he paused and took a step inside the room.

"Best leave that be," he told them. "Or Miss Lily"—he used the stage name which Ophelia was known by among the other girls—"will likely have your heads."

"I'll be surprised if she comes back anytime soon, 'er nor 'er sister Clara, neither!" one of the actresses told him, smirking.

"What?" Ransom demanded, feeling a frisson of alarm.

The second thespian pushed a strand of hennaed hair back from her rouged cheek. "Yeah, dearie. What's wrong, she didn't tell ye? Too bad fer ye. She's got bigger fish to fry, now, I wager."

There was a chorus of laughter, and Ransom backed out of the dressing room, feeling vaguely foolish but also suffering a strong feeling of apprehension. Where had Ophelia gone and why *hadn't* she told him? Surely she would have, if she'd had the chance?

At the doorway, he bumped into the fair-haired actress that Ophelia had befriended, Venetia.

"Oh, where have you been?" she cried. "That lord—the high and mighty marquis—he took them away!"

"What?" Ransom stiffened. "What do you mean?"

"Just as I said, o' course," the young actress said, sniffing. "'E walked into the theater, waited for Miss Lily to come in, looked 'er over—I always said she was the most beautiful o' the lot—and 'e grabbed 'er arm and wouldn't let go. Took 'er sister, too; maybe one of those twisted gents who like a pair, you know? They didn't want to go, neither, honest girls that they are, but he wouldn't hear no never minds." She sniffed into her twisted bit of kerchief. "You got to 'elp them, gov. Ol' Nettles, 'e didn't do a thing."

"I just bet he didn't," Ransom muttered. "Do you know his name—the man who took Ophe—Miss Lily and her sister away?"

"A marquis, 'e said 'e were. Worthington, or some' un like that." She sniffed and dabbed at her red-rimmed eyes. "Too good for 'im, marquis or not, the old sod!"

Worthington? The name didn't resonate. Ransom felt a tremor of panic rise in his chest and pushed it back. He considered confronting Nettles, but the manager would likely claim ignorance, and it would be impossible to know whether it was true or not. Where had the anonymous nobleman gone with the two girls? Dammit, turn his back for half an hour, and he had failed the girls again—

Guilt heavy on his shoulders, he ran for the side door. Old Nobby was in his usual posture, sitting in the rickety chair, leaning back against the wall.

With one gesture, Ransom pulled him up and held him with one hand around his skinny neck.

The old man almost choked. "Wha-a-a—"

"Why did you let him take the girls, Nobby?"

The old man made gasping noises. His face was turning blue. In a moment, the rage faded a little from Ransom's mind. It occurred to him that the doorkeeper really couldn't speak. He lowered the slight body until the man's patched shoes touched the floor and loosened his grip a little. Nobby drew several long breaths, and Ransom shook him.

"Now, tell me!"

"I-I didn't see nothin' wrong."

For a moment Ransom's grip tightened again, and the old man bleated in alarm.

"Do you know his name?"

The doorkeeper shook his head. "Ne'er seen 'im afore. I swear!"

Ransom swore, briskly. How on earth was he going to find this damn kidnapper, and in time to save the two sisters?

He pushed open the door and stepped out into the alley. Darkness was falling, and there was nothing to mark the passing of the carriage that had taken away the Applegate sisters, except a few lines in the mud, but they merged with countless others and would disappear as soon as the vehicle merged into the pavement of the street.

He didn't even know—

Ransom heard footfalls behind him and turned. It was the raw-boned magician who had joined the company not long ago. He looked concerned.

"I heard about Miss Lily," Druid said, breathless from his hasty run. "Perhaps I can help."

"How?" Ransom demanded, his tone more savage than he had intended.

The man winced but persisted, falling into step and almost running to keep up with Ransom's long-legged pace. "I know many of the street boys, Mr. Sheffield. Perhaps I can find out something about the carriage that came to the theater."

Ransom stopped in his tracks, for the first time feeling a stirring of hope. "I hope to God you're right!"

So now, even though he wanted to hurry, he was forced to hang back and watch the street magician revert to his old routine, setting up an impromptu performance and luring the passersby to pause and watch, especially the children who roamed the streets when they had nothing better to do, amusing them with his sleight of hand, his juggling and his patter.

And inserted deftly amongst all, he asked them questions.

"Hi, Jemmy, been a long time. Happen to see that fancy carriage that stopped by Malory Road this afternoon? No, what about you, Shortstuff?"

The first queries drew only negatives. The boys shook their heads, stayed a while to watch the tricks and then drifted on.

But Druid persisted, quietly, as if his questions were of no import.

Presently a boy with a scar on his ear and a torn blue coat said, "Aye, I saw it. Polished brass lamps gleaming like the sun, and a team fine enough to make all our fortunes at Tattersalls. Me old man would snuff a baker's dozen for 'em, 'e would!" The child gave a long sigh at the mere thought of such a prize.

"Ah." The conjuror kept his voice calm with some effort, but in his excitement at finding someone who had seen the carriage, he sent one of his colored balls flying wildly.

The children exclaimed and ran to fetch it back.

When he had all the balls circling again, Druid said, his voice and his hands controlled, "Yep, I'm sure 'e would indeed. Any idea where it went?"

"The ball?" The boy who'd seen the carriage had gone running off with the others, but when he returned, he looked thoughtful.

"The carriage and the bang-up team."

"They turned toward the west of London, o' course, where all the nobs live, with the big squares and fancy houses."

"We would have guessed that," Druid agreed. "But you don't know which square, do you?"

He shook his head, and it occurred to Ransom, as disappointment sank through him like a leaden wave, that the child most likely couldn't read.

The boy raised a narrow face, and his eyes were shrewd. "The carriage had a crest on it," he added.

"Did it now?" the conjuror said. "Think you could describe it for us?"

"'Ow much is it worth to you?" the boy asked, narrowing his eyes.

"Maybe a tuppence," Druid said, keeping his voice even.

Ransom found he had balled his fists. He wanted to grab the

boy and shake the information out of him, but he might scare
the child off, and offering the lad too much might frighten him,
too. He forced himself to wait while the other two dickered
solemnly and settled on half a shilling.

Then the boy described the coat of arms in reasonable de-
tail. And Ransom handed over the agreed-upon sum, plus a
bonus that made the boy's eyes widen. He looked at the coins
put into his palm, then gripped them tightly and took to his
heels before they could be taken away again, in case Ransom
decided he had overpaid.

The conjuror tucked his colored balls into the pockets of
his coat.

"Good job," Ransom told him.

"I pray you can find them, sir," the other man said, his eyes
worried. "She has a sweet nature, as does her sister, too. She
helped me out of the goodness of her heart when there was no
reason for her to bother. And I fear—" He took out his handkerchief and wiped the street dust off his chin to hide the fact
that his lips suddenly trembled, and he didn't finish what he
was about to say.

But he didn't have to. Ransom knew his fears. He shared
them.

Nodding, he turned and waved to a hackney. Climbing inside, Ransom set out to comb the West End of London for a
house marked with the same crest as the one described by the
urchin, and yes, he prayed that he could find it, and in time.

Ten

After Ransom Sheffield had disappeared backstage, the girls had parted, too—Cordelia to go to her sewing room, while her twin turned toward the dressing rooms. Ophelia passed Madam Tatina's private dressing room. Its door was closed; was their prima donna entertaining some wealthy male guest? No, in a moment, she could hear the woman's voice upraised; she seemed to be castigating the theater manager. At least that would keep her away from the other actresses for a while.

The dressing room that the rest of the females shared seemed quieter than usual. She wasn't late? No, there was no sound from the stage itself, but still, she had best hurry up about it.

Ophelia quickened her step and came through the door with a burst of speed. The other actresses were in their usual places as they prepared for rehearsal, tucking up their skirts so that they could dance when their parts called for it.

But no one chattered or laughed. The drafty room was strangely quiet. At once, Ophelia saw why.

A stranger sat in one of the rickety chairs placed at the far side of the dressing room—a man. And what a man!

His form was massive. He must be enormously tall when he stood. His shoulders were broad and his body big-boned, though he did not seem to be at all fat, just well-shaped with muscle. His coat had been made by expert tailors, though she thought not English. It had a subtle air of sophistication that spoke of the Continent, and he held a wide-brimmed hat loosely in one big hand that also showed elegant lines shrieking of both taste and more money to devote to headgear than most men had in a year.

Who was he?

She knew that some of the actresses chatted about occasional admirers, titled rich admirers, even, who had noted a pretty face or form onstage and come back to express their admiration and to pursue a courtship or—she blushed to admit that the girls had admitted freely—an easy conquest. But the new play hadn't even opened yet. And who was he here for? None of the girls seemed flushed with the pride of a new conquest; instead they darted uneasy glances as he sat in the dressing room. Somehow even when he sat quietly, he seemed to dominate the whole chamber.

When he turned his head to stare directly at her, Ophelia stiffened.

His face was scarred from a long ago bout with smallpox. The pockmarks had faded somewhat, but they were still noticeable. His eyes were a deep brown, wise and understanding, she thought, and they knew quite well why she had to fight to hide her instinctive desire to step back. But she managed to overcome her aversion. While he continued to regard her, she pulled herself together and gave a fairly smooth curtsy.

"Sir."

Venetia leaned over to poke her in the ribs. " 'E's a marquis!" she hissed in Ophelia's ear. "Not any plain *sir*."

Good heavens, Ophelia thought. "I beg your pardon," she said quickly, trying to remember how one addressed a marquis, who came second only to dukes, who ranked after princes. She'd never set eyes on such a beast before. "Your Grace?"

He smiled suddenly, lighting up those dark, somewhat brooding eyes. Rising, he bowed, as deeply as if she were a great lady. "John Sinclair, marquis of Gillingham, but John will do," he said. "I believe we have a connection."

"But," she began, "you're not even—" Then she paused. She was no kin at all to John Sinclair, the lofty marquis. It was Gabriel Sinclair, his younger brother, she had a connection with, a totally illicit connection, but she was of no mind to explain how that had happened, the long-ago affair between Gabriel's mother and her father, in front of a roomful of listening ears. John Sinclair's knowing gaze told her that he understood—understood and concurred.

"Your esteemed father sent an urgent post by special messenger to my brother Gabriel's London house, and also, to be quite sure of reaching him, another to his country estate in Kent. Unhappily, my brother has taken his wife and her sister, who is recovering from a bad case of measles, to the south of France to enjoy the gentler climes. However, the servants at the country house directed the messenger on to my estate, and for once, I was actually at home."

Ophelia knew that she was gaping.

The marquis added, almost apologetically, "My wife is something of a world traveler, you see, and she has converted me to her wanderlust ways. But her sister has just had a new baby, so we have came home so that Marian could check on her sister's well-being and visit her family. And I had gone down to inspect my estate and talk to my estate manager. So I happened to be on hand when your father's post arrived. I thought I should step in for my brother and answer your father's plea."

"Oh," Ophelia said, her voice faint. She felt a sudden premonition of doom. "But—"

She tried to gather her wits and marshal all the arguments as to why she could not, should not, be prevented from pursuing her stage career. Having come so far, endured so much—

They were excellent arguments, too. Sadly, the marquis never gave her the chance to voice them.

John Sinclair offered her his arm.

Shaking her head, Ophelia did step back this time. "No,

no," she tried to explain. "I can't, I must—" She felt herself trod on something soft, and she heard a squeal.

Jumping, she looked around and saw for the first time a small, somewhat bedraggled spaniel. Where on earth had the little dog come from? Mr. Nettles did not allow animals back-stage, unless they were trained beasts for a novelty act.

Nobby must be asleep at his post. Afraid someone would beat the little animal, she waved her hands at the dog to shoo it back outside, but John Sinclair spoke first.

"Heel, Runt."

The spaniel trotted back to the man's side.

She saw to her amazement that the small dog, who had been sniffing her shoes, apparently belonged to the marquis. While she was still working this out, the marquis moved up, placed her hand on his arm and held it firmly there, turned her and somehow they were leaving the dressing room.

She darted an alarmed look at the other girls, but she saw that they eyed her with expressions of envy and the occasional sly grin. One of them gave her a thumbs-up and then rubbed her fingers together, as if to say, "Make some blunt, dearie."

Ophelia blushed and looked away.

Venetia alone looked concerned, but what could she do?

"But my role . . . what will Mr. Nettles say? I cannot let him down—" Ophelia protested again, trying to slow their rapid pace toward the door.

"I will send a note to the proprietor of the theater, offering him whatever compensation he desires. I'm sure he will be satisfied," the marquis said in his calm deep voice. "Where is your sister?"

Ophelia felt as if she were being pulled along by a tidal wave. She had heard about such elemental forces of nature happening out at sea. John Sinclair seemed just as impossible to fight. But her acting—her chance on the stage—no, no, he must not do this! She protested again, but he didn't seem to hear.

It seemed nothing would prevent him.

She did not respond to his query, and was still trying to

think how to thwart his determined rescue attempt, when the marquis tossed a coin to a scene shifter. He repeated his question about the other Applegate twin and was readily answered.

In a few minutes, Cordelia looked up from her sewing to see them filling the doorway of her small room. Her mouth dropped open.

"Good morrow, my dear Miss Applegate." The marquis bowed, but without letting go of Ophelia's arm, as if he knew that she would bolt at the slightest opportunity. "I am the marquis of Gillingham, John Sinclair, your, ah, relation. At any rate, I'm standing in for my brother Gabriel Sinclair, who *is* your relation, and of whom your father has requested aid. And I am duty bound to answer such a call, and certainly bound to stand in for my brother, not to mention aiding two ladies of good family who find themselves in uncertain and unsafe surroundings."

"We are quite safe!" Ophelia would have pulled away if she could have, but his grip was too firm. "We have a gentleman here who looks out for us, if we need protecting, and who sees us back and forth from the rectory."

"Really?" John Sinclair's tone was politely skeptical, and his glance bland.

"It's true," she protested.

Dammit, where was Ransom?

Ophelia saw her twin look wildly around, but with the two of them in the doorway, she knew Cordelia could see very little, and screaming for help . . . Well, they'd look like fools and make the marquis think they were soft in the head as well as childish and half daft. He was treating Ophelia now like . . . like a runaway child, she thought, swallowing hard.

"If you would come with me," he requested of Cordelia, "I will escort you both back to my London house, and we will discuss this matter in a more civilized milieu. This is really not a suitable setting for two young ladies."

No, no, tell him no, Cordelia, Ophelia tried to direct her twin. She shook her head slightly and glared at her sister.

But looking slightly pale, Cordelia stared at the big, elegantly dressed man who possessed such an air of command, not to mention a firm hold on her sister, and she nodded.

"No," Ophelia blurted. "We will not—this is not necessary!"

"I fear that it is," the marquis said. He was moving again, sweeping her out of the theater with the same easy force that he had displayed through this whole mad encounter. Ophelia was carried along willy-nilly, even if she were stepping like a crab, sideways, trying with no luck at all to slow their progress. And still she could not glimpse Ransom Sheffield, or see anyone to give a message to; and what could she expect him to do, anyway, she thought bitterly, call out a marquis? Who was following our father's request, some part of her mind added. But . . . her role in the play, her chance at a career on the stage—it couldn't end like this!

She wanted to burst into tears.

Ophelia looked back and saw that Cordelia followed silently behind them. It had all happened so fast. She saw, as if she were in a nightmare, that people moved around them. A scene shifter carried an armload of two-by-fours, staring at the marquis's rich clothing, but paying little heed to his two feminine companions. And her sister . . . they had moved so quickly Cordelia had not even removed the faded apron that she wore to protect her dress from the dusty costumes she mended daily.

Ophelia's last forlorn hope, that the doorkeeper might protest, ended when she saw Nobby grinning as he held the door wide for them, scooping up the coin that the marquis handed over.

"Two of them, eh? A big appetite for a big man." The old man cackled, but John ignored him or didn't hear, though his little dog growled briefly.

An impossibly elegant carriage, its brass lamps polished and gleaming, with a crest on the door, waited at the edge of the street, and John helped them both inside, then followed and sat opposite them as they rode toward the more fashionable part of London.

Only once did Ophelia speak. "Our clothes are at the rectory," she said, her voice strained. "And how can we depart without a word to the vicar, who has been so kind?"

"You can write him a thank-you," the marquis said. "And I shall send a servant to collect your things. I'm sure the good parson will be pleased to know that you have family who have returned to the city and offered you a welcome."

This was, in fact, a side of the city that Ophelia had not yet seen. Under other circumstances she would have been excited to view the wider avenues and bigger, more handsome houses, which sat on spacious squares that held in their centers green gardens surrounded by iron palings.

But today she had no interest in scenery. Instead she sat mute and strangely empty, as if she were a china vessel that a careless maid had overturned and abandoned.

Her stage career had ended before it began. And she had not even had a chance to say good-bye to Giles . . .

The house, which the marquis's carriage drew up in front of, was grand, indeed, and in other circumstances, Ophelia had no doubt she would be have been gratified to have been the houseguest of such a noble and gracious lord.

Because really, she was not even related to John Sinclair. The fact that he was so punctilious in his sense of obligation, feeling that he must honor his brother's responsibilities and Gabriel's duty to his birth father and his half siblings, must reveal John's strong sense of duty and should reflect well on the marquis's own personal honor. A proper young lady would no doubt feel grateful to him. No doubt.

Right now, Ophelia wished he would go to the devil!

She shared a glance with her sister, and wondered if she looked as wan and dejected as Cordelia. If so, they looked about as happy to receive the marquis's munificent hospitality as two wharf rats fished out of the flooding Thames. She, for one, was ready to jump back in and swim for it!

As if he knew this full well, John Sinclair seemed determined to keep a keen watch on her. He showed the two sisters into the big house, where a dizzying number of servants in full livery awaited their pleasure.

The front hall was two stories tall and had a circular stair-case that made Ophelia's mouth drop open for a moment; she closed it hastily. The butler was so intimidating she thought she perhaps should curtsy to him and only stopped herself at the last moment. They were taken up to two bedchambers to "wash away the dust of their journey," as if they had been trav-eling all the way from Yorkshire. Did the marquis think they had brought some irksome fever with them from the dressing room of the theater?

The guest chamber was almost as intimidating as the front hall, and Ophelia thought she might get lost amid so much grandly trimmed furnishings.

When the other servant who had escorted her up the stairs departed, a haughty-looking lady's maid stayed and seemed ready to torment her further, but Ophelia was in no mood to be polite.

"If there's anything at all I can do for you, Miss Applegate," the woman said. "We shall send for your effects from the, ah, rectory where the housekeeper says you have been staying. In the meantime, the master says you are to have anything you de-sire, so—"

"Good," Ophelia said, marching over to the door and pulling it open. "I desire to be alone."

"But, Miss Applegate, you must surely be—"

When the maid didn't move, Ophelia turned and marched out into the hallway herself.

This had the desired effect. The maid hurried out after her to see where she had gone. As Ophelia had suspected—the servants had orders to keep a strict eye on them, damn the marquis's conniving heart! While the maid crossed the thresh-old and paused to look up and down the hallway, Ophelia slipped behind her back into the room and pulled the door closed. She turned the key in the lock.

"I can at least have some time to think!" she told the door. To what end, she had no idea, except perhaps to wallow in her own misery. She walked across and frowned into the large looking glass over her dressing table. This bedchamber was twice the size of the small spare chamber she had inhabited at the rectory, as well as being much more lavishly furnished, and yet she found that she missed her old room with a physical ache. And she missed Giles Sheffield. What a cruel fate to be separated so abruptly just when she had begun to be aware of him as a person, as a man—and such a man!

Sighing, she thought of the note of thanks she must write to the vicar. He had taken them off the streets of London when they had been almost destitute and in real need, real danger. He was so kind, even beyond what his church position might call for.

And now—this precipitous removal—how would she explain? To tell him that they had been virtually kidnapped was too embarrassing, and yet, she would not have Giles think that she had willingly left without saying good-bye or thanking him in person when he had done so much for them, been so kind, made such a difference. True, he had pretty much forced them to write letters home, but if not for that timely and well-meant interference, her poor father might actually have taken his invalid self to London and died of the rigors of the journey, and then she would likely have killed herself with remorse! No, Giles had been quite right, and she had been a selfish fool not to realize what her wicked unthinking flight from home would do to the family who loved her.

Sighing, Ophelia sat down on the edge of a plushly upholstered chair and tried to think. She felt like beating her fists against her velvet-lined prison. Her life was over. What on earth was she to do now? Stay here in this beautiful and luxurious palace until the marquis managed to send them back to Yorkshire?

Her eyes filled with tears just thinking of it, and she rubbed her cheeks. Turning her head, she stared aimlessly around the room, but she could not contain her weeping, and the roses in the vase on the table beside the chair blurred as her eyes continued to fill. She drew out one rose, wishing she could send it to Giles, explain how contrite she was, how sorry for all she had done in so many wrong ways. . . .

She gasped. A sharp pain pricked her finger, and she looked down to see a drop of blood where the thorn had pricked her.

Served her right. She deserved many more such stabbing pains, Ophelia thought, sobbing and wiping her cheeks again. But despite her genuine grief, a line of dialogue popped into her mind. "Alas, how I have tempted Fate, and Fate has repaid me in just but painful blows . . ." That would work in the Second Act, she thought. She hadn't the energy to get up and look for pen and paper, but she tucked the words away to think about later.

In a few minutes she heard a soft tap on the door. Ophelia raised her head.

"Yes," she responded, her tone cautious. If the marquis was back to lecture her further, she would scream!

To her relief, it was Cordelia's voice she heard.

"Ophelia?"

"Oh, just a moment." Ophelia rushed to the door and turned the key in the lock, and in a moment, the two sisters clung together.

"I couldn't get rid of my maid; she kept wanting to bring me things, make me tea, brush my hair. I used to think being rich would be nice, but I think the servants would drive me mad!" Cordelia muttered, glancing about as if to be sure they were alone. "How did you manage it?"

She told her sister about the small trick, and Cordelia laughed. Ophelia managed a smile, but it soon faded.

"What are we going to do?"

They looked at each other, and Ophelia threw her arms about her sister once more, needing her support. "I don't know, but I don't know how I can bear it. How can I lose my chance onstage? And, and I miss Giles, Cordelia."

"The vicar?" Her sister looked at her in surprise. "Oh. Then I can tell you that I miss . . . I shall miss seeing Ransom Sheffield every day; I have kissed him, Ophelia."

Ophelia felt her eyes widen. "Was it . . . was it nice?"

"Beyond nice." Cordelia's smile was mysterious, and her eyes took on a dreamy look that made Ophelia, who had been kissed by at least two, no, three boys back home feel a sudden stab of jealousy more potent than any rose's thorn. Not one of the awkward Yorkshire lads had made her feel like that!

She thought of Giles, his strong arms, his well-muscled torso. Would a vicar stoop to the scandalous act of kissing an unmarried lady? Probably not, she thought with regret.

But she found that her twin was regarding her seriously. "Ophelia, we have to do something!"

They discussed possible plans, such as shredding their sheets and tying them together and escaping out the bedroom window—there was a nice little ornamental iron balcony . . .

"Except, if we go back to Malory Road the marquis will know exactly where to find us," Ophelia pointed out, her tone glum. "And if I don't go back to the theater, what would be the point of escaping from our rescuer?"

"Perhaps we should refuse to eat or drink," Cordelia said, her expression a bit wild.

Ophelia looked at her sister with admiration. "Oh, well done. Do you think that the marquis would let us go back to the theater if we gave up eating?"

"Honestly, no," her sister answered, collapsing onto the edge of the bed. "From what I've seen of him so far, he's more likely to force food down our throats. And by the time we had convinced him we were serious, Mr. Nettles would have long ago replaced you in your part. And the Sheffields—goodness knows what they will think of us!"

"Oh!" Ophelia jumped up and paced up and down the room, wringing her hands. "This is intolerable!"

There was a timid knock at the door. Ophelia paused and, on the bed, her sister stiffened.

"Yes?"

"Pardon, miss, but dinner is in 'alf an 'our. Shall I 'elp you change?" To Ophelia's relief, it was a different voice from the lordly lady's maid who had been here earlier. This voice sounded more human and less like a royal personage.

"Into what?" Ophelia demanded, her tone caustic.

"The marquis 'as 'ad your things sent over from the vicarage, miss. If you open the door, I will put them away for you, and you can pick out a gown for dinner."

"Already?" Cordelia said, dismay coloring her voice.

"I haven't even written to Giles!" Ophelia added in distress.

"And what must Ransom think of all this, to waltz off and leave him without a word, after all he has done for us!" Cordelia added. They shared another look of despair.

"What are we going to do?" Ophelia shut her eyes; she couldn't seem to think. Her usually vivid imagination seemed as blank as the empty space inside her chest where her heart should have been.

Cordelia reached over and took her sister's hand—her fingers felt cold to the touch—and they gripped hands again, as tightly as if they had only each other against the world. Once more, it seemed they could only depend on each other.

"I don't know," Cordelia admitted, her voice strained. "But we will think of something. And I know what I am not going to do: I am not going to change for dinner!"

They agreed on that small act of rebellion, although it was not as if they had a great variation of outfits available, anyhow, Ophelia thought. They had had room to bring only a couple of extra gowns with them and, indeed, owned few that were more elaborate than the faded muslins on their back. So when it was time to go down to dinner, they had washed their faces and hands and smoothed back their hair, and Cordelia had taken off the ancient apron, but otherwise, they still wore the gowns that they had worn all day. The dresses were hardly suitable for dinner with a marquis, but then they were not here by choice. When they came downstairs, they walked side by side, and Ophelia had to fight the urge to reach once more for her sister's hand.

The white and blue wall panels of the dining room were gilded in the French style, and the high ceiling had been painted with scenes from Greek mythology. The table was laden with so many foods in silver-lidded dishes and platters that Ophelia blinked. The candelabras and the chandeliers flashed from so many candles that the light reflected from the gleaming dishes was quite dazzling.

She felt like a naive farmer's daughter who has wandered into some king's palace. But still, even this flamboyant display did not lift her spirits.

She found that the marquis was waiting for them just inside the room.

"You must forgive the somewhat ostentatious display," he told them, bowing. "My servants are so delighted to have my wife and me back in town for a few days that they have out-done themselves to indulge our every whim."

Yes, she thought, the marquis and his wife might well con-sider themselves indulged. And where was the marchioness, anyhow?

Even as she thought the question, a handsome woman of more than average height, with smooth brown hair and intel-ligent blue eyes came into the dining room. She moved with a queenly grace, and her pale blue silk dress had been made by a couturier with a master's skill, even Ophelia could tell that. The shawl that hung so gracefully about her shoulders was the most beautiful bit of silk that Ophelia had ever laid eyes upon.

"And this is my wife, Lady Gillingham. My dear, Miss Cordelia Applegate and Miss Ophelia Applegate."

"Oh, call me Marian, do," this perfectly accoutered lady told them, her tone as smooth and cultured as her appearance. "I'm so glad we were able to be of help to you. My husband tells me you were in a bit of a contretemps?"

Ophelia threw a glance toward her sister as they took their seats around the large table. No doubt that was how the marquis saw it, a genuine act of charity. He had no way of knowing that she and her sister felt more as if they had been kidnapped by a highwayman than rescued by a charitable stranger. Or perhaps he simply didn't care. Did he think them simply unmannered children who had to be taught what propriety was? Either way, they were still trapped.

"It's . . . it's very kind of his grace," Ophelia managed to say, though her lips felt stiff, and she had to take a sip of her wine before she could manage to speak.

Dinner proceeded with what Ophelia felt was agonizing slowness. Their hostess kept up a light conversation with amusing anecdotes about their travels, which Ophelia tried her best to attend to, and she also told them about her sister and brother-in-law in Bath. Her sister had just had their seventh child.

"Fortunately, she births easily, though this time I admit we had some worries, and my mother swore that if she had not had an excellent midwife in attendance . . . However, it has been a fortnight now, and everyone is doing well. The new baby seems to have my brother-in-law's chin, which my sister claims is the infant's only misfortune."

Ophelia dutifully laughed, though a bit weakly. She could think of not a thing to say in return, however, except to make polite good wishes for the mother and baby's health. When the conversation lapsed, she put a fork into one of the vegetables on her plate and pushed it about. The food, which she knew must be excellent, since a man like the marquis would only employ an exemplary cook, was tasteless in her mouth.

The footmen passed an unending number of silver dishes containing meats and vegetables and savories and sauces, and eventually there would be sweets and pastries and nuts and Lord knew what. She stopped trying to keep up with it all, and she certainly couldn't eat it all, or even pretend to taste it, good manners notwithstanding.

In fact, she had no appetite at all.

When the meal had stretched at least till next spring, Ophelia was happier than she could say when Lady Gillingham—Marian—pushed her chair back and glanced at Ophelia, then her sister. "I believe we shall withdraw, my dear, and leave you to your port. You can join us presently in the drawing room."

Ophelia and her sister stood and followed their hostess out of the dining room and up the stairs to the drawing room, which was an even more spacious and alarmingly beautiful chamber. Marian walked across the thick rugs to one of the sofas and sat down, and motioned them to two chairs next to her, where they sat, still silent.

"Now," the marchioness said, fixing them with her blue gray eyes. "Tell me, what is the matter?"

Ophelia and Cordelia glanced at each other and then back at their hostess. How did one tell such a gracious lady that her husband had, with the best of motives, abducted them? But he had done it at their father's bequest, so no one would listen to their complaints. It was hopeless.

"No." Their surprising chatelaine shook her head. "You are passing thoughts back and forth like a couple of Arabian genies newly released from their bottles. I should like to be part of this conversation, please."

Startled—it was true that they often knew, pretty much, what the other was thinking—they looked at each other again. Somehow that came of being twins, or perhaps it was simply that they knew each other so well. Ophelia looked at Cordelia. Cordelia lifted her chin and faced their hostess.

"We did not wish to leave the rectory. We were quite secure there, you know."

"I understand it was most kind of the vicar to offer you safe harbor," Marian told them, smiling a little. "Since you had not taken care to be sure that Gabriel would be at home when you made your precipitous dash to London."

Ophelia flashed another quick look at her sister. No, they had not, since that had not been the real plan.

"But surely you do not wish to impose upon a stranger's kindness any longer when you have family who can offer you a place to stay?" She smiled so sweetly that Ophelia could almost believe that this beautiful woman was genuinely happy to have two unruly, rebellious hellions from the wilds of the North Country thrust upon her. Surely not!

Not sure whether it was bad manners to point out that they were not really family, she said instead, "I-I don't think that he felt we were imposing . . ."

"And I know my husband spoke, at dinner, as if you were going to be rushed back to Yorkshire, but I don't agree that this is necessary."

"You don't?" Startled that anyone could stand up to the forceful Lord Gillingham, Ophelia blinked at their hostess.

"You came all this way. Surely your father would not mind if the two of you saw something of London Society. Properly chaperoned, of course." Marian plied her silk fan and bestowed another smile upon them. "We can write and ask his permission for you to remain with us for a few weeks. It's only the small

Season, but still, there are soirees and balls to attend, theater parties, drives in the park."

Ophelia jumped and felt her cheeks go pale at the mention of the theater, and her sister spoke quickly to cover her start.

"We c-couldn't," Cordelia stuttered, "go into Society, I mean, though it's very kind of you to think of it. We really don't have the clothes, and—"

"Oh, faddle." The other lady waved that away as a mere trifle. "I have some deficiencies of my own wardrobe to fill, after having been away from England for so long. I should like nothing better than to take the two of you along, and I should most enjoy seeing you outfitted. It would be such fun." She laughed. "And I brought back so many presents for my sister and my nieces and nephews, I'm sure there must be some embroidered shawls and lengths of silk left in our trunks that could be turned to your good advantage. We'll have a great deal of fun looking through them!"

"You're much too kind!" Cordelia murmured. But although the prospect of new dresses would have once been sufficient to bring Ophelia to her feet, crowing with delight, now she only nodded in polite agreement.

"Oh, come! I refuse to believe that you two do not wish to have new gowns, go to parties and enjoy yourselves," Marian told them. "What is it? You are in love with the wrong men? We have two Juliets here, in spite of your alternate Shakespearean namesakes? What?"

"No, no romance," Ophelia said quickly, not wishing their keen-witted hostess to pursue this line of thought. She seemed rather too quick to ferret out secrets! Better to confess Ophelia's other ambition. And once she had begun, the words tumbled out. "I came to London to pursue the dream of my life, and now they have taken it away! So how can I ever be happy again?"

Her expression grave, Marian listened with complete attention as Ophelia continued.

Ophelia knew the marchioness would likely be shocked, but it couldn't be helped. It was better that she knew, even if she withdrew her kindnesses and her patronage, even her generous offer to take them shopping and buy them new wardrobes and take them into London Society. These benevolent gestures would once have meant a great deal to Ophelia, and to Cordelia, too, but now—to have been so close to her aspirations—Ophelia stole a quick glance at her sister and prayed that Cordelia would not hate her for telling the truth. She could not judge her twin's expression; she appeared close-lipped and pensive, but this time, Ophelia could not judge her thoughts, so she was, for the moment, quite alone.

She lifted her chin. "I know that young ladies are not . . . supposed to go onst-stage." She faltered only a moment. "But all my life I have dreamed of this. And I was so close. The play is supposed to open in a few days. And if I leave now, I'll never know what I might have—"

Unshed tears closed her throat, and she blinked hard, not wanting to show weakness. For an awful moment, the silence stretched. Cordelia moved closer to put her arm about her sister's shoulders, and Ophelia clung to her.

Then Marian broke the silence, and her voice was gentle. "I know about long-held dreams, my dear."

It was the last thing Ophelia expected. "You do?"

"I dreamed of seeing the world, but I was trapped here, never thinking I would be able to make that dream come true. And then I fell in love with John, who had hardly left his estate until he came to London, with the greatest reluctance, deciding he must seek a wife."

"And found you?"

"Ah, it wasn't quite that simple." The corners of Marian's lips lifted, as at a private memory, then she shook it away and seemed to focus on them once more. "But be that as it may, I do know how bitter it is when Society forbids a mere woman her deepest wish. And really, I have heard of ladies who tread the board, though, I admit, not often. One of the gentlemen in the last government had a mother who went onstage. Of course, she could say she did it to support her children. And she was a widow at the time, not an unmarried lady."

"But still—" Ophelia said eagerly, happy for any crumb of support. "Anyhow, I wasn't going to use my real name on the playbill, you know. I had a stage name picked out, Lily de Lac. Don't you think that sounds nice?"

Cordelia rolled her eyes, but Ophelia ignored her. Marian pressed her lips together, and in a moment nodded. "Yes, indeed. A wise precaution, I should say. But your face will become known, my dear, so—"

"Oh, I thought of that, too. I am going to wear a mask, a half mask, as part of my role, so it will be harder to know for sure, though Cordelia says they may still suspect, but as long as they are not sure, and anyhow, we will likely be back in Yorkshire in a few weeks, you know."

Ophelia put all her most heartfelt if unspoken pleas into her gaze, and she saw Marian look back at her and consider.

"I do not believe you should be deprived of your opportunity, especially when you have already risked so much and thought out a good many steps to try to reduce the risk as much as you can."

Ophelia felt a wave of joy rise inside her. But it was stilled abruptly when a new step sounded and she saw the marquis advancing to join them, the little spaniel just behind him, its ragged tail wagging.

"What is that, my dear?"

She half expected the marchioness to demur, to change the subject and to pretend they had been discussing something else. But Marian held out her hand to her husband—he lifted it and kissed it lightly before he dropped into a large chair close to her—and said easily, "We are discussing Miss Applegate's theatrical debut."

"A sad mistake which has been put behind her," Lord Gillingham said, with a note of finality in his voice.

"No, I think not," Marian told him, her own voice calm.

"Marian!" He sat up straighter. "Their father said—"

Ophelia held her breath, and she knew that Cordelia had stiffened, as well. They shared a glance, but neither spoke.

"What exactly did their father say, my dear?" the marchioness asked, her voice still quite level and without heat.

"He . . . he wished me to remove them to the protection of

my home, well, not me, he wrote to Gabriel not knowing, of course, that Gabriel was out of the country . . ." The marquis ran a hand through his thick mane of hair and frowned a little, glancing from his wife to the two girls, then back to Marian.

"And you have done that. You have fulfilled your charge with great promptness. Their father can rest easy."

"So, how can I allow them to go back to the theater—not even one of the legitimate theaters, at that?" their alarming host demanded. "To risk their safety . . ."

"We were not—" Ophelia tried to interrupt, but he ignored her as if she had been a moth circling the nearest candle's flame.

"And even more certainly their reputations!"

"We shall take some precautions on both counts. But Ophelia has yearned for a chance on the stage for years, John. This is not a whim of the moment. And I do not believe she should be denied an opportunity to pursue such a long-held dream." Marian spoke with great firmness, and she held her husband's gaze.

Something passed between them that Ophelia could not gauge, but she knew enough to keep silent this time. She waited for Lord Gillingham to scowl, to raise his voice, to exert the power of his rank and his status as husband and head of his house. Instead he looked a bit plaintive.

"But, Marian, what will we tell her father? It's obviously not proper to allow a gently reared young lady to return to that second-rate music hall—"

"Most people said it was not proper for a sheltered young widow to go jaunting off around the world." Marian, Lady Gillingham, smiled up into her husband's face, and her eyes glowed for a moment with some flash of deep emotion that was reflected by his blunt features, softening them and rendering him almost handsome.

Feeling as if she'd witnessed something very private, Ophelia drew a deep breath and looked away. Staring at the low fire in the hearth, she felt a moment of envy to see two people who felt so much for each other. Would she ever know that kind of love, palatable as heat rising from glowing coals?

Marian continued, her voice brisk again. "We will take

precautions. Miss Applegate has gone about it in a reasonably circumspect way."

The marquis did not seem content. He continued to raise objections, but his wife met them with soothing logic of her own while Ophelia and her sister sat silently and listened.

Ophelia was so astonished to see the overpowering marquis vanquished that she twisted her hands together in her lap, afraid to speak. Was it possible that she might be allowed to go back to the theater, after all? She darted a quick look at Cordelia and saw her sister's look of warning. Don't say anything yet, she knew her sister was trying to signal her. Don't speak too soon and upset the apple cart before the brake is set.

She nodded and almost held her breath as their host and hostess wrangled civilly over the question of their guests' fate.

At last, when Marian turned back to them, Ophelia found she gripped her hands together so tightly that her fingers were white.

"When are rehearsals held?" the marchioness inquired.

"They generally start about ten and last till near five," Ophelia told her meekly.

"That should not be a problem," her hostess said. "We shall have to have some early fittings for your gowns, but that can be arranged. Once the play begins its run, then it will be a bit trickier, but being fashionably late to parties is hardly unknown, so—"

She smiled at Ophelia's expression of surprise. "I am not releasing you from your initiation into London Society, my dear. We must have a compromise on that, especially if I am to plead your case to your worthy parent."

"Yes, my lady," Ophelia agreed, keeping her expression biddable.

"In the long run, you might find an entry to Society more valuable, after all, than even your debut on the stage," Marian suggested.

Ophelia smiled politely and tried not to show how ridiculous was such a suggestion. On the other side of the divan, she saw that Cordelia had a dreamy look in her eye and she knew exactly what, or rather whom, she was thinking of. Going back to the theater meant that Cordelia would be able to see Ransom Sheffield again. Or . . . would he no longer feel compelled to chaperone and protect them, now that they had acquired such an august protector as the marquis? If so, Cordelia would be very unhappy.

At least they would be able to go back to the theater tomorrow and attend rehearsal as usual! Ophelia felt a wave of happiness, followed by a sudden anxious thought. Surely Mr. Nettles would not have replaced her already, would he? And perhaps they could swing by the rectory to explain to the vicar just why they had left so precipitously; she really would not wish to be uncivil, and a note just would not be the same as explaining face-to-face . . .

While she sat silently, deep in thought, a sudden sound of voices in the entryway below caught her attention.

"What in hell—" the marquis said. He stood suddenly, walking toward the doorway of the drawing room.

But their importune visitor didn't wait to be properly announced. Ophelia could hear the sound of rapid footfalls on the wide staircase, and then a familiar figure burst through the double doors.

"What have you done with the Applegate sisters?"

Eleven

*G*ray eyes flashing with anger and his face set with resolve, Ransom Sheffield stood in the doorway. With one hand gripping a serviceable pistol, he looked a trifle out of place in the gilt and coral drawing room. Everyone sat very still and watched him, and Ophelia knew that her own eyes were wide.

Behind him, the stout elderly butler struggled to catch up. He had snatched up a silver candlestick perhaps to use as a weapon, and his powdered wig was askew. "I could not stop him, Your Grace!" he explained, panting and waving his candlestick in the air. "Shall I call for the footmen to throw him out, or go fetch the Watch?"

In answer, his expression defiant, Ransom simply lifted the pistol higher. Despite his misapprehensions, Ophelia thought he looked rather splendid. She was already sketching out a scene in her head where the hero of the play could rush on to the heath and . . . Absently she noted that her sister's color was high, and her eyes very bright.

"How dare you come into my home carrying a firearm and threatening my family!" the marquis roared. "I should call you out!" He took two steps forward, and Ransom braced himself.

"At any time and place you can name," Ransom agreed. "But first, you will allow me to see the young ladies to a place of safety."

At the same time, Marian spoke quietly, "John!"

Cornelia said, "Ransom, wait!"

Neither man gave any sign he had heard.

"I am not accustomed to anyone doubting my words, sir!" The coldness of the marquis's tone made Ophelia shiver. "But the ladies are here; you can see they are unharmed. You may ask them to confirm my words. And then I will kill you."

"You may try," Ransom replied, his voice just as cool.

"No!" Cordelia burst out, jumping to her feet and taking a step forward as if to put herself bodily between the two men.

"Oh, don't!" Ophelia exclaimed as well, though she did not move from the divan.

"That is quite enough!" Lady Gillingham spoke again, her voice as firm as her husband's. "No one needs to speak of killing. We are all civilized, and we can speak rationally, if you please."

Ransom glanced at her elegant figure and blinked, as if seeing her for the first time. "Just how many women do you feel you need—" he demanded of the man who towered above him.

The marquis gave an inarticulate growl of anger, and the marchioness interrupted swiftly. "I think it would be best if you did not finish that question, sir. Cordelia, perhaps you could make introductions? I think we need some civility added to this cauldron of chaos."

That was putting it mildly. Ophelia was glad she had not been called upon; her mouth was so dry she did not think she could speak. She threw her sister a glance of support.

Cordelia swallowed hard and did as she was bid. "Lord and Lady Gillingham, this is Mr. Ransom Sheffield. His cousin is the vicar who gave us shelter, and Mr. Ransom Sheffield has been escorting us to and from the theater and watching over us during rehearsals so that we are not bothered by any of the cast. Mr. Sheffield, the marquis and his wife are, ah, distant connections of our family."

"Lady Gillingham?" Ransom stared at Marian. "Your wife?"

"Yes." She smiled at him. "Will you not take a seat, Mr. Sheffield? I'm afraid you have missed dinner, but I will ask the servants to bring a tea tray for us."

She signaled to the butler, who had continued to ogle them all from the doorway. He withdrew, although seemingly with some reluctance.

Ransom looked down at the gun still in his hand, flushed and shoved it into an inner pocket of his jacket. Then he sat gingerly down on the edge of a chair, as if it might crumble beneath him, as illusionary as the painted backdrops onstage.

Still looking grim, the marquis sat back down and placed his clenched hands on his lap. When his wife gave him a pointed look, he slowly loosened his fists.

"Since this was all a misunderstanding, obviously you cannot call each other out, is this agreed?" Marion continued, looking from one man to another.

There was an awkward pause, then John nodded, and Ransom followed suit.

"Good," she said. "I gather you were alarmed when you found that the girls had been swept out of the theater, Mr. Sheffield."

"Yes," Ransom said. He glanced at Cordelia, who blushed slightly and then looked down at her own hands, which were clenched together in her lap. She seemed to make a conscious effort to open them, just as the men had. "They left no note, and . . ." His mouth pressed together into a thin line. "My first thought was, ah, not a good one."

"I understand. You are a conscientious guardian. I'm sure the Misses Applegate are happy to have so many friends and relations ready to look out for them. And, of course, you are welcome to call on them here."

Ophelia thought that perhaps Marian's eyes danced a bit. Did she see more here than was apparent on the surface, or note that Cordelia and Ransom made a concerted effort not to gaze into each other's eyes?

At least Cordelia had gotten to see Ransom. Ophelia was glad for her sister, but she thought of Giles and sighed quietly.

Perhaps she would find an opportunity to give Ransom a message for his cousin, she told herself.

When the tea tray came, the company separated naturally into smaller groups, and she and her sister were able to talk quietly to Ransom and explain that they would be coming back to rehearsals.

"You're jesting. The high and mighty . . . I mean, your esteemed relation Lord Gillingham allows it?" Ransom gave a veiled glance toward the marquis, who sat with a resigned expression as he listened to his charming wife.

"Yes, I'll explain later," Ophelia almost whispered. "I hope you will still be there, at the theater, I mean?" She asked the question she knew her sister wanted badly to hear the answer to, and got a grateful smile from Cordelia.

Ransom looked down as if considering his reply. "Since I can hardly see the marquis sitting around a second-rate theater all day, yes, I think I should," he said at last. "Besides, I have some unfinished business of my own."

Ophelia could sense her sister draw a deep breath and allow her tension to escape. "Good," she said. "We can be easy. And please give your cousin the vicar our deepest thanks, and tell him we did not mean to depart so precipitously or without a proper good-bye or thank-yous, or without telling him how much we appreciate all he has done to help us!"

This time she thought it was Cordelia who hid a smile, but at least Ransom kept a suitable solemn expression as he nodded. "I will certainly pass on your message."

And she had to be content with that.

The next morning Cordelia and her sister rode back to the theater in the splendor of the marquis's carriage. After today, however, he had promised to rent a plain carriage to send them back and forth daily, in order to be less noticeable. No more sometimes-dirty hackneys, she thought. No more long walks. Although she missed having Ransom squeezed in beside them. The groom helped them down and they knocked on the side door. She took a malicious pleasure in seeing Nobby's mouth drop open.

"W'ot, back already?" he demanded.

"I wouldn't miss rehearsal," Ophelia said cheerfully.

"But w'ot about the rich nabob? 'E tired of ye already?"

"It's not what you think, Nobby," Ophelia told him, her tone reproachful.

Cordelia added, "His wife is there, too, you know, to chaperone."

"'Is wife? The man 'as stamina, 'e does!" Nobby muttered as they hurried past him.

Cordelia heard squeals of surprise as Ophelia entered the dressing room. Apparently the other actresses were not expecting her sister back so soon, either.

It wasn't long before Ophelia turned up in Cordelia's sewing nook. Her arms were full of various pieces of clothing, her expression grimly satisfied. "They had already divided up my costume!" She shook her head in disbelief. "But I have it all back! Except I cannot wear the bustier until it has been thoroughly laundered. The collier's daughter had it, and I've seen her scratching! What?" Ophelia paused to stare at her twin.

"Just thinking how, ah, determined you have become since we became part of the cast and crew," Cordelia told her, grinning.

"You're not going to prose at me about being unladylike, are you?" Ophelia threw her an impatient glance. "Some of the girls are a bit rough about the edges, that's all, and I can't allow them to tell me what to do!"

"Certainly not," Cordelia agreed, but she had to look down at the sewing in her lap to hide her grin.

"I need you to mend the waist of my skirt. The girl who took it has four inches on me, and she has ripped the waistband, the ninny! Just as I had everything adjusted to fit, too."

"I'll do it first thing," Cordelia promised.

A clatter of wooden swords and stamping of feet from the direction of the stage distracted them both.

"What are they doing?"

"Oh, it's the men at their sword drill. Which means our

musical number is up, next. I'd better run," Ophelia said. She set out at a fast trot before Cordelia could ask if she had seen Ransom Sheffield among the male cast members.

Cordelia put down her sewing and rose to stand in the doorway and watch. Within a few minutes the men wandered back, rubbing the sweat off their foreheads, some of them sipping from pocket flasks.

She was gratified to see Ransom Sheffield heading directly toward her doorway.

"Are you all right?" he asked.

"Yes," she told him, not pretending to misunderstand.

"The grand marquis is indeed a relation, then?"

"More or less," she said, knowing that her words were somewhat vague.

He frowned at her, and she sighed and motioned for him to take a seat on the other three-legged stool. "Did your cousin tell you what Ophelia explained about how we came to London?"

He shook his head. "Vicars, or at least my cousin, are quite close-mouthed about sharing what is told to them in confidence."

"I hope you will be the same," she said.

He looked a bit wounded. "I can keep a trust."

So she explained how they had run away from their home in Yorkshire, and then the more complicated tale about why they had an unacknowledged half brother in Lord Gabriel Sinclair. "So my father wrote a letter to Lord Gabriel asking him to retrieve us from this, ah, den of iniquity."

Ransom gave a short laugh as he glanced about them at the dusty backstage area and the low-cut costumes hanging from pegs as they awaited mending. "Yes, I can see a worried father thinking that."

"But Lord Gabriel has taken his family to France just now, and the letter was sent on to his older brother, the marquis of Gillingham."

Her listener gave a slight whistle. "Ah, I begin to see." Something in his voice told her that Ransom had not particularly cared to look foolish—dashing in last night to effect a rescue that was not necessary.

She looked again at her lap and touched the sewing that filled it. "We were alarmed and dismayed when he turned up and took us away so hastily, I can tell you. And Ophelia was in tears at the thought of having to give up the role here she had waited so long to claim. But to our surprise, Lady Gillingham took our side, so we are back, as you see, though we are going to have to make a debut into Society as well. That gives me many more chills than does opening night, let me tell you!" She leaned over and bit off a stray thread, not caring to picture keen-eyed London matrons just waiting for an untried Yorkshire lass to slip up.

"You will do fine," he told her firmly. "I think it's time that you had some pleasure from this trip, Miss Applegate."

"But we have," she reminded him, glancing up from rethreading her needle. "And Ophelia's happiness in her opportunity—"

"I am not speaking of Ophelia—" His tone had become even more insistent, and she found his silver gray gaze hard to meet. "She will have the thrills of venturing onstage, of hearing applause and seeing the bright footlights, of fulfilling a long-sought goal. What about you, Miss Cordelia Applegate, relegated to this dusty cupboard and doing little more than playing doyenne to your sister? Do you ever think about yourself?"

He leaned closer, and for a moment, she felt the strength of the spark that jumped between them at the least provocation. She found she was breathing more quickly, and she wanted to answer the magnetic pull of the man, feel his arms about her again—no, she shook herself mentally. This was folly!

So she pulled her gaze away from him and tried to hide any betraying reaction "Of course," she said, her voice rather small. "It's just . . . I couldn't let Ophelia come alone all the way to London. And . . . and . . . I don't mind the sewing nook, I never wanted to act, you know. And . . . I mean—"

He shook his head. "Never mind."

To her disappointment, he stood and moved away. "I have my own family burdens, too."

"Your brother?" she said, feeling the pressure ease. This,

she could understand. She would like to ask him why he had to find the missing snuffbox but she didn't quite dare.

"I fear I'm running out of time, and if I don't find a way to pick that lock—"

There was a slight sound behind him, and Ransom whirled.

Cordelia felt her heart beat faster, but this time for a different reason. Had someone heard that too-revealing remark who shouldn't?

Then a faded ball rolled across the dirty floor and she bent to stop its escape. "It's only Mr. Druid," she said, her voice quiet. "Don't be alarmed."

But Ransom Sheffield had already pounced with his usual lethal efficiency, pulling the thin man from behind a stack of scenery. "What are you doing back there! Are you trying to eavesdrop?"

"N-no, no," the conjurer said, clutching his other balls and tucking a colored scarf back into his wide sleeve. "I was only looking for a quiet spot to practice my tricks. The girls say I make them nervous, and the men . . . well, the men throw their wooden swords at me and make me juggle them when I'm trying to do my other tricks, which is a wee bit fatiguing, so I came back to this side of the stage—"

He had a bead of perspiration on his forehead, but whether that was from guilt or only because Ransom glared at him, now, Cordelia wasn't sure. She frowned at Ransom, sure, well, almost sure that the street magician couldn't be a danger. But his next words surprised her.

"But if you need a lock picked, perhaps I could be of help?" he offered, his voice timid.

Ransom raised his dark brows. "And how would you know about that? Is that included in a conjuror's bag of tricks?"

"It is, a bit, yes," the man said, wiping his brow with one of his bright kerchiefs, then stuffing it back into his pocket. "But actually, I learned that at an early age, you see."

"And how was that?" Ransom asked, his tone polite.

"I was a street boy, too, you see. A pickpocket, a small-time thief. But I never got very good, and I was nabbed and sent up to gaol." Mr. Druid's pale lashes fluttered, and he stared at the floorboards and sighed. "Not a nice place, gaol. They do dreadful things to you there, the other prisoners as much as the guards." He glanced from Ransom to Cordelia and back again.

"Details are not necessary," Ransom told him quickly.

The man nodded. "I don't want to go back, not ever. But inside, I met this magician, who had been sent up by mistake, he said. He did tricks, and he made people laugh. I wanted to make people laugh, too. It was ever so much nicer than getting yelled at, you see. So he taught me, and I practiced. I had lots of time, after all. And when I finally got out, I didn't go back to stealing. I took a new name, and I took up doing tricks on the street . . . and so you see me today."

"Then you mustn't risk your new life by engaging in lock picking," Cordelia told him, feeling a shiver of alarm for the conjurer.

"Perhaps just once," Ransom muttered, contradicting. "If I could have the door open, I could do the rest. It's really very important."

"I would do it for you," the conjurer told Cordelia. "You got me this job, when I was down to my last . . . my last . . . well . . . no penny at all."

"But he mustn't risk it, didn't you hear?" Cordelia spoke hotly, feeling sorry for the odd man with the long, gangly limbs.

Ransom's eyes were steely, and their gazes met, and neither looked away. The magician glanced from one to the other, as if not sure what to do.

"We will discuss this matter later, Mr. Druid," Ransom told him, his tone easy again. "Just do not mention this to anyone else, if you please."

"Oh, no, no," the other man agreed. "I'll just go and work on my tricks in the dressing room; the girls will be onstage by now." He picked up his last scarf and wandered off.

Cordelia bit her lip till the magician was out of earshot, then snapped, "How could you put that poor man at risk?"

"I only want his help getting into Nettles's rooms," he said. "Then I will send him away, and I will go through the contents of the apartment myself. If anyone is caught and endangered, it will be me."

"And you will not even tell us what this is about? I told you my secrets. You are not willing to share yours!"

He met her angry stare without dropping his gaze. "It is not my secret to share," he said at last.

"So you say," she said slowly. "Perhaps there is no secret at all. Perhaps you are, after all, simply a thief and a house-breaker. Possibly that is how you make your income."

"Perhaps," he said, refusing to rise to her bait., His expression closed, he turned and walked away.

Cordelia thrust the needle too hard and stuck herself again. Swearing briskly, she feared that Madeline was not going to be pleased with the colorful new terms she had added to her vocabulary since coming to London, Cordelia tossed the garment she had been repairing back into the basket.

Was it possible that what she had said was true? Could Ransom Sheffield really be an ordinary thief? He had spent all this time trying to get into the stage manager's rooms just to steal—what? What on earth could the man have in his apartment that could be worth that much trouble?

She found that she didn't believe it. Ransom was a gentleman. Yes, he could have made the twins' safety an excuse to get into the theater; yes, they had seen him trying to break into the upper floor of the theater's rear building before they had ever met him. But he could hardly have known that they were about to provide him with a likely excuse when he had intervened to save Cordelia from the white slavery gang.

She just couldn't imagine him as a thief. Which meant he had to have some compelling reason for what he was doing. And if it was not for himself—if it wasn't his secret—who else could it be about? Who would he risk his life or his freedom for?

Who had tried to climb into her bed in the middle of the night?

His younger brother—his foolish younger brother! Foolish younger brothers could get into other scrapes, too. Did the theater manager have some connection to Avery Sheffield? And how on earth could she find out?

Staring into space, Cordelia eventually realized she had

promised to mend Ophelia's damaged costume, so she fished it back out of the sewing basket and set to work once more. But she thought hard while she sewed. When it was time to go home, Ophelia came to find her and brought her costume with her to have laundered.

"Actually, I will do it myself," she confessed to her sister. "Rather than have that haughty maid turn up her nose at my, ah, theatrical costume."

Glancing at the somewhat garish and low-cut gown, Cordelia hid a grin. "I understand," she said.

The marquis's elegant carriage was waiting, and Cordelia, in her faded muslin gown, feeling dusty from her hours in the theater, allowed the groom to hand her up, conscious of the irony of it all. Clutching her armload of costume, her sister followed.

When they reached the marquis's spacious home, they went into the double doors, and Cordelia tried to feel that they belonged there. She still wished secretly that they could return to the rectory, but it was impossible, so she did not voice the thought. A glance at Ophelia's wistful expression showed Cordelia that her sister had to be thinking much the same.

Inside they climbed the wide staircase without speaking. On the first landing, the marchioness looked out from the drawing room. "Ah, there you are. Since you were occupied, my dears, I took the liberty of visiting some of the warehouses without you. If there is anything here you do not like, however, I will have it sent back, so you should just say the word. My modiste is coming early tomorrow to take your measurements before you leave for the theater."

Gracious! Marian was a lady of decisive action. The settees were piled high with bolts of fine muslin and soft silks and satins, along with trims and laces and other delicious accoutrements. Ophelia's eyes were wide, and Cordelia knew her own expression must be mirroring her sister's.

"This . . . this is much too generous of you, my lady," she stammered.

"Oh, nonsense," their hostess said. "You must have sufficient new gowns to be allowed some mild jaunts into Society."

If this was what Marian considered a mild jaunt, Cordelia wondered what a serious expedition would entail. She reached to feel a bolt of soft sea green silk with just the tip of her finger, then hesitated, afraid her hands were too dirty and she might soil it.

"We must be in heaven," Ophelia muttered. "Or dreaming."

Marian laughed. "I'm glad you are pleased," she said. "And I'm planning a small dinner party for Thursday night. I thought we should invite your hospitable vicar, as a small thank-you for his kindness to you both, and his cousin, of course. Would that be to your liking?"

"Oh, yes, what a splendid idea!" Ophelia said at once. "We shall be so deeply in your debt, Marian, we shall never be able to repay you."

Marian's eyes sparkled again with that hint of mischief. "I don't wish any repayment, my dear. You are keeping me from the boredom which I was afraid would overtake me on our return to London. And really, my husband is not fond of the city, so you do us both a favor by distracting him from his grumbling about the crowds and the noises and the smoky air."

Cordelia was even less sure of the veracity of that last statement. After all, if they were not here, the marquis could have taken his wife down to their estate and have escaped the city completely, which is what he probably would have preferred. But she kept her doubts to herself. And anyhow, she had suddenly had a—perhaps—brilliant idea.

"Marian," she said slowly. "If it is not presumptuous, since you have already been so very very kind, might I ask one more favor?"

"Of course, my dear," their hostess said, turning to look her way.

"Mr. Ransom Sheffield's younger brother Avery is also staying at the rectory. Might he be invited to the dinner party, too? If it does not upset your numbers, of course."

"Certainly, I did not mean to leave anyone out," Marian said. Perhaps a moment of curiosity glinted in her eyes, but she hid it quickly.

Ophelia glanced at Cordelia in surprise, but Cordelia sent

her a quick look of warning. I'll explain later, she mouthed. Her sister blinked but said nothing and soon was exclaiming happily over the lovely fabrics.

When they went up to bed, Ophelia came across to her sister's room. "Why did you want Avery to come?" she asked.

Cordelia explained her hunch that Avery was connected to Ransom's search for the snuffbox.

"Of course, it's just like one of my plays," Ophelia said at once.

"You *cannot* write this into the play, Ophelia," Cordelia said in alarm. "Anyhow, I don't know for sure. I simply thought if I had a chance to talk to Avery, I might find out something."

"A good plan," her sister agreed. "Perhaps I can use it in my next play." She giggled at her sister's glare. "Oh, be a dear and let me say my lines."

So Cordelia, as she did most nights, listened to her sister recite her lines, prompting her when she faltered, until Ophelia was sure she had them all secure in her memory.

"If you didn't rewrite them so often, you would have known them all much sooner," Cordelia pointed out mildly.

"But you must admit, my changes have strengthened the play," Ophelia said. But the confidence of her words was belied by her anxious look.

"Oh, no doubt at all about that," her sister agreed, and was rewarded with a broad smile.

Ophelia hugged her and then left for her own room.

The next morning Marian's dressmaker arrived as scheduled while the family was still at the breakfast table. It was no imposition to leave their ham and shirred eggs to go stand on a stool and be measured. Thinking of the crisp muslins and smooth silks waiting to be made up into new gowns made Cordelia, for a few minutes, put aside her worries about more weighty matters.

New dresses! She was still human and still decidedly feminine at heart, and thinking of what Ransom Sheffield might think of her on Thursday night if she ~~none~~ a new dinner gown— well, she felt a secret thrill just imagining what his expression

wore

might be. If she could lift that usual guarded look from his face, ease the cynical cast from his silvery‾ gray eyes, it made her heart beat fast just picturing it . . .

They finished in time to pick up their shawls and climb into the new hired carriage for their ride to the theater. A cool breeze blew, and the sky was cloudy. But Ophelia seemed in a good mood, too.

"I have my costume back together," she said, nodding toward the bundle on her knee. "I dried it overnight in front of the fire. And no one is touching it, if I have to do some hairpulling myself!"

Cordelia grinned.

At the theater, they parted. Cordelia went to her sewing nook, tied on her apron and applied herself to her mending. She saw Ransom Sheffield several times that day, although from a slight distance. He did not, as he usually did, come and talk to her, though he nodded when she caught his eye.

Flushing, she looked away. She had not meant for him to see that she somehow could not seem to keep from watching when he walked past. She told herself it did not matter that he did not stop to chat, but somehow the day seemed to drag on much more slowly than usual. Drat the man!

The rest of the week continued in much the same pattern, while, in addition to other worries, Ophelia fretted openly and Cordelia privately that their new dinner dresses would not be done on time. But the modiste must have had plenty of assistants to help her with her needlework. When the sisters stepped out of the carriage after rehearsal on Thursday, they hurried into the entry hall. This time Cordelia did not pause at the sight of the butler's austere expression, and her twin was even less formal.

"Did they come?" Ophelia demanded without preamble. "Our dresses, did they come?"

The butler took his time in answering. "Yes, miss," he said at last. "You both received parcels. They have been sent up to your rooms."

Ophelia squealed in delight. For a moment Cordelia feared she would throw her arms about the butler's neck. He seemed to think so, too, and drew back slightly in alarm, but she merely clasped her hands and danced about the black-and-white tile of the entry. Then she turned to Cordelia and grabbed her hand. "Oh, come, we must see them!"

Cordelia needed no urging. They hastened up the wide staircase. Upstairs they separated and literally ran into their rooms. Cordelia found that the maid had opened her parcel and laid the new dress neatly out upon her bed.

She paused and put one hand to her mouth. Oh, it was a sight to see! Her first new gown in several seasons—she could not even think how many—and such a dress! Made of palest green, the color of sea foam that might have formed atop a tropical sea, and trimmed with frothy white lace at the throat and green silk roses at the hem, it was the most beautiful gown she had ever seen.

From down the hall, she heard Ophelia shriek with happiness, no doubt in raptures over her own gown; but for herself, Cordelia was left speechless. After a long minute, she moved forward to touch the silk skirt with one hand, luxuriating in the softness of it, thinking how it would feel on her body . . .

She was still standing there when Ophelia appeared in her doorway, holding her new dress in front of her. "Oh, Cordelia, look. Is it not a dream?"

Cordelia turned to smile at her sister. Ophelia's gown was of a delicate copper hue, trimmed with matching lace. It would set off her hair and eyes admirably.

"It's beautiful," Cordelia told her. "And you will be beautiful in it."

"As will you in your gown," Ophelia told her happily. "Oh, I am so looking forward to tonight. They will come, don't you think?"

Cordelia had no trouble guessing to whom the *they* referred. "Marian said Giles sent a note accepting," she reassured her sister. "So, yes, I think the Sheffields will come, and I think we'd better get ready."

"Oh, yes!" Ophelia agreed, her tone changing. "I always look a fright after rehearsal, and I know I have dust in my hair!"

So her sister disappeared, still clutching her new dinner

dress, and in a few moments was replaced in the doorway by a maid carrying a pail of steaming water. "Shall I set up the 'ip bath, miss?" she asked.

"That would be lovely," Cordelia agreed.

After bathing with lavender-scented soap and washing her hair, she sat in front of the hearth, enjoying the warmth from the fire as she brushed out her long hair until it dried. Having a fire in her bedchamber was another unaccustomed luxury on this cool early autumn day, but the marquis seemed to think nothing of it.

She suddenly remembered her half brother, Lord Gabriel Sinclair. As the second son of a marquis, he had grown up in luxury like this, taking such things as new clothes and warm bedrooms and bountiful dinners for granted. Then he been cast out abruptly when he was barely an adult, sent to wander the world and live by his wits.

Her older sister Juliana, the first one of the Applegate girls to come to London, had said that she suspected that perhaps he understood, because of that, more about what it was to be poor. She did not see that Lord Gillingham could, however. Perhaps Marian did, somewhat. Lady Gillingham had not always been wealthy. Either way, the generosity she had shown them made Cordelia's eyes moisten, and the anger she had felt at being virtually kidnapped, even if it had been for their own good, or so John Sinclair had assumed, had eased.

As long as Ophelia's dream had not been snatched out of her grasp, the fact that they were now living in such opulence could not be considered a hardship! Of course, that they had been allowed to go back to the theater at all, they owed to Marian, and her grasp of what a cherished dream could mean. Their hostess was an amazing woman.

A look at the small clock on the mantel pulled Cordelia out of her musings. She began brushing her brown locks again until a knock at the door made her jump.

It was Ophelia in her shift and petticoat, her new dress over her arm. "Shall I help you with your hair?"

At home, they always aided each other with their toilettes, and even here, with plenty of maidservants available, it was to each other that they turned at the most important times. So they finished their preparations, Ophelia chattering nervously, Cordelia more apt to be silent but nodding in understanding. They laced each other's stays, buttoned up the tiny buttons at the back of their wonderful new dinner gowns, brushed and pinned up each other's thick brown hair until it was piled in lustrous twists on top of their heads. Cordelia had a jade pendant and Ophelia coral beads to wear about her neck, and both had matching ear drops, gifts Juliana had sent from her honeymoon trip abroad with her handsome new husband.

When Marian herself came and tapped at the door, she smiled to see them. "You are both quite lovely!"

"The gown is lovely; it is so generous of you!" Cordelia told her.

"So kind!" Ophelia agreed, her smile lighting up her face.

Marian waved away their thanks. "Not at all, I'm happy to see you looking so splendid. Shall we go down? I believe the first of our guests is arriving."

At this suggestion, Cordelia felt her stomach quiver, and she and her sister exchanged glances. Would the Sheffields appreciate their new trappings of outer beauty? She murmured as much to her sister as they followed their hostess down the stairwell to the drawing room.

"Of course," she added, grinning. "I'm sure a vicar is above such earthly concerns."

Ophelia shot her a mischievous glance. "He darn well better not be, or I shall try my best to bring him down a notch or two to a more human level!"

The first callers to knock at the door and be led upstairs by the footmen and announced in suitable pomp and ceremony were several old friends of the Sinclairs, the next a count and countess, to Cordelia and Ophelia's private frustration. The sisters exchanged glances but could not express their thoughts. Instead, they smiled and went through the necessary introductions, answering politely to each of the new people they met.

Several carriages later, Cordelia felt a spark of happiness inside when she looked toward the wide doorway and saw the tall, wide-shouldered form of Ransom Sheffield, with his brother and his cousin just behind him. And my, he looked even more handsome than usual in his evening dress, his well-cut dark coat and spotless linen. His expression was austere, his eyes hard to read. Was he still nursing his grievances over their quarrel because she would not countenance his use of the street magician to open Mr. Nettles's locked door?

But he was here; he had come.

She drew a deep breath, not aware until then that she had had doubts that he would honor the engagement.

When the introductions were made, he made an easy bow to the marquis and his wife, then moved down the line to Cordelia and her twin.

"Mr. Sheffield," Cordelia said, trying not to sound too happy that he was here. Besides, he might snub her, and what would she do then? Of course, he had never actually been cruel, she told herself, even as sardonic as he sometimes could be. So she met his gaze squarely, and did she imagine it or did something in the veiled gray eyes soften?

But she knew that Ophelia was waiting impatiently for his cousin to come down the receiving line, and anyhow, Ransom could not linger without looking conspicuous. And perhaps—perhaps she would be able to talk to him later. So she watched him move on and she greeted Giles and then Avery, who looked merry and as carefree as any young man of two and twenty could be.

When they went into dinner, some young stripling was given the task of escorting the twins to the dining room, but Cordelia's heart leaped to her throat when she found that Ransom Sheffield was seated on her other side.

Oh, bless Marian!

For a few minutes she was forced to listen to the young man who apparently saw himself as a tulip of fashion natter on about the latest styles in gentleman's hats. Before her eyes had totally glazed over, she thought to say, "Yes, I would agree that yellow might be the newest thing in walking hats. This soup is excellent, you know, and I believe yours must be getting cold."

At last the man put his spoon into his mouth and, perforce, ceased his yammering for one moment, and she was able to turn to her other side.

Watching her with his calm, sardonic gaze, Ransom was waiting.

And of course, now Cordelia could think of nothing at all to say. "I'm happy you were able to honor us with your presence," was the best she could manage.

"And I," he agreed. "Since I am invited to so many marquis's mansions, it was good of me to fit you in, don't you think?"

She giggled and had to put her spoon back into the dish of soup before she disgraced herself and spotted her beautiful new gown. She nodded to the footman who was hovering, waiting to take away her dish.

"Very good of you," she agreed.

"I suppose you are happy to be housed in such luxury," he noted, glancing at the ornate chamber about them, as long and as tall as many churches.

She answered his implied thought rather than his words. "My sister and I would give this up and go back to the rectory in a minute," she told him bluntly. "So no, we are not swept up in a quest for luxury, Mr. Sheffield, even though the marquis and his wife have been very generous to us, and we are certainly grateful. But that does not mean we are forgetful of old friends, nor do we forget who rescued us when we first came to London."

The woman on the other side of Ransom looked at her curiously, and Cordelia lowered her voice, but, really, the man would annoy a saint!

"I was not fishing for renewed expressions of gratitude," Ransom told her, but the edge in his voice seemed to have faded. "I am only surprised that you and your sister still are determined to return to the theater every day."

"You should not be; you know, or I thought you understood, how much Ophelia's ambition to be an actress means to her."

"I know about her ambitions. But I asked you once, and you never gave me a satisfying response—why are you there, Miss Applegate? What is it that drives you to dare such a risky undertaking?" His eyes had narrowed again, and he seemed to look inside her. Why did he persist in wanting to turn her inside out like this? Why would he not be content with her answers?

"Do you not understand caring about other people, Mr. Sheffield?" she retorted, taking up a piece of pudding, light as a feather—the marquis had an excellent chef—and wishing she could toss the bit of food into his face.

"But—"

"I know, I know. You are going to tell me I should think more often about myself, my desires, my goals. Perhaps, just as with my sister, the theater holds something I seek."

Then, afraid she had revealed too much, she looked down at her plate. From the corner of her eye she saw the stout matron on Ransom's other side tap him with her fan and claim him for conversation, so he had to turn away from Cordelia. The young tulip reclaimed her, as well, and she nodded absently and tried to eat the rest of a delicious dinner as he extolled the virtues of his tailor. At least the young man required few responses, being happy to provide all the conversation himself.

She was able to say little more to Ransom before the ladies left the table and gathered in the drawing room, although she was very aware of his nearness. And it was a wrench to leave him behind, though she made sure she did not show it, keeping her expression even as she stood and walked away with only a nod.

In the drawing room she sat down quietly near two ladies of her own age and waited for Ophelia to join them. Ophelia was beaming; her dinnertime conversation had obviously been more felicitous.

"He misses me; he admitted it," she whispered to her sister. "And he said I looked like a delicate autumn aster in my gown. . . . Oh, life is so sweet."

Cordelia smiled at her sister's giddy good mood and hoped to hide her own more complicated feelings. They chatted with the new acquaintances and all was merry until one of the young ladies brought up the subject of the theater.

"Have you heard about the new play at Malory Road?" Miss Hardy said, waving her fan in front of her face.

Obviously ready to respond, Ophelia sat up straighter, but Cordelia darted a quick glance toward her sister. They had to remember their double lives and not give too much away.

"No, what have you heard?" Cordelia asked politely.

"Malory Road, not Drury Lane?" the other young lady asked. "That's an unfashionable venue, my dear. Why are you going there?"

Ophelia bristled, but again, Cordelia threw her a warning look.

"Yes, but just as fancy. You will never guess what their new play features!"

"A man-eating ape?" The other lady guessed. "An elephant?"

"No, no. You will never guess, so I will tell you. When they open the new play next week"—Miss Hardy paused for effect and waved her fan in emphasis—"it will have a lady of quality in a supporting role! Now, just fancy, how scandalous is that?"

Twelve

*C*ordelia stiffened. *She felt a quiver of alarm run* through her entire body.

Mouth agape, Ophelia stared at the speaker and didn't utter a word. Cordelia hoped the other two young women would think her sister's reaction only a response to the surprising news.

"No, really?" Cordelia said, hoping to keep their attention on her instead of her twin. "That's very hard to credit. How did you hear such a wild rumor?"

"Oh, someone told me, I forget who, but still, it's a strange notion, is it not? They're charging a scandalous fee for box seats on opening night, but really, I shall have to go, just to see!"

Cordelia answered, she wasn't even sure later what she had said, and the other two ladies continued to discuss this surprising gossip with avid interest. Looking pale, Ophelia added little to the conversation.

When the men rejoined the ladies, Cordelia took the chance to draw her sister aside so she could speak more privately.

"What are we going to do? You shall have to withdraw from the play!"

"No!" Ophelia said at once, even if her voice sounded thin. "I will not."

"But somehow, the news has gotten out," Cordelia whispered back. "You cannot risk it! If anyone finds out who that unknown lady is—"

"The gossips didn't know my name," Ophelia told her, as if holding on to one last hope. "You heard that they don't know my name. And I shall be listed on the program under my stage name. So there is still plenty of reason to feel that my identity is safe."

"I don't know, Ophelia, I think—"

"Hush," Ophelia said.

She saw a handful of young men moving toward them, so Cordelia had to smile through set lips and change the subject quickly to something more innocuous. She would have to talk to her sister again later; it was impossible to have a real discussion just now.

The gentlemen who flocked about them seemed intrigued by two ladies with identical pretty faces, and they made jesting compliments about how hard it was to tell the two ladies apart and how provident it was that they were wearing different colors.

While Ophelia flicked her fan and offered coy replies, it reminded Cordelia, offering absentminded responses, that Ransom Sheffield had never once confused Cordelia with her sister. How had he, from the beginning, known the difference?

Perhaps he had looked more closely, understood her more intimately. . . .

In a moment Ophelia made a laughing excuse to cross the room. "I must pay my respects to the marchioness," she said. And the fact that the vicar was standing near their hostess doubtless had nothing to do with it, Cordelia thought.

The disappointed would-be suitors turned to Cordelia, but she made as if to follow her sister.

"What, our second Venus follows the first? Will all the beauteous stars in the night sky desert us? The heavens shall be dark, indeed, and weep from their despair!" One of the young gallants bowed with an exaggerated flourish.

Shakespeare, he was not, Cordelia thought, but she kept her observation to herself and merely smiled politely. She did not, however, follow her sister all the way across the big room; she had remembered her other objective for the evening.

Young Avery Sheffield had been talking to a young lady in a pale pink dress and a slight tendency to freckles. Cordelia paused beside them and smiled at the young man, who obligingly turned his attention to her. The young lady with freckles sniffed and drifted off to find another gentleman whose notice she might hope to keep.

"Oh, I say, it was jolly good of you to include me in the invitation. I know it was your doing. My brother's been on me to stay out of sight, but really, a fellow can't spend all his time indoors skulking in the attic. I'm been aching to get out for a good game of cards and a little bit of frolic, but at least this got me out of the house, don't you know?" He told her, quite ingeniously.

"Of course," she agreed. "It must be quite tedious, being forced to stay out of sight, like that. How long do you think you'll be forced to continue?"

"Oh, God, I don't know. I thought he'd find the blasted thing by now. If I hadn't been so mutton-headed, and I do admit freely it was all my fault—"

"Losing the snuffbox, you mean?" Cordelia put in, keeping her voice quiet.

"Oh, you do know about it. And here he's been harping on about me keeping my clapper shut!. Then he tells the first pretty girl. Well, I admit, you're not quite the common . . . well, anyhow. Yes, that's what Ransom's been about, but it's been harder to track down than we thought it would be. If I hadn't been such a lackwit . . ."

"How did it happen?" Cordelia forced herself to keep her tone sympathetic and not at all urgent, like an understanding older sister.

Avery seemed to need little encouragement to unburden his soul. Perhaps Ransom had not been terribly gracious about his younger brother's role in this fiasco.

"It started with a small, ah, indiscretion up at Oxford, don't you know? An innkeeper's daughter. But likely you don't want to know the details on that."

"Probably not," Cordelia agreed.

Avery looked a little flustered. Relieved, he hurried on. "So I was sent down for the rest of the term, and Ransom gave me a regular chewing out. I thought I could get a little town bronze, don't you know, but he told me I should go and make myself useful at the rectory with Cousin Giles and do good works and all."

He looked so downcast at that memory that Cordelia had to bite her lip not to laugh.

"So I did," Avery said solemnly. "I ladled out soup at the soup kitchen, and I talked to the unemployed men. Did you know they hire little children to work in the factories and leave the men without work? Shocking thing to do!"

"I had heard rumors of that," she agreed.

"So when some of the labor organizers decided to arrange a march, I thought it was a jolly good idea, and I was going to march with them. Thought it was the least I could do, you know. I've never worked in a factory. Some of the men had dreadful scars from their times when they were employed. Can't think why they want to go back, really, except they need the jobs I suppose, and it can't be any better for the poor little brats, but—"

"And you marched . . ." Cordelia prompted, trying to get him back to the main part of the story before they were interrupted. She still didn't see what this had to do with the missing snuffbox.

"Oh, yes," he said, and he lowered his voice and looked around him. "Well, we had the misfortune—everything started out orderly and peaceful enough, and that's all it was supposed to be, I give you my word of honor! But things got a bit out of hand. Some of the men had been drinking, I think. And then, as bad luck would have it, ol' Prinny himself was coming out of Whitehall and turned right into our flank. And some of the men threw stones—"

"Oh, my!" Cordelia breathed, appalled.

"Oh, yes," Avery said again. He looked grim. "That's, ah,

treason, you see, attacking your prince, your future monarch. Not even big stones they were, but they broke the glass panes in his carriage."

"Did you throw them?" She stared at him.

"Of course not!" He raised his voice, then lowered it quickly again when a matron standing nearby raised her lorgnette to stare at him. "I'm not that much of a bloody . . . oh, sorry . . . fool! But in court, they said I did—got some poor fool of a miller who was trying to save his own neck to testify against me. Didn't work; they strung him up anyhow."

Cordelia shivered.

"Then the prince's guard charged the mob, and everyone ran away."

"But you weren't fast enough?"

"I didn't run!" Avery said, his tone indignant. "Sheffields don't run away from a situation of honor."

"You stood there and waited to be captured?" Cordelia suggested, her voice faint, trying to comprehend his amazing blend of honor and naivete.

"Of course." Avery frowned, remembering. "They accused me of all sorts of things. I kept trying to tell them I didn't do it, but no one wanted to listen. . . . They hauled me off to prison."

His voice sank so low she almost couldn't hear it, and he reached for a silver tray that one of the footmen was passing, snagging a glass of wine and lifting it to his lips for a hearty swig.

The servant offered the tray to Cordelia, but she shook her head.

"So, what happened?" Surely he had not escaped.

"Awful place, prison, even though they did allow me a private room, and some amenities. I waited all night and the next and the next for the bloody fools to make up their minds. I got—well, I got stinking . . . um—"

"You had too much wine?" she suggested politely.

"Yes," he agreed. "And since I was about to die, I thought the honorable thing to do would be to write an apology to my prince. So I did."

She gazed at him in horror. "I see."

"And then I drank more wine and went to sleep with my head on the table."

Passed out, he meant.

"So when they came up to say that the charge had been dropped for lack of evidence, I was . . . I was still asleep."

"Oh, no!" Cordelia exclaimed despite herself, then lowered her voice when a matron glanced at her curiously. "Did they see the confession . . . I mean, the note of apology?"

"No, the only other person who knew it was there was my old valet, Helborn, who had been allowed in to wait on me. He had sense enough to know the note had to be got rid of, you see; apparently I had told him what I was writing, or I'd be on my way to the gallows once again. But there was no way to destroy the note. It was summer and there was no fire in the hearth. And who knew if they would search me before they let me out, even then? So our good Helborn thought of the snuffbox, a legacy from our grandfather, which I always carried with me. He folded the note very small and hid it inside the secret compartment. Then he slapped me about a bit, and propped me against him and half-carried me out of the prison."

"Oh." Cordelia felt weak. "But—"

"Good ol' Helborn tried to get a message to my brother and tried to tell me what he had done, too, but I fear I wouldn't listen. I was still a bit, ah, giddy and now crazy with relief. I'd been sure that I'd not see another dawn, you see, so to celebrate my release, I threw myself into a night of more drinking, gambling, and other, ah, activities. As bad luck would have it, I lost all the blunt in my pockets, and being still very foxed, I found the jeweled snuffbox, and pledged it in a round of cards, losing it to Nettles."

Cordelia couldn't speak. She stared at him.

He nodded miserably.

"I know. Only later did I remember writing the note and learn that Helborn had inserted it into the box. Now Ransom gives me a tongue-lashing every day and twice on Sunday and tells me to stay out of sight in case the guard are on the lookout for me again. But I cajoled him into allowing me to accept tonight's invitation—such an important man. I haven't been out of the rectory in days, and anyhow, who would dare take one of the marquis's guests away?"

Cordelia hoped he was right. She stared at the young man's feckless grin with some horror; how could he even sleep at night? And no wonder Ransom had not wanted to share such a secret. "You must be careful not to tell anyone this story, Avery!" she told him, keeping her voice very low.

"But you already knew," he pointed out.

"Oh, of course," she said, feeling a flush of guilt. "But no one else!"

"Oh, I won't. Come along, let's listen to that pretty girl playing the pianoforte. She's got a speaking pair of eyes, and I'm not allowed to flirt with you. Ransom said if I did, he'd have my hide and wear it for bedroom slippers."

A little startled at this matter-of-fact pronouncement, Cordelia followed the young man across to stand near the musical instrument and admire the fair young lady who was singing ballads and running her hands across the keyboard.

Ransom would not allow his imprudent younger brother to flirt with her? Because he was not inclined to think about the consequences of his actions, no doubt that was all. . . . Or because Ransom had other feelings, other reasons? She dared to sneak a quick look across the room and found that Ransom Sheffield's silvery gaze was fastened upon her. Blushing, she bit her lip and pretended to be intensely interested in the music.

When the tune ended, she parted from her young escort and left him trying to strike up a conversation with the ballad singer. She wandered past several groups of chatting guests and then looked up to find Ransom Sheffield approaching her. She paused and waited for him to come up to her.

"I supposed you got it all out of him? How my idiot brother"—Ransom shook his head—"came very close to giving the authorities the only proof they needed to send him straight to the gallows."

"You don't really think he'll still be . . . be at risk?"

"Do I think he could still be executed for treason? It's easily possible. The government would love to make an example of a few more troublemakers," Ransom spoke quietly, as they stood close together near the large chimney piece. He leaned one hand against the white marble and stood perhaps somewhat closer to her than propriety might smile upon, but in her concern for Avery, she forgot to scold him for forgetting the social dictates.

"Then you must recover that letter," she said, her voice firm. Young Avery did not seem very well endowed with common sense, but he also did not deserve to die for one mistake, she thought. She could not see that the younger man had an ounce of real meanness in his entire body. "I will ask Mr. Druid if he will help you get past the locked door."

He lifted those arching brows in surprise as she added quickly, "But you must take care not to let the conjurer get caught. I don't wish the poor man to go back to prison!"

"Nor do I," he agreed. "Neither would I wish to visit the place, myself. His Majesty's gaols are said to be unpleasant, unwholesome abodes, beneficial neither to the body nor the spirit." He flashed one of his brief sardonic grins, but his eyes had warmed and seemed to linger on her face.

She tried not to blush again, hoping that Marian, or—worse, the marquis himself—was not observing this exchange. They were not alone, of course; the drawing room was crowded with people, all chattering loudly, and under cover of the noise she and Ransom could talk in relative privacy. Across the room she could see Ophelia chatting merrily with Giles Sheffield, who smiled back at her.

But surely no one else was plotting a robbery while nattering in this elegant nobleman's buff- and coral-colored drawing room. It was strange enough being here at all; despite her new clothes, she felt like a cuckoo in a lark's nest. All around them, conversations hummed as young people flirted and laughed. Turbaned matrons discussed fashions and faux pas, and gentlemen talked politics and sports.

And she and Mr. Sheffield quietly planned a crime which she only hoped would not make them the topic of the most lurid gossip at the marchioness's next dinner party!

When the guests began to depart, the Sheffield party took

their leave, and she and Ophelia made polite farewells to all the guests. When it was time to climb the stairs, Ophelia clasped Marian's hand and said impulsively, "Oh, thank you for such a lovely dinner party, Marian, you are the most wonderful almost relation we ever have had!"

Their hostess laughed, a clear melodious sound which made her husband's expression soften.

"Yes, thank you," Cordelia agreed, "you have been so kind."

"No need for thanks, my dears," Marion told them, her smile kind. "Why do I suspect that my guest list helped make the evening so enjoyable?"

Ophelia only grinned, and Cordelia looked away, hoping her expression did not reveal too much. It was true; it had made all the difference that the Sheffield cousins had been invited. And having Avery there so that she could extract a missing part of the puzzle had advanced her understanding wonderfully.

Now they had to act upon it!

The next day at the theater, she added a trim of wide lace around Ophelia's half mask, less to embellish the mask than to add to its ability to hide her twin's face.

"And if the manager objects to this mask, you will drop out of the play, Ophelia, no if's, and's or but's!" she told her sister firmly.

Ophelia looked unexpectedly meek. "I'm sure he will not; it's an essential part of the plot line now. I have explained it all in the dialogue. And anyhow—"

"Just be sure you keep the mask on!" Cordelia told her sister, biting off a stray thread with a snip of her teeth.

Then, ignoring the always high pile of mending in her sewing basket, she went to find Mr. Druid.

She located the conjurer in a corner of the backstage area, working a trick which seemed to involve two ropes and three tarnished gold-colored rings. As she came up, he dropped one of them and it clattered across the floor.

"Oh, dear," the man muttered.

She reached down and retrieved it for him and received his thanks. Then she explained her errand, adding that Ransom had promised to take the greatest care. "And when he gets inside, you must come back down to the stage level and have nothing more to do with it, Mr. Druid. Neither of us want you to get into any trouble. If it were not deeply important to . . . to a member of Mr. Shetfield's family—a matter of life or death—he would not risk it, either."

The magician nodded glumly. "Of course," he agreed. "I will take the greatest care. But there are others at risk here, too, you know. Are you aware that Mr. Nettles is putting out broadsheets advertising that the play opening next week will feature a lady of quality treading the boards?"

"What?" Cordelia gasped. "Mr. Nettles is the one who is spreading the word?"

Mr. Druid nodded again. "He's been sending the papers out with street boys. I saw a couple of boys I know and I read them." He took a grimy sheet from an inner pocket and tried to smooth out the creases so she could more easily read the lines of print.

MALORY ROAD THEATER PRESENTS MUSICAL
AND NOVELTY ACTS FOR YOUR AMUSEMENT
and
A PLAY OF CUNNING AND HUMOROUS INTENT
WHICH WILL FEATURE FOR YOUR ENTERTAINMENT
A GENUINE AND BONAFIDE
LADY OF QUALITY
ACTING FOR THE FIRST TIME UPON A LONDON STAGE
TO BE SEEN
ONLY
AT THE MALORY ROAD THEATER . . .

The dates and admission fees were listed, and they were just as exorbitant as Miss Hardy had told them last night at the dinner party.

"That rat!" Cordelia fumed. "Why would he do this?"

Mr. Druid didn't reply, but Cordelia answered herself. "To

get a bigger audience, of course, to make more money. Oh, he is a devil!"

"I fear the god Mammon will make devils of us all, my child, if we are not vigilant," the conjurer said, rubbing the front of his much patched green coat.

Cordelia drew a deep breath to calm herself. "Thank you, Mr. Druid. Don't tell my sister just yet. I'll explain this to her tonight when we're alone. I don't want her to rush into the manager's office and make a scene so that everyone hears."

The magician nodded. "Just so you know that you can't trust him," he said, his voice barely above a whisper. Then he withdrew to return to his practice.

Cordelia stared grimly at a cobweb in the corner and was still sitting there unmoving when someone else appeared in her doorway. She looked up to see Venetia.

"You got my petticoat mended yet?"

"Oh, yes, I think I did that yesterday." Cordelia rummaged through her basket and found the article of clothing. "Here you are. Is your sister with you today?" She looked past the fair-haired actress to the younger girl who stood just behind Venetia, dressed in plain muslin, her hair pulled back without adornment. She peeked shyly around her sister, but hadn't spoken.

Venetia sighed and nodded. "Yeah. I don't like to, don't like the way ol' Nettles looks at 'er and she's too young to be on the stage no matter what 'e says. But she don't like to stay alone in our room, neither. The man across the 'all, 'e's been bothering 'er, like, and I don't want 'im putting 'is grimy 'ands on 'er!"

"Of course not," Cordelia agreed, startled. The child didn't look older than ten or so. "You don't have any family whom you trust for her to stay with?"

Venetia shook her head. "We 'ad an auntie, but she died last week of the consumption, poor old dear."

The girl sniffed at the reminder.

"I'm so sorry to hear it," Cordelia said. "If you need somewhere to sit while your sister is rehearsing on stage, you can come and sit with me."

"That's right kind of you," Venetia flashed a quick grin. "'Er name is Sal. Say thank'ee, Sal."

Sal bobbed a quick curtsy but still couldn't seem to find her tongue. Cordelia smiled at the girl.

When the two left, however, Cordelia went back to worrying about her own sister. What other tricks did Nettles have up his sleeve? She was beginning to suspect that he was as full of artifices as the conjurer and much less trustworthy!

She told Ophelia about the handbills in the carriage on their ride home, and they had a brisk and unproductive argument.

"I don't care," Ophelia said. "I am not dropping out of the play, Cordelia."

"But if the whole of Society recognizes you—"

"How can they recognize me if they have never seen me?"

"They are going to see you! If Marian persists in taking us into Society, we are going to meet people as ourselves. And then these same people, or some of them, are going to come to the theater—they are bound to, Ophelia!"

"I have a mask—"

"Which only covers part of your face!" Cordelia wanted to grab her sister and shake some sense into her. "You can still see your mouth, your nose, the shape of your chin, your hair, so much that makes you who you are. There will be an immense amount of gossip, Ophelia. It's not worth it!"

"Yes, it is!" Ophelia raised her voice, too. "I have waited my whole life for this moment, Cordelia. No one and nothing will take this away from me. I do not care if Mr. Nettles hires a town crier to climb the Tower of London and proclaim it to the entire City. I am going to perform my part in the play. No one can stop me!"

Cordelia found her nails were digging into her palms. She wanted to slap her sister's face so badly; she wanted to scream. And she could do neither. They were pulling into the square where the marquis's house sat, and the carriage was slowing to a stop.

The groom opened the door of the carriage. Flushed with emotion, they had to smooth their expressions as best they could, climb out of the carriage and enter the house. Thank heavens Marian was not there to greet them, and they could hurry up to their own rooms. Cordelia heard Ophelia's door slam. She shut her own door quickly and leaned against it.

Ophelia was the most stubborn, exasperating, mule-headed—

And if there was a scandal, and no one in the Ton would recognize her ever again, if the scandal followed her even into Yorkshire and Ophelia's reputation was ruined, she would be so devastated. She said she would not regret it now, but she would, someday . . .

Cordelia threw herself down upon her bed and pressed her palms against her eyes, not sure whether to scream—at last—or to weep.

Thirteen

*Being launched into Society by a marquis and mar-
chioness*, even by means of a quiet dinner party, seemed
to guarantee two attractive and, thanks again to their generous
hostess, well-dressed young ladies an easy entree to as much
of the Ton's entertainments as they wished to enjoy. The notes
of invitation came pouring in.

Marian opened the letters and read them to the girls as they
all sat at the dining table the next morning. "Lady Roberson
is giving a small supper dance this Saturday. She begs us to
excuse the short notice . . . And in fact, I think you would enjoy it."

Cordelia exchanged a glance with her sister. How could
they possibly manage a social life in Society while trying to
keep Ophelia's secret life as an actress hidden? Just the thought
of it made her heart beat fast, and her twin must be nearly
frantic.

But Ophelia, as if guessing her sister's thoughts, lifted her
chin. "Of course, if you would like us to attend," she said, her
tone more polite than enthused.

Marion shook her head slightly. "You are the most unusual

young ladies I have ever met," she said, chuckling. "Oh, I know, I know. Your play is of paramount importance. And I was never a typical young lady of fashion, myself, so who am I to judge? But I do think you should have some taste of Society, so yes, I will tell Angela we will come, and there are more amusements for next week."

The play would have opened, by that time, Cordelia thought, suddenly having no appetite for her excellent omelet. She put down her fork and had to swallow hard to get down the last morsel. Oh, how would this real life imbroglio—so much more tangled than even the ins and outs of Ophelia's concocted storyline for the comedy about to open—play out?

Who could say?

The butler appeared in the doorway. His expression was slightly disapproving, but then, it always was.

"Is the carriage ready?" Ophelia asked, putting down her napkin and rising even before he could answer.

"Yes, miss."

Cordelia bade farewell to Marian and followed her sister to the vehicle. Once inside, she turned to her twin. But Ophelia looked already lost in thought, withdrawing deep inside herself. Cordelia gave up. Any further attempts at persuasion were useless.

When they reached the theater, she set herself to thinking of ways she could further disguise her sister. Ophelia refused to allow a bigger mask.

"I can barely see as it is. Do you want me to fall on my face in the middle of my biggest scene?" she had demanded. "And I have to be able to speak and be heard!"

No, she didn't want to make her sister look ridiculous—or risk her pulling off the mask in desperation!

They had discussed a wig; there were a few among the costumes, but they had been worn many times by many actors and looked mangy as a result. And Cordelia feared they teemed with lice, so she could hardly blame her sister for giving a decisive thumbs-down to that idea.

So she set to work to construct a large floppy cap that would cover most of her hair. It might not be the most flattering head-wear, but just now, she simply wished to conceal as much about her sister which would give away her identity off the stage as possible—and to hell with obscuring her natural beauty!

So rehearsals continued as usual. Mr. Nettles stayed out of Cordelia's way, which was just as well; she feared she might give way to her anger and accost the man. How Ophelia contained emotions Cordelia couldn't imagine; her twin was so far into her role by now that she almost didn't think of herself.

And on Saturday evening after reheasal, the girls did a quick wash and change into new gowns. They were soon back into the carriage with Marian—the marquis had bowed out of this pleasure, not, his wife said, being fond of dancing—and soon were being handed down by their groom.

The house whose steps they climbed was another grand edifice, all its candles flaring, the entry hall crowded with guests in silks and satins, and the noise from the upper levels already high. If this was what Lady Roberson called a small dance, Cordelia thought, she would hate to see a large one!

They climbed the staircase behind a few other latecomers and then paused in the doorway as the footman bellowed their names. A number of faces turned to regard them with curiosity in their expressions.

"Lady Gillingham, Miss Cordelia Applegate, Miss Ophelia Applegate."

Their hostess was a short stout woman who seized on the marchioness, smiled briefly at the twins and hooked her arms through Marian's. "Oh, so glad you made it, Marian, you and your lovely guests. I am more than ready to sit down; my feet are killing me. Come, let's have some champagne. My butler assures me this is a very tolerable batch."

Marian smiled at the sisters and allowed herself to be swept away.

Left on their own—at least they had each other—Cordelia glanced at the crowd and then back at her sister.

"I could have stayed at home and learned my new lines," her sister grumbled under her breath.

"If you would stop rewriting the script, you wouldn't have new lines to learn," Cordelia pointed out mildly. "And don't speak about that here. Someone may overhear you."

Since Ophelia lived, breathed and practically had the play coming out her pores, that was easy to say but hard to enforce, Cordelia knew. Then she spied a familiar face amid the many strange ones and it drove her apprehensions out of her mind.

"Mr. Sheffield! What are you doing here?" she blurted.

Ophelia turned swiftly to see which of the Sheffields approached them, then her face fell. It was Ransom Sheffield who gave them an easy bow.

"You're surprised. I was somehow sure it was to you that I owed this sudden demand for my company among the more lofty reaches of the Ton," he pointed out with his usual sardonic grin.

"Lady Roberson was one of the dinner guests on Thursday," Cordelia explained, hearing the stiffness in her own voice. "I suppose she thought, or Marian told her . . . oh, I don't know. But it's . . . it's nice to see a friendly face, I admit."

"Yes, indeed," Ophelia agreed. "I don't suppose—" She looked over his shoulder for a moment.

Ransom read her thought as easily as Cordelia did herself.

"My cousin was invited as well, although thankfully not my incorrigible younger brother. But at the last minute, Giles was sent word of a widow and her children about to be turned out into the street by their landlord for not paying their rent. So he lightened my pockets of all my spare coin—I shall have to walk home tonight, I fear—and left to save the family from losing the roof over their heads."

"Oh." Ophelia's expression still revealed disappointment but now it was mixed with pride, as well.

"He's good man, your cousin," Cordelia said.

"Yes, a better man than I, any day," Ransom agreed, his tone almost a warning.

She looked at him curiously. Why did he persist in trying to dissuade her of any positive opinions that she might form of him? Was he not risking his own neck to save his brother's? Was he allowed no credit for that?

The soft music that had been playing in the background faded, and the unseen musicians, hidden by the crowd, now struck up a graceful dance tune.

"Shall we indulge?" Ransom offered her his arm.

With one glance toward her sister—Ophelia nodded and motioned to her to go on; two young men were already moving toward Ophelia, so she would not miss her chance if she wished for a partner—Cordelia did not hesitate.

She took his offer even as she thought what a mass of contradictions he was. But she would have taken advantage of any excuse to lay her hand upon his arm, to enjoy the feel of his firm muscle beneath the smooth superfine. He was so purely masculine, such restrained energy just waiting to be released, that she could almost feel the vibrations of his just contained strength, as if he were one of her new brother-in-law's wild beasts held in check behind a barred door.

Juliana's new husband had showed her sisters exotic beasts from Africa and Asia, safely housed in spacious enclosures, before he and Juliana had set out on a long honeymoon voyage. Juliana had confided they would like as not come back with a cargo of even more unusual creatures. At the time Cordelia had wondered that anyone would be attracted to such wild and dangerous animals.

Now, perhaps, she understood.

Ransom Sheffield was dangerous, too, in his own way. His odd-colored eyes could be cold one moment, hot with nascent passion the next. He could warn her off one moment and seem to tease her with invitation a second later. She had never met a man quite like him—and she did not even want to think about letting him go!

Too soon they reached the dance floor and she was forced to let go of his arm. They had to part, he to stand with the line of gentlemen, she with the ladies. He made his bow, she her curtsy as the dance began.

It was a dance familiar to her. Even in Yorkshire, they had gone to small assemblies. Her older sisters had sacrificed to allow the twins to have presentable gowns, to go to dances in a nearby town or at their neighbors's house parties. It occurred to her almost for the first time that her sisters might have wished to go to dances, too. Cordelia felt a twinge of guilt.

But of course Lauryn had married young and attended assemblies and parties with her husband. Juliana, to everyone's surprise, had come to London and found a husband, too. And Madeline, their eldest sister, dear stern Maddie, swore she would never leave their father and apparently found all her contentment in being the mistress of her father's house, so—

The dance brought them together, and the warm touch of his hand, even through their thin gloves, seemed to send a spark of feeling that resonated through her body and left a quiver of emotion deep in her belly. Cordelia forgot everything else. They turned and twisted and then she had to step away and let go of his hand. Feeling strangely breathless, she went back to her place in line and watched the next couple go through their paces. But in her mind, she still felt the echoes of the effects that Ransom Sheffield always produced in her.

He was a dangerous beast, indeed!

No, she told herself, trying hard not to catch his eye, afraid he might somehow guess what she was thinking, and then how would she ever face him again? He was no beast; this was insane to even jest about. He was a man, she told herself sternly, only a man.

The whole line of males and females came together now, and she was able to reach for his hand, to feel his other hand on her shoulder as he guided her easily through the next steps. And every touch thrilled her.

Oh, yes, he was a man—and such a man!

And again, she did not dare look up into his face. But she felt his breath on her cheek, and somehow he seemed to be breathing more quickly than usual. She was sure it was not the stately steps of the dance which fatigued a man in such good form.

Was it possible her closeness affected him, as well?

This was such a remarkable thought that she forgot circumspection, threw away her sense of caution and glanced up into his face. And the silvery tint of his gray eyes caught her as surely as any trap had ever closed upon a song bird, cutting off its trill. What he saw in her eyes, she couldn't have said, but she knew that her breath seemed to stop in her throat, and the shivery ache deep inside her grew and swelled and made her knees weak and her pulse jump, and she felt what she had never ever felt before.

God, yes, he was a man, and he could teach her to feel what a woman should feel. She knew it by some instinct which men and women from the dawn of time had felt, and she, for the first time, knew in every corner of her soul.

She reached to touch his face.

Only because he quickly grabbed her hand and kissed it lightly before he gave her a precise bow did she realize that the dance had ended, and all the other couples were bowing and parting.

Flushing, Cordelia felt as if she were coming out of a trance.

"Oh," she said. "I-I beg your pardon. I don't know what I was . . . I was about."

It was a lie, and they both knew it, but she could hardly admit the truth. And he hardly needed to hear it. Her pulse was still pounding, and she felt a strong need to sit down before she fell.

"Perhaps," he said, his voice quiet, "you are overwarm?"

"Yes," she agreed, "that's it. Perchance if I had a breath of air?"

He turned her toward one of the long windows that stretched down to meet the hardwood floors and putting his arm—such strength he had—behind her back to half support her, they proceeded toward it. Managing to move without fuss through the crowd, he brought her to a partly open window and they stood in the shadows of the long draperies, half hidden from the rest of the guests.

By this time Cordelia was able to fan herself with her small silk fan. She felt like a fool. How did one admit to being overcome by pure passion? What was wrong with her? Juliana had told her a little about her own courtship, and how strong one's body could react to a man one had feelings for, but still . . .

Cordelia stared out the window into a dark garden where occasional torches lit up shadowy shrubbery and little else. She could think of nothing sensible to say, so she pressed her lips together and said nothing at all.

The silence stretched. Accustomed to sophisticated London coquettes and suave flirtations, Ransom must think her ridiculous. Cordelia hoped she would not burst into tears. Would Marian let her go sit in the carriage until they could go home? She didn't want to ruin the party for Ophelia, but—

She blinked hard, but one unbidden tear slipped out anyhow. Damn!

Unfortunately, he noticed. Ransom caught the drop on one fingertip before it slipped down her cheek. "Are you still feeling unwell? Shall I call for Lady Gillingham? Or fetch a maid servant?"

"No!" she said. "I-I'm sorry to be such a . . . such a . . . well, such an idiot."

She looked up at him for the first time since they had entered the window enclosure, and he lowered his head, merely in sympathy, she thought. His eyes were not as cynical as they often were, and he smiled back at her.

"I don't see anything idiotic here," he said softly. He bent his head.

And he kissed her. This time it was, if possible, even better. His lips and hers seemed to fit perfectly together, and the feelings that surged through her body . . . She leaned into him and all trace of doubt and anxiety slipped away, like smoke up a chimney.

But the flames that he always kindled, merely by the touch of his hand, leaped into a raging bonfire, and the hunger that lay just below the surface now howled for more, grew to famine proportions.

When at last they broke apart, both were breathless.

"As much as I would like to pursue that embrace, my d— Miss Applegate," Ransom said, his voice tight. "I fear we would be seen. Some keen-eyed matron may have already spotted our transgression, in which case, this time I may truly be called out by the marquis."

Cordelia felt a stab of anxiety. "Oh, surely not!"

"We shall hope not." He grinned briefly at her. "But we must go back into the public view, as much as I would wish not. And for the next set, you should dance with someone else."

As little as she wished for a different partner, Cordelia could see the sense in that, to avert malicious gossip, so she nodded reluctantly. She also found she had to exercise all her self control to keep from leaping on the man beside her and throwing her arms about his neck and shoving him to the floor . . . and talk about wild beasts!

Sighing, she wondered just what instincts she had awakened inside her own body. Gracious. She should have spent more time talking to her married sisters!

But she allowed Ransom to take her back to her twin, who had danced with a young man they had met at the marchioness's dinner party, and then they were both approached by new partners.

Cordelia chatted politely and managed to get through the next set, although when her partner, an otherwise pleasing young man whose shirt collars were so high he could barely turn his head, remarked, "I say, have you heard that the new play opening next week at Malory Road has a lady of quality in the cast? Everyone's buzzing about it. I've got a wager on that it's the earl of Bainbridge's second daughter—the scamp will try anything! I've bought a box if you would like to go, you and your lovely twin and the marchioness, of course."

Cordelia promptly stepped on his toe. "Oh, I beg your pardon!" she said at once. "I'm afraid I wasn't attending to the form." For a few moments she minded her steps and made sure that she was breathing steadily again; she had thought herself inured to the talk about the play, but it still sent arrows of alarm through her.

"About the play—" her partner said again.

"Oh, thank you for the invitation," she told him, as they met once more in the dance. "But I'm afraid I have already made plans for that evening."

"But I didn't tell you which evening it was," he protested, his expression wounded.

"I'm busy all next week," she said, her tone firm.

It was some time before Cordelia had the chance to talk privately with her sister. She saw that her sister also seemed only civil as she danced with other partners, even though the next man had a well-formed face and, as Marian, who had performed the necessary introductions, informed them, even a baronetcy to add glamour to his name.

This pulled her thoughts away from their own predicament. Surely Ophelia was not serious about the handsome young vicar? Ophelia as a clergyman's wife, doing good deeds; how would that compliment her ambitions as an actress? Cordelia could not imagine anything more unlikely!

No, Ophelia must be thinking about her role or writing out new lines for the script in her mind, Cordelia assured herself. That was much more likely.

She herself dearly wanted to dance again with Ransom, and at the same time deeply feared getting close to him. Yet when he did not ask her again and she found the choice made for her, she felt both peeved and deeply disappointed.

And as for her other concern, when she could at last get a moment alone with Ophelia in a corner of the room, she told her about the young man's comment about the play opening.

"Yes, I know, I heard someone mention it, too," Ophelia agreed. "Happily, Marian has not, so far. But no one has brought up *my* name, you see."

"Only because so few people know you," Cordelia predicted. "Yet!"

But her sister refused to fret. Still, when it was time for the carriage to be called, both Cordelia and Ophelia were quiet on the ride home.

"Did you not enjoy the dance?" Marian asked.

"Oh, yes, it was very pleasant," Cordelia said.

"Very nice," Ophelia agreed, yawning.

Marian laughed and shook her head.

When they reached the marquis's home and went inside, the footman handed Cordelia a note. "From Yorkshire, miss. It went first to the rectory, but the vicar sent it on here."

Ophelia stopped to stare. Cordelia, after one anxious look at her twin, ripped the wax seal and pulled the letter open.

"It's from Lauryn," she said, scanning the short note. "Oh, dear. Robert, her husband, is ill, and not responding well to the local physician's treatment. He has bled him twice, but to little effect. She asks if we can procure some medicines which the village apothecary is not able to obtain." She held out a smaller sheet of paper. "The doctor thinks that these might help him, and in London they should be more easily available."

"Of course," Marian said. She handed the note to her butler. "Send this out to our own apothecary at once, and then we will send them to Yorkshire by special messenger, so have the man standing by; Miss Applegate will furnish you with the address."

"Oh, you are so good to us," Cordelia said, giving their hostess an impulsive hug. Ophelia came to join in, blinking hard, and tried to offer more thanks, but the older woman shook her head. "I am surfeit with thank-yous," she told them firmly. "I could hardly do else, when your poor brother-in-law is ailing. Go on upstairs; I know you're both tired and you will likely wish to write to your sister before you retire."

"Yes, indeed," Cordelia agreed, as Ophelia tried to smother another yawn. They hastily climbed the stairs, and Ophelia came to her room and looked over her shoulder as Cordelia penned a hasty note to her sister, promising that the medicines would soon be on their way.

It did not seem to phase Marian that her own apothecary, who most likely lived over his shop, would have to be awakened in the middle of the night. But for such an important customer, he would not likely object, and knowing Marian, she would make it worth his while, Cordelia thought.

She got out paper and an inkwell, sharpened a quill and sat down to pen a short note to her sister, explaining why they were staying with the marquis, in case their father or Maddy had not written about their change of address, and sending loving messages and their hope that Lauryn's husband would soon be on the mend. Ophelia hung over the back of the chair and added her own messages.

"Tell her the play opens next week. Tell her we send all our love to Robert. And tell her to be sure to try Grandmother's goose grease poultice."

"I don't think it's his chest, Ophelia; she speaks of pains in his side."

"Oh," Ophelia said, sounding downcast. "But it's the only remedy I know of. I just wanted to help."

"I will put it in," Cordelia promised.

They both signed the letter and Cordelia sent Ophelia on to bed, then ran it downstairs herself to give to a footman.

"Be sure it goes off to Yorkshire with the potions," she told him.

"Yes, miss," he agreed.

The next morning they all went off to church, and by special request—Ophelia's, of course—they went to Giles's parish and were able to listen to a short but sincere sermon by their former host. Gazing up at the podium, Ophelia attended to the speaker with unusually close attention.

Sitting beside her sister, Cordelia observed the glow that lit up her twin's face and bit her lip. Oh, dear. It must be true. Her sister was developing feelings for the young vicar. Was she aware of it? Did the handsome churchman share her feelings? Cordelia still could not see her twin as a clergyman's wife . . . She was so abstracted that when the vicar finished his discourse, she almost missed the cue to stand for the next part of the service.

Listening to the marquis's deep voice booming beside her, and Marian's pleasing lighter voice, Cordelia tried to put aside her disquiet. The play was about to open. She had to worry about Ophelia being recognized by half of Society. Ophelia's maybe infatuation would have to wait. Cordelia only had so much energy for her anxieties!

"Perhaps," Giles had said, "we have kept him closed in too long. A healthy young man cannot be kept in a box, Ransom."

"Better than having his body, *sans* head, interred in one!" Ransom fired back, knowing his tone was savage but finding it hard to hold on to his temper.

"Why don't you take him out to your club for a while; at least it will get him out of the house, let him be around other people, without him getting too rowdy or being tempted to make too much fuss," the vicar persisted.

So on Friday night when Ransom knew that White's would be crowded and few of the members would remember who was about, he told Avery of his treat and was a little ashamed of how pathetically grateful the boy was to learn of his few hours of proffered freedom.

He was only trying to save the lad's bloody neck, he told himself, as his brother hurried to pull himself into a decent coat and to tie his neckcloth into a perfect Oriental, or whatever the young sprigs of fashion thought was the style of the moment.

They took a hackney down to White's. Ransom had left his own carriage in the country; Giles had little room at the rectory to house a carriage and the small gig that the vicar used around the parish took up his only space in the carriage house.

Ransom left Avery to look around and was greeted by a few of his own friends. He had just been invited to sit down to a hand of cards when he saw one of the servants come up and speak to Avery. His brother gave start of surprise.

Ransom made an excuse to turn away and went to see what had made his brother pale.

"What is it?"

Avery showed him the note. "Someone left a message here for me."

"What? You're not even a member!"

Ransom turned to the footman. "The note was left for my brother?"

The servant nodded. "Yes, sir, it was for Mr. Avery Sheffield, sir. I made certain of that, not Mr. Ransom Sheffield. I did think it strange, sir, but I supposed it was acceptable."

"Do you know the name of the man who left it?"

"'E didn't say, sir, just, ah, left me a coin to deliver it the next time Mr. Avery came in. You'll recall that you brought 'im in a few weeks ago with you, sir, so I thought 'e might be back."

"Do you remember what he looked like, this man who left the note?" Ransom persisted.

The footman wrinkled his brow. "'E was shorter than you, sir, and a bit stouter, but that's all that I recall."

Ransom gave the servant a coin and let him return to serving glasses of wine and spirits.

Then his brother showed him the note. When the paper was unfolded, the message inside made Ransom grit his teeth.

> *If you wish the letter inside the snuffbox to be return'd to you, and not given o'r to the Prince Regent and his hangman, ye must bring 10,000 pounds to exchange in a week's time. Ye'll get a ms where to bring it, all in gold.*

It was written in a clumsy block script, probably to prevent the handwriting from being identified.

"Who—" Avery began, though his lips seemed to want to chatter. "Who could have sent it, do you think?"

"Who else but the man you lost the snuffbox to? Nettles is shorter and stouter than I am."

"So are most of the men in London," Avery pointed out, his tone plaintive.

"True. And he could have sold the box to someone else since he won it. I shall have to find the bloody thing right away and see if the letter is still there," Ransom said, crumpling the letter into a wad inside his palm and tossing it into the fire where they both watched it go up in smoke.

For a moment they stood in silence, then Avery said, "I don't have ten thousand pounds, Ransom."

"I could raise that much, I suppose, if I sold off most of my shares in the Fund, or let go the smaller estate in—"

"No!" Avery interrupted, his voice just a little squeaky.

Ransom looked at him in surprise.

"I'll not see you beggared to save me from my own stupidity," his brother continued more quietly. "You will not pay off a blackmailer for my sake."

"I was about to say, it would stick in my craw to reward a snake like that," Ransom agreed, his tone grim. "We shall have to retrieve the note, that is all, before he can use it to harm you.

And the first thing we have to do is find out if it is Nettles who has it or not. And we don't have any time to waste!"

On Monday, the twins found the tension at the theater had escalated to a significant degree. Tuesday was the dress rehearsal, and Wednesday was opening night. Their resident diva, Madam Tatina, the lead heroine in the play, had absolutely forbidden Ophelia to make any more changes in the script.

"Yes, I will say it, even me; your dialogue is very clever and the new lines should get me more laughs," the often tempestuous leading lady admitted with her slight Italian accent. She fixed Ophelia with her handsome brown eyes after stopping her on the way to the dressing rooms on Monday. "But no more! I have strained my poor brain as much as it will take, and with so many plays to memorize during the season as it is, enough is enough!"

For once sounding suitably meek, Ophelia agreed.

Cordelia could hardly blame her. She herself had to finish all the last-minute costume alterations as the actresses and actors hung over her, every one claiming that it had to be done now, now!

"Then why didn't you bring it to me last week?" Cordelia asked in annoyance. "I thought I was all caught up. You can't have all ripped out your hems just this morning!"

The scene shifters practiced moving the scenery about as fast as possible and in between swept out the stage and the areas in the wings, too, until dust rose in clouds and made everyone cough. Zeus's gilt-painted chariot zoomed in and out of the heavens on rusty wires until they couldn't walk across the stage without checking to see if their heads were in danger of being sliced off. Even Cordelia caught the excitement of it, and Ophelia was near to floating away, even without the help of the wires that powered the special stage effects and machinery that they were told the audience enjoyed so much.

Toward the end of the day, Ransom Sheffield appeared in

the doorway of her sewing closet. Her first reaction was a thrill of joy, just seeing him there filling the narrow doorway, her second a surge of apprehension.

"We're going to do it on opening night," he told her quietly.

"What?" she said, even though she knew a second later what he must mean.

He lowered his voice even more, so that she almost had to read his lips. "Break into Nettles's rooms. I'll find the snuffbox, extract the letter and be done with the threat to my brother. While Nettles is occupied with overseeing the performance, you can watch the stairs, Mr. Druid can get the lock undone, and I will comb the apartment."

"But what about your part? How long—"

"Trust me, I can move swiftly," he promised. "I don't go on until Act Two, and there's the other musical numbers between the First and Second Act. My, ah, talent as a performer is not terribly marked, so they have not made a great use of me."

"I wonder they have kept you on at all," she pointed out.

He grinned, showing the usual sardonic glints in his gray eyes. "I regularly grease the assistant director's palm. He thinks I am stage mad and enjoy spending my time lounging about with the actresses."

Laughing, Cordelia thought of something else. If she had to play lookout upstairs, she hoped she would not miss all of Ophelia's performance. Still, there would be more performances nightly, and Avery's life could depend on retrieving that damning confession, so she nodded. "And you will send the conjurer away immediately?"

"Of course, I said it, did I not? I always keep my word, Miss Applegate."

She nodded. But it still seemed an enterprise fraught with peril, and perhaps something in her face revealed her anxiety because he reached for her hand and pressed it gently.

Her heart leaped.

"I will see you both safe," he promised. "Although, speaking of dangerous endeavors, you do know that you and your sister are risking social condemnation. Did you know the Ton are already gossiping about the lady of quality who will appear in the show?"

Sighing, she told him about Nettles's handbills.

Ransom swore briefly beneath his breath. "Something else to add to the list of crimes for which Nettles must face accounting," he noted, his expression dark.

"But Ophelia said she does not regard the risk."

"And you?"

"I worry about my sister, I admit—" she began, but he shook his head.

"Not about your sister, Miss Applegate. About you. The two of you share the same face, or near as peas in a pod. If she is ruined socially, do you think you will not be tarred with the same brush? Among people who do not know the two of you well, who will be able to say which sister trod the boards in this, ah, delightful musical extravaganza?"

"Oh." She stared at him blankly. For some reason, that peril, which should have been obvious, had not occurred to her.

"Have I not said it before? You must think more about yourself, Cordelia," he told her.

She had heard few sweeter sounds than her Christian name on his lips. She flushed and defying her awareness of the danger, looked into his eyes. Her name on his lips, the arousing pressure of his hand, the awareness of the man standing so close . . . He took another step. Would he kiss her?

She lifted her face—

Something crashed nearby.

Ransom uttered an oath beneath his breath and stepped back. "I'd better go," he said. "Anyhow, the male dancers are about to do their bl—their wretched sword dance, and Jutes will be shouting if I'm not in my place. Just so you know, I fear I am never going to earn my living as a dancer."

She smiled reluctantly and he strode away. The scene shifter who had dropped an armload of wooden frames watched him go, then gave Cordelia a broad wink before he retrieved his burden once more.

Flushing, she ignored him and picked up her sewing again.

Oh, she wished this whole thing—opening night and all—were safely over. Would the Ton recognize her sister; and if so, what would her father, what would the marquis, say? And how would Ophelia ever live it down, not to say Cordelia herself, since as Ransom had pointed out, few people could tell them apart?

And she wished Ransom had kissed her again.

Perhaps she should stop worrying about the state of Ophelia's heart and worry about her own!

That night when she and her sister and Marian were alone in the drawing room after dinner, their hostess looked at them both with a concerned expression. "I had lunch with a few friends today, girls. Did you know that gossip is already circulating about a lady playing a part in your production?"

Oh, dear. How did they think Marian would not hear the whispers, too, when the whispers were rising into a roar as they swept through the Ton?

Cordelia shared a glance with her twin, and Ophelia rushed to answer. "It's nothing. They do not know my name, and only my stage name will appear on the playbill. I will still be wearing my mask. You must not be concerned."

"It's more than nothing, and I am concerned, but I can see that nothing short of the much touted wild horses will keep you from stepping onto that stage in two nights' time." Marian sighed. "And I dare say even if I locked you in your room—"

Ophelia looked so alarmed that Marian gave a reluctant laugh. "It was only a figure of speech, my dear."

The marquis joined them, and to Cordelia and her sister's relief, Marion changed the subject. The sisters were more than happy to make up a quiet table of whist before going up to bed early.

And then it was the day of dress rehearsal. Cordelia didn't blame her sister for her rush of excitement; she felt almost the same herself.

"'Tis the day," Nobby greeted them with uncharacteristic cheeriness.

"I'd say someone must have given him a new bottle of gin," Ransom muttered.

The theater had been swept and dusted, the rows of boxes

along the sides polished until their gilt looked almost like real gold, and even the benches in the pit seemed cleaner than usual.

The actresses bustled about backstage, and the men marched up and down swinging their wooden swords about in dangerous bursts of energy. All the actors appeared overflowing with optimism. It was a pity that everything else seemed to go wrong.

Two of the wooden swords splintered and fell to pieces when the actors practiced a sword fight in act one with a bit too much vigor, and the assistant director had to be sent to construct replacements.

"Didn't I say he was dangerous?" Ransom told Cordelia, who was given the delicate task of pulling out several splinters from his hand as he winced and looked the other way. "The next time I'm going to throttle the man and be done with it."

Then, when Madam Tatina, Ophelia and several of the junior actresses gathered onstage for an important scene, and Jutes had shouted twice for quiet, the diva waved her arms with theatrical flair and prepared to emote.

Then Zeus's chariot came off one of its wires and in its wild rush to the stage almost beheaded their diva.

Everyone, including Cordelia, who had come to stand in the wings and watch, screamed a warning or simply shrieked in dismay. Fortunately, the lady, who was stout and fairly short, ducked in time.

But when the heavy chariot at last stopped swinging on its single wire and was tackled by two scene shifters and restored to its usual double track, she sat down flat on the stage and had a noisy attack of hysterics.

"Trying to kill me—me, the most important person in the play! I am beside myself, me!" she shrieked.

"Now, me dear, now, now—" Mr. Nettles tried to pat her shoulder, but she threw him a hostile glance and continued to screech.

"'Ow about a nip of Nobby's gin, with a little chaser of rum?" He tried again.

"Gin? You think that I drink gin like a common street

'hore?" She looked so outraged that the manager quickly tried a new tack.

"No, no, what I meant to say was, I'll just run to my office and you shall 'ave some of me own wine, the best bottle I 'ave."

When, after several large glasses of wine, Madam Tatina had calmed down, she found she had ripped her skirt, and she turned on Cordelia as if it were her fault.

"This must be repaired at once," she said, lifting her Roman nose as if she were a direct descendant of the Caesars, instead of the daughter of a Cockney butcher and an Italian seamstress.

"Yes, Madam Tatina," Cordelia said, having already learned the futility of argument. The diva could quarrel all day and still have energy left to chew up half the cast.

Resigned, she watched their lead actress drop her skirt in the middle of the stage and walk off in her petticoats, still carrying her glass and the bottle of wine, with Mr. Nettles shaking his head.

When she had gone, the manager clapped his hands. "Next scene, let's go, girls!"

Cordelia picked up the wide flounced skirt and headed back to her sewing nook. Ophelia winked at her as her twin took her place onstage, and Cordelia grinned.

The show must go on.

An amazing amount of last-minute rips and tears continued to appear, so Cordelia sewed rapidly and somehow finished by the time Ophelia was ready to leave. From the roars she had heard Mr. Nettles give from the stage, the dress rehearsal had not been a great success.

"But that is supposed to guarantee a good opening night," Ophelia assured her as they rode home in the hired carriage. "And goodness knows, I'm tired enough to sleep. I was afraid I would be too nervous. I do hope we do not have guests for dinner."

Marian seemed to have thought of that, and there was no one at the dinner table but the four of them, and the sisters were able to go up early to their rooms.

Ophelia had an attack of last-minute nerves, and Cordelia

listened to her say her lines for over an hour, then she persuaded her twin to drink a glass of warm milk and go at last to bed.

And then it was upon them, the day of the play's opening night—the night Ophelia had waited so long for, the night that Ransom would finally, if all went well, retrieve the letter that threatened his brother. And both Ophelia and Cordella would learn, soon enough, if their gamble with the Ton's sagacity, and sharpness of vision, would be won or lost.

Cordelia woke early, but though she rose at once, bathed and dressed with the aid of one of the maids, she found that her twin was already downstairs.

"There is no rehearsal today, Ophelia," she told her sister, whom she found at the breakfast table, regarding a plate of eggs and beef as if it might attack her. "There is no need to go in early."

"I know, but who could sleep late?" Ophelia explained, her voice plaintive. "It is my debut on the London stage. Oh, my stomach is in knots, Cordelia!"

"Just try a little toast," Cordelia told her, patting her sister's shoulder. "Perhaps after breakfast we should take a walk about the square. A little fresh air might—"

"No, no. You must listen to me say my lines again!" Ophelia implored.

"Of course, if you wish it," Cordelia agreed at once. "But drink some tea and try to eat just a little; it will help your stomach."

So when Marian came down, Ophelia was chewing on the end of a piece of toast, her expression wan.

Their hostess sat down and chatted on a variety of innocuous subjects, and Cordelia blessed her silently for her tact.

Ophelia's tension seemed to ease a little, and she finished half a piece of her toast and several swallows of tea.

Unfortunately, when the marquis returned from an early morning walk with his small spaniel frisking about his legs, he came in to join them. His first words were, "So this is the big day, eh?"

Ophelia moaned and set her cup down so abruptly that the tea sloshed over the delicate rim. She had gone very pale.

Marian gave her husband a reproachful glance.

He looked guilty. "Oh, I see. A bit of nerves, is it? I'm sure you'll do splendidly. We have a box purchased to come along and show support, even if the theater is such a . . . well, never mind that. It's sure to be better than . . . remember that time in India, Marian, and the tiny playhouse where they were doing Romeo and Juliet with an all-male cast—bearded, yet—when the balcony collapsed and we had to run for it?"

"Yes, they tried to hide the beards behind a veil, but the veils weren't thick enough, which made Juliet a bit much to accept!" Marian laughed, and she and the marquis shared stories from their travels for several minutes while Ophelia's complexion slowly returned to normal.

When Ophelia swore she could not eat another bite— though she had barely managed half a dozen—Cordelia followed her upstairs and back to her guest chamber and listened to her again go through her part through most of the morning, until it was time at last to proceed to the theater.

Even in the carriage, Ophelia sat close to her sister and clutched her hand.

"You're going to be wonderful," Cordelia tried to reassure her. "You've been marvelous in rehearsals; you know you have. And you've waited so long for this."

Her sister nodded.

Nobby let them inside, and the backstage seemed to bustle with a new surge of energy. Cordelia accompanied her sister to the dressing room, and even though she knew that the same number of women filled it, it seemed more crowded than usual, simply because all the actresses appeared to be filled with the same nervous energy that made Ophelia stiff with anticipation.

Cordelia helped her don her costume, watched her twin powder her face and arch her brows and paint her lips, then don the mask that Cordelia had sewn so carefully. Last came the floppy cap that would hide most of her lustrous brown hair.

"You look wonderful," Cordelia told her sister, and got a tight smile in response. Ophelia tugged nervously at the low-cut neckline and adjusted the mask. "I can barely see," she muttered, as she had done many times before.

"You'll do fine," Cordelia told her.

One of the younger actresses had apparently been out to peek past the edge of the closed curtain; she came back to the dressing room all atwitter.

"The theater's packed! We've never 'ad such a crowd. We're gonna 'ave a smash 'it, unless we mess up really bad."

Ophelia quivered, and Cordelia pressed her hand. "You're not going to make any mistakes, and if you do, you'll cover them—you're good at that," she whispered.

Ophelia looked pale, but she nodded bravely. With a certain grimness, Cordelia remembered Mr. Nettles's provocative handbills and the resulting gossip among the Ton. But there was no time to worry about that just now.

A bit of melody drifted backstage and they could heard the music for the first musical numbers. Cordelia saw Mr. Druid go by the dressing room door. Had Mr. Nettles rearranged the order of the acts again? Would that throw off Ransom's timing for his attempt to get into the manager's rooms? She hadn't seen him since they had entered the theater. Worried for a moment about more than her sister's nerves, Cordelia bit her lip. She should be on her way upstairs, right now!

But how could she leave Ophelia until she was sure her sister could cope? She rose to check on Mr. Druid and see if Ransom had already moved toward the stairwell, but Ophelia, as if in answer to her thought, clutched her hand. "Don't leave me," she begged.

"I won't," Cordelia promised, now really worried about her sister—she would never have expected the usually self-confident Ophelia to have a sudden attack of nerves—as well as her own quandary.

Ransom might be waiting for her right now to play lookout. But Ophelia's hand was ice-cold, and she held to her sister with a grip of pure fear.

And now she saw the conjurer go in the other direction. She called his name, but the magician didn't seem to hear her.

"Oh, rats," she muttered. She looked around and saw Venetia, with her little sister behind her helping as the fair-haired actress dressed her own hair and pressed powder on her nose.

"Venetia, could you do something for me?" she asked. "You don't go on right away, do you?"

Venetia shook her head.

Lowering her voice, Ophelia explained that she must go to the stairwell and look for Mr. Sheffield and tell him that Cordelia had been delayed but would soon be on her way.

The other woman looked mystified, but she agreed to go, telling her sister to stay in the dressing room and not to wander out. Young Sal, who was as fair and pale of skin as her sister, nodded.

Now it was time for Ophelia to take her place in the wings, ready for her cue. Once she was onstage, reveling in her role, Cordelia would go and join Ransom, take up her place on the stairs, ready to warn Ransom if anyone came close enough to catch him inside the manager's rooms.

But first, Ophelia had to make her long-awaited debut onstage.

Her twin looked out past the side curtain, past the oil-fired footlights that danced and glittered, past the orchestra just below, past the packed benches of the pit and the boxes along the side walls that were packed with members of the Ton who stared through opera glasses and lorgnettes, eager to identify the "lady of quality" who dared to tread the boards.

Cordelia felt her sister quiver—she thought for a moment she was going to swoon; she was as pale as mist . . .

Onstage, the young man who played the lover of Marabelle, the name of Ophelia's character, said, "I think I see my beloved approaching!" He turned expectantly.

It was Ophelia's cue.

Cordelia gave her sister a tiny push.

Instead of floating gracefully onto the stage, as she had done in every rehearsal, and spouting her line of dialogue, Ophelia turned on her heel and ran back toward the dressing room.

Mr. Nettles, who had been watching the stage from a few feet away, pacing up and down as he oversaw the critical opening night—one eye on the packed house and the other on his nervous actors—gawked.

"What the hell—" He stamped after her.

Cordelia ran, too, and got there first.

"Ophelia, what is the matter?" she begged. She found her sister in the dressing room sitting in front of her portion of the looking glass. The room was now almost empty as most of the actresses were either onstage or waiting in the wings for their cues to go on. Only two minor players and Sal, Venetia's sister, watched, their mouths open.

"I can't do it," Ophelia wailed. "I can't do it, Cordelia. I never thought I would be afraid, but when I look out at all those people, all those eyes staring at me! Oh, I will die, I will die. It all goes out of my head. I can't do it."

Cordelia could think of nothing to say. She wanted to tell her sister that she would be all right once she started—but what if she were not? While she tried to think of a reassuring comment, the theater manager threw open the door and blustered into the dressing room like some tropical hurricane.

"What the hell are you doing? The actors are having to make up lines around your bloody absence! Why the hell aren't you onstage, you bloody amateur? This is what I get for giving you your big chance?"

"I'm sorry!" Ophelia was crying in earnest, now, her makeup running in rivulets down her cheeks behind her mask. "I'm sorry, but I can't do it."

"Listen to me, you stupid twit!" the manager roared, taking her by the shoulders and shaking her until her teeth chattered.

Cordelia winced, and her sister trembled even harder.

"You will go onstage if I have to strip you naked and toss you out there myself! I've advertised a lady of quality on my boards, and I will provide it! There's no way in hell I'll be forced to refund their tickets and give back a purse the size of tonight's crowd! I'd cut your damn throat first! Here, have a drink of Dutch courage, if you must, but I want you onstage in five minutes or I'll be back here to keep my word!" He drew out a pocket flask and thrust it into Ophelia's hands.

With that, he stomped out.

Dropping the flask onto the shelf that ran in front of the

looking glass, Ophelia looked as if she might faint. Her voice was the merest whisper. "Oh, what am I going to do?"

Cordelia made up her mind. "Take off your costume."

"What?" Opening her eyes wider with alarm, Ophelia swayed again on her stool.

Cordelia grabbed her sister. "Don't swoon! I'm going to take your place."

Fourteen

As he had done every day for three days, Avery Sheffield walked through the room with a silver tray, offering glasses of port to the men in the club chairs. His wig itched. He couldn't scratch beneath it until he was back in the kitchen, dammit. He tried to keep his expression impassive, even when one of the gentlemen, face hidden behind a newspaper, caught his foot and almost tripped him.

Good thing his tray was empty by now, or the wineglasses would have gone flying! He'd had the devil of a time learning to balance full glasses on a tray as it was. That would make a good bet when he went back to Oxford, he told himself, filing that idea in the back of his mind.

He'd never realized how hard, and how damned boring, the life of a servant was.

It had been his idea to keep a watch on White's and try to catch the man when he came back with the note with information on where to deliver the blackmail money. The problem was, Avery wasn't a member. Otherwise, he could have lounged in the famous bow window and eyed St. James Street at his ease, observing who came and went and keeping an eye out for any suspicious person who left a note with the servants.

But since he would only be admitted with his brother, and since Ransom was already committed to that silly theater troupe and would not beg off—it was that girl, Avery was sure of it, the actress, or maybe her sister, they looked just alike, so who could tell? Anyhow, Ransom would not help, but Avery had decided he could do it himself. He'd come up with the clever idea of posing as one of the club's servants and watching for the man this way.

He'd hadn't realized he'd actually have to *work*.

Sighing, he headed back toward the kitchen. That was when he caught sight of another footman handing a folded paper to the small man in the green morning coat. Avery's heart leaped. At last! Dropping the tray without ceremony into an empty chair, he ran forward and grabbed the plump little man and swung him about.

"Got you!" he snapped.

"Here now, have you lost your wits?" the man sputtered. "I'll see you discharged!"

Avery ignored him and snatched the paper out of his hands, holding it closer so he could decipher the cramped script. "What the hell does it say?"

"Id's my wife's special receipd for a hod doddy—she ford-dod to give id do me when I left de house," the man said. "I habe a cold in my head." And then he sneezed heavily into Avery's face.

Wiping his face on his sleeve, Avery released the man without a word and handed him back his sheet of now-drenched paper.

Looking up, he saw a small man in the doorway regarding him with alarm. And, yes, he had a folded sheet of paper in one hand.

"Wait!" Avery called. "Wait right there!"

But the drab little man turned and ran out the door and up the cobbled street.

Avery ran after him.

∼

"What?" Ophelia stared at her.

Cordelia nodded. "You know Nettles can't tell us apart. It's the only thing we can do."

"You're not afraid? All those eyes—and what about the lines?"

"I've listened to you say them for weeks. What I can't remember I'll have to fake," Cordelia said grimly. "I can't let him carry out his threat; he means it, Ophelia. He would put you out there without your mask and your gown, too, if you don't go on voluntarily. Now, hurry!"

It was the fastest change of clothes they had ever performed. With the tawdry costume in place, she didn't bother with makeup, just donned the mask, pulled on the cap, and ran for the stage, leaving Ophelia still sobbing quietly behind her and Venetia's sister patting her sister's shoulder and looking on with big eyes.

Oh, what about Ransom? But she had no time to think about that now. How would she carry this off? No time to worry about that, either, just do it.

Picking up her skirts and resisting the urge to tug at her low-cut neckline, Cordelia ran past Mr. Nettles who growled at her as she passed. "About time!"

She skidded to a stop at the edge of the stage, drew a deep breath and gave the actors onstage, who were still frantically ad-libbing, time to register that she was there. Marley, her "lover," gave a visible sigh of relief. "Ah, now I am sure I see my lover approaching."

Aware that her legs were shaking and hoping it was not obvious to the audience, Cordelia walked onstage.

Good God, there were so many people! She heard a murmur rise as the packed house looked her over.

For a moment, she felt a frisson of fear ice its way up her spine, and she felt frozen to the spot. But even as Marley watched her anxiously—he'd been forced to make up dialogue for at least ten minutes already, and she could see drops of sweat on his forehead—some leering gallant in the pit whistled in appreciation of either her short skirts or her low-cut cleavage.

That, added to Mr. Nettles's high-handed tactics, sent a surge of anger through her, and the fear receded. The line came to her. "Why, it is my own sweetheart. Perchance you came to linger on the path in hopes of finding me here?" she proclaimed, remembering to speak out, trying to make her voice as audible as possible to the people in the back of the theater.

Marley answered her with enthusiasm. "Yes, yes, my dear girl. You know my heart is true only to you!"

Recalling just in time that she was supposed to walk upstage and speak directly to the audience, she forced her feet to move. Her steps sounded hollow on the wooden stage, and the few steps sent her heart beating fast all over again. She looked out into the watching faces and said clearly, "His heart may be true, but the nether reaches of his male form I am not so sure of!"

The laugh that greeted this piece of crude humor sent a surge of adrenaline through her. Almost, she could see why some people did love performing in front of an audience. Her heart ached for her sister, who had longed for this moment and not been able to carry it out. Oh, would Ophelia be able to go on tomorrow night, or would her stage fright be permanent?

But the scene moved on, and right now Cordelia needed to concentrate; she could not even worry about Ransom and how he and Mr. Druid would make out without her help. Every moment, every line was a new challenge. She came up with most of Ophelia's lines, and when she could not remember, she made them up.

Despite his relative youth, Marley was an experienced actor, and he carried her with him through the rest of the scene. The plot of the play, which Ophelia's rewriting had improved considerably, was the usual lovers' tangle, much of it borrowed from Shakespeare, which only seemed fair as he had borrowed his own plots originally from other writers. Marabelle's lover was secretly entangled with their diva, the lead actress, who was playing fast and loose with her own lover, and they would, of course, find themselves caught in comic predicaments and engaged in noisy recriminations until the last scene, when the lovers would reunite and all would be forgiven.

Cordelia grasped in her mind to retrieve her next line. She watched from the corner of her eye as, in the nearest box, a stout matron in a diamond tiara stared at the "mystery lady" through a pair of gold encrusted opera glasses as though to fix Cordelia's face in her memory, she thought the last scene seemed an eternity away.

Ransom had stood guard on the landing while Mr. Druid put his expert fingers to bear on the lock at Mr. Nettles's door.

"Ah, quite a bit of blunt 'e's expended on this one," the conjurer said. "Not your ordinary lock, this ain't, Mr. Sheffield."

"So I gathered," Ransom said, his voice barely above a whisper. Where the hell was Cordelia? And would even Mr. Druid be able to get past this damn lock?

After what seemed an interminable time of twisting and probing with long hair-thin slivers of metal, at last he heard a faint click, and the doorknob turned.

A faint look of satisfaction on his face, the other man nodded.

"Thanks," Ransom told him. "I'm only looking for something that belongs to my family. With any luck, Nettles will not even know I've been inside."

The magician hurried toward the staircase. "I must be ready to go on after this act ends."

Hardly had he disappeared around the bend in the hall when Ransom heard soft footfalls. He stiffened. About to enter the apartment, he pulled the door almost shut and waited. Was it Cordelia, at last? She was usually prompt; what had kept her?

To his disappointment, it was the fair-haired actress that Ophelia had taken up. "Clara says 'as 'ow to tell you she's been 'eld up."

He swore beneath his breath. "Venetia, I need you to stand just here at the corner of the stairwell and whistle if anyone comes up."

"But I got to go on in a 'alf an hour," she protested. "Mr. Nettles would put me back on the street if I missed my cue."

"You don't have to stay that long," he told her. "I won't make you late. Just stay long enough to, um, count slowly to a hundred."

"I can't count that 'igh," she told him.

"Then how high can you count?"

"Um, twenty," she said, with some pride.

"Then count to twenty ten times," he instructed. "Slowly!" And he went back to the theater manager's rooms and, at long last, slipped through the doorway.

The rooms were opulently furnished but very dirty—hardly a surprise, given the manager's generally unsavory mien. Ransom wasted no time; he went through the bedroom first, starting with the bureau drawers, searching through their contents, then for anything taped beneath them or to the sides, searching next for hidden compartments. He checked the bed, under the pillows and mattresses, beneath and behind the frame, and went next to the clothespress. He patted the clothes and ran a thin knife into the linings of the man's coats and hats but could find nothing that should not be there. The boots and shoes he examined carefully, but could find no hidden compartments. He rolled back the rug and checked for loose floorboards or any secret panels in the floor, but found nothing.

The sitting room and study came next, and every piece of furniture that might hold a hidden compartment had a look, even though he had to be swift. The mantel he probed for secret cubbyholes, but again, nothing. Any piles of paper, of course, he checked, though he doubted very much that Nettles would leave such a document out in plain sight, and Ransom knew he would recognize his brother's handwriting instantly.

He spent extra time on the big desk in the study. He found the snuffbox tucked away neatly in a secret drawer in the middle section of the desk. His heart beat faster when he saw it. He paused for a moment, even though he knew he was running out of time, and touched the knob that opened the secret compartment—and then inhaled slowly . . .

Ophelia was too caught up in her own wretchedness to be aware of how much time had passed. But eventually she became aware that someone was sobbing. And this time, it was not her.

The sound was so plaintive that she lifted her head. Women had come in and gone out of the dressing room, and once Mr. Nettles himself had stormed in and out, and even the manager had failed to rouse her from her fog of misery. But this sound—

She saw Venetia sitting in front of the looking glass, drawing a thick line of kohl around her eyes, but she was crying so hard that the dark makeup ran down her cheeks as fast as she put it on. The actress wiped it off and drew it on again, but to no avail. She couldn't seem to stop weeping.

"Venetia, whatever is the matter?" Ophelia asked. She rose and went to place her arms around the quivering shoulders of the other woman.

"My sister," Venetia said, her voice faint. "My sister, 'e's sent 'er to Paradise."

"Who? What has he done to your sister? Sal was just here." Ophelia looked around for the young girl, who had been so sweet to her earlier, trying to comfort her.

"Mr. Nettles, 'e was in such a rage, 'e's sent 'er to Paradise, 'e's been threatening . . . wouldn't let 'im put 'er onstage yet—"

"Sent her to Paradise?" Trying to understand, Ophelia gasped. "He didn't . . . he didn't kill her?"

Venetia shook her head. "Paradise . . . it's one of 'is brothels, deep in Whitechapel."

"A brothel!" Ophelia shrieked, then lowered her voice hastily, glancing at the doorway to the dressing room. "Mr. Nettles owns a brothel, as well as a share in the theater?"

Venetia nodded. "'E's 'inted at it afore, but I didn't think 'e'd really do it. This time, I wasn't ere to beg 'im not to do it."

Oh, dear lord, Ophelia thought. It was her fault Cordelia had sent Venetia to Mr. Sheffield. It was her fault Mr. Nettles was so angry; it was all Ophelia's fault. And to send such a child to such a place. . . . "Surely she didn't want to go?" she faltered.

"'Course not." Venetia sobbed again. "When I got me job 'ere, I thought I could keep 'er off the streets, you know. Keep 'er safe. But now—and I got to go on in a few minutes . . . if I miss my cue, Nettles will fire me, and I'll be on the streets anyhow, and no 'elp to Sal, nohow. Even if I went myself, they got this bruiser at the door—'e'd never let me take 'er away. But me poor sister . . . oh, God 'elp 'er . . ."

She sobbed again, and Ophelia felt her mouth go dry with horror. This could not be allowed, it could not.

"I will go," she said, sitting up straighter. "Tell me how to find this place, Venetia."

"You'll never be able to get 'er out, Lily," the actress pointed out, using Ophelia's stage name. "They might just keep you captive as well. It's too dangerous!"

"I'll take a man with me," Ophelia promised.

"But Mr. Ransom is still upstairs—and I don't wanna know w'ot 'e's doing—so don't tell me," Venetia said quickly. "And who else is brave enough to face the bully boys that Mr. Nettles 'ires?"

"I know someone," Ophelia promised. "Just tell me where to find this horrid place."

Venetia rubbed at her by now black-stained cheek and gave her directions, which Ophelia tried to fix in her memory, then she told the actress not to breathe a word.

"Oh, I won't," the other woman promised, a faint gleam of hope in her eyes.

"Go on and take your place," Ophelia told her. "Oh, and wipe your face again."

After hastily powdering her cheeks, Venetia hurried away. Ophelia pulled out the small lap desk she had brought with her from Yorkshire, and on which she wrote the changes she made in the script, from beneath the curtained shelf. One of the pieces of practical advice Venetia had given her was to hide any valuables from the other girls. Ophelia took out her small store of shillings that represented her salary to date and put them in her pocket. She had to hire a hackney—she had no time to waste.

She pulled a threadbare shawl over her dress—good thing she had already changed into street clothes when she gave Cordelia her costume. Goodness, she hoped her sister was making out all right onstage, but she had no time to check on that now. Ophelia ran for the side door.

Outside, the street was thick with carriages, and there was no hope of finding the marquis's carriage, even if she had had the nerve to take away his vehicle with the owner inside the theater.

For an instant she paused. Should she try to find the marquis and get his help? But she didn't know where in the audience, in the boxes, the marquis and his wife were sitting. And if Nettles saw Ophelia searching the audience, he might suspect something. No, it was safer to go straight to Giles—

There were plenty of hackneys in the area waiting for theater patrons to emerge and she had no trouble hailing one and hiring it to take her back to the rectory. She needed a knight who would not quail at a very large quest, and she felt sure she knew where to find him.

The ride seemed very slow, but it was only her own impatience, Ophelia thought later. When the hired vehicle drew up in front of the church, she paid the man and then ran past the church itself to the vicar's residence beside it.

Ophelia prayed that Giles was home; she had not even thought that he might be away! She knocked loudly, and it seemed a year until at last someone opened the door. It was the motherly housekeeper that they had gotten to know well while she and her sister had stayed in the rectory.

"Miss Applegate," Mrs. Madigan said in surprise. "Are you all right, miss? I thought you were at your fancy relation's 'ouse these days."

"No, I mean, I am, but I need the vicar's help for a poor girl in dire distress. Is he in?" She waited for the reply, wanting to shake the words out of the woman's throat.

The housekeeper pursed her lips. "Ah, yes, miss; 'e's in 'is study. I'll just fetch 'im for you."

"No need, I know the way." And she slipped swiftly past the servant, running down the bare hallway.

Opening the door and skimming over the threadbare rugs, she almost threw herself into his arms. "Oh, Giles!"

He turned, and she was gratified to see that his face lit up, though just as quickly his brows knit when he took in her agitated expression.

"My dear Miss Applegate, is something amiss?"

"Oh, it's dreadful. You must help me save her!" The words tumbled out as she told him about the child and her abduction into the brothel. "I have the directions. We must go at once. Her sister is almost in hysterics but she dare not leave the theater or she will lose her job and she depends on it for the only honest living she can earn."

Hesitating, Ophelia had her first moment of doubt.

Giles looked concerned, yes, but he had not yet spoken. Was it possible that he would think an actress's sister not morally elevated enough to be worth retrieving from vice, not worth saving, in other words, when her retrieval would be so admittedly dangerous?

"I know it is a bad part of the city, Giles, Mr. Sheffield, but—"

"It is, indeed," he told her. "I am regretting very much that Avery is not at home and cannot accompany me. But while I wish I had another man at hand, I do know that you cannot go along, Miss Applegate. There is no way I can take a gently born female into such a part of the city and certainly not into such an establishment."

"What? I have to go. I know what the girl looks like!"

He stood and walked toward the back of the house, taking a well-worn jacket off a hook and pulling it on without slowing his steps. He hurried out the kitchen door and on to the small stable in the back of the rectory where he hooked up the gig, hitching the mare that he always drove in his errands of mercy around the neighborhood.

Ophelia knew about horses and their rigging, she lifted one

of the traces as he checked that the buckles were fastened. And all the while she argued her case.

"How will you know which girl to bring out?"

"You can describe the young woman to me," he told her patiently.

"What if she is unconscious, drugged, dazed with terror?" Ophelia demanded, her writer's imagination fertile with possibility as she imagined dreadful scenarios.

"I shall have to do the best I can. Tell me the color of her hair and eyes, if she is slim or stout, frail or sturdy," he suggested, climbing into the vehicle and picking up the traces.

"It is not enough," Ophelia told him, clambering in on the other side. "I'm sorry, Giles, I must come!" She reached for the driving rein and flicked it across the horse's back sending even the staid mare into a fast trot.

She thought he would pull up the gig, but something in her face—the desperation in her voice or her swollen eyelids, something held him back.

"I must do this!" she said simply. "To redeem myself. And we must not waste any more time arguing!"

And so they set out for Whitechapel.

When Ophelia saw the narrow filthy streets they were driving into and the ramshackle houses that lined them—and that was before it became too dark to see at all—she felt a finger of fear slip down her spine, but she refused to give in to it.

She had already let down too many people today, and it was her fault that Venetia's sister had been sent to this terrible fate. They must rescue her, even if Ophelia had to risk her own safety to do it. And looking at how tightly Giles Sheffield pressed his lips together and how his shoulders hunched over his reins, she saw that he was likely already regretting that he had allowed her to come. So she kept quiet and tried to make herself as small as possible, watching for the landmarks that Venetia had described.

She saw the ruined inn and then the tavern on the corner of the street, and at last the scarlet door and the burning tabards and the painted sign that ironically proclaimed Paradise above the doorway.

Giles drew up the gig a few houses away as, yes, she made out the burly doorman, with shoulders as wide as two men's and a face whose nose seemed to have been pushed in by a brutish hand; he looked just as formidable as Venetia had said. One of his ears seemed to have been ripped off; the other sported a large gold earring. Would Giles be able to get the kidnapped girl past him?

First they had to get in and then they had to find her.

She voiced these thoughts, and Giles looked at her sharply. "You cannot enter a brothel."

"I certainly don't want to wait out here," she pointed out.

He frowned. "You *should* have waited at the rectory," he noted, his voice only mildly accusatory. "And I should have made you."

He stared at her, and Ophelia for once did not argue; he could not very well send her back. "We need that mask right now," he said, as if thinking aloud.

"Lend me your neckcloth," she suggested.

He looked startled. "But—"

"Are you really worried about proper dress?" She met his gaze until he smiled grimly.

"I see your point." He unwound his carefully tied neckcloth, tied in a clergyman's simple fashion, and gave her the piece of white linen. She fashioned a scarf for herself which hid part of her face. She must look rather odd, and quite Puritanical, but if he wanted anonymity—

"Clever girl," he said in approval, and she beamed.

He flicked the driving reins and pulled up in front of the brothel, tossing a coin to the doorman. Patting his mare and muttering, "I hope to see you again," Giles told the man, "Take care of my horse; I don't mean to be long," and he helped Ophelia down from the high perch.

"Oh, I got more faith in you than that, gov," the man said. "A little of the ought-five brandy'll cure ye. Whatcha bringing your gal for? We got plenty."

"Personal idiosyncracy," Giles told him, his tone solemn.

"Wuh?" The man peered at them and scratched his bald

head, but he didn't try to stop them. They went through the brightly painted door and inside the brothel.

Sounds of drunken laughter, loud talk and shouts and a few clinks of a pianoforte sadly in need of tuning came from a doorway beyond.

"Stay behind me," Giles muttered. Knowing her eyes were big, Ophelia obeyed. Giles strode to the doorway and glanced in, taking a quick but comprehensive sweep of the room. Several people hailed him with drunken jollity, but he shook his head to invitations to come in and join them and instead stepped back into the hall.

"Upstairs," he said, and they quickly mounted the narrow staircase. On the first landing, he paused, and Ophelia stopped, too, a few steps behind him. She could hear a woman speak, and Giles answer her.

"You lookin' for somethin' special, dearie? Mother Nell can 'elp you."

"Maybe," he answered. "I heard you had some new girls in, young girls."

"We always 'ave new girls," she said, her giggle high-pitched. "You like them fresh, untouched maybe? Some men have a special yen for virgins, I know. Cost you more, of course!"

"Could be worth it," he answered.

Behind him, Ophelia shivered, and she could see Giles clench his fists at his side as he struggled to hide his disgust.

"Come along then, we got a pretty little redhead and a brunette," the woman said, her voice fading as if she were walking away.

"No fair-haired girls?" Giles asked quickly.

"Well, we did, but someone 'as already claimed that one," the woman said.

"Oh, God," Ophelia breathed. "Don't let us be too late."

She hurried up the rest of the steps and peeked around the corner in time to see the woman, a slatternly older woman whose red hair obviously came from the henna pots, glance at one of the rooms where the door was pulled shut. Then she kept walking and after a moment's hesitation, Giles followed.

But Ophelia stopped and put her ear to the door. Someone was sobbing. She turned the knob and, before her fear could stop her, stepped inside.

A stout man wearing only his shirt and waistcoat and an irritated expression was saying, "Here now, don't make such a fuss! How am I ever going to get—"

And curled up in the corner, clutching her cotton gown, which was ripped in several places, in front of her nude body, was a shivering blond girl—it was Sal!

"Oh, at last! Giles, in here!" Ophelia shrieked at the top of her lungs.

"What are you doing—get out of here!" the half-naked man shouted. "I only paid for the girl. I mean, if you want to be part of a threesome . . . well, I can't always perform with an adult . . . that is, maybe, but I don't know—not that it's any of your concern, but . . . just get out of here and stop making such a commotion. She's being difficult enough already!"

Seeing a familiar face, Sal's desperate expression eased and her eyes lit up. She rushed into Ophelia's arms, and Ophelia hugged the child—cradling the thin shivering body and trying to share her own warmth, wrapping the child's naked torso in her wide shawl.

"You should be ashamed of yourself, you devil!" she said to the man, who stared at her in confusion.

"Here, I'll have you whipped!" he said, his befuddlement turning to anger. "You can't address me in that manner."

"And how should she address you, Sir Geoffrey?" Giles's deep voice came from the doorway. "How do you think your wife and your neighbors would address you, if they could see you now?"

"V-vicar?" The man went white with shock, and then a wave of red flooded his face. He stuttered for a moment in dismay. He fumbled on the bed and around it for his abandoned trousers. He had, Ophelia noted with a curiously unembarrassed detachment, what were surely very unimpressive masculine accessories for such an otherwise rotund man.

Then he paused and said. "Here now—what are you doing here? Having a bit of feminine pleasure on the side yourself, eh, vicar? I think we are even, then, in our sinning." His voice was smug, and his moment of chagrin had faded.

"Why, you—" Ophelia sputtered, but Giles shook his head at her, just as she was about to engage in some highly unchristian commentary.

"I am here to rescue a kidnapped child, Sir Geoffrey. Would you like to assist us?" he asked politely. "I fear there is some danger involved. There often is, in good works."

The other man narrowed his eyes—making him look even more piglike; they were already narrow enough. "What child?" His tone was suspicious.

"This one. Did you think she volunteered for this kind of life?" Ophelia snapped. "To be abused by monsters like you? How could you treat a mere baby this way?"

"Shut your mouth!" he roared. "I've told you, I will not be lectured by a two-bit whore in a cheap whorehouse!"

And to everyone's surprise, certainly Ophelia's, the always moderate and restrained vicar took two quick steps, drew back his arm and punched Sir Geoffrey neatly in the jaw, knocking him back over the only piece of furniture in the room. The rotund Sir Geoffrey fell back over the narrow bed, clipping his head against the wall with a hollow sound like a melon hitting a wooden cutting board.

It was most satisfying, Ophelia thought.

Even the child watched with wide eyes.

"Oh, Giles," Ophelia said. "That was splendid!" If she had not still been holding Sal tightly, she would have applauded.

The vicar was breathing quickly. "I fear . . . I fear I lost my temper. However, perhaps it will be for his own good, in the long run. I think we'd better get out of here, however."

She nodded. "What about those other children, Giles?"

"Yes, I thought of that. She showed me the room they're in; come on—we must be quick before someone gets suspicious. I gave her my ten shillings, but we've made a bit of a noise here." He eased the door open and looked up and down the hall, then, when it seemed empty, led the way to another room several doors down.

"Be very quiet," Ophelia whispered to Sal, and the little girl seemed to understand. She nodded and clung close to her rescuer. Giles eased this door open, and they all crowded inside.

Two little girls even younger than Sal were huddled together on another bed, and a woman sat beside them, her back to the door. She was dressed only in a dirty shift, her sagging breasts visible beneath, and her hair was a tangle of brown which seemed not to have known a comb in years.

Ophelia tensed. Would the prostitute give them away? She had been sitting quietly, easing the redheaded child's tangled curls back from her face as she slept. The other girl, whose heritage might have been West Indian, was awake. She stared at them with large brown eyes.

But when the woman turned to stare, she did not make an outcry. "Who're you?"

"We just want to help the children," Ophelia said. "I came to rescue Sal, here; I know her sister, who was most distressed when Sal was taken away. But when we heard about these two—well, we couldn't leave them here, either."

"You're gentry, ain't you?" The woman looked them up and down with eyes that might have been a hundred years old. "W'ot about 'im?"

"He's a clergyman and a good man, I promise you. We'll see they are well cared for," Ophelia told her.

Giles said, "We will do our best to get them away safely, and then they will not be abandoned or mistreated, I give you my oath." He met her skeptical gaze with his own steady one, and she seemed to make up her mind.

She nodded and looked down at the two girls. "You'd best go, then. If you go to the third floor, you might be able to get out o'er the roof and down the outer staircase."

"Thank you," Ophelia told her, adding impulsively, "Do you want to come, too?"

The woman sighed. "Too late for me, missy. You better 'urry afore they call out the Brute on ye."

Ophelia suddenly remembered she still had two shillings tied into her handkerchief after the hackney ride; she handed it to the woman. "For looking out for the children."

Giles picked up a child in each arm. The sleeping child

woke but seemed too timid to protest, and the other put her thumb in her mouth.

"It's all right," he told them, and Ophelia patted their arms.

"You're going to be safe," she said, hoping it was true. If they could get out of this place and this neighborhood, she thought. With one arm around Sal, she followed Giles to the door, checked the hallway, and they hurried out.

They found the stairwell and, hoping the woman had advised them well, went up instead of down. On the third floor, after only a few minutes wasted, they found the trapdoor that led to the roof, and just in time, too. Shouts of alarm from below suggested that the children had been discovered to be missing.

"I believe our madam has discovered her high-priced merchandise is absent its box," Giles said softly.

The two children in his arms clung to him more tightly, and Sal shivered. Ophelia tightened her grip on the girl. They had to get these innocents out of this awful place!

With Giles to help her climb, Ophelia managed to pull herself through to the roof. Then he handed her up each child and pulled himself up.

The roof was slick with soot and gloomy with the accumulated grime of years. It was treacherous going in the dark, only a half moon occasionally showing a wan light from behind fleeting clouds, and looking for the promised outside staircase proved to be even harder. When Giles at last made out a narrow set of wooden rungs going down the side of the building, Ophelia was aghast.

"Surely she did not mean this?"

He bade the children sit quietly a few feet back from the edge, and Ophelia kept one eye on them and one eye on Giles who knelt to check the stability of the skeleton stair.

"I think she must have. But whether it will support us—"

Still on the rooftop, he leaned to test the ladder-like projections, putting weight on them with his arms. The second one he touched crumbled beneath him. He pitched forward.

Terrified that he would tumble over the side of the building, Ophelia flung herself toward him. Grasping his legs, she held on as, with a muffled curse, he slowly pulled himself back from the abyss.

When his upper body was again safely on the slippery tiles, he lay there for a moment, looking up at her. Ophelia was breathing just as hard as he partly from exertion—he was a solidly built man and bigger than she—and partly from the rush of fear that had gripped her when she'd thought he was falling.

"Well done, Miss Applegate," he said softly. "I believe you have saved me from an early demise."

On the point of tears, from relief if nothing else, she blinked hard. She mustn't frighten the children, she told herself; they'd had enough to deal with already. She couldn't fall apart now!

She gave him a tight smile, but did not trust herself to answer. Then she turned her head—was that the sound of voices from inside the brothel?

Her heart beat rapidly once more. If someone else opened the trapdoor to the roof, they would be easily seen!

Giles sat up quickly. "We must get out of sight," he said, his thoughts obviously the same as hers. "And if the ladder is not an option, then—"

He looked around. The houses were built close together in this slum, so close that they appeared only a few feet apart. He walked to the edge of the roof again, so that Ophelia held her breath, hoping he would not slip.

"I think we can jump it," he said calmly over his shoulder.

Ophelia gasped. Jump that yawning chasm, over the gap which led to the alley below, a fall which would mean certain death? And the children—their legs were not so long; which meant they would have to carry the children!

"Oh, my God!" she breathed.

He came back to where the little ones were sitting and bent down to speak to them. "Sal," he said. "Do you think you can jump to the other roof, just there? It's not really a very big distance. We have to get away from the people inside this house."

The girl measured it with her eyes, then nodded, lifting her chin. "I'm a prime jumper," she said.

She sounded quite calm, making Ophelia ashamed of her own fears. If the little girl was willing to risk her life so calmly, Ophelia could hardly do less.

"I will carry the two younger girls," he said. "I don't think their smaller legs would make the jump."

Ophelia nodded. "I will go first," she said. Or she would lose her nerve completely, she thought. Do it quickly before she could think about it, or she might freeze, as she'd done before going onstage. No, don't remember that now.

"All right, but wait just one moment."

To her mystification, he bent and picked up a pile of cinders that had collected in a mound against a chimney pot, then spread it to the edge of the roof.

"To make it less slippery," he explained. "We need a running start." He gave her a smile that, even in this dark and dangerous corner of hell, lit up her soul. "You can do it, Ophelia."

And with that to buoy her, she thought that, just maybe, she could. She smiled back, picked up her skirts to give herself room to run, then she drew a deep breath, took several long strides to the edge of the rooftop and jumped.

She made it with, well, inches to spare, falling forward onto another grimy rooftop and gasping from the impact. Her pulse beat so loudly in her ears that she could hear nothing else. In a moment or two, when she could find her breath again, Ophelia rolled over, rubbed her hands where she had scraped them in her fall and sat up, waving to Giles to show him she was all right. She didn't dare call out; the people searching for them in the brothel might hear.

He nodded and waved back. Then, it was Sal's turn.

Now Ophelia felt her heart beat fast in anxiety for the girl. "Oh, please," she prayed, and her hands clenched. She inched closer to the edge of the roof as the child started her run.

Sal sprang like a young cat and she was so close—oh, God, she wasn't going to make it! Ophelia felt her heart contract . . . no, Sal's foot just touched the edge; Ophelia leaned dangerously over the gap and grabbed Sal's arm, jerking the girl toward safety.

Sal cried out in pain and Ophelia felt the stabbing strain in her own arm, too, but she had her. They rolled together back onto the dirty rooftop. Ophelia hugged the child to her, and this time she did sob out loud.

Sal clung to her again, and Ophelia wrapped her arms around her. "You're safe, you're safe," Ophelia exclaimed. "You're here, you made it! Oh, brave girl!"

She looked up to see Giles, wasting no time, starting his run with a child in each arm. Oh, could he do it burdened with so much extra weight? But there was no question of leaving the children behind. Ophelia felt a fierce pride in him, his courage, his compassion. There was no such man to compare to Giles Sheffield in all of London, all of England, the entire world, she thought.

He leaped.

Too terrified to think, she watched him cross the empty space—it seemed to hunger for victims—but his momentum carried him on and he alit, with his two wide-eyed innocents looking too terrified to scream . . . a few feet from her.

"Oh, we've done it—" Ophelia began.

But even as he hit the roof, the weight of a grown man and two children on the decaying timbers bore its own result.

The roof gave way beneath them.

Fifteen

They plummeted, amid a rain of rotten timbers, sooty roof tiles and cinders. Buffeted by heavy wood and sharp fragments of cheap tile, Ophelia knew she cried out, and the children screamed.

In a moment she found that she lay, dazed, on a cold bare floor, covered by fragments of wood and tile. One of the children whimpered. Where was Giles? It was so dark, the moonlight barely penetrated the opening in the roof above them; she couldn't make out much of their surroundings.

"Giles?" she whispered. When there was no reply, her pulse leaped. Oh, God, don't let him be dead, she prayed. "Giles, are you hurt?"

She felt about her cautiously, first finding one of the little girls, whom she patted, finding cuts but no apparent serious injury, then another. They scooted closer to her. "Sal, where are you?"

"Here, miss," the older girl called, her voice quivering.

"Are you all right?"

"I'm a bit scraped up, but nuthin' worse than me ol' auntie used to give me wid one of 'er 'idings," the child said, sounding unexpectedly cheerful. She, too, crawled closer to Ophelia, seeming to take comfort in her closeness. Well, it was very dark in this wretched place, wherever they were. She smelled mold and the scent of a closed-up house; she wondered if it were abandoned. She hoped the floor was stronger and in better repair than the rooftop had been!

But where was Giles?

"Stay where you are, girls," she told the children, then she patted the floor around her, wincing whenever she hit a sharp piece of tile or a splintered piece of wood, seeking his larger frame. "Giles?"

At last she felt his leg. She felt her way up his body to his torso, anxiously checking for bleeding or any limb bent at an unnatural angle that would speak of broken bones. He must be unconscious, but—

She put her hand on his chest and was relieved to detect a definite rise and fall. He was breathing.

"Ophelia?" His speech sounded slightly slurred, but she was so happy to hear him speak that she felt tears flood her eyes. Glad he could not see her weakness, she blinked hard.

"How are you?" she said quickly. "Are you hurt?"

"I don't think so," he said. "I got a good blow to the head, and I'm a little woozy. What about you and the children?"

"They seem to be all right, and as for me—" She suddenly realized that one of her legs hurt quite a lot. "Um, I believe I have a cut on my upper leg; it seems to be bleeding—a good deal." She touched her thin muslin gown, what was left of it, and found it drenched with blood.

Groaning, he sat up. "Let me see . . . well, let me, with apologies, let me try to determine how bad it is."

Without comment she found his reaching hand in the darkness and guided it to her thigh. He swore beneath his breath when he found her gown wet with blood.

"We must stop the bleeding. Can you take one of your petticoats and fashion a bandage, do you think?"

She smiled. "I only have one petticoat, Giles, but I will try." At any rate, she did not have to ask him to turn his back. Moving awkwardly, she slid off her undergarment, part of it already damp, and folded it, then tied it around her upper leg, hoping it would staunch the bleeding.

"Is it helping?" he asked presently.

"I believe so," she told him.

"Try not to move," he suggested. "Here, lean on me if that helps."

It would certainly help her spirits, she thought. The children were whimpering again, however, and she called to them. "Over here, girls, just be careful of the debris on the floor; some of it is sharp."

The children crawled to them and curled up next to her other, unwounded side.

"Did anyone heed our fall, do you think?" Giles asked her, his voice quiet. "I think I blacked out briefly."

"If anyone heard, there was no sign," she told him. "I detected no outcry from the brothel."

"Then perhaps they had not gotten to the roof yet. Unless the trapdoor was open, I don't imagine the sound of our fall would have been obvious," he said. "We will hope not, anyhow."

"How," she asked, keeping her voice low, "are we going to get out of here, Giles?"

"When we can't see anything about us?" He sounded rueful. "I think we shall be forced to wait until daybreak. When we can see more, we shall try to make our escape."

Of course, then the thugs across the alley would be able to see them, as well, Ophelia thought, shivering, but it was the best they could do.

Presently, the children's breathing became even and she could tell that they slept. The two smaller girls dropped off first. Sal sighed once, and Ophelia wondered if she was reliving her terrible time in the brothel.

"I am so sorry for what happened to you, Sal. You should never have been sent to that place. Did that dreadful man hurt you?" she asked once, not sure if the girl wanted to talk about it.

She felt rather than saw the youngster shrug. She seemed to have recovered her composure.

"Naw," the child said. "Not really. He shouted at me a lot, though, a 'cause I wouldn't do what he wanted, and he waved his dillydang at me. And he ripped my best dress a 'cause I didn't want to take it off."

Ophelia swallowed. "We shall get you a new dress," she promised. "And he was a very bad man to do that."

"I hope," Sal said darkly, "a big dog comes and chews him up."

"An excellent notion," Ophelia agreed, thinking, dillydang and all. She felt Giles shake with silent laughter.

When Sal's head, too, drooped against Ophelia's arm, Ophelia shifted the girl into a more comfortable position.

"Are you all right? You seem to be a pillow for all three," Giles asked.

"How can you tell?" she asked. "It's dark as Hades in here."

"I can read your small motions," he told her. He put one arm around her. "Here, lie back against me; you must be aching from the weight of the children. How is your leg?"

"The bleeding has almost stopped, I think," she told him, shifting to lie closer to him. His body felt reassuringly firm. She was not half so frightened as she would have been in this strange adventure if he had not been here. She tried to tell him so.

"It was so good of you to come with me, Giles. I do not know what I would done, if you had not."

She felt him shake his head. "I wish to God I had not allowed you to come," he said, his voice grim. "You would not be in such mortal peril now. You would be safely back at the rectory, or at the marquis's residence—"

"Worried out of my head about you and the girls," she interrupted. "No, you needed me here, Giles, you know you did!"

"Yes, I rather think I did," he agreed.

It was an odd thing, lying so close to him in the darkness, feeling the warmth and solidity of his body and hearing the pleasing timbre of his voice in her ear. It was a strangely intimate experience. She had never felt like this with any man before, never been so close, physically or . . . or what . . . what did she feel for him that she hardly knew how to express?

"I had to come," she repeated, somehow compelled to be sure he understood. "You don't know what happened today at the theater, Giles. I had an overpowering case of stage fright.

I couldn't go on. Opening night, my lifelong dream, and I panicked. I looked out at that theater packed with people, with all those staring, judging eyes, and I couldn't do it. I wasn't good enough, and I failed everyone—me most of all."

Her voice fell away, and some of the desolation she'd felt earlier rushed back. She felt the prickle of tears behind her lids.

"That happens to many thespians, Ophelia," he said gently.

"But it shouldn't have," she protested. "I came to London to go on the stage. I ran away from home, distressed my father, my whole family, shocked the shire, or I will, when the story gets out—and heaven knows, I've done it countless times before. We're the terrible Applegate twins at home, you see. And it's really my fault, it's always been my fault. Cordelia just comes along to try to prevent me from even worse scrapes, although most people don't know it . . ."

He made no comment but his silence was somehow not censorious, and she was able to continue. Speaking into the darkness was easier than seeing his face where she might have seen condemnation, or worse, pity.

"She was the one born first, the responsible one . . . I'm the one who rushes into trouble, the dreamer, who doesn't think about consequences," she said, her voice dropping to a whisper. "I prefer stories I can make up to real life."

There, she had said it. She felt his arm tighten around her.

"Why, Ophelia?"

"Real life is too painful," she said, feeling the old familiar misery. "Our mother died after our birth, you know. Perhaps bearing two babies was too much. So, you see—"

"Ophelia, I'm so sorry."

"I've never known a mother, so, I began to make up stories . . ."

He put his hand to her face. She had been holding herself very stiff so that he would not detect it, but somehow, he had sensed, anyhow, the tears that had been slipping past her lashes and sliding down her cheeks.

He caressed her cheeks and rubbed her temples where they ached, and she sobbed aloud this time and hid her face in the

curve of his neck, feeling the warmth of his skin like a balm
soothing an old pain. And the darkness did not seem so dense
and cold, and in a while, she, too, slept.

⌒

When Cordelia had remained backstage, the play had
never seemed so long. Now, waiting for her part in Act Two to
be concluded, it seemed to go on for a year. But Marley
winked at her and offered encouraging grins, and somehow
she got through it. Between the memories she pulled up, from
all the times she had gone over Ophelia's lines with her twin,
and an occasional improvisation when she couldn't dredge up
the right words, she stumbled through it, and the laughs from
the audience seemed to indicate that her first time ever on the
boards was not a total disaster.

Oh, poor Ophelia. What she must be feeling, stuck backstage when this should have been her night!

When Cordelia had gone back to the dressing room briefly,
Ophelia had not been there, but she thought her sister might
have had to visit the necessary; her sister didn't have an attack
of nerves often, but when she did, it often affected her stomach
that way. She would have gone to see, but Mr. Nettles barged
into the room, yelling at the junior actresses to get ready for the
musical number.

"Oh, good God," Cordelia muttered. Now what? She had
not practiced the musical acts at all except for the once.

Venetia grabbed her arm. The fair-haired actress seemed to
have been crying; her face was blotchy even beneath her face
paint and her powder was caked. "Come on," she muttered.
"Just stay in the back and watch me."

Ophelia must have told the girl about their switch, Cordelia
deduced. Glad to have an ally, she nodded. But she found this
number more nerve-wracking than her acting role. She stumbled through the dance as best she could, trying to hide behind
the other dancers, and mouthing the words to lyrics she didn't
know, devoutly glad when the last notes of the song were
played.

At last the final curtain came down. Applause sounded, and around her, the other actors were flushed with the triumph of a successful opening night. Pushing the mask, which became annoying after a time, down to hang below her chin, Cordelia was mainly thankful to have fumbled through it all, but she thought of her sister with an ache in her heart. Poor Ophelia, to have missed her long-awaited night. But where was she?

They trouped off the stage, and Cordelia looked into the dressing room, which to her puzzlement showed no sign of her sister. Chattering happily, the other actresses flocked in around her and began to rub off their makeup and step out of their costumes.

Where was Ophelia? Cordelia drew Venetia aside, "Do you know where my sister can be?"

The actress lowered her voice and looked over her shoulder before she spoke. "She has gone to get help for my sister."

What had happened to Sal? She would ask later, if Venetia didn't wish to talk openly about it. Cordelia knotted her brows. She found herself whispering, too, without knowing why. "Don't leave, Venetia. I will take you home."

The actress nodded.

Cordelia barely noticed. Looking to the doorway, she glimpsed Ransom Sheffield for the first time since the beginning of Act One, and the expression on his face was grim. Her heart contracted. She hurried across the few feet that separated them.

"Did you get caught?"

Shaking his head, he motioned for her to lower her voice.

"Mr. Druid, then?"

"Your conjurer did his part and got away cleanly." But his voice was tight with tension.

Her thoughts leaped ahead. After all their dangerous skulduggery—"You didn't find the snuffbox?"

"Oh, I found it," he told her, his brows pulled together over his silvery gray eyes. "I left it where it lay, in a secret compartment in Nettles's desk drawer, no need for the villain to know we were searching his rooms. It was empty."

She found her mouth dropping open. "The note was gone?"

He nodded. "Nettles has found the secret compartment. He has the damning letter that can send my brother to the gallows, and he is trying to blackmail him with it. Worse, yet, although I took those rooms apart, I cannot find the letter itself. I don't know where he is keeping it."

She gazed anxiously up at him. "Perhaps Mr. Nettles has secret compartments of his own?"

He shook his head. "I don't think so. I checked out his desk and his bureau, his mantel and around his bed, the paneling in his rooms, every place that would be logical."

"So where could the note be?" Cordelia demanded.

"I fear he's carrying it on his person," Ransom said. "He's out front of the curtain just now, talking to some of the more influential patrons and rubbing his palms as he figures how much blunt he has made tonight."

"Wait for me," she urged. "I'll be right out."

She told Venetia she would look for her outside the side door, then prepared to change quickly into her street clothes, hoping devoutly that Ophelia would be able to take over the role tomorrow night.

But a sudden intrusion stopped her, even as her hands moved to the buttons on her bodice.

A young gallant dressed in the height of fashion, with a companion behind him, barged through the doorway without so much as a "beg pardon." "Here she is—our delicious masked mystery lady!"

At the sight of the strangers, Cordelia hastily pulled her mask back into place and tightened the ribbons. Now, to her acute embarrassment, the first young man dropped to his knee in front of her, while the other actresses giggled and called comments.

"Hooked a live 'un already, 'ave you, Lil?"

The young man took off his hat and waved it as he spoke. "Will you be my beloved, oh, darling mystery lady, and fill my heart, not to mention my bed, with love and entrancing moments of passion?"

"Certainly not!" she said, her tone sharp. "Do get up. You look ridiculous."

"Alas," he said, not moving. "She spurns me. You have a go of it, Adolphus."

As far as Cordelia could make out, his friend's idea of persuasion was to emulate a donkey and give peals of high-pitched laughter. Before he was done with his fit, three more men burst into the dressing room. Oh, heavens, what on earth was she to do? She tried to edge around them, but they had her surrounded.

And every one of them spouted nonsense, all babbling more loudly than the other. The other actresses were no help. Giving her cold looks, they seemed to think she had more admirers than her fair share and, instead of laughing this time, had turned away. Cordelia thought wildly that she would be glad to give all these silly men away if she knew how!

She was still trapped.

To her enormous relief, she looked up to see a face she knew. This time Ransom cut through the men encircling her with the ease of a practiced warrior amid a company of raw recruits. "Here you are, my dear. Your carriage awaits."

He held out a long enveloping dark cape that he must have found in the costume wardrobe. Wrapping her in it, he put one arm about her and guided her through her erstwhile admirers, who groaned and protested but were not strong enough to stop him.

Outside the dressing room, he did not pause but propelled her on toward the door. "I have spoken to the marquis and his wife and told them of the situation," he spoke quietly in her ear. "They are waiting for us in the carriage."

"Thank heavens you came to help me," she said. "I couldn't get away." She held tightly to his arm. "Oh, and we have to collect Venetia, too. She's waiting by the door."

He nodded. When they went out of the side door—quickly, so as not to allow any of the men milling about to get a look at Cordelia, who kept her head down and the hood of the cape pulled low—Ransom beckoned to Venetia, who hovered nearby.

They all slipped out the door and headed down the alley in the darkness until they came to the marquis's elegant carriage, softly lit by its carriage lamps. Ransom helped Cordelia in first and she paused to look back at him.

"Ransom . . . Mr. Sheffield . . . I have not thanked you—"

He grinned at her. "I have been invited to dinner. I will be there shortly. Now, go."

"Oh, good," she said, and ducking her head, went into the carriage without further delay.

Inside the carriage, she found the marquis and his wife waiting, Marian looking anxious.

"My dear, thank goodness," Marian said.

But when Venetia was the next to enter, the marchioness looked startled. "Hello. But, Cordelia, where is your sister?"

At the unfamiliar name, Venetia blinked. She perched on the edge of the seat, looking awed by the richness of the carriage.

Cordelia hastened to explain. "This is Venetia, one of our other actresses. Venetia, Lord and Lady Gillingham."

Venetia's eyes widened. "Cor . . . ! I mean, nice to meet 'cha, I'm sure."

"Now tell us what happened to your sister, and why Ophelia—I mean Lily—has gone and where," Cordelia told the actress.

"I don't rightly know where, Clara," Venetia said. "I told Lily that Mr. Nettles had sent me little sister to Paradise, to 'is brothel in Whitechapel, that is, and she said she knew someone who would 'elp to get 'er back. She went off, and that's all I know." She twisted her hands together in her lap, as if remembering her anxieties about her sister. "Begging your pardon for talking about brothels, my lady."

"That's quite all right." Marian bit her lip and looked at her husband, whose expression was grim.

Cordelia thought she must look just as horrified. "Oh, Venetia, that's dreadful. Sal is a child—she's only ten! And, well, it would be dreadful in any case, kidnapped for such a reason!"

"Indeed," Marian said. "John, we must do something."

"Of course," he said. Cordelia could not see his face as well in the far corner of the carriage where the darkness was more dense, but his tone would have sent shivers down a braver spine than Mr. Nettles, she thought.

"But where is, ah, Lily?" Marian continued.

Cordelia was thinking. "She would have gone to Giles for help. You both were in the audience and out of reach, practically speaking; she and Venetia could not alert Mr. Nettles to what they were doing."

Marian looked relieved. "Then let us go at once to the rectory and see if they have had success; we shall certainly pray so."

The marquis knocked on the front panel and gave new directions to the coachman, and the carriage changed direction. No one spoke, although Cordelia thought that several hearts must be beating as fast as hers.

When the church tower first came into view, then the stone wall and rectory, she breathed a sigh of relief. With any luck, Ophelia would be here, sipping a cup of tea with Giles and Sal, waiting to be collected, and they could all go back to the marquis's home and have a good dinner together.

So when they knocked at the door, and only the housekeeper was there to open it, she felt cold inside.

"The vicar ain't back yet, miss. I don't rightly know what to tell you. Oh, Mr. Ransom Sheffield is upstairs changing clothes. I'll fetch 'im."

"Please do," Cordelia said, wishing the good-natured woman were not so slow of wit.

The housekeeper showed them into the parlor, where a fire burned fitfully on the hearth, and the marquis and his wife looked as out of place as hothouse flowers in a rocky Yorkshire garden.

Yet, perhaps she wronged them. Marian took off her cloak and her husband added a log to the fire as naturally as if he had not had servants at his disposal all his life. She thought of their many treks around the world and reflected that perhaps they had had to rough it now and then and were more adaptable than she knew.

But right now, she wanted to know where Ophelia was.

Was she safe? What about Sal, sent off to a dangerous hell-hole? Oh, dear God, what had happened?

She heard a rapid clatter of steps descending the bare staircase and then in a moment, Ransom Sheffield was in the doorway. "My lord and lady, welcome to my cousin's rectory. I'm sorry he is not here to welcome you himself. I'm not sure where he has gone, but he's no doubt been called out on some errand of mercy."

"Ransom, it may have to do with Venetia's sister," Cordelia explained rapidly what they had been told and saw Ransom's expression darken. He pulled the bell rope and waited for the housekeeper to come back from the kitchen.

"Mrs. Madigan, Giles did not tell you where he was going?"

"No, Mr. Ransom, 'e didn't. You know 'e's always going off at odd hours." The woman's expression was as placid as always.

"Did he go on foot?" Ransom asked.

"No, sir, 'e 'itched up the mare and the gig," the housekeeper said.

"So he was going some distance."

She nodded. "I did think as 'ow it would be a bit of a squeeze, with the young lady along, but—"

"The young lady?" Cordelia interrupted. "Did my sister go, too?"

"He would not have allowed her to accompany him if he were actually going to this whore—to this place," the marquis barked. "Surely not!"

"You don't know how persistent, or stubborn, Lily can be," Cordelia said, her tone grim. "Oh, dear heavens."

Sharing a glance with Marian, she felt a weakness in her knees and sat down suddenly on the closest chair.

"Are you sure he did not leave me a note, Mrs. Madigan," Ransom demanded, staring hard at the housekeeper. "I cannot think why he would not leave word of his plans."

"No, sir," the servant said.

"You're quite sure?"

She shook her head.

"I looked in his study," Ransom said, as if thinking aloud. "On his desk and bureau. He left me no message at all?"

"No, sir," she repeated. "Only the note for Mr. Avery."

Everyone in the room stared at her, and Cordelia had to bite her lip to keep from exclaiming. Ransom let out a long breath. "I see. Where is *that* note, Mrs. Madigan?"

She withdrew a folded sheet of paper from her apron pocket. "Right 'ere, sir; I was keeping it safe till your brother got 'ome. 'E was supposed to be back by dinnertime, but you know your brother."

"Oh, yes, I know my brother," Ransom said, his voice tight. "Why don't you give it to me, and I will deliver it to Avery when he comes in."

"Yes, sir," she said. "If that's all?"

"You might fix the ladies some tea," he told her.

She went out the door, and as soon as it closed behind her, Ransom unfolded the note.

"My brother will understand!" he said succinctly and scanned the note.

Cordelia didn't even have to ask what Giles had written; she saw Ransom's expression change, and fear flooded her like a cold rain.

"They have gone to this place to try to find the child," she said, knowing it had to be true, as much as she wished it were not.

Ransom nodded.

Cordelia felt her chest constrict; she thought she could not breathe. Ophelia had gone into the worst part of London's underworld, with only Giles beside her, in a small open carriage and likely no defenses.

Venetia gave a small sob.

Marian said, "John, what shall we do?"

The marquis took several steps up and back on the threadbare carpet and pounded one large fist into his other hand. "Venetia, do you know where this bloody place is?"

She nodded.

He took her aside, and they talked in low voices for several minutes. Ransom came to join them and listened intently. When she had finished, the two men talked briefly, then the marquis shook his head.

"I don't think we can find it in the dark," he said. "And even if we take a small army with us, it will do no good if we merely blunder about. In fact, it would give us away and raise an alarm, giving them time to spirit away the child—and your sister and the vicar, too, if they should be captives by now—to some other location. We daren't risk it. We shall have to wait till sunrise."

Cordelia bit back a protest. She knew his words were logical, but she wanted to go after them now. What might be happening to Ophelia right now—this moment? Oh, it was just like Ophelia to dash off without thinking! And for once, she had managed to go off without Cordelia beside her, and look what had happened!

Disaster, that was what.

She had been busy saving her at the theater, taking on her role onstage, and Ophelia, her ungrateful twin, had managed to risk, not just her reputation, but her bloody life! She wanted to wring her neck—and if she were not already dead, she probably would! Cordelia was not sure whether to laugh or cry at the thought. Putting one hand to her mouth, she tried to swallow a sob.

"My dear," Marian said, coming up and putting an arm around her. "I think we need that tea. Where is the housekeeper?"

As if she had conjured her up, the door opened again and Mrs. Madigan came in with a tea tray. Marian poured out for all of them—or for the women; Ransom refused politely and found some brandy for the marquis and himself.

Cordelia drank some strong tea, and Venetia also gulped down the tea, though she eyed the brandy wistfully until Ransom almost offhandedly brought the bottle by and tipped some of it into her teacup.

"I think we should go back home and see about dinner. You need some food inside you," Marian told them.

"Yes, and I have preparations to make," the marquis added. "Sheffield, you should come."

Ransom nodded. "I will add a few words and leave the note for my dear brother, if he ever returns from his partying. This is what he thinks is staying out of sight and living a quiet life, I take it!"

However, Venetia drew Cordelia into the corner of the room and begged to be spared a visit to a marquis's home. Seeing her discomfort—even the rectory was more luxury than Venetia was accustomed to, and the grandeur of the Sinclair residence would likely leave her speechless with nerves—Cordelia agreed to her request. She spoke to the housekeeper, who was accustomed to the vicar bringing home waifs who needed nurturing. Mrs. Madigan agreed to feed Venetia a good dinner and give her a bed for the night.

Cordelia left her enough coin to get a hackney back to the theater the next day. Despite everything, Venetia could not lose her job.

"And I will let you know as soon as we hear anything about your sister, on my oath," she told the actress. "There is still hope, so don't give up; try to get some sleep tonight."

Venetia wiped her eyes. "Thank'ee, Clara. You and your sister've been way kind," she said. "Don't know why you and Lily're wanting to go onstage, when you don't need to, with good food and homes and folks like this around you." She glanced at the plain room of the rectory as if it were a palace.

Cordelia nodded. "Sometimes I wonder, too."

And when she—oh, please, God—saw her twin again, perhaps she would try to shake some sense into her, as well!

When Ophelia opened her eyes again, she saw that the blackness had softened to gray. She blinked twice and tried to focus her eyes. To say that sunlight leaked past the hole in the roof above them would be too generous, but there was a little more light in this cavernous space. She looked about her. The girls were still asleep, but Giles gazed back at her.

"Is it dawn?"

"Almost, I think," Giles answered. "Let me slip out and reconnoiter."

Nodding and trying not to wake the children, she leaned away and propped herself on one arm so he could sit up. Let the girls sleep as long as they could, she thought. Lord only knew what further peril they might face before this day had ended.

Giles got to his feet, careful of the fragments of fallen timber and tile all around them. As the light increased in almost imperceptible increments, he inched toward the far end of the long narrow space.

They must be in the attic of the house, but did it even have a window? No, there, at the far end, hidden behind some pieces of junk . . . Giles shoved the broken furniture aside and found a tiny aperture. The small square formed a slightly lighter space against the rest of the grayness. Yes, daybreak was dawning, even on this miserable street.

"Do you see anything?"

"No one is moving below," he said. "We need to go, now, before the locals awake."

Perhaps everyone next door was still asleep, Ophelia thought, with her first real stab of hope. Perhaps they had searched the brothel last night and thought that she and Giles and the girls had already made their escape and were long gone. She hoped.

She shook the children and when they woke with little cries, she did her best to reassure them.

"It's all right," she said. "But we have to go now. You must be very quiet, and watch your step. Don't step on a sharp tile. Follow behind me."

"I could carry them," Giles said.

"And if the stairs are as rotten as the roof?" she suggested.

"Good point," he admitted. "Better to spread out the weight."

So they headed for the narrow staircase in single file, Giles going first to test, gingerly, each step. Several gave way beneath him and had to be stepped over, carefully.

The children whimpered now and then but mostly followed bravely, the redheaded girl, the smallest, with her finger in her mouth. Ophelia ached for them, but she couldn't think about it just now; they had to get out of here first.

They wound their way down several levels of dirty, decaying stairs. Coughing at the dust they stirred up, no one spoke. When they reached the ground floor, Giles paused for a moment to look around, making sure there was still no sound of any inhabitant, then led the way to the front door. Here, an ancient lock gave them trouble, as no one had left them the key.

After trying without success to force it, Giles shook his head. "We'll go out one of the windows," he told Ophelia. He led the way to a window on the side of the vacant house away from the brothel. Here one of the panes was already broken, so it was easy enough to push open the window frame and climb through. No doubt all the valuables in the house, if there had ever been any, had long since been looted.

Giles jumped down, and Ophelia lowered the girls to his arms, then climbed through herself. Were they going to make it to safety?

"Do you know which way to go?" she whispered as they walked toward the alley.

"I think so," he muttered in answer. "Let's run for it as long as we can, then when we're out of breath—"

He never got to finish.

She heard the sound of a low growl, and the hair on the back of her neck rose. She saw Giles's expression and heard one of the children shriek, and she knew the worst had happened even before she turned.

Sixteen

A bulldog with a mangled ear stood planted in the dirt of the alleyway behind them. Growling, it eyed them as if just waiting to sink its teeth into their skin. And looming over the dog was the giant of a man whom Ophelia had last seen at the door of the brothel. He had pulled on a worn coat over a nightshirt, but even this incongruous outfit did not make him seem less intimidating. The gold ring in his left ear seemed to make up for his missing right ear, and his bald head shone as if it were greased; perhaps it was.

The children clung to her. Giles stepped forward in front of them.

"Thought you was so clever, did ye?" the big man taunted them. "Me dog is worth two of ye, 'e smelt ye trying to get away. I'll 'ave the small ones back now—we paid good blunt for 'em, if ye please, and I'll 'ave the woman, too, as a bonus for me bother. And just maybe I won't kill ye for all the trouble ye've caused us—maybe I'll just chuck ye around a bit, as a lesson, like."

Ophelia found her throat was too dry to swallow. She reached down and patted the younger children, who were sobbing, but then unfastened their grasping hands and, trying not to be obvious about it, pressed them upon Sal, instead.

Giles took another step closer to the hulking figure. "I'm sure God will forgive you for your sins," he said, his voice steady. "I fear I cannot."

The man laughed in surprise, but the guffaw was interrupted as Giles's fist smashed into his mouth.

The big man's head snapped back, but, to Ophelia's regret, he did not fall. He rocked slightly on his feet, and the dog barked, a sharp volley of sound. The doorman spat a mouthful of blood and then a tooth onto the dirt.

"Damn you!" he roared. "That were a good sound tooth, too!"

He swung furiously. Giles dodged the attack and struck again, but this time, the blow only glanced off the big man's ribs. Fists raised, the two men wove back and forth in the packed dirt and refuse of the narrow street.

Ophelia told Sal, "Stay here and hold onto the girls!" Then she ran back to the edge of the abandoned house and pulled up a piece of wood that lay against the foundation. Running back, she stood a few feet from the men and waited for her chance.

The big man threw another powerful blow, enough to slay a dozen men, but Giles ducked.

Giles found his opening and punched. The other man swayed from the impact, but again, he kept his feet.

Now! Ophelia stood on tiptoe and brought down her crude weapon with all her strength. Alas, the sound was more impressive than the blow. As rotten as the rafters had been, the piece of lumber cracked uselessly over the man's head, doing little damage except to startle and anger him.

Eyes wide, he turned and stared at her, roaring. "What ye be doing there, bitch?"

Giles delivered a powerful left hook, hitting the man hard on his golden earring. This time, the man went down like a sturdy tree at the last stroke of the ax.

Ophelia gasped, and the dog whimpered. Hoping the animal would not attack, Ophelia kept an eye on the dog, but he seemed to wait for his command.

Giles had his attention on the man on the ground, but the doorman seemed dazed.

"Let's go," Giles said.

But before they could take more than three steps, they were forced to turn once more and face more threats from behind them.

The big doorman still lay in the dirt, but he seemed to have called for reinforcements before he'd emerged, as now three, no, four, five other half-dressed men were pouring from the door of the brothel. Oh, God, what were they to do?

The big man pulled himself to one elbow. "I'll see you dead for that, ye miserable—" He paused, eyes going wide.

What? Ophelia held her breath. She heard something—more than one man's footfalls. Surely the brothel's inhabitants had not an entire army to call out against them? She wanted to clutch Giles's arm as the girls tugged at hers, but she restrained herself, knowing he needed to be free. She wished desperately for another weapon more reliable than the rotten wood.

Then she heard the rattle of a carriage and the pounding of horses's hooves. She looked over her shoulder and saw the most beautiful sight of her life: the marquis's carriage, although its crest had been covered, and, pistol in one hand, his expression fierce, Ransom Sheffield, spurring his horse on. There was the marquis himself astride a dark horse, his face as grim as Ransom's, and yes, what seemed an army of men behind them, jamming the narrow street.

"Oh, Giles, we are saved!" she exclaimed. And she sat full down in the muck of the street as her legs turned to jelly.

Only when Giles turned and saw their rescuers coming at full speed did she scramble up. He helped pull her and the children to the side of the way so that they might not be trampled by the same people who had come to deliver them.

The next few minutes passed like a dream, but at least this time, it was no nightmare. Ophelia was helped into the carriage, the children huddled around her on the seat, with several men stationed to guard them.

Then, before they left this godforsaken street, the marquis and his men, with Giles's help, went back through the brothel to be sure that no one else was being held against her will. The madam and the doorman, still barely able to stand, and several others were sent to the local magistrate to be had up on charges.

"And if he turns out to be a 'trading magistrate,' I'll see what can be done about that, too," John said darkly.

"What is that?" Ophelia whispered to Giles when the men had come back out to the street.

"A magistrate who takes bribes," he told her, shaking his head.

"Oh," she said. After tonight, she did not think she would be surprised at any corruption in the world.

"What about Mr. Nettles?" she asked.

"We will see that he is dealt with, too, but not just yet. We have to think about Avery's situation, first," Giles told her, his voice grim.

"Will Nettles not be suspicious at the raid on his brothel?"

"Perhaps, but he won't know for sure about the cause; it could have come from any of the children's relatives in search of them," Giles told her.

Sighing, she set herself to reassuring the children. They were all now in the marquis's carriage as it rumbled through the uneven streets. Learning that Venetia was at the rectory, they had asked to be taken there, first, and John had agreed. He rode on to let Marian and Cordelia know that all was well.

When they reached the rectory, the sun was full up, but the actress, accustomed to late hours, was still asleep. Ophelia took Sal, and the other two girls, too, as they did not want to be parted from her, up to the guest room where the actress slept, and so witnessed the happy reunion.

Venetia was ecstatic to see her sister safe. "Oh, Sal, my sweet girl!" She sat up in bed and hugged her sister to her. "Oh, Lily, I am so thankful. You are an angel, you are!"

Ophelia blinked back tears. "It was all Giles, Reverend Sheffield, really, and the marquis and his men," she told her. "I am just so happy that Sal is safe. But we shall have to talk about how to keep her that way. Come downstairs when you are dressed. Let me get the girls something to eat."

Alerted by her master, the housekeeper had bowls of hot soup ready for the children, and they tucked eagerly into the soup and the thick slices of brown bread that she put out for them. By the time they had finished, Ophelia and the maid had warm baths prepared.

"A bath?" Sal complained.

The children were not as enthused about this, but Ophelia was firm.

"You'll feel much better with the grime off you, trust me," she told them. "We are all of us as black as chimney sweeps." So despite some protests, they were scrubbed, and their hair washed and combed. Soon all three were toweled dry and tucked into worn but clean flannel nightgowns from the rectory's supply of emergency clothing, and they were put into a guest chamber.

"I think a nap wouldn't be a bad thing," Ophelia said, seeing the girls' heavy eyelids. "Yesterday was . . . eventful."

Venetia had come to help with the bathing, and she sat on the bed beside her sister. She nodded. "I'll 'ave to leave for the theater in a few 'ours. What we gonna do about Sal, Lily? I can't take 'er back to the theater and let ol' Nettles know we got 'er out of that place. 'E might snatch 'er all over again!"

"No, indeed." Ophelia shivered. "And you said she doesn't feel safe in your rooms, either."

"I have a suggestion, if I may."

Ophelia looked up. Marian and Cordelia had arrived.

Ophelia went to hug her sister. Her eyes damp with emotion, Cordelia returned her embrace, but her expression was strange.

"What?" Ophelia whispered.

"We'll talk later," Cordelia murmured back.

Ophelia pulled her attention back to the marchioness. "Yes?"

"My sister-in-law, Lady Gabriel Sinclair, is away just now, but I'm familiar with the foundling home whose board she serves on. It was not the best of places when she took it on, but she has turned it around completely. Now you will find it very homelike. The girls there are well taken care of, well fed and clothed and happy, and they get an education and end up with a means of making an honest living."

She looked down at the smaller children and touched the damp chocolate-colored curls of the nearest child, who had already closed her eyes. "When they are calmer, we will talk to them and try to trace their families. If the young ones have been abducted, we will see they are reunited. If they are orphans, the foundling home would be a safe haven for them. And for Sal, it would be a safe place for her to stay, as well, while her sister works, and she could get an education there. If her sister approves, of course. Venetia could come and visit whenever she has time off. We will make sure she has transportation."

"Oh, my lady, that would be bloody . . . I mean, that would be awful nice," Venetia said, her face clearing. She put one arm around her sister and gave her a hug.

Sal looked uncertain, but she hugged her sister back. "Nobody gonna cane me?"

"No, indeed," Marian promised. "Tomorrow we will start early and all go out to the home, so you can see it, and we will still get Venetia back in time for her performance."

Ophelia sighed. It seemed it would all work out, thank heavens. And as for Cordelia, surely she was simply . . . oh, goodness, the play!

"Did it go all right, the role, you stepping in?" she took her twin to the door so she could ask quietly. "It was so good of you, Cordelia, to rescue me."

Cordelia raised her brow. "I muddled through. But I hope you can take the part back tonight."

"Oh, no, I can't." Ophelia felt the panic rise inside her, just at the thought of it. "I can't, Cordelia!"

"But, Ophelia—I'm not the one who wanted to be an actress!"

"I know, I'm a wretch." Ophelia groaned. "I'm a disgrace to the family; I can't even be bad and do it right. But I just can't do it. And now the children need me; let them get settled in, and maybe . . . no, I just don't think I can, Cordelia. Maybe Mr. Nettles can put another actress into the part. He has more time now to get someone ready. Some of the girls are very quick studies. I mean, it's not as if it's moments before the play starts. . . ."

Her sister sighed in exasperation. "Oh, Ophelia, when I think what we went through so that you could go onstage—"

Ophelia looked away. "I know. I feel very guilty, honestly, I do, Cordelia. It's all my fault. And I was having a wonderful time, all the way till opening night when I looked out at that sea of faces—" She shuddered at the memory. "Please don't ask me to do it, Cordelia. Just the thought fills me with terror."

Her sister pursed her lips but she drew a deep breath. "Oh, very well. I'll go and talk to the manager. With what we know about his brothel, I don't see how he can complain about you dropping out of the play."

On her way to the theater, Cordelia remembered that she could not bring up the brothel, since, until they had the incriminating note and Avery was safe, they were not supposed to know about Nettles's ownership of the disgraceful house of prostitution. So what was she going to say? She'd have to think of something.

When she walked into the manager's office, she was still grappling for a good argument, and her statement was short and succinct.

"What'd you mean you want to quit?" The man frowned at her and leaned forward in his chair.

"Just what I said." Cordelia lifted her chin, refusing to be intimidated by this horrid man. "I find I don't care for acting, after all."

"And I don't care, missy, whether you care for it or not. I gave you a chance, as you begged for, and I've advertised a lady of quality on my stage, and that's where you'll be, or the whole town, the whole of the Quality, will know that Miss Applegate has not so much nerve as she thought she had," Nettles snapped, the expression in his narrow eyes sly.

"I don't intend—" Cordelia began, then paused as his words sank in. A chill wave of alarm ran through her. How had the man found out their real name? If he spread it among the Ton, they would be ruined, for sure!

"Don't think you can keep secrets from Tom Nettles."—the manager smirked and leaned back in his chair again—"it's bloody hard to maintain a stage name."

Of course. He'd no doubt had someone follow them back to the Sinclair residence and ask the servants about the visitors staying with the marquis. It would have been laughably simple to learn their real names. So much for all of Ophelia's precautions. . . .

"You'll stay in the show as long as I say you will," Nettles told her. "So get into your costume, missy, and be ready to go on, and don't make such a shambles of the dance number tonight."

Icy cold with anger, she stared at him as Nobby came in with a paper in his hands. "This the sheet you want taken to the printer, Mr. Nettles, sir?"

The manager glanced at the playbill and nodded. "Aye, that'll do."

Cordelia made up her mind. Before Nobby could turn, she took the sheet of paper away. "Not yet. There's a change that needs to be made."

"If you take your name off, so help me—" Nettles threatened.

"No, indeed. I have an addition in mind," she said coolly. She picked up a quill and stuck it into the ink pot on his desk.

Nettles tried to see what she wrote on the paper but she shielded her writing with her other hand until she had finished, then held it out for him to see. She had marked out the earlier name and written in, "*Play authored by L. de Lac.*"

"What?" Nettles snapped.

"People may come to see the novelty of a masked lady onstage, but if they keep coming, it will be because the play is, after I have rewritten ninety percent of it, actually funny. So I wish to have credit for my work, and I wish to be paid for it."

She thought rapidly, having no idea what one would be paid for penning a play, then named a sum.

He shrugged. "I suppose."

Too low, obviously.

"A week," she said quickly.

"What!"

"I'll take the first payment tonight," she told him sweetly. "Nobby, you can take this to the printers now. I have to go get into my costume."

She left the office with her head high, but her heart still beat fast. It was only until they found the note, she told herself. Then they would haul Nettles off to gaol and . . . and how would they manage to stop his tongue?

Somehow, they would have to find a way!

It was a good thing she had left her bag with Ophelia's mask and cap and the costume in the carriage. She retrieved them and looked with repugnance at the gaudy and revealing outfit. She had an hour or more till the play commenced. She could go over her lines, or practice that infernal dance or—

She got up suddenly and went to the sewing nook where she had once spent most of her time. She found another actress there, with a ripped petticoat in hand. "Lily? Or Clara, is it?"

"Clara's home sick," she said at once.

"Oh, 'ell, I've got a tear in my petticoat," the other woman said.

Cordelia found a needle and thread and handed it to her, but didn't offer to mend the garment; she had sewing of her own to do. She took the sewing basket back to the dressing room, and before she reached it, she looked up to see Ransom Sheffield waiting for her.

"You're still here? Why did you come back?" He frowned as she motioned him to lower his voice. He followed her to the side where they could talk more privately.

"I don't"—she said with some bitterness—"have much choice." And she recounted her interview with Nettles.

"Damn and blast the man!" Ransom swore briefly.

"First, we have to find your brother's note," she muttered. "Even then, how are we ever going to keep Nettles from exposing our names? If our identity is known, we'll be ruined!"

Would she be trapped for the rest of her life in this grimy second-rate theater, in a role she had never wanted? She didn't even share her sister's excitement in being onstage, exposed to staring matrons eager to unmask her identity and leering men who eyed her body as if she were a plucked chicken in a butcher's window.

Thinking of her upcoming performance filled her only with renewed tension and a dull headache like a tightening band across her forehead. She rubbed her temples and swallowed an urge to sit down and cry. For the first time she felt genuine despair, and it must have showed in her face because, instead of his habitual cynical response, Ransom's expression showed an unusual gentleness.

He cupped one hand gently against her cheek. "We will find a way to stop Nettles, I give you my oath, Cordelia," he whispered, his breath soft against her ear. It sounded almost like a lover's vow.

She had been among actors too long; she was thinking in storybook terms, Cordelia scolded herself. But she wanted to believe him, wanted to believe that miracles could happen, that heroes could produce fairy-tale results. She shut her eyes for a moment and enjoyed the light and reassuring touch of his hand.

Something moved inside her that was not at all childlike, and she was intensely aware of how close he stood. He was so deeply male, Ransom Sheffield. He had ridden to save her sister—he would do that; he would come to save her if she were in need of saving. He was a man one could depend on . . .

He stroked her cheek again, then she felt—without even opening her eyes—when he moved back.

Two scene shifters walked past with a cheerful bustle. Sighing, Cordelia blinked and stood up straighter. "I must go and work on my costume," she said. "Thank you for . . . thank you."

He nodded. "Don't trouble yourself," he said, his voice still low. "We will find a way."

She nodded, but she paused at the doorway to the dressing room and looked back once, and was reassured to see that he watched her, his expression serious. She felt immensely better just knowing that he was still at hand in the theater.

Although Cordelia took a few minutes to look over the script, she spent most of the time before she had to dress and apply makeup working on her costume. She managed to sew a wide ruffle of lace onto the neckline of her costume, so the people looking down from the boxes at the side of the theater would not be able to see all the way to her navel.

Tomorrow, she would add a ruffle or two to her hemline, so that not so much of her legs were exposed. Nettles would no doubt be annoyed—a pleasing thought.

Marley came and made sure she was at the side of the stage, ready for her cue. After yesterday, she didn't blame him. But she was prepared, had donned her mask and cap, and although a cold spot had settled in her middle, she walked onto the stage and said her line, and managed to get through the next one and the next one. Then it was easier, and Marley smiled at her, and she relaxed a little and the scene moved on.

Her scenes with their diva were not as easy, and Madam Tatina not as helpful as Marley. But, unlike Ophelia if her sister had stayed in the role, Cordelia didn't care if she was upstaged by their leading lady—and she *was* the leading lady—so she hardly objected if the temperamental diva skipped over Cordelia's best lines.

All Cordelia wanted was to get to the end of the play. When they did, once again, the applause was loud, so that she supposed that Nettles should be happy. The other actors were. And this time she and Venetia had no overpowering anxiety about missing loved ones, so she could be thankful for that.

But she rode home alone in the rented carriage and was chagrined to find that Ophelia had stayed another night at the rectory. She had wanted to talk to her sister further about their quandary with the manager.

"She didn't want to upset the children; they are still clinging to her, you see," Marian explained as she whisked into Cordelia's guest room in her dressing gown. "We're taking them out to the foundling home in the morning, and we want them to be as settled as possible before we show them another change of scene, poor babies."

Cordelia nodded, then wished she hadn't. She went off to find a cold cloth to put on her forehead, before, at last, falling into bed.

The next morning Ophelia, Venetia and the children rose early to join Marian as they rode out to the foundling home. It was large and clean and well-run, as the marchioness had promised. Sal took to it right away. Some coaxing was required for the two smaller girls to leave Ophelia's side but fortunately, they took a liking to one of the younger nursemaids, so Ophelia was spared the bout of tears that she had feared might occur.

Afterward, the carriage took Marian home first, then dropped Venetia back at the theater and finally took Ophelia to the rectory, although she planned to return to the marquis's residence before dinner. She had made an excuse to return. She felt, since she had turned the place into a nursery for the children, that she should help the two female servants straighten it up again. And really, she just wanted to see Giles one more time.

And to her surprise, he had asked her to come back. Perhaps he was making an excuse for more private time together, too. Or a girl could hope!

When the groom helped her down, she said, "You can return to fetch me at six o'clock," before she knocked at the door of the rectory.

She was surprised but pleased when it was Giles himself who opened it.

"Please come in," he said. He sounded strangely formal.

Ophelia hoped he had not regretted asking her to come. The carriage had already pulled away; he was stuck with her. She smiled a bit anxiously at him.

To her relief, he smiled back, but his eyes were still . . . what? He led the way to the parlor and motioned her inside.

Still puzzled, she followed and sat down in one of the chairs beside the hearth when he waved her toward it.

Giles did not sit. He turned to face her. "Miss Applegate—"

"Really, Giles," she interrupted. "After all we have been through together, don't you think you can go on calling me Ophelia? You did so during our adventure."

"Our adventure was scandalous," he pointed out mildly. "That is the subject of what I wish to say, Miss . . . oh, very well, Ophelia."

She rewarded him with a quick smile.

"First, how is your, ah, wound?"

Marian had sent their own family physician to the rectory to have it tended to yesterday. The neat bandages were hidden beneath her petticoat and gown. "It seems to be healing," she told him. "I hardly notice it."

"Good," he said. "I have written to your father, Ophelia, explaining why under the circumstances, I think we should not wait for the bans. I have obtained the special license this morning from the bishop."

"What?" Ophelia stared at him blankly. What did this have to do with her leg injury?

"As to why we should not wait to be married, Ophelia," he said steadily. "Since we were forced to spend the night together—"

"But nothing happened!" she protested. "It was quite innocent. Giles, you could not have been more of a gentleman if we had been in church!"

"I know that and you know that," he told her. "But as far as Society is concerned, I would not see your reputation besmirched, Ophelia. And I know your father will expect—as a gentleman, I still must offer . . ."

She gazed at him with horror. "Me—a clergyman's wife?" And for him to be forced into such an offer, even worse, she thought. "I'm sorry, I couldn't!"

"I see," he said quietly, his face without expression. "Then I shall say no more about it." He gave her a short bow and withdrew a little abruptly.

Ophelia blinked. He didn't have to just walk away . . . that is, it wasn't that she couldn't ever consider marrying him. Giles was really the most wonderful man, but—a vicar's wife?

Oh, dear, it was the most incredible tangle. What did one do, and how did one separate a man from his position, when you cared about one but were put off by the other?

Left alone in the narrow room, she stood and paced up and down, coming to a bookshelf on the wall and glancing at a shelf full of collections of sermons. She shivered. Oh, dear. Not a good omen. If anyone needed sermons, lectures, it was certainly her very imperfect self, but that was not what she wanted from a husband, someone to lecture and scold. . . .

If he were her husband, would Giles feel compelled to point out all her flaws? she asked herself as she did her best to wear out a path in the thin carpet.

Had he ever? she argued with herself. Hadn't he already seen some of her imperfections?

But he didn't know the half of it, the other voice in her head said. When he found out what she was really like, how defective she really was, he would doubtless not wish to be bound to her for life. He would thank her for saying no, really, he would. She continued to pace.

After a time it occurred to her that she had been alone quite a while, and she might have to sit by herself until six o'clock. At least she could have some tea. She pulled the bell rope, but no one came. She pulled it again.

Still, nothing. What was going on in the kitchen?

Ophelia opened the door and listened. The hallway was empty; she didn't want to run into Giles just now. She hastened down the passage and down the stairs to the basement.

But in the doorway, she paused in bewilderment. The housekeeper was sitting at the table, mopping her face with a large handkerchief. The maid sat on a three-legged stool, her face also red and blotched, her eyes wet.

"Whatever is the matter?" Ophelia demanded. "Are you ill?"

The maid wailed, and the housekeeper blew her nose like a trumpet. "Worse, miss."

"What is it?" Ophelia drew up another stool and sat on it, trying to sound comforting. "It can't be this bad."

"It's the reverend," Mrs. Madigan said, her voice doleful. "The best vicar I've ever laid eyes on, miss, and I've served my share. 'E's upstairs in 'is study writin' out 'is resignation."

"What?" Ophelia jumped to her feet. "He can't do that!"

"'E is! 'E's resigning 'is living," the housekeeper said as the maid wailed again. "I don't 'ave any notion why. 'E's the best man I ever seen, and the good 'e's done wid the poor folk in this parish . . ."

"Oh, no." Ophelia forgot about her urge for tea and ran for the stairs. By the time she reached the study, she was breathless, but she barely paused before knocking at the door. Not giving him time to speak, she snatched the door open.

"Giles, what are you doing?" she demanded.

Sure enough, he was sitting at his desk, quill in hand, a sheet of paper before him. His expression was grim. He didn't immediately answer.

"The housekeeper said—"

His lips tightened. "That was not for your ears."

"But Giles, you put your heart and soul into your work, it's obvious. And you do so much good! What will the poor people here do without you? You can't resign!"

"Sooner or later we will bring Nettles to justice, and when we do, I fear news of the whole episode is bound to leak out, Ophelia, and the night I shared with you will likely bring you to social ruin. And yet you can't bring yourself to consider marriage even to save your good name . . . No, you don't have to answer, my dear. If I am so repellant to you as that, I must not be doing an adequate job either as a man or as a vicar. So I must try to change one." She saw the expression that flashed across his face, and his voice faltered.

"Giles, you must not change anything. I would not have you be any less than you are!" She knelt beside him on the rug and touched his arm. "And of course you don't repel me!"

He raised his brows and did not speak, but something eased in his eyes.

"I think you are the bravest, kindest, most wonderful man in the world! To come to Sal's rescue like you did, to refuse to leave the other children . . ." She swallowed, remembering. "I was so glad that you were there, having you close was such a comfort. And I love being close to you, at any time. If we had not had three children with us, perhaps it would not have been such an innocent night." She smiled a bit ruefully at him. "But, Giles, I am not cut out to be a clergyman's wife."

"And what do you think a clergyman's wife must be?" he asked her, his expression still unrevealing.

"Oh, someone who does good works, I suppose," she said vaguely. "You don't know me very well. Back in Yorkshire, I was—"

"Yes, you told me. Very wild, you said." His tone was still strange.

"It's true." He didn't seem to believe her, and she found herself sounding defensive.

Giles put down his quill and met her gaze squarely. "My dear Miss Applegate. You are a fraud."

She gasped. "Of all the things to say! If you mean I am not sufficiently ladylike or proper . . . I just admitted I was too wild—you don't have to cast it into my face."

It was just as she had thought. She could *not* marry a clergyman. For some reason, having this proved to her satisfaction only made her totally miserable. Ophelia stood and backed toward the door, hoping she could get out of the room before she burst into tears.

But he was too quick. Giles jumped up and rounded the desk, with two long strides reaching the door and shutting it before she could slip out through the open doorway. And now he stood with his back to it, holding her prisoner.

His eyes glittered. Cruel, too? She had never seen this side of him, never even guessed at it. Bewildered, she stared up at him.

"No, I mean you are a sham. Wild? You have tried so hard to be a wicked woman. There is no harm in your soul."

His voice caressed her. She felt a shiver run down her spine.

"In fact, I think you are quite the most conventional lady at heart as any well-brought-up young miss that I know."

She shook her head. "No, indeed. My sister can tell you—"

"Bosh." He took one hand and pushed back her long sleeve. She felt a prickle of sensation as he stroked her wrist. She felt a callous on his hand; what strong fingers he had.

"When we ran off with our brother-in-law's landeau, it was I—"

"His horses no doubt needed the exercise—" He brought her arm up to his lips and kissed her wrist lightly.

The sensation made her a thrill run through her; no man had ever done something so intimate! What was he doing?

"And . . . and the time we dressed up as . . . as"—it was harder and harder to order her thoughts—"as maids and went into the village, and the miller's sons chased us through the orchard for a kiss. It was all my idea!"

Now he was nibbling on her palm. Oh, dear lord! Surely he wasn't supposed to be doing this—

"And how old were you then?"

"Twelve," she admitted. "But we knew it was forbidden."

"They were probably not very good kisses," he suggested.

"Dreadful," she agreed. "They had no clue how to kiss."

He put his lips against her palm, now. His kisses would not be dreadful, she knew suddenly, and her stomach seemed to shiver with that knowledge, and she felt her knees go to jelly again, this time not from fear or sudden relief, but from a re-action so much more complicated . . .

"But I couldn't marry you, really, Giles, I couldn't; you would be sorry. You would regret it, eventually, and then I could not bear it!" she said, her voice too loud.

And this time he lifted her hand to his cheek and pressed it there for a moment as gently as if it were a tender rose, then kissed it again before releasing it, and then . . . then, he put his hands on both sides of her face, turned her toward him and bent down to meet her lips.

And he kissed her.

And it was so much beyond some sloppy adolescent buss that Ophelia immediately forgot any attempt at comparison. His mouth was firm and warm and sure, and she allowed his lips to guide her. Her lips parted in surprise and joy, and when his tongue slipped past, that was a new pleasure, too. She was floating on sensations she had not dreamed of. And the feeling deep in her belly grew, and she leaned into him until she thought their bodies would grow together, too, and—

And suddenly he had pushed her a little away, and she found they were both breathing quickly.

"Did I do it wrong?" she asked, frowning.

He laughed, even as he opened the door and propelled her quickly into the hall.

"No, indeed, my wild and scandalous Miss Applegate," he told her quietly. "Only, I am going to call you a hackney."

"But the marquis's carriage is coming back for me at six," she protested.

"My darling Ophelia, if we wait until six for the marquis's carriage, we will have had the honeymoon before the wedding. Even my restraint has its limits." He bent and touched her mouth again just for one instant, and she felt the hunger in his lips and saw that he ached for her, too. So that was what troubled her belly!

In the comparatively public space of the hall, he called for the maid. When she came up from the kitchen, still rubbing her eyes, the vicar sighed and said, "I am not going to resign the living, Annie."

"Oh, thank the Lord," the girl muttered.

"Please go hail a hackney for Miss Applegate. She finds that she has to leave earlier than planned," he said, keeping his face straight.

Ophelia bit her lip to keep from laughing. Suddenly, everything seemed worth smiling about. But even so, when the maid had hurried out the door, she looked up at him again.

"You're sure? If you regret this—"

"If you were the most wicked woman in all of Yorkshire, in all of London, my darling Ophelia, if you possessed all seven of the deadly sins—"

"It's not just to protect my reputation?" She gazed at him, needing to be sure, totally sure.

"To bloody hell with your reputation," he said, lowering his voice and giving her one more quick but hearty kiss. "I want you, my improper Miss Applegate, now and forever."

Ophelia was still laughing when Bess came back to report a hackney was waiting.

∼≈∽

Cordelia came home from the theater in a foul mood, and it didn't help to find her sister strangely detached. Even though she poured out her alarm over Nettles now knowing their real name, she could not seem to awake Ophelia to an awareness of their peril.

"I expect we will find some way around it," was all her twin would say.

"But, Ophelia—" Cordelia stared at her sister.

"By the way, I'm getting married at ten tomorrow. Giles's bishop wants to perform the ceremony, so it will be at St. Paul's," her sister said, her gaze far away. "You'll likely want to wear your best gown. The maize-colored silk looks very nice on you."

"What?" Cordelia shrieked.

But Ophelia had gone off to confer with Marian about topics of dress and didn't look back.

Cordelia had to sink down upon the nearest chair. She felt as if the world had turned upside down. Nothing that Ophelia had done or planned in the past, no scandalous undertaking, no disguise or midnight escape from parental authority, had been as shocking as this—to accept an offer of marriage without even conferring with her twin?

Cordelia felt . . . she felt strangely betrayed.

Sitting alone in her room, she fought back a desire to curl up on her bed and give way to angry tears. How could her sister not think about Cordelia, leave her trapped in the theater playing a role she didn't want at the mercy of Nettles, while Ophelia planned a wedding—a wedding!

Gritting her teeth, Cordelia told herself that self-pity was as ugly as it was useless. Pushing herself up, she followed her sister and found that Ophelia's own room was empty. She had gone to the marchioness's bedchamber.

Standing in the doorway, Cordelia found the two, with their hostess's dresser and two other maidservants hanging on every word, deep in conversation. Marian had known about the wedding for hours, apparently. Of course she would. She hadn't been stuck at the theater, Cordelia told herself, then pushed aside those thoughts as too bitter.

"Excuse me, miss," a footman said.

Startled, she found one of the menservants, his arms full of large bundles, trying to get past her. She stepped aside.

"Oh, good," Marian said. "Put it here, please." She turned to Ophelia and explained. "I didn't wish to raise your hopes, my dear, but my dressmaker has come through for us. This was a gown she was making for me, but this afternoon when you told me the wonderful news, I sent a note and asked her to alter it for you and change the trim for some more appropriate for the occasion. She has your measurements, of course, and she promised to put all her staff on it, and that they would stay late if necessary. And here it is; I am so pleased. You shall have a new dress for your wedding!"

Ophelia squealed and clapped her hands, and everyone watched as the dresser carefully unwrapped the brown paper that had protected the gown, spreading it carefully on the bed.

The white skirt and bodice was trimmed with lace edged in gold. The skirt had white silk roses adorning the flounces that revealed the delicate underskirt.

Cordelia's sight of the gown blurred just a little as Ophelia picked it up and held it in front of her, turning first to the looking glass. She looked at her reflection with the same kind of awe that she used to show as a young girl when they had dreamed of just such an occasion. Except they'd always meant to have a double wedding . . . And they'd promised that one would never fall in love until the other twin could do so, as well . . .

Dreams, she told herself, childish dreams . . . Real life did not pay heed to such juvenile fancies.

When her sister turned to her, her expression anxious, Cordelia found the strength to blink quickly and smile. "You look quite beautiful," she said, and was glad to hear that her voice sounded normal and her words sincere and to see that she'd made her twin smile.

So Ophelia turned back in time for Marian to take out a velvet-covered box. "A small wedding present," she said. "From John and myself."

"You've been much too kind already," Ophelia protested, but her eyes sparkled. When she opened the case, she exclaimed once more, then held up a lovely circlet of pearls. "Oh, they will be perfect with the dress, and there are matching ear drops. Thank you so much!"

"I found them on our last visit to the Orient. I thought they were exquisite. I'm glad you like them." Marian looked pleased at Ophelia's response. "Cordelia, you must not get betrothed too quickly; I must have time to find another set for you."

She smiled, and Cordelia tried to laugh at the mild jest, but just now, it was hard to frame even a chuckle.

And when the jewelry had been exclaimed over and put back into its box, and the wedding gown hung up carefully, and the conversation turned to the important subject of undergarments, Cordelia was able to murmur a few words about needing a bath before dinner and slip unnoticed out of the room.

That night Cordelia slept fitfully, tossing in her bed. She kept thinking how it would never be the same. Even when she returned to her father's house, Ophelia would not be there. Cordelia would be in Yorkshire, and Ophelia in London, untold miles away. Even on a rare visit, Cordelia would never share a bedroom with her sister again—they would never argue over who was hogging the blankets or who had poked an elbow in whose side in the middle of the night . . .

All their lives they had been together, from the time they had learned to toddle about, from the time they had fallen into the brook together, had muddied their petticoats together, had been scolded by Maddie for dunking their dolls in the maids' wash water or chased the hens until feathers flew—

She had never not had Ophelia beside her. She had always been the one looking out for Ophelia, keeping her out—well, mostly out—of the most serious kinds of trouble. She still felt obscurely that if she had been there, Ophelia would not have been trapped in that horrid place in Whitechapel, she would not be forced to marry now in such haste to save her reputation—

Was she being forced, really forced?

Alarmed, Cordelia sat up in bed at the thought.

Oh, Ophelia pretended to be happy, and she was thrilled enough with pretty dresses and new jewelry, but was she really thinking about the consequences, about what it meant for the rest of her life? The vicar seemed a nice enough man, but Ophelia as a vicar's wife? Of all the most unlikely persons to fill such a role . . .

And if she regretted it later, she would be helpless to change her position.

She would be trapped.

And to rush into this marriage at such a breakneck speed, it was madness! Ophelia could not—must not marry before talking it over with her sister.

Having made up her mind, Cordelia drew a deep breath and felt somewhat calmer. Tomorrow morning, she would take her sister aside and they would talk privately, calmly, and she would make her see sense . . .

Except that when she finally shut her eyes, it was so late that she overslept. Instead of waking early, as she had intended, Cordelia found when the maid brought her tea that it was well on toward nine. She had to gulp down the hot drink and splash water on her face and hasten to dress and get herself ready.

When she went to see her sister, Ophelia was already dressed and sitting in front of the looking glass having her hair dressed high on her head. Two maids were in the room, and Marian was in and out, and any private conversation was impossible.

"Oh, Ophelia," Cordelia said. "I wanted to speak to you, alone."

"Oh, I know." Ophelia gazed at her sister in the glass. "I'm a bundle of nerves, too. You must ride with me in the carriage and hold my hand."

But even there, Marian and John rode with them, everyone looking very fine in their best clothes, and Cordelia had to hide her feelings, although she was seething inside with frustration. And Ophelia seemed very pale—was she already having second thoughts?

She could not see her sister sacrificed on the altar of propriety! If she had to denounce this marriage of convenience herself, she would.

Wilder schemes than any Ophelia herself had ever hatched floated through Cordelia's head. She would pull her sister out of the church and borrow a chaise and run—to where?

But something had to be done! Surely Marian would not wish to see Ophelia made unhappy for the rest of her life over such a small thing as one night spent unchaperoned with a man?

But everything seemed to rush ahead. Now they were arriving, now they were being helped out of the carriage. Now they were escorted into the great cathedral. They paused in an anteroom where Marian helped Ophelia adjust the skirt of her gown, then handed her the bouquet of flowers and kissed her cheek.

"I will take my place in the pew," Marian said. "John will be here in one moment to walk Ophelia down the aisle; he is checking on the arrangements. Cordelia will precede you. You both look beautiful, my dears."

Marian went out, and it was just the sisters, alone at last. Ophelia looked as white as her dress.

Cordelia gathered all her courage. For her sister's sake, she must tell her what a dreadful mistake she was about to make!

Seventeen

$\mathcal{A}$ figure appeared in the doorway. It was not John Sinclair, but Ransom Sheffield, looking very handsome in formal morning dress.

Startled, she paused, and they both looked at him.

He grinned. "Not to worry. The bishop has managed to misplace the special license which Giles spent a fortune on yesterday. We'll be set to begin in just a moment. Giles is helping him tear his study apart to find it; it has to be there."

Ophelia giggled. Cordelia looked at her sharply. If she had hysterics—

But to her surprise, Ransom turned to Cordelia herself. "Are you going to swoon?" he muttered. "You look very strange."

"Of course not," she said sharply. "I was just about to talk—privately—to my sister. If you'll excuse me . . ."

But now John Sinclair had entered. The marquis walked over to Ophelia, smiled and offered his arm, chatting amicably with the bride to be.

Ransom turned Cordelia toward the far window. "Come and talk to me. I'll pour you a glass of sherry."

"I don't need any sherry," she snapped, miserable that once

again she had lost any last chance to bring her sister to an understanding of the rashness of the too-quick marriage. But Ransom did just that, taking a carafe from a sideboard and pouring it into the glasses that sat beside it. He took two across to Ophelia and John, and then brought one to her. "Good for wedding nerves," he told her. "What's wrong, Cordelia?"

That he should be the only one to see that something troubled her made tears sting her eyes. Damnation, why did she keep wanting to cry?

"You're not really losing a sister," he said, his voice low. "It must be hard, however, being a twin, seeing her marry first."

"It isn't that!" she protested—and suddenly hoped fervently it wasn't that, that she wasn't simply being selfish. "It's just . . . I don't want her making a mistake. Ophelia a vicar's wife . . . it's just so not . . . not Ophelia."

He grinned. "Open your eyes, Cordelia. Don't you see how besotted she is with my cousin? Who is, you must grant, a very good, very kind, very loving man—and very much in love with your sister and has been for some time. He has a reasonable income of his own, apart from the living, and she will likely stop him from giving it all away and make him remember that he is a family man now. He will make her an excellent husband and a very happy woman. And whatever you fear it is that vicar's wives must do, I'm sure he will grant her a dispensation."

Cordelia bit her lip, and this time her eyes did brim over. Oh, God, what a fool she was being, and how close she had come to saying all the wrong things, and perhaps . . . perhaps even ruining her dearly beloved sister's wedding. She sniffed, wondering if she had even put a handkerchief into her sleeve.

As if reading her thoughts, he withdrew a clean handkerchief from an inside pocket and handed it to her. She wiped her eyes. "Thank you," she told him, sniffing again. "Does it show?"

"It doesn't matter," he told her. "Women always cry at weddings. It's de rigueur."

She made a face at him, but then grinned, feebly, and took another sip of the sherry.

Now a young clerk hurried in to say that the license had been found and the bishop was ready to begin the ceremony. Ophelia, who seemed to have gained some color in her cheeks, paled again and then blushed.

Ransom smiled at Cordelia and winked, then left to take his place beside his cousin, and Cordelia prepared to walk down the aisle in front of the bride. She had time only to kiss her sister's cheek.

"Thank goodness you are here, Cordelia," Ophelia whispered into her ear. "I could not be so happy without you at my side!"

Cordelia smiled and tried not to tear up again.

And in a few minutes when she watched Ophelia and Giles join hands before the bishop and repeat their vows, "for better or for worse," she could easily witness the love that flowed between them.

How had she not seen it before? Perhaps she had been afraid to, afraid to admit that someone else had become so important to her twin.

So she smiled through the ceremony, smiled as the newlyweds kissed, smiled with determination as the guests hugged and shook hands and repeated their good wishes afterward until she thought her cheeks would crack. And when Ransom murmured to her, "Brave girl," only then did her fixed smile fade, and she grinned at him ruefully but more naturally.

The bride and groom rode in Giles's new carriage—an unexpected wedding gift from the marquis complete with a handsome team of matched bays, which he said was to replace the gig that had never been found after the night spent trapped in Whitechapel—on the way back to the wedding breakfast at the marquis's residence. Cordelia rode with Marian and John, who held hands and reminisced about their own wedding. Cordelia sat quietly and, at last, could cease smiling.

Her other sisters would regret missing the wedding, she thought, but they would be happy to hear about her sister being settled. They would all be surprised to hear that Ophelia, of all the sisters, had wed a vicar. . . . She sighed. No, she could not start those thoughts again. . . . She must trust that Ophelia knew what she was doing.

She, too, had a surprise for her sister. Cordelia slipped up to her room and brought down her gifts hidden in her pocket. When at last she had a moment when the bride was free of other distractions, she took Ophelia aside and showed her.

"The new playbill," she said.

Ophelia looked blank, but she scanned the page, then looked more closely and gasped. "Oh, Cordelia! How did you do this?"

"It was part of my big scene with Nettles," she said, grinning. "He thinks I'm you, of course. But I argued for author credit. And here is the first installment of my—your—fee as playwright."

She handed over the bag of coin and was gratified to see her twin's eyes widen. "Oh, I earned it myself! With my own words and ideas—my story! Oh, Cordelia," she whispered. "This is more exciting than even a string of pearls, though I value all the gifts our generous cousins have given Giles and me."

She hugged her sister impulsively. Cordelia felt rewarded for all the toil and peril of their mad escapade. If Ophelia's storytelling had found its place at last—

Ophelia took the playbill, handling it as carefully as if it were stamped with gold, and the money, and put them aside. "I will show them later to Giles in private," she told her sister.

They turned back to the rest of the guests, and then it was time to sit down to the well-filled table, to toast the health and happiness of the couple and then to fill their plates.

And after the wedding breakfast had lasted into the early afternoon, Cordelia had to go off, as usual, to the theater. She and Ransom still had a show to put on.

The play went as usual; she seemed more at home in the role, and even her part in the dance was less of a calamity, but the performance seemed to drag on and on. And even worse, they had an engagement afterward, so she had to hurry and change and play Society miss, as if she had not just stumbled through a play.

"But really, it will help alleviate suspicion, you see, if anyone should try to connect you to the person on the stage, so yes, you really need to come, my dear," Marian insisted, her voice kind but firm.

Cordelia knew that her hostess was likely right, but it was the last thing she wanted to do just now. She was bone tired after the stress of the play and the wedding, and was ready to wash up and fall into bed. Instead she had to wash, then change into a dinner gown and redo her hair. Then she and Marian and John climbed into the carriage and were off, to be among the last of the arrivals at Lady something or other's tea dance.

After they were announced, Cordelia found her hand claimed at once, and this time she was led into a dance where she did know the steps. Her only problem now was to smother a yawn and to make polite conversation.

It was alarming to hear that the play at Malory Road was still being discussed. Her partner, a feckless young gallant of exactly the same cut who still flocked backstage after performances, told her bets were being passed around on the identity of the masked lady onstage.

"Oh, really?" Cordelia muttered, trying to sound bored. Her heart beat faster just at the idea. Surely he was not peering at her trying to decide if she resembled the masked lady?

He took her hand and turned her as the dancers revolved about them.

"Oh, yes, I have ten crown riding at my club, and my cousin Terrance says it may be his second cousin once removed, who lives in Surrey, but I say that her nose is too big, so—"

Everyone had a theory. When her partner led her off the dance floor, Cordelia found that the group of young ladies she next stood beside were also discussing the mystery lady, some with simply curiosity and others with open envy.

"I don't really see what all the fuss is about," a short young lady with an unfortunate tendency to spots remarked. "She's really not all that pretty. Not that one can tell behind that vulgar mask, or that vulgar costume."

"Is that why your fiancé has been there three times to see

her?" the second young lady asked, her tone arch. "He must be an expert on her appearance by now."

The first lady bristled and flicked her fan. "Don't be vulgar," she snapped.

A third lady, somewhat older and plainer than the other two, said, "Appearance is such an overrated part of one's charm. If gentlemen would only learn to value one's spiritual and mental attributes—"

"Then fewer spinsters would pine," the second lady agreed. "And masked ladies with good limbs and bosoms would lose their appeal."

The first lady gasped and clutched her fan so hard she broke a rib. Cordelia heard the distinct sound of its click as it snapped. "Agatha, really!"

"That was what your fiancé said, at any rate," Agatha answered, her expression serene.

Not sure what her own face must reveal, Cordelia turned to look toward the other side of the room. To her immense relief, she saw Ransom Sheffield making his way toward her. The other young ladies must have seen him, too; she felt rather than saw them all stiffen.

But it was to her that he bowed and offered his arm. "May I have the pleasure of this dance?"

The sighs behind her were faint, and for the sake of the other women, she pretended not to hear. "Yes, thank you, Mr. Sheffield."

He led her to the floor. When they were a safe distance away, she whispered, "Everyone is talking about the dratted play—and the mystery lady! What am I going to do?"

"Smile," he told her. "Dance. Enjoy the moment. We will not allow them to best us."

So she did, emboldened by the thought that she was not alone. With his hand on her hand, her shoulder, her waist, her tension eased, her heart lifted, and if her pulse quickened, it was for an entirely different reason. His gray eyes gazing into her own—the lift of his lips—she remembered their touch, too, and just the thought of it awakened the softening ache of her stomach.

Mind your steps, she scolded herself, as only his guidance kept her from falling behind the other dancers. Or you will look as clumsy here as you do in the musical number onstage!

"Sorry," she muttered, feeling her cheeks flame. "I am not the best of dancers, I fear."

He had to release her as the lines of men and women parted, but when next they came together, he took her hand again and squeezed it lightly. "You give yourself too little credit," he murmured. "I would prefer no other partner."

She flushed again, but this time not from embarrassment. Glancing up once into his silvery eyes, she met such warmth there—lately his usual sardonic facade seemed to be missing more often than not—that she hardly knew how to respond.

Nor I, she thought, but had not the nerve to say it aloud. But she found she had stopped worrying about the rumors floating about the room and the speculation on the masked lady who tread the boards at the Malory Road Theater.

When they returned home, however, her anxiety surfaced again, that and the sudden thought that tonight was her twin's wedding night. And that, she told herself sternly, was no one's business but Ophelia's. To change the direction of her thoughts—for some reason she kept thinking of Ransom Sheffield and the kiss they had exchanged—she went down to the library and found the driest and most boring book of philosophy that she could and took it up to bed. But still, it was a long time before she could sleep.

At the rectory, they had had an early supper. The maid and housekeeper's delighted congratulations and beaming, but also suggestive, looks had had Ophelia blushing several times, so she had gone up to the bedroom early.

And then what did one do when it was still broad daylight outside, and you were a newlywed, and both eager and nervous about the fact?

Giles's bedroom was larger than her guest chamber had been. There was a small dressing room attached, and one of her bags had been set inside it. She had not moved all of her clothes over as yet, just the ones she thought she would need right away. She found that Annie had brought up warm water and Ophelia bathed and changed into a nightdress, hanging up her gown, glad to have some time alone.

Her thoughts seemed to skate around like a frightened hen who senses a fox lurking just behind a bush.

Her new husband was not a fox!

No, she thought, glancing at a worn Bible on top of Giles's bureau. He was a vicar. Did vicars . . . what did vicars think about lovemaking?

Should she do . . . what should she do?

He had kissed her with considerable passion yesterday in the study and sent her home so that they did not get carried away too soon, but still—

Oh, looking at the bishop in his robes, today, and the grandeur of St. Paul's with its amazing dome and splendid architecture, she had been reminded again of the audacity of what she was doing, she, Ophelia Applegate, daring to marry a man of the cloth.

It had brought back all her feelings of being not good enough . . . And besides—the door opened, and she jumped.

Giles stood in the doorway. He smiled at her, and her heart seemed to turn over. For a moment, she forgot all her fears.

Shutting the door, he crossed the room and put his arms around her, pulling her closer for a kiss. She shut her eyes and enjoyed the rush of feeling that his lips always brought.

"I'm sorry to be delayed, my love. A goodwife in the parish has a sick husband."

"Oh," she said, all her other worries flowing back. "If you need to go, I understand."

He shook his head. "It does not sound serious. I told her I will call first thing tomorrow. But I appreciate your tolerance, my dear." He kissed her again, but Ophelia knew that she had stiffened, and this time she did not return his embrace with the same enthusiasm.

Drawing back, Giles regarded her with an anxious crease on his forehead. "What's wrong, Ophelia; are you concerned that my role as pastor will take me away too often? I will do my best not to allow my duties to cause me to neglect you, I give you my word."

"Oh, I would not be so selfish as that," she assured him, flushing a little. "It's just that—"

"Just that what?" He drew her toward the bed.

Feeling more awkward than ever, she sat down somewhat primly, her back straight, keeping her feet on the floor. He sat beside her and did not attempt any more lovemaking, she noted with a sigh, but waited patiently for her to continue.

She wasn't sure how to explain. She wasn't even sure she understood it, herself. "It's just—you're a most good-looking man, Giles, and when you kiss me, I feel all sorts of things I've never felt before." She blushed at the spark in his eyes.

"This is promising," he observed, his voice solemn, although she saw his eyes dance with mischief and something more.

"But you're also . . . you're also a vicar, and when I think of that, I feel that I shouldn't be feeling all the other things I feel, so how can I kiss you and . . . and . . ."

"Ah, I see." He frowned for a moment, and then sighed. "My darling Ophelia, we must sort this out now, or I fear it will plague us for many years to come."

Afraid he might be correct, she bit her lip, not sure how they would sort it out when her feelings were so confused. It was like trying to kiss someone in church—quite improper— and yet Giles, one part of her mind insisted, was carrying the church's roof with him.

"My love, I pray every day to be the best vicar and the best Christian I can be. I think you know me well enough to know that I take my position seriously."

"Oh, yes," she agreed, meeting his straightforward gaze.

"The robes that I wear on Sunday and other high holidays are hanging in the clothespress in my office in the church; the housekeeper is kind enough to keep them cleaned and pressed for me. But when I leave the church, they are carefully closed inside. Can you picture that?"

"Yes," she agreed.

"And of course, there is more to my office than simply officiating at church services. I visit the sick, tend to the poor, help anyone who asks for my aid," he went on in his warm voice that always seemed to wrap her in its mellow tones. "But, Ophelia, when I sit down at the dining room table with you, and certainly when I come up to bed with you, I come only as your husband, nothing more. And then my only role is to be the best husband I can be—to love you and make you happy."

"Oh," she said, and could think of nothing to add.

"There are verses in the Bible about that, too. Not that I'm going to quote them to you just now, but God also gave us wonderful natural instincts to lead us, and I look forward to guiding you if you will allow me. I want you to show you all the ways we can please each other—if you would like me to?"

He lifted her hand and kissed one finger, than another. His touch was warm, and suddenly her feelings of constraint seemed small and silly, and the wonderful ripple of sensation that always ran through her when he touched her was back.

"Oh," she repeated, this time even more faintly, but the stiffness of her back had eased, and she founded herself leaning toward him.

As he had done before, he pushed back the sleeve of her nightdress and kissed her wrist, and Ophelia felt the delicious ripples continue. Suddenly, moving easily and yet swiftly, he lifted her legs and shifted her farther onto the bed, laying her back against the pillows.

He stood back and stripped off his coat and shirt and neckcloth with rapid but efficient movements.

Abashed but deeply interested, Ophelia lowered her lashes and watched through their veiling as her husband's body appeared, no longer cloaked by its covering of daywear. My, she had made an interesting acquisition! His chest was broad and covered by a sprinkling of dark blond hair, and his shoulders were broad, too, and well-muscled. His arms were nicely corded—all that chopping of wood, she thought demurely. And now, oh, heavens, he was dropping his trousers. She shut her eyes for a moment, afraid she would turn cherry red . . .

Gazing straight up at the pale muslin that draped the bed, she thought of those natural instincts that Giles had mentioned. Was that what stirred inside her and made her feel so trembly, a little bit frightened and nervous, her heart beating fast? She wanted to hide her face, and yet she would not have been anywhere else for all the gold in a Spanish pirate's treasure trove.

Her view of the top of the bed was cut off by her husband's handsome face. "Ophelia?"

"Yes, my love," she said.

He leaned down to kiss her lips, and she responded—a little timidly at first, then, as his lips coaxed and soothed and then encouraged her, with rising heat. And his arms went round her, turned her toward him, ran up the back of her torso, gently kneaded her back and shoulders till she shivered with delight and put her own arms about his neck and pulled him nearer. For long minutes they kissed, then he drew back and untied the knot at her neckline that held the gown closed.

"I believe it's your turn," he murmured.

It took a moment for her to follow his meaning, then she saw that he was drawing off her nightgown. Blushing, she lifted her arms to allow him to ease it over her head, and—for the first time in her life—she was naked before a man. She held her breath.

"You are so beautiful, my darling," he said, smiling down at her. "I can hardly believe how lovely you are."

Ophelia found that she could inhale again, although she still fought the urge to pull a blanket over her bare body. Was it true what he had said before, that she was not truly a wicked woman? That was a trifle disheartening. She would have to try harder.

He leaned closer and kissed the side of her neck, just below her ear. Ophelia's eyes widened. Oh, my! The tremors of feeling that ran through her from such a simple caress! Perhaps it was worth getting naked, after all.

"You may do that again," she suggested.

"I will be sure to," he agreed. So he did. He kissed the tender skin, even nibbled a bit lower on her neck, which sent such chills down her back that Ophelia found herself moving against the linen sheets, not sure what one was supposed to do with all these sensations that ran up and down her body—her still naked body which she was so alarmingly aware of . . .

He continued to rain kisses and small nibbles all the way down her neck and shoulder, and every single one sent charges of sensation through her, and as he did, his left hand almost casually reached across and touched her other shoulder, rubbing it lightly. And her body didn't seem to know which sensation to savor most, and her brain—her brain had apparently stopped functioning altogether.

It's all right, Ophelia told herself. It's Giles, my husband. Husband . . . what a lovely word; she had never appreciated it fully before. It was a word wrapped up with love and trust and now—oh, he had let his hand drop lower and now it stroked the upper curve of her left breast, even as his lips moved to touch the upper curve of her right breast, and the parallel play of sensation was almost overwhelming.

Her brain gave up the fight, and her body gave itself over to pure sensation. Ophelia moved beneath his hand and his lips, and when she found that she was making little gasps and moans of delight she hoped that this was acceptable, because she didn't think she knew how to stop. . . .

The circles of pleasure that grew from his lips flowed out from his kisses and on throughout her body. He pressed his lips against her breast, even as he pressed gently with his hand on the other side, massaging lightly, and when his mouth touched the nipple, she almost came off the bed. But he pressed her back gently, and his tongue touched it again, surrounded it, eased it into his mouth, suckled, sending ripples of pleasure deep down into her body until her stomach ached with an increasingly urgent need.

All the while his hand mimicked much of his lips' and tongue's actions on the other side, and she thought nothing could induce more feeling, nothing until he moved his head and applied his lips and tongue to the left breast. And she gasped again, and found herself muttering, "Oh, yes, darling, yes, yes, yes."

And then his hand had strayed down to her stomach, tracing

light patterns over the skin there, skin so ultrasensitive that she drew up her legs a little and moaned deep inside her throat. But Giles's hand moved in ever widening circles until he could ease her legs apart and then—oh heavens—his hand slipped into the curly dark triangle between her legs and touched areas so sensitive that Ophelia thought she truly honestly could not bear the sensation; she was moving on the bed linen, her body rising and falling as if to evade his knowing touch for an instant and then hastening back for more.

He paused only long enough to kiss her again, and she put both arms around his neck and pulled him tightly to her. And this time she felt his own response, and she paused in surprise.

She opened her eyes to look into his face and saw his clear blue eyes crinkle at their edges. "You are allowed to look, my love," he said. "Even touch."

So, blushing, she ran her hand down the warmth of his chest, loving the soft touch of his chest hair, liking that he inhaled sharply as she reached his stomach. Apparently she could affect his body, too! When she ventured farther down yet—there . . . his male member stood stiff and alert. Did she dare touch him?

Timidly, at first, she closed her hand around it and felt the pulsing energy of all his masculine force—this then would fit inside her?—and she trembled with excitement. But she was no longer afraid.

"What do we do?" she whispered.

"I will show you," he told her. He knelt over her and lifted her hips a little so that it was easier to slip inside her, running his hands down her belly, one more time tracing the sensitive places that longed for his touch till she moved with eager anticipation. Her body ached with need and yet she knew only vaguely what she ached for.

And then he pushed inside her where she was damp with the need for him.

It was a unique sensation. He felt so big and yet so right, and so good, filling the space exactly as it should be. For a moment she went very still, savoring the feel of him, then she felt a deep need to move against him, pushing him deeper, grasping with her muscles to hold him inside her in ways she hadn't known she would know.

Yet he seemed to meet resistence. What was wrong? Was she not big enough?

He leaned forward to kiss her forehead. "There may be a little pain, my love," he said. "But not for long."

She bit her lip and stayed very still.

He pushed forward, and she felt a pang deep inside. Well, not too bad. He drew back, which felt good, and pushed forward, and she waited for the pain to strike again, but this time his movement brought only pleasure. She breathed again and moved with him. In and out, up and down, there was a rhythm to it, and she found it without thinking, found it more easily than she had any pattern on the dance floor and without any need for prompting.

And oh, the rippling waves of pleasure that flowed up from deep inside her, how incredible were these sensations, how amazing that these hidden parts of her body and his body could provoke so much feeling.

Giles moved ever more quickly, with an easy strength that she'd always known he had. The rising circles of pleasure were drowning them both, but showering them not with death but with a life-affirming joy that would follow them through their marriage, bless every day they shared together, Ophelia thought faintly. They were being swept up into a maelstrom of passion that was more than she had ever dreamed of—rising and growing, more intense and glorious with every movement of his hips, every thrust, every spasm that she seemed to echo through every grain and freckle of her body. And when he surged into the fullness of his passion, she felt his completion even as her own exploded past all knowledge or limits into expanding circles of ecstasy like fireworks bursting outward again and again, into colors brighter than the naked eye could see.

Joy was inside them, and love bound them together—they seemed to have melded into one. Poets had written about this, she thought dimly, in soaring stanzas that lay in the back of her mind, just past memory's reach. But she knew the truth of the poems now, in the deepest part of her heart and soul, even though her tongue was mute and her body sated.

Her hair damp and clinging to her face, she lay her head against his chest. She could hear his thundering heart slowing to a more sedate beat, and his breathing returning to normal. Did her own body also reveal similar signs as the stages of their love retreated from riotous to languor?

He put one arm about her, and she lay inside the circle of his embrace, content to curl up next to him and listen to the soft sound of his breathing. There seemed no need for talking, though she also felt she could have said anything and he would have listened.

Presently, she turned and looked at his face, wondering if he slept. But his eyes were open, and he raised his brows.

"Do we do this every night?" she asked quite seriously. "Or only now and then?"

"What would be your preference?" he asked.

"Every night," she told him.

His smile broke across his face like dawn on a Yorkshire moor. "I would not argue with that, sweet lovely Ophelia," he told her.

She smiled back at him and started to lay her head back in the circle of his arm, then a sudden thought made her pause. "I have something to show you," she said, and, feeling the languor pulling at her limbs, she went to the bureau.

She came back with the playbill that Cordelia had brought her. She showed him the paper, and Giles scanned it politely but without comprehension. She pointed out her pen name. "This is me," she explained. "As author of the play. I have the credit, Giles, *me*. It is my writing, my words, my story! And I also received pay, real money.

"It is a nom de plume, of course, but it is not impossible that it might somehow be linked to me. And although I should enjoy earning the money, it is more exciting to see my stories produced. But Giles, I am aware that some of your parishioners are likely not going to think it proper for a vicar's wife to write comedies—somewhat bawdy comedies, if the truth be known. Perhaps you don't, either?"

She had not thought of that before.

His fair hair tousled, he looked blank for a moment.

She faltered, and it seemed to her that the world itself paused for an instant on its axis. Her mouth seemed very dry.

Pushing up on one elbow, he smiled at her. "My darling Ophelia, if it is your comedy, I am sure it is delightful, and if bawdy, bawdy and delightful. Didn't Shakespeare do the same? I would never seek to deny you your talents or make you less than you are. And my parishioners will learn to deal with it, I am sure."

The world seem to resume its rightful movement. She drew a deep breath and leaned over to kiss her husband.

The next day Cordelia had a brief note from her sister.

> *Marriage is delightful, dear Cordelia. The only mystery is I do not see how married couples ever tear themselves out of bed! But since we must rise, today I am discussing receipts for Giles's most preferred dishes with the house-keeper. I have written to Maddy for some of our mother's favorites for me to try, as well. Happily, the servants seem to have no problem accepting me as the new mistress of the house.*
>
> *We will talk soon!*
> *Yours as ever,*
> *Ophelia*

Except it was not as ever, and it would never be again—she was no longer the closest person in her twin's life, Cordelia thought. Oh, she was very happy for her sister, really, she was. But still, the note left her feeling strangely lonely.

"How is your sister?" Marian asked at the breakfast table as Cordelia refolded the sheet of paper.

"Very well," Cordelia said, then cleared her throat, afraid her voice had sounded too bleak. "Marriage seems to suit her." This came out more cheerfully, and she smiled. "Although if Ophelia takes up cooking, I'm not sure even the vicar will retain his saintly demeanor."

Marian chuckled. "Her enthusiasm for the mixing bowl will likely soon wear off, and she will go back to her quill and paper."

"Indeed, and a good thing for the household! I must get ready, however. I have an early meeting with Mr. Sheffield and Mr. Druid before tonight's performance to discuss . . . a possible new act for the show," she said.

Actually, that was not quite true. They had agreed to meet at a coffee shop, away from the listening ears always found at the theater, so they could discuss the still missing letter.

When the marquis's carriage let her off at the appointed meeting place, Ransom Sheffield was waiting to escort her inside. He took her into a room reserved just for the three of them, and she was glad to see that their privacy was indeed assured.

The waiter brought them steaming cups of coffee sweetened with brown sugar, and while Cordelia waited for her steaming brew to cool, she listened to Ransom summarize where they had come so far.

"I turned the apartment inside out," he said. "I do not believe I could have missed it. And although I know it's possible that he has stashed it somewhere else, that seems to me unlikely. For one thing, where?"

"In his office?" Cordelia suggested.

"That is even more accessible and less securely locked than his rooms," Ransom pointed out. "Anyhow, I went through his office the first week I was there. I saw no sign of my brother's note. No, I'd rule that out, too."

"Oh," Cordelia said.

"The whore—ah, excuse me, my dear," the conjurer blushed. "The establishment in Whitechapel? I don't think so, either, dear boy. That place is full of people with darker hearts than our Mr. Nettles, if such a thing is possible. I tend to think that he is keeping it close."

Cordelia took a cautious sip of her coffee. "On his person, you mean?"

"Indeed. It could be in an inner pocket, inside his leather wallet, even sewn into the lining of his coat or his hat. Or, and I rather favor this one, he might have a secret compartment in his shoe." Mr. Druid's eyes gleamed. "I've done some rather nice tricks with that type of hidden cache."

Cordelia looked at him with admiration. "Indeed. You mentioned you had been a pickpocket in a more nefarious period of your life. I don't suppose, if the paper were inside one of his pockets—"

The conjurer sighed. "Alas, my dear, my skill is quite limited. Why do you think I ended up in gaol to begin with?"

"Oh, I see," she said. "Forgive me for suggesting it."

He nodded. Ransom seemed deep in thought.

"Unless we can find a way to induce the man to strip off all his clothes . . . I don't suppose he is a devotee of Turkish baths?"

Cordelia shuddered. "I don't think he bathes at all. Have you stood close to him, or even a few feet away? He smells like the alley before a rain."

Ransom wrinkled his brow. "Yes, I'd noticed. And if he has any amorous interests, we'd have to assume he pursues them in his own, ah, establishment in Whitechapel. And since they have already seen my face and a copy of yours—not that I would dream of allowing you near it, Cordelia—I don't see that we have any hope of catching him without his clothing or getting the chance to search his clothing for concealed pockets, there. What is it?"

Cordelia stared at him. "It's just that, since the marquis was able to have the madam and several of the men sent up before the magistrate, I'd hoped that perhaps—"

"That perhaps the brothel had been closed down?" He quirked one brow. "I'm sorry to say, these places are like the classical Hydra, cut off one head and they grow another."

Sighing, Cordelia nodded her understanding and took another sip of her coffee. "So," she said. "What do we do now? If we cannot force our recalcitrant manager to remove his clothes for our convenience in searching—"

"I suppose, we must look for a way to persuade him to hand over the note," Ransom said.

And since that seemed as likely as the Prince Regent handing over his hope for the throne, presently it was time for all of them to make their way to the theater. They did not seem to have arrived at any great illumination or theory.

Ransom did share the story of Avery's attempt to track down the delivery of the second blackmail note. "I will say this for my brother, it was a brave attempt," he pointed out. "But although he followed the messenger across half of London, and thus missed being at hand to help Giles storm the brothel, which likely was just as well; he lost him in the end. He has resumed his post at White's; if nothing else, he will make a capital footman by the time this is over."

Cordelia shook her head at him, although Mr. Druid chuckled.

Ransom hailed a hackney, and Cordelia was handed in, escorted in the somewhat crowded vehicle by her two fellow thespians, and she rode back to Malory Road in a less than hopeful spirit.

At least she could sit side by side with Ransom. With his tall frame, handsome rakish face and ready glance—how did he always seem to know what she was thinking and when she was concerned or disturbed?—she always felt more secure when Ransom was nearby. Thank heavens that he had decided, quite without persuasion, to join the theater troupe, too, to look out for their—now her—welfare.

She tried to tell him how much his presence meant to her.

As usual, he turned away her expressions of gratitude.

"Not at all; been good for me to have something to do," he told her, his silvery eyes glinting with humor. "I haven't been down to my estate for weeks. My agent has likely gotten twice as much done without my interference. And I'm sure I will win three times as much money the next time I have time to play cards with my new acting skills."

She laughed. "Oh, yes, no doubt. At least no one has had handbills pasted up announcing that a gentleman of good name will be acting at Malory Road. Although, I'd like to know why not? Why is it such a scandal when a lady treads the boards and not a gentleman? That is hardly fair! Does no one wish to know how a gentleman performs?"

She had begun the sentence in mock censure before she realized how it was going to end. She bit her lip as his face lit up with mischief.

"As to that, I have several ladies who could give me good references," he murmured into her ear. "Although if you really would like to know, I would be happy to give you a private performance and allow you to judge."

She blushed, feeling the heat in her cheeks. "I did not mean—"

"Oh, I know what you meant." He shifted his arm and allowed it to rest on the back of the seat, caressing her shoulder. His grip felt warm and strong, and she wanted badly to lean into it. On his other side, Mr. Druid seemed lost in his own thoughts, as the conjurer often was.

As a chaperone, the man left much to be desired.

Or perhaps he was ideal!

Turning his head, Ransom met her glance. His own gaze was half teasing, half serious. "I had no idea you were concerned about the quality of my performance, Miss Applegate. But now that I know, I will make certain not to falter. I want to be ready to exhibit only my best efforts for your enjoyment."

She knew her cheeks must be the color of a flaming sunset. "You enjoy tormenting me," she said, trying to maintain the dignity of a lady who is above such childish banter.

"You have no idea what I would most enjoy, dear Miss Applegate," he murmured, and the hand that lay on her shoulder, the hand that Mr. Druid, on his other side, could not see, reached up to caress her cheek with the slightest of touches.

She jumped, then sighed with pleasure. Without thinking, she turned her face into his hand; allowing him to brush her cheek, her jaw, trace the outline of her lips with his strong fingers, his touch as gentle and yet as knowing as—

The hackney was rattling to a stop. They had reached the theater.

Damn, she thought and in her confusion almost said the word aloud.

They went inside and she hurried on to the dressing room to change into her costume. When she sat down in front of the looking glass, she stared at her flushed face. How did the man have such an effect on her? Her heart still beat fast.

Oh, ask a stupid question, she told herself crossly and reached for the powder puff.

The theater's pit and boxes were still packed, although Madam Tatina took credit, to anyone who would listen, for the play's popularity. But it was not the diva the audience still pointed their opera glasses at or leaned over the balconies to scrutinize.

Cordelia made sure her mask was tied on securely before she walked onstage.

If Cordelia had ever wished to be a successful actress, she would have been gratified. The fact that she was trapped in her role only made the play's success more ironic.

After their final bows tonight, Marley commented on how her skills were improving. "You're speaking out nicely," he told her. "And your timing has improved. You've learned not to speak into the laughs but to wait for the audience's laughter to almost fade before you begin the next line."

She thanked him gravely, again thinking of the irony of it all. Still, she had a plan for her eventual freedom.

She spent any extra time coaching Venetia, who she hoped might someday be able to take over Ophelia's part when Cordelia was free to leave the production. She had worried that the actress would have trouble learning the lines, since she didn't think the girl could read. But she learned, to her surprise, that Ophelia had been teaching the streetwise but otherwise uneducated actress to read and write since they had struck up their unlikely friendship.

"Lily said I were doing right well, too," Venetia explained, pride evident in her voice. "Only the bigger words give me trouble. She said I need to know 'ow to read if I want to get on. I was lucky to get a job 'ere at all fooling Mr. Nettles."

"She was right, too," Cordelia agreed. "And you're doing

very well." Perhaps, she thought, her sister would make a better vicar's wife than she had realized.

Tonight Cordelia found herself not wanting to go back to the marquis's home. They had another social engagement. She would have to hear more gossip about the mystery lady, dance with more idiots who would tell her their theories, and from a comment Ransom had made, she'd gathered he wouldn't be there . . .

She sent a note out to the marquis's carriage for Marian, offering apologies but telling her hostess she had an extra, late rehearsal and to please return the carriage for her in a couple of hours.

She just didn't want to face another tedious social affair. And anyhow, she had made a promise to Mr. Druid. Didn't she owe him a favor after he had risked his own freedom by jimmying the lock to get Ransom into Mr. Nettles's room?

Bubbling with enthusiasm, he had come in just before the play began. "It has arrived at last! Come see, dear girl!"

She'd followed him to the prop room in the back of the theater where, to her bemusement, she saw him point to a large wicker basket as big as an apple barrel. It had a top made of the same material.

"What is it, Mr. Druid?" she asked. He looked as excited as a child with a new toy, and she thought that his breath held just a hint of wine.

"It's a new trick! I seldom imbibe, as I must have my wits about me to do my juggling and my other tricks, but today I have been celebrating my good fortune." He sighed happily.

"I cannot wait to try it out! I saw it two days ago down near the docks, performed by a gentleman of Indian extraction. One of the scene shifters told me about it, and I went down to see. The magician was Hindu, I believe; he wore a turban of really marvelous construction—but I digress.

"He had this large basket, and an assistant: a slip of a boy, who wore a turban, too, and nothing much else but this sort of loincloth. The boy went into this basket, and then the master put swords through it, and then he pulled out the swords, and out came the boy with not a scratch on him! Marvelous, and the crowd just showered him with coins. It was most impressive! And I have bought the basket, and the swords, of course, and I mean to master the trick myself."

The conjurer beamed. She nodded, hoping that the real trick was not in the coins that the other magician had taken from Mr. Druid.

"Did he, ah, tell you how the trick was executed?"

"No, but I'm sure we can figure it out, my dear."

"We?" She stared at him.

"I need someone to be inside the basket," he explained, as if it were obvious. "To take the boy's part. I thought you might wish to assist me?" He seemed to be confident she would think it an enormous lark, and she found it difficult to find the heart to dissuade him. And she did owe him a favor.

"I suppose I could try," she said doubtfully.

So, when it was quiet backstage, when Venetia and the other actors and actresses had departed, and even the swells and other gentlemen admirers had faded from around the stage door, Cordelia made her way to the prop room. She found Mr. Druid waiting, with a portable set of wooden steps so that she could climb easily into the enormous basket.

"You will probably want to remove your dress, my dear," the conjurer told her, "or perhaps don a pair of trousers. If you recall, the boy wore very little. And I think the point is that you are going to have to squeeze yourself into rather odd positions to avoid the swords."

"I see," Cordelia said faintly. She went back to the pegs on which hung assorted costumes from old productions and eventually found a kind of harem outfit that was not totally revealing and had a pair of wide-legged trousers and a loose-fitting top. She went behind a tall wooden screen and exchanged her muslin gown for this strange getup. When she returned, Mr. Druid was so matter-of-fact about her garb that she felt less conspicuous. His mind was intent upon making the new ruse work.

"This will be an enormous hit with the audience, mark my words, my dear," he told her, his enthusiasm still strongly evident. "Now, if you will take your place inside the basket—"

She climbed the steps and, with no easy way to climb down, finally jumped into the dim depths of the basket, hoping that there were no many-legged-surprises awaiting her. But she found only a slight layer of dust, which made her sneeze. The interior was not as large as it had first looked, and she tried to find a comfortable position, eventually setting on a semi-crouch as the conjurer put the lid on top of the basket, making it even darker inside.

How was she supposed to see the swords when they came? Cordelia was about to ask when suddenly, the magician announced, "The first one will be up by your head, so watch for it toward the left." And he thrust the first one through.

It slide through the basket—she could see the bigger openings in the wicker, now, and saw that there were slits prepared for the swords to travel. So there were ways for one to survive this trick, somehow. If one knew the right ways to avoid them, which she did not.

The glint of metal in the dimness showed up more than she had expected. And she had not expected metal! Cordelia realized that she had been expecting wooden swords, like the fake weapons the actors used in the sword dance that had so bedeviled Ransom in Act Two. Their fake swords were painted with a gilt-colored paint, and were perfectly convincing from a distance. Why did this Hindu person have to use metal swords? Surely they were not sharply honed?

She ducked her head a little more, eying the blade with distrust.

"Now, down at the near side," she heard the conjurer say. Another blade slide into the basket, and she drew her leg back in alarm. That had come too close!

Good God. It had ripped right through the thin gauze of her costume. It *was* sharp. It was a sword, a real sword. The man was mad! Whatever the Indian magician had done—

"Now, up to the top again, on the right."

She leaned to the other side, almost hitting the first sword, as another one came through dangerously close to her throat. Cordelia gasped in alarm. She tried to scream but couldn't find the breath.

"Now at the side, on your right." Another blade—

She pulled her leg up sharply, till she was balancing precariously on one foot, and that leg was cramping already. If she lost her balance and fell—she felt as if she wavered on the edge of a pit full of vipers.

"Mr. Druid," she cried at last. "Stop, I can't do this!"

"Oh, you're doing fine, dear girl," he said, and she heard the unaccustomed tremor in his voice. "The lad at the docks had no trouble. I'm sure you can do it. We're just getting started. I have a dozen more swords to insert before we're done. Then I will draw them all out, one by one, and help you out, to thunderous applause, I'm sure. You will be a great hit." He spoke as if they were already onstage before the audience.

He would draw out only a bloody corpse, she thought, panic clutching her throat.

"Now one at the side, just here."

"Stop!" she cried.

Her pleas only seem to convince him to go faster, as if he could finish before she changed her mind. This sword ripped through so close to her ribs that it left a fine cut under her arm; she felt the sting of it and drew a deep breath.

"Now at the top; mind your head."

She could mind it, but there was nowhere else to put it! She was helpless, unless she wished to slit her own throat by pushing into the sword in front of her. The sword that came through next nicked her ear; she gasped at the sting and felt a trickle of blood run down her cheek.

"Mr. Druid," she cried, "you must stop! You're going to kill me!"

This time he didn't answer. She heard a thump and then a muffled thud.

Had the man passed out? Oh, God help her, no. If he had, she would never get out of here alive!

Eighteen

Then the lid was lifted from the top of the basket and someone held a candle over her head. The flame glinted on the swords crisscrossing inside the basket.

"Good God! Don't move!" It was Ransom.

She had never been so glad to see anyone—and never had any advice been so unnecessary!

The swords slid rapidly back out of the basket. She held her breath until they were all gone, then, trembling, she allowed herself to breathe again. Ransom reached down to help lift her out. All the strength seemed to have leached out of her limbs; he had to almost drag her out of the big basket, then he lifted her into his arms.

"Where is Mr. Druid?" she asked, while clinging to Ransom. He nodded toward the corner.

He appeared to have knocked out the magician. Eyes shut, body limp, the man lay crumpled against a pile of discarded fabric. "It was faster than arguing," Ransom told her. "How did this happen? Never mind. We need to tend to your wounds, first."

She nodded, still too weak to do more than lay her head

against his chest and be thankful that she was, for the most part, in one piece.

The silly outfit she had donned to play magician's assistant—never again, she vowed—was shredded and spotted with blood.

Ransom carried her back to the actresses' dressing room, where a couch gave him a place to lay her down. Shaking his head and swearing, he looked at the small cuts and scratches that marked her body. "What the bloody hell was he thinking?" He stood again. "Don't move; I'll be right back."

When he returned, he had a basin of water, clean cloths and a bottle of wine. He removed the remaining shreds of the harem costume and bathed and treated the gashes, bandaged the larger cut on her side, and then brought her a silk dressing gown of a bright scarlet and gold pattern, which smelled heavily of lavender, to put on. It looked familiar.

"This," Cordelia pointed out, glad to have something innocuous to say—she had been blushing hard and trying to pretend she wasn't aware of his hands on her bare body— "belongs to the diva. We will both be in enormous trouble if Madam Tatina finds I have been wearing it."

"True," he agreed. "But then, after your ordeal at the hands of our slightly mad conjurer, I thought you needed something pleasant to brighten your evening."

So he was aware of it, too, the tension that danced between them. But he was only doing what anyone would do, Cordelia told herself, staring at the end of the worn couch. She had been hurt, he had tended her injuries. Just because her clothes were falling apart . . . it wasn't really as improper as it seemed . . .

Ransom cleared his throat. He moved the basin of water to the floor and took the wine, which he had been using to dress the wounds, found a couple of glasses and poured out the rest of it for them to drink. "Now why don't you tell me how in hell you agreed to get in that basket in the first place?"

She tried to explain. Somehow, it was hard to make it sound even halfway logical. "You know how enthused he is about new tricks," she said, afraid she sounded defensive. "And he did help us get into the manager's rooms, so—"

"So you were ready to offer yourself up as a pincushion?"

"I didn't expect it to be so . . . so . . ." Cordelia frowned at him.

"And why were you here so late, anyhow? I thought you had a dance to go to." He raised his dark brows, that sardonic gleam back in his eyes. She had begun to think that he was protecting himself when he retreated behind that sardonic humor. If so, why did he withdraw now?

"I sent word to Marian that I had rehearsal. Really, I didn't want to go," she said bluntly. "I felt, well, it would be more gossip about the mystery lady onstage, more silly men asking me to dance. I would be alone. And you wouldn't be there." Then she wished she had not been quite so honest about that last. She looked away from his expression, which for a moment had seemed startled. Picking up her wine, she gulped some down. "My sister is married, and I . . . I feel . . ."

She was going from bad to worse. She drank more wine and refused to look at him. Perhaps he had not wanted to dance with her again. She was certainly not going to ask him why he had chosen not to go to the party!

But he seemed to hear the question anyhow. "I stayed because I heard Nettles tell Nobby he was going to Whitechapel tonight," Ransom said quietly. "I thought perhaps I would have another look at his office."

"Oh," she said. "Did you find anything?"

"Not the note, certainly," he said. "An interesting set of books. And I had to wait for Nobby to nurse himself to sleep with a bottle of gin, so . . . and by the time I finished searching, I heard sounds from the back, so I came to check. Just as well that I did!"

"Yes, I am most thankful you did," she agreed, and shivered at the memory of the swords sliding so close to her. Somehow, she couldn't seem to stop shaking.

"It's all right now, Cordelia," he said.

But she still shook, as if all her fear had been stored up and now erupted at once.

"I can't st-stop," she stammered. "Wh-what's wrong with me?"

"It's all right," he told her, his voice steady. "I've seen men come off the battlefield and do this. You will be all right in a while."

Ransom pulled her up and put his arms around her, holding her close to him, trying to warm her with his own body heat, she thought.

"Let it go, Cordelia," he murmured into her ear. "Let it go."

He wrapped himself around her, holding her tight, and for the first time since her sister had left, Cordelia did not feel alone. She felt the strength of his body, the hard tightness of his arms, the tautness of his limbs and the muscled torso against which she leaned. She knew the keen intelligence and sharp wit of his mind, and how he had always been there when she needed him; and the cold fear inside her finally began to seep away. . . .

She lay her head on his shoulder and sobbed dryly, without tears but with a somehow greater need than mere tears would have conveyed. It was more than losing the companionship of her sister, Cordelia thought. Having her twin by her side was one thing. But meeting Ransom had taught her that there was a greater loneliness aching inside her, an emptiness she had only lately begun to suspect.

He was the kind of man she had not known she would find, not realized she might be fortunate enough to encounter. The energy that flowed between them . . . surely he felt it, too . . .

Her tremors had faded. But now he might let go; Cordelia found she did not want to be released. She had her arms about his neck. Did he only care to hold her when it was for medicinal purposes?

"Ransom?" she spoke into his ear. "May I kiss you?"

"Cordelia," he said, "Miss Applegate. We are alone in the theater. Unchaperoned. It would be better, wiser—"

"I didn't ask what was wiser," she told him, her tone grave with reproach. "I have a great need to kiss you."

He turned to meet her gaze, and she saw the sardonic gleam glint briefly in his silver-gray eyes.

"And they said that your sister was the wild one?" he murmured. "Cordelia, I give you fair warning. I am not, like my esteemed cousin, a temperate man. If you do not flee now, you will not have the opportunity to go."

Smiling with relief, she pulled him closer. His kiss felt hard against her lips, and she met him with equal strength. The weakness in her limbs was slipping away; her hunger was un-abated.

Unlike her sister, Cordelia had never longed to go onstage, had not spent years making up stories in her head. She'd always felt a bit prosaic next to Ophelia. But now, for the first time in her life, Cordelia felt as if she knew what she wanted. She wanted this man—she wasn't sure about how or exactly in what manner, her notions about lovemaking were vague—but she wanted him, here and now and without any further fuss about propriety or chaperones or . . .

When you were lucky enough to find a man like Ransom Sheffield, you didn't second-guess your fortune. Cordelia wrapped her arms about his neck and kissed him with every ounce of her being.

Eventually, it was, she found, necessary to breathe.

When they broke apart, she found she was breathing fast, and he, too, seemed to breathe quickly. "They do say, among the troupe, that you are a quick study," he murmured. "I am so glad."

She laughed out loud.

Then he was kissing her neck, and she shivered with de-light and the laughter faded. Somehow, the silk robe had come untied, and his hands were drifting down, running lightly over her shoulder blades and down into the hollows of her neck where the skin was sensitive to every nuance of his fingertips.

She shivered again from the intensity of her feelings. The tremor of sensation that his strong hands induced seemed to run through every ounce of her body, leaving her as shivery as if a gale of autumn wind had sailed through her bedroom. And still his hands moved over her body, dropping lower to caress the curves of her uncovered breasts.

Cordelia gasped and found that new hungers were grow-ing; she leaned forward into his hands—large capable hands, which knew their way here, as they had known earlier how to ease her hurts. She felt their light touch on her breasts, held her breath as they moved in easy concert to her nipples, and arched her back as the delicate touch sent ripples of sensation through her entire body.

The rings of feeling seemed to echo through her, floating over and through her until she quivered from it, until she felt the resonance deep in her belly. She felt confused and almost overwhelmed, yet she didn't want him to stop. In fact, she reached up for him again, kissing him when he leaned close enough, kissing his hands when he paused, running her own hands over his chest and pushing his jacket and waistcoat aside to feel the hard muscle beneath.

"You have"—she pointed out, her tone reproachful—"a great deal of clothing on. It hardly seems fair."

"You're quite right," he agreed, grinning. He unbuttoned his coat, pulling it and his waistcoat off, then unwound his neck-cloth and pulled his white linen shirt over his head. The rest of his garments followed, although he had difficulty with his boots, which necessitated a certain amount of jumping about.

She tried not to giggle.

"If you laugh, I will make you play bootjack," he threatened. But in a moment, he had the footwear off, too, and then his trousers and undergarments, and then he came back to the couch.

Cordelia was trying not to stare at his masculine parts—it was not only his hands which were large and well-made—when he leaned over her and kissed the tender skin of her stomach.

She gasped, and felt sensation ripple across her skin like a wave on the shore. And now he leaned farther and kissed her right breast, letting his mouth find her nipple. Cordelia almost sat up, the feelings were so strong, but he caught her and pushed her gently back.

"Just enjoy, my darling," he said, his voice low.

The tone of his voice, the endearment, was as much a caress as the delightful feeling of his mouth on her skin. All of it sent shivers of delight through her. She felt as if she might dissolve from sheer pleasure. And it continued to come, wave upon wave. He sucked the nipple, ran his tongue over the tender flesh and played with the most sensitive bits of her breast. And just when Cordelia thought she could take no more, he switched to the other breast, and began again, and again she felt the rings of delight begin, rising, falling and flowing outward to crest and sweep over her, leaving her speechless with ever increasing need.

She had no idea how to tell him how wonderful this felt. And how did she do something similar for him?

She tried to ask, but he only smiled. "I am happy when you are happy," he told her. "Just now, let's make you fly, lovely Cordelia."

She thought she had left her body behind some eternity ago, except that it still glowed with pleasure whenever he touched her. And somehow, it seemed they had only begun. He reached lower still, touched her stomach and, with a delicate touch that almost made her moan, traced circles in the tender skin.

She was aching for more—more of what she didn't yet know, but she knew her need was deep and intense, and she kissed his lips, ran her hands up and across the defined muscles of his chest and the dark hair that clustered across it.

"Ransom!"

She found that her hips were moving; she could not be still on the narrow couch, and she wondered if she were again having some reaction from the ordeal in the basket. But when she looked up at him, concern in her eyes, she saw that he grinned down at her.

"You are well, dearest, more than well—you are exquisite!"

He moved one hand down to touch the place between her legs where the ache was deepest. Cordelia gasped. "Oh, Ransom!"

Without thinking, she moved her body toward his hand, and he slipped his fingers deeper into that secret place, already wet with her hunger for him. And the feel of his hand as it searched for the right spot—just the right spot—left such tingles of sensation that she gasped again.

"Ransom!"

"I said we would make you fly."

She would fly to the damn moon if he kept that up! Gasping once more, she flung her arms about his neck and moved even closer into his embrace, unable to be still when he did such amazing things to her body. For a few moments, he slid his fingers in and out, sending charges of pure energy surging through her body, pleasing her and yet exciting her to greater need at one and the same time. She found that she was making soft inarticulate sounds in her throat. Then he lay her back against the couch and pushed her legs apart as he placed himself over her.

"Now, my love—"

And he slid inside her. She gasped at the feel of him—this sensation was even more intense, more right. He pushed against her tightness, again and again, and the pulsations of pleasure were so deep, echoed through her being with such exquisite intensity until she felt she might shatter like a crystal goblet at the clarity of a high-pitched note. The joy was almost too much to bear. Cordelia shut her eyes and allowed all thought to fall away.

There was only feeling, only the rhythm that bound them together, as basic and elemental as the old humors that had pulsed beneath the core of the earth. Like the Titans that once ruled the universe, or the Greek gods on Mount Olympus, there was only ancient primal instinct, but surely of the purest and best . . .

And it was Ransom, whom she would trust with her life, whom she would give the best part of herself to, freely and willingly, with whom she would share her heart, her body, her soul.

He continued to move in and out, and the sensation was so amazing that she fell easily into the rhythm with him, finding it again the most elemental, the purest of life's secrets. The pleasure that it brought was so acute that she found it almost unbearable, and she gasped, biting her lip to keep from making too much noise.

Ransom bent closer and kissed her. "You're going to make your lips bleed," he told her. "It's all right; no one will hear you."

She gazed at him. "You don't mind?"

"My darling Cordelia, I have waited for this day from the first moment I met you!"

He grinned down at her. Now he pushed harder and faster, and she found the strength of her pleasure deepen. Oh, bloody hell, could it get any better? She reached behind her to find something with which to brace herself, grabbed the edge of the couch and gripped it so hard that she found the worn fabric ripping in her hands. But still his body pounded against hers.

They had come together so fiercely that they were slipping off the narrow sofa; she found they were sliding onto the thin rug. Too impatient to wait to climb back up, she pulled him down with her, and they lay together on the hard wooden floor where she met him with an unabated vigor.

But when they fell back, he rolled onto his back, and to her surprise, she found herself on top, but still joined. For a moment, she paused, then she found that he still moved inside her, and this change in position had certain advantages. When she moved . . . ah, when she moved, she could control the angle and the speed of their tempo: She slid her knees to the sides of his body, ignoring the cold of the floor, only aware of the heat rising from their linked passion, the heat that they made together, and she arched her back and moved with rapidly increasing joy as passion and pleasure joined over them like colors in a sunset deepening into dusk, colors that swirled about them as the circles of pleasure rose and consumed her, surely consumed him—and she was as intent as he was on the pounding rhythm that held them together as one being. She felt as if she were being turned inside out and every bit of her were drenched in pleasure, dripping with joy.

And when the speed and almost savage motion of their splendid manic dance made her near giddy, he grasped her hips and rolled them again, easing her back onto the rug and rising once more above her, kissing her quickly and then thrusting even more quickly, even more powerfully as she moaned aloud. "Yes, my love, yes!"

The force of their union sparked a wild and primitive joy

inside her, a spiraling rise of passion and deep sparking sweetness until she felt as if pure flame ran across her entire body, arcs of fire and ice spreading through her, taking her breath and coloring the universe.

Spasms rose from deep inside and raced over her body like lightning through a summer sky, bursting outward in silent explosions again and again. She heard him cry out, even as her lips parted in soundless exclamations until she fell back, limp and sated and more content than she had ever felt.

He pulled her close and wrapped his arms about her, and she lay within his embrace, too spent to seek—or need—any words.

For a few minutes, both damp with perspiration, they lay together on the rug, and no one spoke. Then he pushed himself up and leaned over her to kiss her forehead, her cheek, her lips. "My darling Cordelia, what a woman you are, to your core. I always knew it would be so."

She smiled up at him, still marveling at what they had shared. Ophelia was right. It was a small miracle.

"And you are such a man," she murmured. "Dearest Ransom."

"Will you marry me, sweet?" he asked, with one finger tracing the arch of her brow even as it rose in surprise. "Aside from my tendency to break into theaters, I am of good character—you may ask my cousin for his reference— sound family and respectable income. Then we can reenact this splendid drama every night without risk of falling out of bed. I promise to provide a couch of more ample proportions."

"Ransom!"

"Why are you surprised? Do you think I would devote weeks of my time frequenting a second-rate theater just to learn to do a poorly choreographed sword dance?"

She shuddered. "Do not mention swords to me! But marriage . . . why did you not say something before?"

"Before," he said, his tone wry, "you had thoughts only for your sister, my love. That is easy to understand; you have grown up taking care of her. But she has someone in her life now also devoted to her welfare; so I hope that you, too, will permit a new person to enter your life. I would very much like to be that lucky man."

She felt a lump rise in her throat and for a moment could not answer. She thought his gaze sharpened. She managed a watery smile and blinked hard.

"It is I who am fortunate, my love," she told him.

He leaned forward to kiss her. "We can argue that point after each embrace," he told her when they moved apart.

"But what about the missing note, Ransom?" she reminded him. "We still have to establish your brother's safety and release him as well as me from Nettles's blackmail, and we are running out of time!"

"Yes," he agreed. "And now that my marital bliss depends on it, not to mention my hapless brother's fate, I am more intent on a speedy release than ever. And just when I think I have examined even the most farfetched of notions, I believe you have given me an idea."

"I?" She stared at him.

He pulled her closer and told her what he had in mind, and Cordelia's eyes widened.

Ransom waited with her until the carriage returned with a maid for company on the ride home. Then he kissed her quickly and handed her up. Apparently the marquis and his wife were still at their social engagement, but Cordelia didn't mind. She greeted the servant civilly but didn't feel constrained to make conversation on the ride home. She could sit quietly and think of her extraordinary evening and how her blissful heart seemed to be drifting above the carriage beside the stars in the night sky—at least, until she remembered Nettles, and the dangerous situation in which they still found themselves ensnared.

Would they ever be free of his blackmail and his nasty little schemes? Only that seemed to stand between her and ultimate happiness. Social ruin was bad enough, but for Ransom's brother, exposure would mean his life.

How could she be happy just yet?

So while one part of her wanted to hum with new contentment, the other half of her still felt tense with fear. Sighing, Cordelia wondered if she would sleep at all that night.

The next morning, Ophelia came down to breakfast and was surprised to find a note already waiting from her sister.

"At this hour?" she said. "After being up late at the theater last night? I'm surprised she's even awake."

She stopped to bend and kiss her husband, who seemed to have already almost finished a plate of ham and steak and eggs and who kissed her heartily back, with a knowing look in his eye that made her blush, knowing that the maid watched them with a grin. Then she sat down to unfold the paper.

She skimmed the few lines of script and yelped like a startled puppy.

"My dear." Giles looked up in alarm. "Is everything all right?"

Without answering, she read it again.

Dearest Ophelia,

I know you will not judge me if I tell you I have sampled the sweetness of the marriage bed before actually taking the marriage vows—but that will come soon, as well, and you are quite right about the joy of it! Ransom loves me! And I adore him, and there is hope that we will work out this tangle yet. I am happy and fearful, both, but I will explain all soon. And for now, just share my happiness!

Your loving sister,
Cordelia

Ophelia found that her mouth was agape. She realized that Giles had spoken. And she certainly believed in honesty between husband and wife. On the other hand—

She cleared her throat. "Cordelia and Ransom are betrothed," she told him. "At least, they will be officially, I suppose, when

Ransom is able to ride into Yorkshire and see our father. I am so happy for them!"

He grinned. "That is most felicitous news. I admit, I had some suspicions about Ransom's feelings. I will congratulate my cousin as soon as I see him."

She nodded, pushing back her chair. "And I must go visit my sister! Nothing for me, Annie, thank you."

After a long giggly talk with Ophelia, Cordelia went into the theater early so that she could give Venetia one more lesson on taking over her role. She had decided she had to behave as if all would be well and she would soon be able to leave this role to someone else who would actually enjoy it.

Mr. Druid greeted her with a bashful diffidence, profuse apologies and a knot on his aching head. Ransom had given him a thorough chewing out, it seemed, when the conjuror had finally come to.

Cordelia accepted his apology, though she had to draw him to the side and tell him not to speak of it before anyone else, but she also told him she was done with being his assistant.

"Yes, yes," he agreed, though he sighed. "A shame, that. It was a splendid trick."

Cordelia bit back any comment and went off to warn Venetia against accepting any extra work with the magician.

When the two women finished their private rehearsal, Cordelia passed two scene shifters who were swearing briskly. Zeus's chariot had come off its wires again. "Bloody thing is fine one day, and off balance as 'ell the next," one of the men told the other, who nodded in agreement. Their words would once have shocked her; now she hardly noticed the foul language.

The same could be said for the young actor who walked past in his trousers and undershirt, his braces hanging down his front and a fake beard about to slide off his chin.

"Who took the gray wig from the costume store?" he was demanding. "I need it for Act One!"

Being part of the troupe had been a unique experience, Cordelia thought. She didn't really regret it, though she was ready to say good-bye now. And she would do it again for Ophelia's sake. But she didn't want to be exposed before all of London's Ton. . . . If Nettles talked . . .

When Marley came to the edge of the stage, adjusting his costume, she smiled at him and thanked him for all his help with her part.

"You're not leaving, are you?" he said, not quite meeting her eye.

"No," she said, then wondered that he seemed a little uneasy. He was staring down at the mask that she held in her hand, ready to don before she went onstage. "Not that I . . . is something wrong, Marley?"

"Hush," he said, looking over his shoulder. "It's just that . . . well, not here. Come back to the . . . come to the prop room and help me find that sword."

Shuddering a little at the word, she nodded. But once they were in a more secluded spot, with less people around to hear, he dropped his voice to barely more than a whisperer. "You know I don't want to do you a bad turn, Clara. But 'e's been on at me, and if I don't do it, someun else will. And I need the money. And anyhow, 'e says 'e won't give me any more good parts this season if I don't do what 'e says!"

A hard knot in her stomach warned her what was coming. Cordelia swallowed hard. "What does Nettles want you to do?"

"Rip off your mask," Marley told her, his voice miserable. "In front of a packed 'ouse, a'course."

Nineteen

C ordelia swallowed hard. They should have foreseen this, she told herself.

" 'E's been spreading rumors all over town that the 'mystery lady' will be unmasked," the young actor told her. "Tickets 'ave already near sold out, and the prices 'e's asking you wouldn't credit!" Marley wiped his brow. "And really, 'e may 'ave one of the other men ready to take action in case I don't."

Feeling grim, she nodded. "When?"

He looked miserable. "Tomorrow night, just before the end of Act Two."

"I see. Then I will have to be ready." She lifted her chin. "Do what you must, Marley. I will understand. We'd better get back to our places."

They hurried back to the front of the stage, ready to go on. But her brain was spinning so furiously, Cordelia wasn't sure she'd remember her lines. Another crisis to cope with—after all this, she'd be damned if she'd let Nettles have the last laugh now!

Not until the interval between Acts One and Two was she able to speak privately to Ransom.

Swearing briskly, her new fiancé took off his cumbersome helmet and slapped his wooden sword. "By God, I'll have his whiskers for tinder!"

"Yes, but what are we to do! And how is this going to affect our other plan?"

"If we frighten him enough—"

"This is not like the note, Ransom," she said. "Your brother cannot be tried without evidence, but a reputation is a fragile thing. Nettles's fright will wear off, and his tongue could still wag. Oh, I know you would love me, anyhow, but . . . but it would be, at the least, annoying, distressing even, if my sister and I are snubbed by half of Society." She sighed.

He stared at her. "I don't know," he said slowly. "I think you have hit on it again, Cordelia. Evidence. What if we gave them evidence? If we showed them the proof with their own eyes? I think it's high time that Avery did more than pass drinks around at my club, don't you?"

And she began to see, too, and she put one hand to her mouth at the audacity of it.

"Places for the sword dance," the assistant director called.

Ransom gave her a quick hard kiss before he ran for his mark.

They had a great deal to do that night and the next morning to prepare, and it had to be done in secrecy, using only people they could trust. They called in Avery, and of course Giles, the two servants at the rectory whom the vicar swore were as tight-lipped as anyone could wish for. They had the marquis and his wife, and Marian's dresser also was let into the plan.

Even the clothes the ladies would wear took a considerable amount of discussion.

"But," Giles pointed out, "it always seems to, and you might as well become accustomed to that, Ransom, I tell you now."

Ransom grinned. "As long as I can become accustomed to taking my lady wife to bed every night and lying beside her between the same sheets, I will put up with any amount of chat about gowns," he promised, although he kept his voice low. "And hats and gloves and whatever lacy stuffs, as well!"

The marquis sent his agent out with a fat purse to purchase the tickets, and the amount he had to pay for three boxes was scandalous, Giles said, but Marian said this was not the time to carp over a few pounds.

"Soon enough, we will make Mr. Nettles rue the day," she predicted.

Cordelia only hoped she was right. At last, they parted. Ophelia and Giles went back to the rectory, and Ransom said a polite good night under everyone's eye. The marquis and his wife went upstairs, and Cordelia also made her way to her bedroom. But she found herself tense with anxiety over the coming encounter with their villain and she expected little sleep.

Lying awake and watching the shadows crawl across the wall as the moon shifted, she wondered if Ophelia, too, was wakeful. But if so, she could turn to her husband's waiting arms.

Damn. That was the advantage of marriage, Cordelia thought, envying her sister. Was Ransom thinking of her now, wishing they were already wed and lying together instead of apart? She hoped it might be so. Thinking of him made the deep ache inside her awaken, those new awarenesses that their one night together had spawned, and now—now she wished he were here, sharing her bed. She shifted restlessly, turned and pounded her pillow. Sighing, it was a long time before she shut her eyes.

The next afternoon it was not just her imagination that seemed to imbue the stage with extra tension. The actors were all jumpy, and the scene shifters swore even more than usual and struggled to keep Zeus's chariot from falling off its wires and dangling to one side.

Cordelia got ready early and kept her mask nearby; she had already strengthened the ribbons and made sure they were sewn on with extra thread. When Mr. Nettles walked by, she pretended not to notice how the manager stared at her with a certain avaricious gleam in his narrow eyes. She could hear the sounds of the packed house, more crowded even than usual in the pits, all the boxes along the sides jammed with spectators. She knew that John and Marian would be there, and, for the first time, Ophelia and Giles.

She hoped that Ophelia would think that Cordelia represented herself adequately in Ophelia's role!

Oh, it was almost time. The small orchestra was tuning up. Her stomach was tightening. She had not seen Ransom, but she usually didn't at this time, and she had to go take her place for her first entrance.

And now she could glimpse Mr. Nettles being given a note by one of the scene shifters—just at the time they had planned.

The timing had to be just right—she closed her eyes and said a quick prayer—then opened them again.

He was walking away.

She licked her lips and checked the tightness of her mask. She was more nervous than she had been since the very first night she'd gone onstage. But now it was her cue . . .

She walked onstage, she said her first line.

"Why, it is my own sweetheart. Perchance you came to linger on the path in hopes of finding me here?"

And they were off again . . .

What the hell did the bloody conjurer want with him now, Nettles thought, stamping down to the prop room. Stupid man was more trouble than he was worth, and he didn't even get that many laughs, though he did work cheap. Druid was getting his notice this week, that was that. He'd tell the idiot on Friday.

Right now, he wanted to get this done quickly. He didn't want to risk missing any of the Act, and for sure not Act Two. He had to see her expression, the snooty little bitch, when he exposed her face—and her name—before all the hoity-toity Ton. Oh, mincing around and turning up her nose at him, like she was too good to give him a tumble on the dressing room couch like most of the actresses were willing to do. . . . You didn't muck around with Tom Nettles and not regret it!

Nobody messed with Tom Nettles. He grinned with a grim satisfaction at the thought, then turned into the prop room, its interior dim, at the end of the hall. The scene shifter had faded away, and where in the bloody hell was the damn magician, anyhow?

A noise from the back of the room made Nettles turn. What the hell was he doing over—

Something black came down over his head, there was a strange odor, and he had a feeling of suffocating; he couldn't breath. He struck out instinctively, but his arms were caught up in some kind of fabric or netting. He was flailing uselessly and then he was falling—

When he came to himself again, he couldn't see. The darkness brought him a feeling of panic, and he felt the beads of sweat break out on his forehead. He tried to shout for help, but he couldn't talk, either, much less yell. Something was stuffed into his mouth, and there seemed to be a band of cloth tied around his lips. His wrists were tied together in some way, as were his ankles and he was crammed down into a narrow space.

Of course. Something was tied around his eyes. He wasn't blind—no one had put out his eyes—he had a cloth around his eyes, that was all. The relief was enormous. He let out a great gusty sigh and tried to pull himself together. If this was someone's idea of a joke . . . he'd strangle that damned magician. If he could get this gag off. Yes, he could move his head. He tried to lean sideways and found he could bring his arm partway up toward his head. He rubbed his jaw along the side of his arm and moved the bands on his head a little way.

Encouraged, he did it again, and within a few minutes, he had shifted both the gag and the blindfold. He blinked in the dimness, and his first impression was that he was inside a hedge. He stared. No, he was definitely inside some enclosed space, maybe in some kind of wicker box?

He spat out the folded rag and cleared his throat. He was husky both from fear and from the dryness that came from having a rag stuffed into his mouth. He shouted. "Help, help, I've been kidnapped!"

Nothing.

He tried to listen. There seemed to be a faint noise from faraway, but he couldn't make out what it was. There were smells of mildew, old smells, as from an old building, but that could be any building in London.

"Help!"

"Shout all you like," a cold voice said. "No one will hear. You are in the basement of a warehouse near the Thames."

So that's what the faint noise was he heard now and then, rising and falling, water washing the foundation. A good place to get rid of a body, he thought, and felt beads of sweat prickle his forehead.

"Druid, is that you?" he muttered, covering anxiety with anger. "If this is some kind of trick—"

"The magician is dead," the voice in the darkness continued. It had a strange accent he couldn't place. "You will shut up and listen. We want the paper."

Nettles paused and swallowed hard.

"Wh-what paper."

"You know the one. You are a blackmailer, but you possess only one thing of importance just now."

Nettles snorted. "You think you'll get anything out of that young idiot? I already tried. He hasn't enough income to be worth any trouble."

"The young man is not our objective. Nonetheless, we want the note."

Nettles stared into the dimness. Who the hell . . . ? He'd missed an angle somewhere, he thought, intensely annoyed. Something to do with the Prince? But what?

"Where is the note?" the voice said again.

"I don't have it!" he said.

"You're lying. It's not in your rooms, nor in your office. You're carrying it on your person. If you're wise, you'll hand it over now."

The voice out of the dark was not just cold but icy, and almost, he could believe . . . but that note must be worth even more than he'd thought. Hell's bells, the unseen person wouldn't have gone to all this trouble if it weren't so. If they killed him, they'd never find it, he told himself and tried to believe it. Likely they'd already searched him . . .

"Don't have it," he repeated stubbornly.

"We shall see," the voice said.

A sword suddenly slid through the wicker, just inches from his head.

Nettles yelped in surprise. "What the hell!"

"A clever trick, yes?"

Another sword came through further down. He leaned hastily to the side. It nicked his knee, and he swore again.

"Are you an agile man?"

His gaze swung wildly back and forth, but it was impossible to predict from which angle the next sword would come. And anyhow, he was a well-built man, priding himself on his ample girth; didn't it show the prosperity he had achieved? And there wasn't much room in the basket to sidle back and forth to avoid the damn swords. Another came through at his head and another by his legs. He was nicked again, and then his jacket was slit, and he felt blood seeping down from a stinging cut on his forehead.

"Wait, wait, damn you," he shouted. "Wait! Even if I had the note, how could I give it to you. My wrists are tied, and—

With an almost noiseless passage, another sword glided through the wicker. With a frisson of pure panic, he thought it seemed to head straight for his heart.

He screamed. "No, wait! It's in my shoe, damn it all to hell! It's in the heel of my shoe!"

The sword paused. He felt sweat dripping down his forehead, down his back, down beneath his armpits. And blood, too, mingled with sweat. He gulped for air.

"Take off the shoe and toss it out of the basket," the voice said, expressionless.

"How the hell am I going to—"

"Do it!"

The sword was still pointed at his heart.

Reaching down with bound hands, avoiding the swords

already poised all around him, tugging off the shoe and then pushing it up and over the top of the basket. He sweated and swore for several minutes before it was done. And when he heard the shoe clatter to the floor, and the sword did not after all pierce his heart, it occurred to Nettles to use the sharp side of one of the swords to saw the rope that bound his wrists until it broke.

Then, to his relief, someone pulled the other swords out, and he was no longer imperiled by the sharp blades.

"Are you done with me?" he asked.

No one answered.

So he pushed against the wicker until his jail overturned and he could scramble out. He fumbled around in the darkness until he found a door and a doorknob—to his great relief it was not locked.

They were fools, he thought—he was a great one for the best locks his blunt could buy, himself—so he turned and pushed it open, hoping he could get away without being spotted and that he didn't have to walk too far on one bare foot . . .

And he found to his fury that he was not situated at the foot of the Thames at all, but still stood in his own theater; he had been in the prop room all the time. The sounds he had taken for the ebb and flow of water swirling against wooden piling were instead the faint rise and fall of the audience's laughter and applause.

"Damn their bloody lying hearts!" he growled. He stopped at the men's dressing room where a couple of actors lounged inside. They gaped at him, and he looked in the glass and saw that he was indeed a sight. He stopped long enough to throw water on his face and wipe away the dust and sweat and blood and find a new shirt to hide the embarrassing signs of his fake kidnapping.

He had another coat in his office, he thought with satisfaction. Because Act Two was coming up very fast and no matter if the damned note had gone, he would still get to witness the little bitch get her comeuppance and in front of a packed house, too. And remembering the details about that, he rubbed his palms and smiled.

He had seen her give her first lines in her clear pleasing voice and walk across the stage with those well-made legs that made him hungry to touch them—damn if only she'd just been more amenable. If she'd been sensible about having a bit of a romp with the manager, he could take her a long way . . .

Putting aside those thoughts with a sigh, Nettles positioned himself where he could see when Marley ripped off her mask. He hoped she screamed, cried, begged for mercy—the crowd would go wild, he thought with satisfaction.

He paused just at the edge of the stage and waited.

Act Two was racing along, tension was unusually high. The actors were on edge, the woman herself seemed stiff with tension, and her voice sounded shrill. The audience looked on the edge of their seats, as well, as if everyone were waiting for something to happen . . .

And then Marley moved suddenly toward the actress in her scarlet dress and mask. The young actor grasped the mask and pulled it away from her face.

Lily—no, Miss Ophelia Applegate—screamed and put her hands to her face.

The audience burst into a dozen spontaneous conversations.

"Can you see her face?"

"Who is it?"

"Who wins the bet?"

"Oh, be a sport, let us see your face?" one young man called.

The young actress continued to cower and cover her face.

This was not good drama, and certainly not according to the script he had fashioned in his head! Irritated, Nettles stomped onto the stage. With a sweeping gesture like the born showman he knew that he was, Nettles boomed, "Allow me to introduce our lady of quality and newest actress at Malory Road Theater, Miss Ophelia Applegate!"

A buzz of speculation filled the theater, then a man's voice cut through it all.

"I beg your pardon!" A tall young man stood in one of the middle boxes, his grave good looks drawing the crowd's eyes. "If you persist in defaming my wife's good name, I fear, well, as a clergyman, I cannot break the law by calling you out, but

I can certainly take you to court! My wife is at my side, as everyone here can see." He held out his hand, and the woman beside him stood. She had brown hair dressed elegantly on top of her head, and she wore a modish silk evening gown and a pearl necklace.

It was his actress, Lily—Ophelia Applegate. How the hell . . . ?

The audience was chattering again, talking loudly to each other.

"What are you pulling, Nettles?" someone yelled.

He had just seen her onstage a few minutes ago! He felt sweat break out again on his forehead. What—

No, no, she had a sister, of course, of course.

"She has a sister, a twin sister," he shouted over the heads of the spectators in the pit who were frowning and calling out at him. "They've switched places, that's all. They're trying to, trying to—"

"I would stop right there, Nettles," another man cut him off. It was a cold voice, almost familiar as was his face. He was speaking from another of the boxes. A tall man with a cutting gaze, he was dressed in evening clothes, too, but this man was dark-haired instead of fair. "You're speaking of my fiancé, Miss Cordelia Applegate, and not in a way of which I approve. I am not a clergyman, and if you would like to be called out, it could most assuredly be arranged. Pistols or swords, as you prefer."

Beside him, another young woman stood, lowering her fan to reveal her face. She was identical in her face and form to the first, except for a different colored gown, but she was sitting in another box, several tiers over, so how could they have switched places if they were trying to fool him, like streets boys playing switch the shells and find the pea? Were both the sisters really up in the boxes? If so, who the hell was playing the part?

"And I am John Sinclair, marquis of Gillingham, if I must be so vulgar as to announce it," another man said, standing in another box, a big man who positively reeked of power and wealth and authority. He stared down at Nettles, who felt as if he shrank a little just looking up at this hard-eyed nobleman. "These young ladies are my relations, and I should strongly suggest that you leave off casting aspersions on their good names! If not, I promise that you will be certain to regret it."

Nettles found nothing to say. His mouth felt as dry as it had when the gag had bound it.

The audience was booing now, and someone lobbed a rotten lime and a half-blackened tomato at him. He hardly winced as the missiles hit his second best coat.

"Who's the masked lady, Nettles? What trick are you pulling? Do you have a lady of quality up there or not?"

Nettles stamped across the stage, grabbed the figure who had not moved from her quivering semicrouch and jerked her hands away. "I demand to know—"

And paused in horror.

Grinning back at him was one face he knew all too well.

Avery Sheffield, his pencil-thin mustache no longer hidden by the mask, smiled broadly and gave a deep, theatrical bow to the crowd. And his wig fell off.

The audience gasped and then roared with mingled shouts of both laughter and fury.

Avery reached behind him to unfasten the ties that held on his costume and stripped it off a piece at a time. "It is I who have won the bet, ladies, gentlemen," he told them grandly. "And you have been gracious enough to endure my acting and my singing—"

"Caterwauling!" some wag called from the audience.

"That, too," Avery agreed calmly.

Nettles watched with a rage bordering on paranoia. "Make fun of me, will ye? I'll wring yon bastard's throat," he muttered. "And no doubt with 'is note back in 'is pocket after I won it fair and square . . . well, almost, at the cards, too."

So angry he was shaking, he took long steps toward the young man and stumbled over the discarded skirt from the lady's costume that Avery was still stripping away, revealing a shirt and pants with their cuffs rolled up underneath. Swearing furiously, Nettles picked up the long skirt and tossed it aside.

"I'll 'ave your 'ead on a platter, you damn young fool," he snarled. "And you can take that—" He swung furiously and Avery ducked.

The audience roared and applauded. The rest of the scene still had not been enacted, but the actors had stopped, standing onstage looking at each other uncertainly and not knowing what to do.

Not until he smelled the burning fabric did Nettles realize he had tossed the costume into one of the oil-fired footlights. The fabric was burning, and now so was the edge of the wooden stage.

"Fire!" One of the men in the pit shouted, and the people on the first bench jumped to their feet in alarm.

The actors onstage ran to get buckets.

Nettles swore again and turned. He would throttle that young fool Avery for this—

But the crowd was running and pushing, now, and more of the stage was burning. Women screamed. Smoke gathered above the stage, and already the air seemed streaked with blue haze. He found it catching in his throat. And looking up, he saw that Zeus's chariot swung dangerously low. Nettles gazed at it in alarm.

He ran for the ladder near the stage.

Ransom put his arm around her and half guided, half pulled her through the crowd. People shouted and screamed, the smoke was already making it hard to see. Coughing, Cordelia clung to him. They paused only once to help an elderly lady to her feet. With her on his other side, Ransom got them all out the door and into the alley. Flames shot out the top of the theater.

"It's moving so fast!" Cordelia said, gasping. "Oh, Ransom!"

"I fear the theater's days are done," he said. "This theater, anyhow. Let us get a safe distance away."

The crowd was still dense. They escorted the older woman

until she found the rest of her party amid the milling spectators, then pushed their way toward the line of carriages until
they were hailed by Marian and the marquis.

"Oh, thank goodness," Marian said. "I have seen your sister, Cordelia. She has gone ahead to the rectory in case there
are any wounded who need help. Giles is over by the side; I
hope he will not go too close."

Ransom nodded. "I must go back and check on my brother.
I haven't seen him safe, as yet. If you would take the ladies
home, my lord."

"I will send the carriage on," the marquis said.

Marian looked at her husband, her expression anxious. "Be
careful, John."

He pressed her hand, then jumped down from the carriage
and helped Cordelia up, instead.

Ransom wasted no time in running back toward the theater.
Flames now showed even higher through the roof.

Druid had stayed away tonight, to make their ruse work; just
as well. At least they didn't have to worry about finding him.
Ransom discovered the actors and actresses huddled near the
side of the theater, most of them streaked with smoke. Venetia
was shushing some of the actresses, who were indulging in
mild hysterics.

"The flames grew too fast; they usually do," Marley told
him, yelling to be heard above the crackling of the still developing flames. "These wooden buildings—"

"Have you seen my brother?" Ransom yelled back.

"Here!" Avery answered. Coming closer, he was so black
in face and clothing that he was as well disguised as he had
been beneath his lady's costume. "I made part of the bucket
brigade, but we couldn't do much about the fire."

Ransom threw one arm about his sibling's shoulders in relief. "Young fool!" he said. "No, I guess not."

Then he looked around. "Anyone seen Nettles?"

Avery blinked, showing just a glint of paler skin that was
not blackened by soot. "Last time I did, he was throwing left
hooks at me, but missing me, glad to say."

The rest of the actors shook their heads or shrugged.

"You don't suppose he, ah, went up with his theater, like a captain going down with his ship, do you?" Avery asked delicately.

"Nettles having a finer feeling?" Ransom raised his brows. "I don't think so. But let's have a look around."

Marley came with them, only because it was too off-putting to stay and watch the theater burn, he said, and the rest of his wages for the season go up with it.

They could not come too close to the edges of the building, the heat was too intense. But Ransom skirted the theater itself and walked along the far end of the alley, not even sure what he searched for, only something in the back of his mind—

And it was Avery who spotted it first, the glint of the twisted handles still showing its gilt paint as the man dragged it through the dirty alley, leaving long tracks behind him.

"There!" he called. And they all ran and tackled the portly man now streaked with smoke who lugged the strange contraption through the darkness and muck.

Nettles swung wildly at them, but he was already panting and still coughing from the aftereffects of the fire, besides being winded from pulling the heavy chariot. It was hardly even a fight.

After they had pummeled the manager and trussed him up like a turkey, they stopped to consider how to get their burdens back to the theater. "What the hell did he want with the thing?" Avery asked,

"Has he lost his mind?" Marley asked. "I mean, the only thing left from the theater and he couldn't bear to leave it, was that it?"

Nettles groaned and didn't answer.

"Can we just abandon it here?" Avery added. "I don't want to drag it back. It weighs a ton."

"I should think Marley will," Ransom pointed out, his tone mild. "Considering it's got a good share of the profits that Nettles stole from the cast over the season—"

"What?" Marley jumped.

"Remember what the scene shifters said about the chariot being so hard to balance? It was Nettles's hiding place. He kept stashing coins in it, as it was up in the air and safely out of reach. He was keeping a fake set of books, so that the percentage of profits that you and the other cast members were supposed to get from the ticket sales . . . well, you were being cheated, in a word. I was going to blow the whistle after tonight."

"Why, you—" Marley turned and kicked the former theater manager in a sensitive spot, and the man groaned again. Then Marley picked up the handles of the chariot and, without complaint, dragged the awkward thing back toward the theater, while Avery pulled Nettles to his feet and prodded the man back toward his ultimate justice.

It was very late before Ransom and Avery returned to the rectory. Ransom was surprised to find that Cordelia, the marquis and his wife were there, as well as Giles and Ophelia. They had all gone back to see if anyone needed help after the fire, Cordelia told him.

"We took care of the last of them some time ago. Most of the spectators were not hurt. There were a few burns among the actors, and some in the pit were trampled in their panic and needed tending. And most of all, we wanted to hear what happened. Is Venetia all right and the other actors and actresses? And did you find Nettles?"

He sat down, accepting a glass of wine and taking a long drink—his throat felt as smoke-dried as the chimney itself. Then he, with frequent interruptions from Avery, told them all what had happened.

"Zeus's chariot?" She blinked. "Oh, very good!"

Ophelia clapped her hands. "Splendid! I shall have to put it into one of my stories!"

"You don't think this is too strange even for fiction?" Avery asked, his tone innocent.

"Certainly not," she said, looking wounded. "When you see how I cast it . . ."

"He is teasing, ignore him," Ransom said, frowning at his younger brother. "When I searched his office, I had an intimation of it because his books did not look quite right. Most of the actors perhaps had not had enough education to catch it, but he was skimming the profits and not giving them the correct percentages, but I didn't know where he was hiding the money. Turns out, it was inside the inner wall of the chariot."

"They will be glad of the funds," Cordelia said. "Especially with the theater gone. Do you think it will be rebuilt? I don't like to think of Venetia and Marley without jobs . . ."

"I have no idea." Ransom pointed out, "They will need an investor to replace Nettles."

"My dear," Marian said to her husband, her tone sweet.

John looked at her with suspicion. "Yes, my love?"

"I find I have a burning desire to own a theater—"

Everyone laughed or groaned at the dreadful pun.

The marquis sighed. "I should have known," he said. "I thought you were going to be busy designing a wedding?"

"Oh, I can do that, too." Marian smiled and put her arm through his. "We shall visit the fabric warehouses first thing tomorrow."

Cordelia blushed. "Can we go back to Yorkshire, however, for the ceremony?" she suggested. "I know my sisters would like to see the wedding."

"Of course, my dear," Marian said. "We shall do exactly what you like. I'm sure Ransom agrees."

Ransom, on the other hand, took his affianced bride aside the first chance he found. "Yorkshire? You're not wanting to wait for the bans to be read? Giles and Ophelia bought a special license. They were married in two days! We have to wait?"

"I know." She sighed. "I ache for you, too. But I hate for my sisters to miss both the weddings. And my father . . ." She looked at him, her hazel eyes anxious. "Do you mind terribly?"

"Of course I mind."

Her eyes widened, and her lips parted. He put one finger over her mouth before she could speak. "And we'll do whatever you wish, Cordelia. But I can complain just once, surely? If I have to ache, too . . ."

He grinned at her and leaned over to steal a quick kiss.

Turn the page for a preview of
Nicole Byrd's
next historical romance
A Lady Betrayed
coming in December 2007
from Berkley Sensation!

One

A dagger pierced her temple . . .

Pain washed over her in waves so intense that her body shook with the force of them. Pushing back the nausea that came close to overwhelming her, Maddie fought for every breath.

She had hoped to make it home before she lost control of her limbs, but the weakness had increased too quickly. Staggering along the overgrown path among the trees, she paused to thrust aside a low growing branch. As she did, she glimpsed the abandoned structure; its bare wooden skeleton outlined against the darkening sky. The lone sign of human habitation, it stood in the center of a grassy lea where nowadays only the occasional doe and fawn came to call.

She should have remembered the dilapidated gazebo, she told herself. By now she was almost beyond coherent thought. In happier times Madeline and her sisters had visited here often, bringing baskets of berries and sandwiches, with flasks of lemonade hung over their arms.

Thunder crackled overhead. A drop fell, hitting her forehead, then another, and then sheets of rain followed.

Gasping as the cold flood drenched her, she was happy enough to see the gazebo, even in its current state. It offered an almost whole roof to shield her from the rain that descended in torrents, soaking her light muslin dress and chilling her from head to toe before she could stumble inside. But the pain in her temple drowned out the other less-significant discomfort, bringing her literally to her knees on the cold, shattered tiles of the floor.

How long would it be before anyone thought to come searching for her? Her father had warned her about walking alone through the woods and moors, but now that their servants were few, she had thought they were needed more—

Oh, the pain!

She put both her hands to her head, clutching it, trying to contain the physical torture that spiraled to greater heights, like a pot boiling over, spilling huge drops that would burn and blister everywhere they touched. The pain wouldn't stop, wouldn't slow. Oh, dear God, Why had she chosen to walk to the village today? Why must she fall victim to this assault before she could reach home?

Everything around her spun into a dizzying whirl of unbearable unending torment. Death would be easier than this.

Pain was all—she curled into herself—and if someone sobbed, she no longer noticed.

The first drops of rain fell when he was barely past the village, and Adrian wondered if he should have stopped for the night in the hamlet after all. But he'd seen no decent inn, and anyhow, he had no time to spare, with a would-be murderer hard on his heels.

No time to spare—a good jest, that. They might inscribe it on his tombstone.

He lifted his lips in a grim smile that might as easily pass for a grimace. The last man who had smiled back at him now rested beneath a marble slab, presumably at peace although still bearing Adrian's bullet.

As Adrian did, his.

Inconvenient things, duels. They interrupted one's life so easily . . . as did dying.

And self-pity was an indulgence he would not allow himself . . . did not have time to allow himself.

He glanced again at the lowering sky, the dark clouds heavy with rain that would not be put off much longer. As if the thought had opened heaven's floodgates, he felt another large droplet smack his cheek. Adrian turned up his collar, pulled down his hat and resigned himself to a wet and miserable ride.

His horse—an iron-mouthed, surly gray—seemed to take matters under its own control. Snorting, the gelding plunged into the trees that surrounded the narrow lane.

"What the hell?" Adrian tightened his grip on the reins and tried to turn his mount back toward the road, but it was too late. The horse had taken its head and seemed, as the damned beast sometimes did, to have been momentarily possessed of a devil. Or more likely, it wanted out of the wet, not being fond of rainstorms.

"And what makes you think this way leads to a stable, you fool?" Adrian demanded, as if the dumb brute could understand. But the insane thing was that the animal had, now and then, been right about which road to take when its master had lost his way.

After a moment Adrian realized that they were, in fact, following a narrow but discernable path through the woods. Was this some local gentry's parkland? Perhaps they would find a house and stable at the end of this overgrown pathway.

If it was a park or a gentleman's property, someone had come down in the world, Adrian told himself. The narrow path was poorly maintained. But then he saw the first sign of habitation. A servant's cottage? It was very small. No, he saw now that it was only a roof and frame, a gazebo set out for shelter on a nice summer day, now half derelict, with holes in the roof but still offering some shelter from the rain.

Not until he dismounted and led his steed under what was left of the roof, pulling a blanket from behind the saddle to throw over the horse and giving it a handful of the oats that he carried in his saddlebag, did he turn and make out the body lying motionless on the floor of the structure.

"Good God," Adrian exclaimed. He tied his horse to one of the roof supports a safe distance away so that the animal would not tread on the prone figure, then took several long strides to see who lay so ominously still.

It was—as he had thought—a woman, a young woman, her muslin dress sodden and sticking to her body—a very nicely made body, he could not help but notice. She had soft brown hair, wet, too—she had obviously been caught in the storm— and her eyes were shut. Had she been injured in some way?

She lay on her side, curled up in a semicircle like a babe, and something about the way she lay, the expression on her face—such suffering it seemed to show—caught at his heart. She looked so vulnerable, so helpless. Her cheeks were damp from raindrops or tears.

What had happened here?

Her face was very pale. He knelt beside her and leaned over to touch her hand. It was as frigid as a mountain stream. He drew a deep breath.

Was she dead?

Too alarmed to worry about propriety, he put his hand against her chest, searching for a heartbeat. He was relieved past measure to detect a steady rhythm beneath the skin and then to feel the slow rise and fall of the damp muslin beneath his fingers.

If she had been well and interested in flirtation, his hand might have lingered, but she was not well at all, and he was still not sure what had caused her current distress. One thing was sure, she could not continue to lie on this cold tile floor in a wet gown. If he left the stranger here in such a state whatever her other problems, she would end up with fluid on her lungs and die of congestion and lung fever, as his own mother had done.

He had no idea where her home might lie. He could continue down the path and search for a likely structure or retrace his path to the village, but the sunlight was fading rapidly and the chill in the air deepening and the rain too heavy. And he hesitated to leave her here alone in such an isolated location, with the temperature dropping and without anyone to watch over her while he searched for help.

Pausing only for a moment, Adrian made up his mind. He walked back to his horse and, with an ironic grin, stripped off the blanket he had only just put over the animal. "Sorry, old man, a greater need!" He shook off as many horse hairs as he could, then came back and lay the blanket on the floor next to the unconscious woman.

Leaning closer, he unbuttoned—he'd had some practice removing women's apparel, though never before on a female who could not give him prior permission—the back of her wet gown. Lifting her as gently as he could, he still saw no sign of obvious injury as he stripped off the soaked clothing. The gown stuck to her arms and clung to her full, well-shaped breasts, and he ripped one of the sleeves before he could pull it off, but finally she was free of it. He found that her shift was little better, dripping with cold water, so, with the ruthless determination that his friends—and his enemies—would have recognized, he stripped it off as well.

Her body was lovely, pale as alabaster in the blue of the fading light. Drawing a deep breath, he put aside the surge of passion that threatened to rush through him.

Not to be thought of. But, bloody hell, she was beautiful.

He laid her very carefully upon the blanket, pulled off his coat, and covered her with it, or as much of her as he could, hoping that by removing the soaked clothing and putting dry wool over her and the blanket beneath her would allow some heat to return to the young woman's body.

He knelt beside her and took both her ice cold hands in his, rubbing them and trying to return some warmth to them. But she still seemed ominously chilled. He could not allow the life to seep out of her into the stony ground, not without a struggle, damn it!

"Wake up," he said into her ear. "You must fight!"

He took one hand, then another, into his own hands, feeling like a bear who has come upon a forest nymph in some ancient legend. She seemed so slight, so delicate next to his large frame. Ironically, he had never felt so healthy, so full of life.

He gently rubbed her hands, her arms, feeling how soft her skin was, how delicate the clean lines of her forearms. And the rest of her body—no, she was helpless and in his care. Even in his thoughts, he could not trespass, not now. Nor did he have the leisure for idle fancies, he told himself. He must make sure she survived this ordeal some cruel fate had thrust upon her. He had seen enough useless death . . .

"Live!" he muttered, bending closer.

She drew a breath more labored and more palpable than before. He felt a moment of encouragement.

"Stay with me," he told her. "Lady with no name, stay with me. I will not allow your spirit to fade into the twilight, slipping away like a barely seen face in the mist. Surely if I can just make you warm again, bring back the heat of human blood and bone—"

Her skin was still so cold, especially her hands and feet, which had been as frigid as a corpse's from the beginning, as if the joyless grip of the grave had already claimed her. No, he would not consider such a possibility!

He continued to chafe her hands, gently but firmly, trying to force some hint of warmth back into her limbs. But the air around them cooled even more as the sun dropped behind the horizon, and everything seemed to conspire against him. The breeze had picked up, and as the wind whipped through the trees, the mournful sound made the horse toss its head.

Adrian pressed his lips together. Even he shivered, and he had not been soaked to the bone to start with. Whereas the woman on the ground—

He would not give up! But how could he improve her condition?

Could he start a fire?

The trees and bushes around them were drenched, and the rain still fell, rattling against the leaves. He saw no way to find any brush dry enough to use as tinder, and he had no time to waste wandering through the dark in search of kindling suitable for burning. What else could he do?

Try to ride with her in his arms as he sought help? He did not think he could balance her safely atop the fractious horse. He pushed the idea aside as wild and impractical.

He had to do something. He would warm her if he had to strip off his own skin to do it!

The madness of that notion made him smile grimly once more. Without thinking about the wisdom of his actions, he slid to the tile floor, wrapping his arms about the young woman, gathering her closer and pulling her naked body into his embrace.

His heart beat faster as she came to him, her slight body offering no resistence. It seemed as light as a robin's egg. Smooth and finely made, its softness and pleasing curves were as exquisite as God could ever have created.

She was female in her essence, her breasts were round and soft as they pressed against his chest, and he wanted badly to cradle them with each hand, knowing that his hands would fit easily around each sweet arc. And lower, her hips made a natural curve, guarding within them that vee with its natural softness where his own hardness wanted to press, ached to push harder into than he would allow himself.

He could not—would not—take advantage of her innocence, certainly not in her moment of accident or illness or even assault. Not now, like this. But, dear God, it was hard to hold her so close, knowing that this perfect body was bare and lovely beneath the inadequate shelter of his own clothing, and not pull her nearer, closer, mold her hips into his and—

He could not think like this when she was unaware of their embrace. He had only meant to warm her, save her from illness or death. Feeling the sweat break out on his forehead, on his upper lip, Adrian tried to focus instead on the pale complexion of her face, the delicate blue veins that could be seen in her temples.

"You are so beautiful," he said softly. "If only I could woo you properly, if only I had met you before I started this journey toward death . . ."

Her eyelids lifted.

Startled, he paused and stared into her eyes. They were as

beautiful as the rest of her, large green eyes with the faintest specks of gold sprinkled across the irises. Her lashes were long, and blinked now as if she did not believe what she saw.

For one long moment, they stared at each other as Adrian held her close, held her naked body next to him, with only the barest layer of cloth to separate them. He was acutely aware of how it felt to be this intimate, this near to the unknown woman from the damp wood where mist now rose in foggy fingers—but how did it feel to her to wake thus, in the arms of a stranger?

"Don't be afraid," he said quickly. "I was only—"

And as quickly as she had come to herself, her eyes rolled upward, and she had passed out once more.

Adrian sighed, not sure if he had done the young lady more harm than good.

A few feet away, the gelding snorted.

"I didn't ask you," he snapped. "At least she's still alive. That is, if I haven't scared her to death!"

But her body was growing warmer, less deathly chilled, he was almost sure of it, and even though he might have caused her alarm, at this point, he decided to remain close to the unconscious woman. Night was upon them, the air was colder than ever, and he dared not allow her to become chilled all over again; he would lose all the progress he had made. If she woke again and railed again his ungentlemanly behavior, he would explain, and if she insisted, give her a more proper space.

And, anyhow, he didn't want to let her go, dammit!

How long had it been since he had held anything so precious in his arms? Hell's fire, *Had* he ever held anything so precious as this lovely woman with the look of pain etched into her eyes?

That brief look—he was not sure what her expression had meant, but he would dearly like to convince her to stay, convince her to know him, allow him to know her.

For now, he just wanted to wrap his arms about her, enfold her, hold her tight, hold her close . . .

Rain spattered beyond the roof, the cold wind whistled, the gelding stamped its feet and snorted its opinion of the drafty lodgings and lack of proper provisions. The trees beyond were indistinct, cloaked in the ground fog that made the moors beyond the small pocket of woods too dangerous to travel tonight, even if he had wished to dare the dark road. He would have had to stop regardless, he thought. But who could have predicted such an adventure?

Adrian lay as close as he could to the woman whose name he did not know, tried to endow her with every scrap of warmth that he might, and waited for dawn to break.

For a long time he lay stiffly, afraid to relax in case in his slumber he allowed his arms to relax and drift away from her, permitting the cold to seep in and chill her again. But eventually sleep overcame him.

When the faintest traces of light streaked the sky and the first bird calls rang through the woods, he opened his eyes.

One arm had loosened its grip, but the other still cradled the mystery woman, still held her close to his body. Her eyes were closed, but she seemed to breath more easily, and she had shifted a little to lie with her cheek against his chest. His coat had slipped slightly, exposing her bare arm; he reached to pull it up so that it would cover her nakedness more completely.

And as he did, he looked up to see, past the splintered roof of the gazebo, a trio of staring faces.

Enter the rich world of
historical romance
with Berkley Books.

Lynn Kurland

Patricia Potter

Betina Krahn

Jodi Thomas

Anne Gracie

Love is timeless.

penguin.com